I0787990

AFFLICTED

RD BAKER

CONTENT WARNING

Afflicted is a dark romance. It contains situations and themes that may be disturbing to some readers.

These include but are not limited to:

Explicit sexual scenes, including instances of dubious consent, consensual non-consent, blood play, branding/scarring, anal sex, primal play, fear kink, breeding kink, degradation, somnophilia and free use kink

Graphic violence and gore, blood, decapitation and disarticulation

Sexual Assault and Rape, both on page and described as a past event (not involving the MMC)

Suicide and attempted suicide, both on page and described as a past event

Discussions of addiction, including themes of heroin use and needles

Toxic behaviours such as stalking and intimidation

Blood and biting

Imprisonment and Captivity

Forced contraception

Forced breeding (off-page, not involving the MMC)

Forced medical procedures

Mercy Killing

Forced Removal of children and babies from parents (off-page)

Loss of loved ones

Discussions of depression and poor mental health

Please be kind to yourself, always. Your mental health matters.

PLAYLIST

CHOKEHOLD
SLEEP TOKEN

ALL I HAVE LEFT TO GIVE
THOUSAND BELOW

THE DEATH OF PEACE OF MIND
BAD OMENS

RUNNING UP THAT HILL (DEAL WITH GOD)
LOVELESS

MISSING LIMBS
SLEEP TOKEN

DRINKING WITH CUPID
VOILA

WITHOUT ME
DAYSEEKER

LET IT GO
CHANDLER LEIGHTON, LO SPIRIT)

HAPPIER THAN EVER
LOVELESS

PULL THE PLUG
VOILA

INTO YOUR ARMS
WITT LOWRY, AVA MAX

YOUNGBLOOD
5 SECONDS OF SUMMER

THERAPY
VOILA

TRAPPED IN A DREAM
RUDYWADE

REGRETS
STEVE HOWIE

NO MERCY
AUSTIN GIORGIO

MINE
SLEEP TOKEN

FIRE UP THE NIGHT
NEW MEDICINE

ADDICTED
SAVING ABEL

GO FUCK YOURSELF
TWO FEET

HOTEL
MONTELL FISH

IF I DIDN'T KNOW BETTER
MACK LOREN

SHE THINKS OF ME
LANDON TEWERS

TOXIC
2WEI

EVERYTHING
SMNM

CLOSER
NINE INCH NAILS

SHAME ON ME
CATCH YOUR BREATH

DRAG ME DOWN
LOVELESS

ROSES
AWAKEN I AM

IF IT DOESN'T HURT
NOTHING MORE

SUGAR
SLEEP TOKEN

MY EYE$
TOBY MAI

THE WALLS
CHASE ATLANTIC

TAKE WHAT YOU WANT
POST MALONE, OZZY OSBORNE, TRAVIS SCOTT

MY LIGHT
DEAD BY APRIL

BAD DRUGS
KING KAVALIER, CHRISLEE

I'M THE SINNER
JARED BENJAMIN

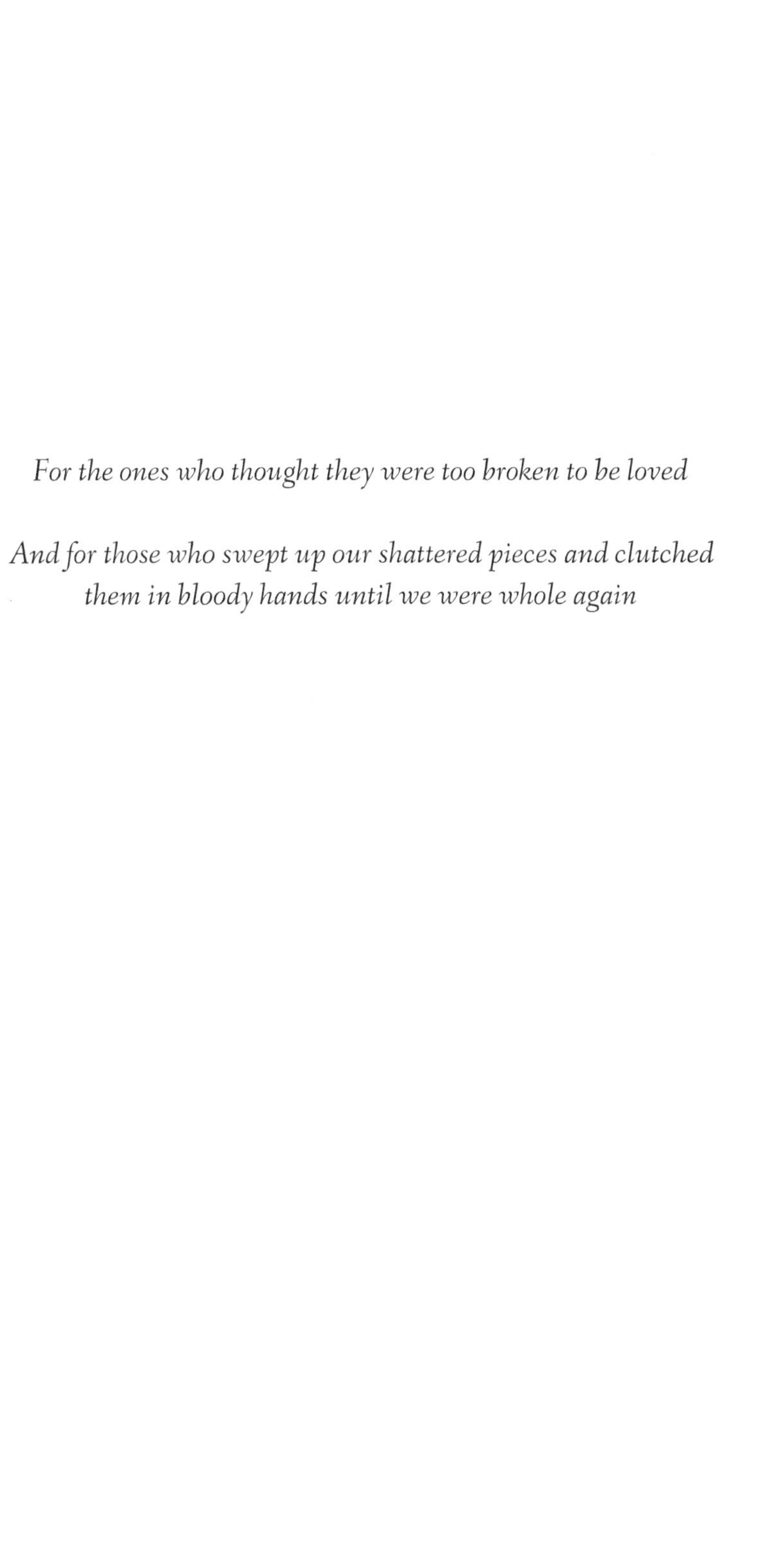

For the ones who thought they were too broken to be loved

*And for those who swept up our shattered pieces and clutched
them in bloody hands until we were whole again*

THE INFORMER

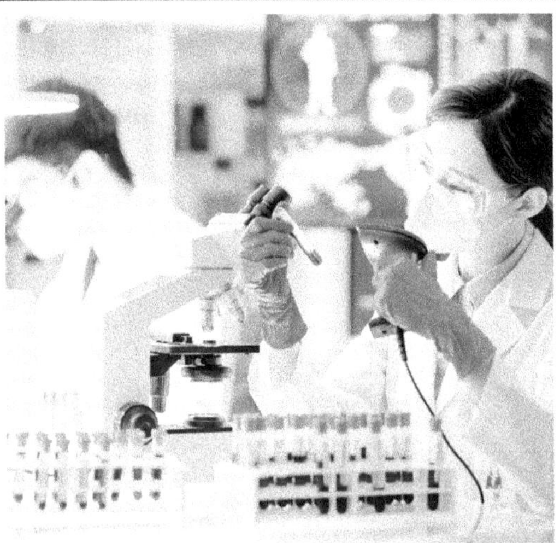

VAMPS MAKE PROGRESS

A VACCINE TO LESSEN THE NEED FOR BLOOD HAS BEEN FOUND, ACCORDING TO OFFICIALS AT THE FIELDS MEDICAL CENTRE IN BOSTON MA. DR JULIAN SMITH CLAIMS THE NEW VACCINE MEANS THE NEED FOR BLOOD IS LESSENED BY OVER 70%, MEANING A VAMPIRE CAN SURVIVE ON NE SINGLE UNIT OF BLOOD FOR MORE THAN FOUR DAYS. "OBVIOUSLY THIS IS HUGE," DR SMITH TOLD THE INFORMER. "IFVAMPIRES NEED LESS BLOOD, IT MAKES LIVING AND EXISTING WITHI HUMAN SOCIETY SAFER FOR US ALL. AFTER THE SUCCESS OF THE HIV VACCINE, WE HAVE HIGH HOPES FOR WHAT THIS WILL MEAN FOR US ALL."

BOSTON LABS CERTAIN VIRUS CAN BE CONTAINED

VAMPIRE OFFICIALS AT THE FIELDS MEDICAL FACILITY ASSURED REPORTS AT THE INFORMER THAT THE OUTBEAK WAS SMALL AND WOULD BE EASILY CONTAINED. IT IS STILL UNSURE WHAT CAUSED THE OUTBREAK OF THE VIRUS OR WHAT THE HEALTH EFFECTS WOULD BE ON THE HUMAN AND VAMPIRE POPULATIONS. REPORTS AN INFECTED VAMPIRE HAD ESCAPED THE FACILKITY WERE VEHEMENTLY DENIED.

CONTACT US
NEWS@INFORMER.GA

ECONOMY

SOMEONE'S FUCKING at the end of the dorm.

It started off as discreet moans and a gently creaking bed, subtle enough to make you think you're just imagining things. But now it's progressed to high-pitched whimpering and the rhythmic metallic scrape of the bed across the concrete floor.

Even though it's against the rules for us to fuck, every so often it happens. When the vampires set up these camps they had to know it would happen, shoving us all in together and expecting us not to act like humans?

Stupid feeders. They really didn't think this through. I puff out a heavy breath into the humid night air as the moans get louder. Both parties involved are clearly having a great time. The woman in the bed next to me, Gina, shifts to her side, raising herself on an elbow and giving a frustrated sigh. She lies back down and pulls the blanket over her head.

Usually I'd do the same, just roll over and bury my head under the pillow, shutting out the sound and try to go to sleep. I don't want to alert the feeders to what's going on and get anyone in trouble, and if I call out one of them might hear. But tonight it's unbearably hot, and there's not a hint of damn air movement in this fucking dorm. The moans get louder again and I can't take it.

"Can you keep it down?" I say without lifting my head. "Some of us are trying to sleep."

A few people nearby giggle abashedly, and the moans quieten down a little. The scraping of the bed sounds in short bursts, then there's a muffled groan. And silence.

Finally.

I shift onto my stomach and curl my arms around my pillow. My skin tingles a little, and I sigh. I'm not just annoyed, and hot. Maybe, just maybe, I'm a little jealous. My body is caught in a sudden rush of heat that has nothing to do with the early Summer night. Hearing those sounds and remembering what *that* feels like has me turned on suddenly. I swallow down a groan. *Goddammit.*

I haven't had sex in years. The last time was my first week of college. Before all of this started.

I chew the inside of my cheek, struggling to remember the guy's name. He's probably dead now, or locked up in a compound just like this one. *What was his name?* Harley? Hadley? Bradley? *Fuck.* I can't even remember his name. Not that it really matters anyway.

I do remember that night though. I was a little drunk, enough to have the confidence to go home with a guy I barely knew. He'd had big blue eyes, and he made me laugh. He'd been on the swim team, so he had nice muscles. Nice dick, too. Average length, but thick. He made sure I came first. Maybe he'd have been my boyfriend if the world hadn't gone to shit.

My nipples graze against the cotton of my t-shirt and I bite back a moan.

God fucking dammit. Why did I have to think about that night? Now I'm hot and really, really horny. I squeeze my thighs together. Great. Fucking great. I hate not having any privacy, ever. The feeders keep us in a nice, tight flock, so we're never alone. We eat together, sleep together, shower together, get drained together. It's a fucking nightmare.

I miss being alone. Being able to just think or read or sleep in a room with no other people, or maybe use a fucking vibrator in the shower.

I look over at my neighbor, the one in my line of vision now, to check he's asleep. Larry is an older guy, in his late 50s. Nice enough, a bit lazy. Snores sometimes. Like right now. Good.

I strain to hear if there's any more sounds of anyone being awake, but all seems quiet. Just soft snoring and shallow breathing.

No one will hear me. I'll just lie here on my stomach and be real, real quiet.

I put my hand in my panties, which are absolutely soaked. I circle my clit slowly, and I bite my lip. Being hot turns me on, it makes my whole body taut with need and I don't even know why. Especially when I'm in a really dark room. Everything feels more heightened. I move my fingers fast, chasing my orgasm, just wanting to feel that heat in my face and that pressure in my belly. I don't need it to last long.

After a minute I feel it rising, but I realize I'm so wet that someone's going to hear if I keep moving this quickly. Shit. I have to slow down, and fuck it's agonising. My toes curl as the arousal draws out, and I bite into my pillow to stop myself moaning. Fuck fuck fuck.

My heartbeat thunders in my ears and I can't help but roll my hips a little. The bed creaks softly under me, but it may as well be a hand grenade going off in this fucking dorm. I whimper as my climax builds, harder and deeper than if I'd just been able to finish straight away.

I breathe rapidly, imagining Harley - Bradley? - grinding himself into me, that thick cock stretching me. Fuck, I just want that weight on me again, the weight of another person, holding me, kissing me, fucking railing me til I scream.

Then it hits me, and I press my face into the pillow. A tiny moan shudders out of my throat, my fingers still moving as I ride out the high. My whole body is buzzing with electricity, and I lift my head from the pillow to suck down a rasping breath.

Thunder rumbles overhead just as the double door at the end of the dorm pushes open.

Oh fuck. I drop my head back to the pillow instantly, praying that whoever just walked in didn't see the movement. My fingers are still in my panties against my throbbing clit and *who the fuck just walked in?* I hold my breath, listening for any movement and wishing I could stop my heart thundering in my chest. It's so fucking *loud.*

For a moment I wonder if I imagined the sound of the door opening, but then footsteps begin to move across the floor. Slow and heavy. I exhale soundlessly, keeping my cheek determinedly pressed to the pillow, my eyes clenched shut. Whoever it is gets closer. And closer. Panic begins to prickle at my lips. Can the feeder smell me?

I was told once that human arousal sends them into a sort of frenzy. But that was just a rumor, right? Just one of those stupid urban myths that humans threw around about the "feeders", to make vampires even scarier. It's not true. It can't be.

But right now with my fingers still coated in my arousal and tucked between my thighs, I can't help but wonder far too hard. Especially when the footsteps stop. Right at the end of my bed.

I hold my breath, trying to stay perfectly still so they just move on. They're just doing a patrol.

But they don't move. They just stand there. The seconds tick by and my heartbeat pounds in my ears. Why won't they go away? I finally have no choice but to exhale, and my lungs rasp as little as I do which sends a fresh wave of panic through me. They saw that movement, for sure. They have to know I'm awake.

Then they inhale. Deeply. Through their nose.

Oh my god. A feeder is standing over my bed and sniffing me out. I just know they can hear my heartbeat, and the blood ricocheting through my body right now. They can probably smell it pooling in my pussy. *Please go away. Oh my god, please just walk out right now.*

The feeder sucks in a heavy breath, through their mouth this time. They make a sound that's covered by the growl of thunder overhead. I swear to god they mutter something. Something that sounded a lot like the word *fuck.*

Pellets of rain begin to ping against the tin roof. The feeder shifts on their feet, boots shuffling against concrete, then they finally move away with a heavy exhale. A few seconds later, the door to the dorm falls shut, the magnetic lock snapping into place. I breathe a sigh of relief, and realize my hands are shaking.

Holy shit.

I roll onto my back, staring at the ceiling where a fan spins around languidly, doing nothing but spreading the thick air around the dorm. My t-shirt is sticking to me, sweat rolling down my neck, and I desperately want a shower. But, like everything else in this place, that happens on schedule. I can't just get up and shower when I want, I'll have to wait til tomorrow. I get a shower before draining. They like us nice and clean for that.

I grimace at the thought. I'm on shift this week, after having eight weeks off. I always dread these weeks. Daily needles, big bruises and feeling light-headed all the damn time. We get a better diet on draining weeks, but not even that is a pay-off anymore. These days, the smell of steak cooking just turns my stomach.

It used to remind me of summer, my dad standing by the grill while we swam in the lake. He'd call us in while Mom fixed everyone's plate. Steak always came with potato salad, because "that's what the Germans do" she told us. I don't even know if that's true. I just believed her.

Now my steaks come with orange juice and iron supplements that give me cramps.

I fucking hate steak now.

I sigh, grabbing the front of my t-shirt and fanning it away from my body to try and get some air against my sweaty skin. I should sleep. They'll get us up early tomorrow. They always do on draining days. If I don't sleep, it makes the dizziness and nausea so much worse. I close my eyes, counting my breaths, trying to relax.

Footsteps sound on the other side of the metal wall, right behind my head. The window above me is open a little, illuminated by a flash of lightning, sending shadowed images of the bars lining the frame across the dorm. Thunder rolls loudly. The footsteps sound again, as though someone is pacing. It's a feeder on their patrols I decide as I yawn. Just like I thought. They didn't smell me after all.

I'm sure I'm imagining it, I'm sure it's just one of those weird half awake dreams, but as I drift off, I'm sure, I'm certain I hear that feeder sniffing again.

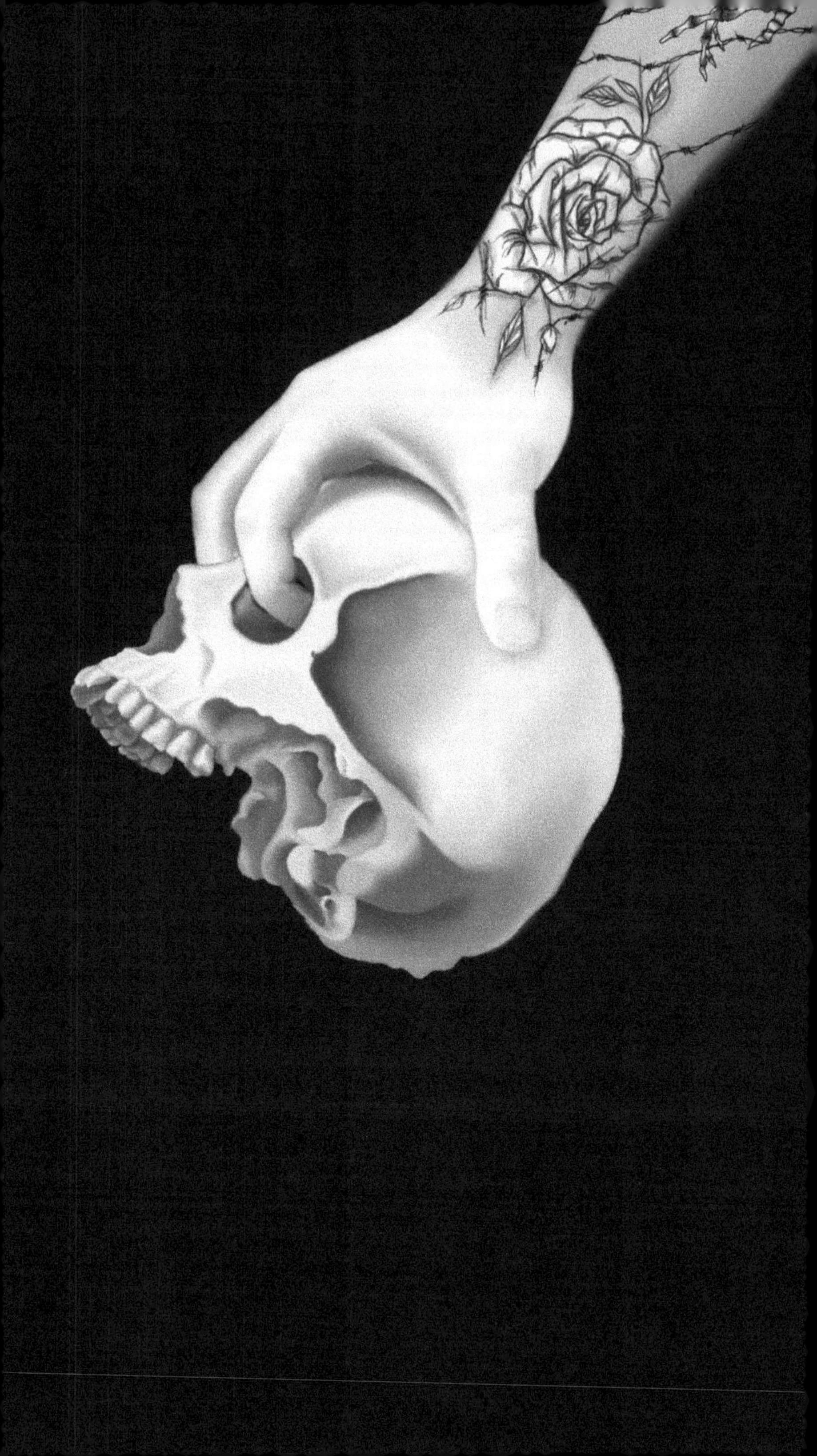

THERE'S a time and a place to fantasize about the smell of a pretty human as she gets herself off. To think about the sounds she made, grinding her hips against the bed because she's so desperate to be fucked. To imagine all the ways you'd make her scream, and wondering how her pussy tastes.

Sitting in a meeting with your superiors while they discuss your promotion definitely isn't it.

And yet this morning, while everyone around me discusses accommodations and protocol and all the benefits I was now entitled to, all I can think about is the pretty blonde and the intoxicating scent of her orgasm. I don't even know her name. It shouldn't even matter. But I've never been the type to just let something go.

This promotion was incredibly welcome. Two years on gate duty had been mind-numbingly boring, but it was better than sitting up in a factory in Boston producing electronics and weapons. So I'd taken it. Rural Georgia was still much as it was before the world went to hell, and I enjoyed the fresh air and the countryside.

Then the higher-ups finally realized that I was equipped with a set of skills that they could use to increase their security systems. Off gate duty, out of the cramped guard compound where I lived with the other grunts, and into officer's quarters of the Milledgeville Human Preservation Complex. The guards were kept separate from the humans, but the officer's cabins were in the human compound. Of course I knew I'd be in contact with humans again. It didn't really bother me.

I just didn't expect the prettiest human I've seen in my life to cross my path.

Being in a relationship with humans is against the rules now. *Against the rules.* That makes it sound so benign. Whenever it's spoken about, it's *against the rules.* It's punishable by something worse than death. Humans are our commodity, our livestock, a precious asset we have to keep secure. Fraternising with them, much less biting and fucking them, is strictly forbidden.

It wasn't always that way.

Before all this started, when the world had just found out about our existence, even I'd tried having a relationship with a human. Back when I'd been determined to hold on to the last shred of my humanity. But a new vamp and a human turned out to be a deadly combination. Realizing you've killed someone while you're coming inside them isn't a feeling I'm anxious to experience again.

And yet, right now, sitting in with my new bosses and other newly promoted vamps, I'm staring at my hands in my lap, imagining fucking her with my fingers, feeling that pussy contract on my hand as I make her come. I imagine tracing pictures on her body, connecting all those heavenly freckles on her skin into myriad shapes as her skin cools after countless orgasms.

Hardly ideal.

I shift in my chair, crossing my legs to hide the very obvious bulge in my trousers, and cross my arms over my chest. I set my face in a frown, nodding so as to appear attentive as I gaze around the room. Sure, I'm definitely listening.

Yes, absolutely the budgets will need addressing.

The food rations for the humans absolutely need adjusting as winter approaches.

I wonder what her blood tastes like.

I exhale heavily, clenching my molars, and my boss, a silver-haired vamp named Anderson, regards me with raised eyebrows.

"Not boring you, are we, King?" He's stern but not unfriendly, giving off an air almost of an english teacher who likes to give you a talking-to over glasses perched on his nose. "Got somewhere better to be?"

I shake my head quickly, pasting a smile on my face. "Sorry, no, not at all. It's just rather hot today, isn't it? There was some talk of the new air conditioning units being installed in the dorms, is that still happening?"

The other vamp looks down at the paperwork in front of him - his name is Peters, I think - and clears his throat. "They'd mentioned it to me but I think Boston was still waiting on parts."

"Ah, right then." I smile amicably, wishing the talk of air conditioning would calm my fucking raging erection.

It's not.

Instead, I run over the layout of the compound to try and distract myself. *Four dorms, containing 40 humans in each. A shower block. Library. Cafeteria. Clinic. Garden. Rec Room and gym. Officer's cabins.*

OK, that helped. Marginally.

Peters leans back in his chair and looks at me thoughtfully over caged hands. "Sorry to get off topic here for a second, but I've always wondered how you ended up here?"

"I applied for the transfer from Boston."

He laughs lightly, waving his hand. "No, I mean how did *you* end up *here*?" He gestures to the ground beneath us. "The states. Your maker, I mean she was legendary, why aren't you kicking it with the elites back in Boston?"

I shift in my seat. "Her assets were seized. For the cause, you see." *The cause.* Those words have the others nodding, looks of understanding being passed around the room. Plenty of well-off vampire families had their assets seized by the most powerful vampire covens, in the name of the cause - eradicating the Afflicted. There's no doubt in my mind some of the vamps sitting with me now come from wealthy families, now demoted to servants, all in the name of the cause.

Ironic, considering vampires are the cause of all this in the first place.

But the mention of my maker drives a cold stake straight through my stomach. I don't want to think about all that, clasping my hands together under the table until my fingers go numb. It's been four years, but the pain still lingers, aching like a long-healed broken limb.

The vamps have started talking again, discussing all the research coming out of Boston, all the advances they've made in the labs. I can't bring myself to care, not in the midst of this swirl of emotions. Everything else fades away and becomes insignificant.

I'll bet she's so incredibly soft when she's asleep. The intrusive thought roars through my brain, and instantly the swirl of emotions centers until all I can think about is the head of blonde hair and the scent of her skin. The first time I saw her, the way my stomach dropped, and the ache of my lungs emptying of air I don't even need to breathe anymore. Imagining her pouty lips against mine, the delicate brush of her tongue as she opens up for me.

Everyone turns to look at me as one, several sets of

confused eyes staring at me, because like a true fucking psycho I've pounded my fist against the table.

"You OK?" Anderson asks.

"Yeah. Sorry, uh…" I get to my feet, running a hand over my head. "I think I have duty now, I should go."

"Oh, of course." Anderson dismisses me with a nod and looks back down at the papers in front of him. "I think we've got everything all cleared and ready anyhow. You go on."

I head out of the office that suddenly feels tiny and cramped, out into the warm afternoon. For a moment, everything feels tight and wrong, like there's a noose around my neck. With a sick lurch of my stomach, I run my hands up and down my arms, trying to scrub away the feeling of track marks. They're gone, long fucking gone. Healed up along with every other scar on my body, every trace of my previous life. The life I was saved from.

But that doesn't stop that old feeling crashing back down when I realize I'm in the midst of a new addiction. I'm reformed, not recovered.

I lied, I'm not on shift at all, I just needed to get the fuck out of there.

I consider heading to the gym, but then I catch a scent on the breeze, sweet and fresh, and I know she's close by. I follow it, rounding a corner and heading down the path to the gardens.

The sun glints gold, and it catches the blonde head of hair currently bent over a garden bed. I lean against a tree, half-hiding myself as I watch her. Her hair is loose, and with a flick of her arm she swoops it over her shoulder, revealing her throat. She rubs the back of her hand over her top lip, dashing away sweat, and her eyebrows knit together in a sweet little frown as she concentrates on what she's doing. After a few minutes, she rolls back on her haunches, tipping her head back, eyes closed, and exhales through pursed lips. She's just fucking gardening, and I'm rock-hard again, imagining her on top of me, riding me, her head tipped back just like it is now as my hand runs down her chest.

Get out of here. My reason tries to make me see sense. I should leave.

Instead I move closer, watching from the long shadows being cast by the late afternoon sun. My senses are in overdrive as the breeze carries her scent to me, I can practically feel every drop of her sweat on my tongue.

As though she can sense she's being watched, her head jerks to look over her shoulder. Her eyes don't quite find my place in the shadows as they scan the yard. She rises to her feet, her movements lithe and easy. Her gaze almost finds me, and I simply stare at her.

Fuck, you're beautiful.

You're perfect.

I need to know what you taste like.

I almost will her to find me, to move closer so she sees me.

Instead she drops back to her knees and continues with her work. I watch until the guards tell the humans to stop and come in to clean up for dinner. I watch as she cleans her hands and runs them through her hair that's so long it hangs to her hips. She braces her hands against her waist and stretches her back.

She goes through all the motions of her evening routine, unaware that I'm lingering close enough to continue smelling that delicious scent. A few times she casts a glance around her, and my heart does a leap every single time.

She can feel me.

My reason is losing.

That night it loses again, as it screams at me not to make the same mistake I made last night. It tells me to go back to my bed as I walk to her dorm. It tells me to take my hand off the door handle. This isn't helping. I should keep my distance. I should stay away. *Go back to bed.* I ignore it, hearing it fade into the background with every step towards her.

I find myself standing over her, watching her sleep, her breasts rising and falling as she breathes, her eyelashes fluttering as she dreams. I know touching her is a step too far. I reach out and yank my hand back three times. I risk waking her, and her screams letting everyone from the bloodbags to the other vamps know exactly what I'm doing. And try explaining *that.*

But then she rolls on to her stomach, taking the sheet with her, exposing her long legs, and a small, pert ass barely covered by white panties. I grit my teeth. I can't resist. She smells so fucking sweet. I reach out and brush the back of my index finger down her calf. Lightly, so she doesn't feel it. But enough for her heat to be blazing through my body. I suck in a shuddering breath, pulling my hand back before I go too far.

You shouldn't have done that. My reason whispers hopelessly in my ear.

No I shouldn't have.

But it's too late now.

WHAT IS it about food that makes people burst into happy noise? Because even on a day where we're about to get strapped down and milked for blood, the cafeteria is abuzz with laughter and conversation. Humans line the rows of tables, sunshine streaming in through the windows. The smell of coffee and bacon wafts through the air, the breeze drifting in through the open windows already warm at 7am. It's going to be another scorching day.

The ridged metal of the bench digs into my thighs, and I wriggle back and forth, trying to get comfortable. I curse how bony my ass is now. I've lost so much weight since they brought me here and I hate it. It's not even down to a lack of food, food production was definitely something the feeders kept up. But it's monotonous. I find no joy in food anymore. Or anything else for that matter.

Goddamn, Juliet, throw yourself more of a pity party.

I sigh heavily, and Gina gives me a wide smile.

"You ok, sweetie?"

"Oh, yeah, I'm fine. It's just hot already," I reply.

"Did you sleep well?" Her smile remains, beaming at me from over the edge of the white cup she's cradling in her hands.

How is she always in such a good mood? She's always smiling and laughing and trying to cheer us all up. It's sweet but jarring. Maybe I'm just tired.

I shrug, pushing the scrambled eggs on my tray around with my fork. "Not really, it was too hot."

"Yes it was," she says, tossing her long dark curls over her shoulder. "I really hope they get that air conditioning fixed, it's been so long since they said they would."

"Yeah." I gaze out of the unbarred window at the sunshine. My hair is frizzing in the humidity. I claw it up on top of my head and secure it with a black band I have on my wrist. It's so fucking long now, but the feeders don't let us cut it very often. They claim something about hair being a good indicator of health, so rather than argue we all just look like Woodstock Reimagined. I wonder what the hippies would think about this future.

I feel eyes on me. I look over my shoulder, and feel a shiver down my back. One of the feeders is staring right in my direction. Just staring, his arms crossed over his chest. I'm imagining it, but the way his gaze intensifies when my eyes meet his tells me he is definitely looking right at me. I quickly turn around and look back at Gina's smiling face.

"Are you sure you're alright?" She asks in that motherly tone that makes my heart flip just a little.

"Yeah I'm fine. Just tired. And not looking forward to draining."

Gina takes a sip of her water and shrugs. "At least we get to sit down and don't have to work outside, huh?" Yep, she always sees the bright side of things. I prefer working outside to being stuck with needles and watching the feeders take as much blood as they can without killing me.

I glance back over my shoulder, and the feeder is still fucking staring at me. His eyes are that weird rusty red color all the feeders' eyes are. He's young, or at least he looks young, maybe 25 or so. He could be 200 for all I know. He's leaning against the wall, wearing that stupid green military uniform all the feeders wear to make it appear that they have some sort of authority. Someone walks by him and I realize how tall he is. He has to be 6'5" at least.

And he's still staring at me.

Uneasiness creeps through me as I wonder if he was the one who paused by my bed a few nights ago, who sniffed me out while I was getting myself off. Fuck. I shiver at the thought. Then I realize I'm still staring right back at him.

The horn sounds above us, signaling that it's time to head over to the clinic, making me jump and diverting my attention for a second. When I glance back at the wall, the feeder is gone. I breathe a sigh of relief. Fucking creep.

Gina hums as we head to the clinic, and I chide myself for finding her positivity irritating. We all have to do what we have to do to get through this, right? I shouldn't be mad just because she's trying to make her day a little easier.

The sun is beating down, dark grey storm clouds lining the horizon. Green fields spread out as far as the eye can see, and I allow myself a chuckle. Whenever I see those green fields, I always think of the label on the eggs Mom insisted on buying because she wanted eggs from happy chickens - "free range".

In the early days after the Affliction took over and destroyed the world, the feeders kept us locked up inside for fear we'd revolt and run away. It was ridiculous and miserable. It didn't last long, because after a few months of no sunshine or fresh air, we were all anemic and delivering low-quality blood. Low quality blood, sick humans, and by default, weak feeders.

They moved us out into compounds just like this one, where we could get fresh air and sunlight, along with a diet of farm-to-table foods to ensure our blood was of the highest quality. Healthy, happy feeders, and supposedly healthy, happy humans.

I wonder just how happy those free-range chickens really were.

We're ushered into the clinic and assigned our royal blue reclining chairs behind white curtains, it's so weird that they put up barriers between us for this but not when we want to shower. Feeder logic, there is none.

Settling down in these blue chairs always reminds me of going to the dentist. Every time it gives me that tiny jolt of almost normality, a distant memory of my old life. I gaze at the fluorescent light above me, watching it flicker ever so slightly. The feeder comes in, dressed in scrubs, thick gloves on. She doesn't say a word, just gestures for me to give her my arm.

First comes the depo shot, and it barely stings. The feeders say it's so we don't have to deal with menstrual hygiene, but I also know the blood of pregnant people can send them insane. They have to know that what happened the other night between the couple in the dorm is bound to happen, no matter how forbidden it is.

She puts the brace around my arm, tightening it almost painfully. "Make a fist," she says sternly.

I obey, not looking at her. I know the drill. It's been almost five years of this.

She puts the needle in my arm, and it stings. These fucking feeders all suck at taking blood, a fact so ironic it almost makes me laugh. But then a shiver breaks out down my spine as I think of the alternative harvesting method, the one that's no longer allowed.

Some girls at school talked about the bite once. One of them insisted her cousin had been with a feeder, and that the bite had been better than sex. There were a whole bunch of folks who got addicted to the high a feeder bite gave them, and the thought makes me sick. Having a feeder touch me in a benign way like this, with gloves while they're taking blood, that's bad enough. The idea of letting one touch me intimately, letting one fuck me or bite me, or make me come?

No fucking way.

The curtain pushes aside, and a figure walks in that has me wishing I wasn't tied down to a chair right now.

It's the staring feeder from the cafeteria. His rust-red eyes take me in curiously, moving over my body almost languidly. It gives me chills. He's looking at me in a way that someone who doesn't know me shouldn't be. He pushes his dark hair from his forehead, revealing a tattooed hand and more tattoos emerging from the sleeve of his uniform. Even his neck is tattooed, and he has a small silver earring in his right earlobe. I don't know why it strikes me as strange, a tattooed, pierced feeder, is that even weird? Maybe he was some sort of rockstar before he was turned.

He's tall, I could see that before, but he's also just so *big*. Broad and muscular, his size so imposing it makes me feel incredibly small and vulnerable. I'd heard that vampires could gain strength from their makers if they were old and powerful, and from the looks of this guy his maker was one of those.

Finally his eyes stop moving all over my body and settle on my face. *Wait.* Did he just lick his lip?

"Everything alright here?" He has a British accent, a deep voice that's almost a little husky. The hairs on the back of my neck stand up.

The female feeder nods absently, filling out a chart, writing my number at the top of a form. We're all just numbers here. No names. Only amongst ourselves.

"Contraception was administered," she says, adjusting the clipboard in her hand to fill out some lines further down the form, "and we will be taking 500 mls of A+."

The man nods, his eyes staying on me. His skin has a hint of tan, and when he grits his white teeth behind his full lips, it occurs to me that I'm staring at his mouth. He's attractive I guess, or he would be if he wasn't dead and didn't have freaky red eyes, or fangs.

"I'll be right back," the woman says, and rises to her feet, pushing through the curtain, which parts with a metallic hiss.

The man watches her go then turns his attention back to me, his hands staying firmly in his pockets.

There are people just a few feet away, but I feel incredibly fucking alone right now. He's just staring at me. My throat goes dry and I swallow, trying to produce some saliva so I don't start coughing everywhere.

"Is there something wrong?" I finally ask him.

He shakes his head, the first movement he's made with something other than his eyes or his lips. "Not at all."

"OK, so why are you staring at me?"

He tilts his head, narrowing his eyes slightly. "Am I?"

"Yes. You were staring at me in the cafeteria too."

"Just keeping an eye on everyone," he replies.

"I'm not everyone." I'm glaring at him now, trying to figure out what the hell is going on. "And you feeders usually aren't this chatty."

"Hmmm." He takes a step towards me, his eyes flickering to me when he sees me flinch. He looks over the needles in my arm, and his mouth twitches for a moment, like he's judging the other feeder's handiwork. Then he shakes his head and takes a step back, his eyes meeting mine again.

And the staring continues.

The woman shuffles back into the cubicle, and checks the bag slowly filling with my blood. "How are you feeling?" She asks me.

I shrug. "Fine, as always."

"Good." She doesn't care, she's just saying it because she should. Even feeders still have residual small talk built-in, saying shit they don't mean in the name of being polite. She's probably not very old.

I look at her for a moment, taking in her blunt black bob and brown eyes, and I wonder who she was before this all started. How long before the Affliction was she turned? Was she a doctor? She has that demeanor about her.

Then I become aware of eyes on me again, and the man's still standing there staring at me. I'm about to ask him what's going on, what's wrong, what he wants, when he suddenly pushes through the curtains and leaves.

Fucking freak.

Once the bag is full of my blood, the woman removes the needle from my arm and puts a band-aid over the hole left behind. She tells me to stay seated, and leans out of the curtain to call for a tray. Another feeder comes in with a tray containing a milkshake and a donut.

"Eat," she says, gesturing at the tray placed by my side.

More things I can't stand now, that I loved before I came here. I remember my brother and I driving to the donut shop in town that was open til midnight, sitting on the hood of his car, him always stealing my strawberry frosted donut even though he insisted the plain glazed were his favorite.

The donut gets caught on the lump that forms in my throat as I think of him, of Kaden, my twin. My dad used to call us Raggedy Ann and Andy, even though neither of us had red hair. "We got one of each," my mom would say lovingly whenever she stroked her hands over our heads, over Kaden's dark hair, just like hers, and my blonde waves, just like my dad.

My eyes sting and I choke down the tepid milkshake. I still remember Kaden's voice when he called. "They're dead, Jules." He was sobbing. "I don't know what to do. What do I do?"

Then he was dead not even two weeks later.

And I was alone.

There's the clatter of metal on the ground, and I'm torn from my memories as shouting erupts from one of the neighboring cubicles. The woman rushes out to see what's going on.

"You can't do this!" It's a man's voice, it sounds like Larry, and he's protesting loudly.

My head spins as I grasp on to the headrest, hauling myself to my feet even as my face flushes and bile rises in my throat. I stumble to the curtain as more shouting erupts.

"What's going on?" I hear the woman's voice as I poke my head out of the curtain.

"His veins are no good," another feeder says, a man in dark blue scrubs. "They're collapsing. He's done."

"No!" Larry is suddenly pulled out of the cubicle, his eyes wide with terror. "What are you doing? I can still work, I'm still of use!"

The woman shakes her head. "No blood, no use. Take him off."

My stomach drops. "What are you doing?" I call out, stumbling out of the cubicle even as my head fills with that floaty cotton wool feeling.

The feeders turn to look at me, and the woman points with her index finger. "Go and sit down," she orders, "this is none of your concern."

"Well, it is my concern."

She glares at me. "How so?"

I take another step out of the cubicle. "Come on, he's one of us."

Larry latches on to this and looks at them with wild eyes. "She's right, I am, I'm one of them and you can't just get rid of me like this! I have people here, who care about me. I can be of use, I can cook and clean and help with the medical equipment. Before all this I was a lab -”

“Off.” The woman points, and two feeders grab Larry, lifting him almost off his feet as they carry him outside.

“Hey!” I move to go after them, white lines floating through my vision. “Hey, where are you taking him?”

I follow them out of the building, making it to the bottom of the stairs of the clinic before a hand grabs me. I look up into the face of the staring man, and flinch.

“Where are you going?” He asks.

I gesture after Larry, who’s screaming and begging for them not to hurt him. “Wherever they’re taking him.”

He shakes his head. “You don’t want to do that, trust me.”

My heart begins to pound in my chest, and I notice the man’s rusty eyes flickering to my chest. “They’re going to kill him, aren’t they?”

“He’s aged out,” the man replies, his voice so neutral it’s almost cold. “His veins are no good. Time to be replaced.”

I shake my head. “You can’t just kill someone,” I say, realizing as the words leave my mouth how stupid they are. They can do whatever the fuck they want. They don’t care about us. We’re assets, bloodbags. Nothing more.

I look over to where they dragged Larry away, and there’s a high pitched shout. I jump involuntarily. I look back up at the man, who’s just staring at me again.

“It’s just how it is,” he says to me, his hand still on my arm.

I try to yank my arm out of his grasp, but his grip is like iron. “Let go of me.” I say in a low voice.

For a second his grip becomes tighter, and I almost think he’s going to draw me closer. But then his hand falls away from me, and he straightens up. “Go back to your dorm.”

“I’m not going back to that fucking dorm,” I snap, and storm off in the direction of the garden. Before I can even reach the edge of the building, a gunshot rings through the air. I don't know if it's shock, or the lack of blood, but the ground sways beneath me. I try to steady myself, but suddenly my feet have left the ground.

I hate draining week.

RAIN DRUMS against the tin roof above me, and for once a cool breeze moves through the dorm. Everyone is at lunch but I've been put on bed rest for some dumb reason. I'm not going to question it because I'm alone and I'm so happy. I've been able to just lie here and read while the rain drums down, and it's blissful.

After I collapsed yesterday the rest of my draining was canceled for this week, and I'm on an extended break. Thank god for that. Bruises are blooming on my skin from the botch job the feeder did, and I don't even want to think about how bad they would be by the end of the week.

I glance over at Larry's bed and feel a pang. I can't believe they just killed him. I should be more upset about it, but I guess the feeders' blase attitude is fueling my own. You care less and less about the sanctity of life when the whole world's gone to shit and everyone's dead.

A breeze blows a sheet of rain against the glass behind me, and I tilt my head to catch a glimpse of the overcast sky. I wonder what the rest of the world looks like now. I know the big cities are all destroyed. The Affliction traveled so fast there, wiping out whole populations in months.

My parents took Kaden and I to Paris once, when we were 12. It was beautiful. I remember making myself sick eating macarons, the green ones were my favorite. It's all gone now, I bet. I wonder if there's some colonies out in the French countryside, like this one, where they farm free range humans for the feeders. There has to be, right?

The door at the end of the dorm opens, and a feeder walks in, gesturing for someone to follow him. A young man walks in, messy dark brown hair hanging over his forehead. He ambles along behind the feeder, a sports bag slung over his shoulder.

I sit up in bed, and the man smiles at me as he approaches.

"Hey, I'm the new arrival," he says jovially. The feeder stops at the bed next to mine, Larry's old bed, and the man throws his bag down. They really didn't waste any time replacing Larry as quickly as possible.

"This will be your bed," the feeder says, "there's a locker underneath for your things."

"Yeah, thanks," the man says, sitting down on the bed and leaning back on his hands. He smiles at the feeder. "You can go now."

The feeder glares at him, then shakes his head and leaves quickly. The man looks back at me and shakes his head, grinning.

"I'm Matt."

"I'm Juliet." I extend my hand. He takes it and smiles, revealing a mouth full of white teeth that glow against his tanned skin.

God, he's fucking gorgeous. His shoulders are broad and his hand is strong and warm. He looks to be about 30 or so.

And he's going to be sleeping next to me. Jesus shitting christ.

"You been here long?" Matt asks, releasing my hand to slouch back on his bed.

I sigh, nodding. "Yeah, almost 5 years now."

Matt raises his eyebrows. "Holy shit."

"Where did you come from?"

"Breeding farm, over near Charleston."

My jaw drops. "A breeding farm?" I've never met anyone from one of those places. The feeders' barbaric program to keep a steady supply of humans. I've spent many nights thanking my lucky stars that I didn't end up in one of those places.

Matt nods, rising to his feet to unzip his sports bag. "Yeah, it was fucking weird. I have like 25 kids and don't know any of them."

My skin crawls. "That's awful, I'm so sorry."

He shrugs as he starts unpacking his things. "I'm out of there now. If I never see another viagra in my lifetime I'll be happy." He grins at me. "And now I get to sleep next to you every night, so, everyone wins, right?"

I give a little awkward laugh. "I don't snore from what I'm told, so lucky you."

"If you tell me you sleep naked my life will be complete." He laughs, then looks at me sheepishly. "Sorry, I don't mean to be creepy. I'll stop."

I shake my head and smile. I'm enjoying the flirting, because Matt is so handsome and I'm also feeling lonely as fuck all of a sudden. "No, it's fine. We have to do what we have to do to get along, right?"

"I guess so." He dumps his things into the locker and sends it back under the bed with a kick. "Are you sick? Is that why you're in here alone during the day?"

I pull my knees up to my chest and wrap my arms around them. "I collapsed after draining yesterday, so I got written off for the week."

"Did they take too much?"

I shrug. "They dragged off the guy whose bed you have

now, took him out back and shot him like he was an old horse or something. It got me a little worked up."

Matt scoffs. "Jesus, that's fucked up. I'm sorry." He leans forward and rubs my arm. "That's awful."

"I guess it's just part of life around here, huh?"

"Still fucked up." Matt replies, rubbing the back of his neck and tipping his head back. "It's so hot here."

"Yeah get used to it, this dorm is like an oven during the night."

Matt looks around the room and shakes his head. "Breeding farm is like a five star hotel compared to this."

I give a cynical laugh. "Think I'd take this over being forced to do... that."

"Yeah that's for damn sure," he replies, and his expression darkens for a second. He gives himself a shake and rises to his feet. "I guess I should let you rest and see if they need me somewhere else."

I reach out for him without thinking, suddenly not wanting to be alone so badly after all. "Hey, no, you can rest for a while, you just had a long drive here, right?"

The dorm door flies open and we both look to see the feeder who wouldn't stop staring at me walk in. I feel a flush rise in my cheeks as a faint memory washes through my mind, of him carrying me to my bed yesterday, sweeping me up in his arms like I weighed nothing.

He walks towards us, his hands in his pockets, he always looks so fucking casual, like he's strolling into a coffee shop or something. He looks Matt up and down when he stops at the end of my bed, then looks down at me. "You feeling better?" He asks.

I shrug. "I guess so."

"I've told them to give you extra supplements for the next week."

"Great. Thanks."

His rusty red eyes stay fixed on me, flickering for a millisecond to my bare legs. "Your donation has been canceled for tomorrow."

"I know, they told me." I just want him to go away and stop staring at me. When he doesn't move, I raise my eyebrows. "I'm fine, thanks."

His lips move, as though he's dragging them against his fangs, then he turns abruptly and heads back out of the dorm, the door falling closed behind him.

"Friend of yours?" Matt asks with a chuckle.

I roll my eyes. "That guy freaks me out. He keeps staring at me."

"Maybe he's hungry?"

"Oh shut up," I say, and I can't help but smile as Matt bursts out laughing.

"Hey, maybe he thinks you're hot." Matt shrugs. "I mean, you are, so..."

I flush again and shake my head. "I'm a mess, are you kidding?" I run my blonde hair self-consciously through my hands. It used to be lighter, back when I could go to a salon and get highlights, now it's just a sandy kind of color, and way too long.

"Nah, you're cute," Matt says, grinning. "I mean it, those freckles." He gestures across his own face, over his nose, indicating the freckles that stray there on my face. "They're real cute. Very girl-next-door."

I scoff. "Yeah, OK. You can stay. You're going to be good for my ego."

"I hope so." He smiles. "I guess I'd better go. I'll see you at bedtime then?"

"I'll be right here," I reply. And then I remember he and I will be scheduled to shower in the same shift tonight because we're not up for draining, and I think I'm going to cringe myself into oblivion.

He leaves the dorm with a wave, and I throw myself back on the bed. The ceiling fan spins around and around. My eyes get heavy, and I drift off as thunder rumbles outside.

THE SIREN SOUNDS JUST as we're being ushered into the bathroom block. The high-pitched wail sends chills down my spine, and everyone begins to murmur in collective panic. Gina grabs on to my hand.

"I was wondering when this was going to happen," she says, her eyes flickering from the feeders back to my face. "There hasn't been an attack in a while."

"Yeah, like 6 months now right?" I just hope this horde is smaller than the last one.

Gina nods, opening her mouth to speak but she's interrupted as the feeders start barking commands, telling us to move out into the yard. The siren drones on overhead as we're herded back to the dorms, and feeders are running towards the gates, guns slung over their shoulders.

I look up into the observation tower, and there's a flurry of activity up there too. A chill runs through me, and Gina grasps my hand tighter like a concerned mother as she no doubt feels me trembling.

Fucking Afflicted. These attacks scare the shit out of me. Last time they nearly made it in, I think one of them actually did, because the next day a few feeders were gone and we never saw them again. I'm guessing they got infected, but no one ever tells us anything.

We're unceremoniously shoved into the dorm, and then the door is closed behind us, the heavy metallic lock falling into place. Gina and I go to our beds, putting our things back into the lockers. Gina must be scared too, because she sits beside me on my bed, holding my hand.

Matt sits down opposite us. "This happen a lot?"

I shrug. "Last couple of years it's been a lot less frequent, the first two years it happened nearly every week."

Gunfire sounds in the distance, and Gina flinches. A few people cry out in surprise, and someone sobs softly nearby. If the Afflicted make it in, we all die. The feeders can survive an infection, even though they'll be outcasts, roaming around just like the horde attacking us now. But we'll all be dead. Either the virus will take us out, or the crazed feeders will kill us before it gets a chance.

Heavy footfalls sound right outside the window, and we can hear shouted commands. The siren stops blaring, and the eerie silence that falls suddenly is somehow worse. We all just sit and wait - what else can we do?

"This ever happen at the farm?" I ask Matt quietly.

He nods, a pained expression on his face. "They only made it in one time, but it was bad. They got to the maternity ward and..." He trails off as Gina gasps, and shakes his head. "Never mind."

Without thinking I reach across and take his hand, which he grasps tightly. We all need comfort right now.

The fact that the attacks aren't happening as often should probably comfort me. The Afflicted are probably dying off, starving to death slowly. They'll all die out eventually, right? But in the meantime, are they getting more desperate?

There's an explosion somewhere nearby, and a collective shriek goes up in the dorm. Fuck, fuck, fuck. They're trying to blow open the gate, that has to be it. Gina throws an arm around my shoulders, clutching me to her to comfort herself as much as me.

We're so fucked.

I should want to die, right? Why would I want to keep living like this? This sucks. It's not a life. It's an existence.

But I don't want to die. I don't want to end my life in agony, suffocating on my own blood as my lungs fill with it. Like my mom, my dad, like my poor brother who fucking died alone on our kitchen floor, the phone clutched to his mouth as he begged me to help him. All I could do was tell him I loved him. All I could do was listen to him die.

Tears bite at my eyes, and I turn my face into Gina's shoulder. I'm scared. I'm fucking terrified.

There's another explosion, and the ground beneath us quakes. Gina and I sink to the floor, Matt joining us quickly. And the others all follow suit, as though being lower to the ground will somehow help us.

There's gunfire right outside the dorm, and there's a sound, a bloodcurdling groaning sound, like something from a zombie movie. Afflicted. They're in the compound. We're thin metal walls away from them. We're going to die. Fuck, we're going to die.

Bullets ping off the outer walls of the dorm and I press my hand to my mouth to stop myself from screaming. Gina is crying now, silent tears rolling down her cheeks as she clutches on to me.

"It's OK," Matt whispers, moving closer to us, putting a hand on my shoulder. "It's going to be OK."

I nod. I know it's not going to be OK. We're fucked. But I nod anyway.

There's a sharp pinging sound, followed by another explosion, but this one is smaller, maybe it's further away? There's a chorus of sharp cries outside, and I can smell something, like bug spray almost, sharp and sweet and deeply unpleasant. It burns my throat and makes me cough, coating my tongue in a furry layer.

Something starts banging and clawing on the door, shrieking wildly. We're all silent but the room is so taut with terror we may as well all be screaming. I clasp Matt's hand on my shoulder, and we keep our eyes fixed on the door.

They're here. They're right here, trying to get in. They know where we are. They've found us. Maybe the feeders have abandoned us now, too worried about themselves. They'll make more humans. They can just breed them, they don't need us. They left us to preserve themselves.

Bullets slam into the door, and I can't help but cry out. There's shouting, so much shouting and so many heavy footsteps outside. More bullets fly, and one of the windows cracks from side to side.

And then suddenly, the shrieking stops. Everything goes quiet, well, as quiet as it can considering what's just happened. The air becomes lighter, and I try to breathe normally, to stop the air rasping into my lungs in a panic. I begin to shiver violently as the adrenaline of the moment floods my body, and Gina hugs me tight.

"Is it over?" She asks after a few minutes.

There are voices outside. Feeders talking. I strain to hear what they're saying, to get any hint of detail, to try and glean what's fucking happening. I swear one of them says "eliminated".

Matt rises tentatively to his feet, creeping up the wall underneath the window, angling his head to peer out. He looks left, then right, then drops back down to the ground. He crawls over to us and shakes his head.

"I think they got them all," he whispers. "There's feeders out there, and they seem pretty relaxed."

The speaker mounted on the wall overhead crackles to life. "Please remain in the dorms and remain calm," the voices announces robotically. "Lockdown conditions will remain until morning." There's a high-pitched whir as the announcement ends, and the speaker falls silent.

We all climb slowly onto our beds, fear etched into the faces around me.

"Shit." Matt sits down heavily, his eyes still widened with mild shock. "What a first day."

"Yeah," I say with a nervous laugh, "welcome to Hell."

CHAPTER 5

JULIET

"ARE YOU AWAKE?"

I open my eyes, and turn on to my side to look at Matt. "Yeah. Just a little on edge."

"Freaked you out a bit, huh?"

I shrug against my pillow. "It's been a while since we had an attack, I don't know, guess it did."

He shifts a little, his eyes darting away before bouncing back to my face. "Did you... I mean, did you wanna come sleep over here?"

"With you?" I smile, trying not to giggle and hoping to god he doesn't see the flush in my cheeks. "You think I'm that easy, huh?"

He clenches his eyes shut and runs a hand over his face. "Ugh sorry, I didn't mean it like that."

The giggle breaks free from me, and suddenly everything feels giddy and even a bit dangerous. I shouldn't go and climb into his bed. I don't even know this guy. But my skin is screaming for someone's hands to touch it, to feel the warmth of another body against mine, and the urge is so strong that I find myself climbing out of the bed and under Matt's waiting arm before I know it.

"Is this weird?" He asks as he presses himself to my back, his arms wrapping around me.

"Everything is weird." I close my eyes, because goddamn this feels nice. I sigh, settling into his warmth. "In case you hadn't noticed."

He chuckles, his warm breath brushing across my ear. "Yeah, guess you're right." He strokes my arms, his fingers moving up over my shoulder and back down again. Goose-bumps rise over my skin. "This isn't a bad way to end a crazy first day though."

"Glad I made it all worthwhile." I smile to myself as he chuckles again.

"You're funny."

I shake my head against his bicep. "Nope, just cynical."

"How old are you?"

"Twenty-four. And you?"

"Thirty-two." He makes a sound in his throat as I shift against him, almost like a groan, and when his hips press against me, I can feel that he's getting hard.

I should go back to my bed. But a little secret thrill wells up in my stomach, sending out a rush of butterflies. I try not to react, just lie in his arms and enjoy his warmth. The night may be hot, but having the heat of another person so close like this, it's different. It's welcoming.

"What were you? Before?"

He strokes my hair, brushing along the nape of my neck, and I can't help but shiver.

"I was a mechanic," he replies in a voice that's way too low and sexy for what we're discussing. "Mainly motorbikes and stuff. I worked for a team, they did all the big races. It was fun. How about you?"

"Just started college." I bite my lip to suppress a moan as his fingers start to trace small circles along my collarbone. He's so close to my breasts, my nipples are brushing painfully against the cotton of my t-shirt. "This all started my first week."

"Well, that fucking sucks." His mouth moves closer to my neck. He's really hard now, his erection pressing into my back. "What was your major?"

I'm hot all over, and I should go back to my bed. I barely know this guy. His lips brush against my neck, and I bite my lip. Getting involved is a bad idea. This isn't going to lead any place good, and I don't need to catch feelings for this guy.

"I-I hadn't decided yet." I finally answer, my voice barely audible.

"No?" He kisses my neck. Actually kisses it. I'm going to melt. Oh god I'm going to be a grease spot in the damn mattress. I'm just touch-starved, that's all. Nothing needs to actually happen. But I really, *really* want it to.

"I thought I had time," I gasp as his hand moves down my side, across my hip to splay across my stomach. "I was just going to take some art classes and decide, because I was there on a scholarship and..." I trail off as he kisses my neck again, a flood of heat erupting between my thighs. "I, um, god, I thought I still had time."

"Didn't we all?" He presses himself harder against my back, the hand that was caressing my collarbone moving down to the hem of my shirt. His fingertips move closer to my breast, and I tense against him as his thumb brushes my nipple. "Is this OK?"

Is it OK? I don't know. I haven't been touched like this in years, and even before that, it hadn't been more than teenage fumblings in the back of a car that my date had borrowed from his parents.

"Yeah, it's OK." I whimper as he gently rolls my nipple between his fingers.

"You're so fucking pretty, you know that?" He growls in my

ear. His hand moves up my stomach until it's cupping my breast. "Can you feel how hard I am?"

I nod, wriggling my ass against him. "Yeah."

"Will you touch it for me, baby?"

I reach down tentatively between us, pushing my hand into his shorts. Matt groans against my shoulder as I wrap my hand around his dick. I don't move for a second, and he shifts so his mouth is against my ear.

"That feels so fucking good." His chest vibrates as I feather my hand gently up and down his length. He inhales sharply as I begin to pump him awkwardly, the tip of his cock meeting my back as he pushes my tank top up. This angle sucks, but he seems to be enjoying it anyway. One of his hands works my nipple, and the other moves down into my panties. His finger rubs up and down my clit, and I bury my face in his arm.

"I need to be inside you." His voice is ragged with desire.

This is a mistake. I should go back to my bed. But then one of his fingers slips inside me, and my need takes over. I just need him to fuck me. My eyes dart over to Gina, just a bed away, but she's sleeping peacefully. No one else seems to be moving. Maybe it'll be OK. No one will notice.We just have to stay quiet.

"OK." *God, Juliet, what a fucking answer.* I release his dick, frantically pulling my panties aside as his knee parts my thighs. He fists himself and guides himself inside me, slipping all the way in easily because I'm so wet. I bite my lip trying not to moan.

He groans again. "Fuck, you feel good."

I don't respond, just close my eyes and try to let go and sink into the feeling of him being inside me. He thrusts as hard as he can without alerting the others, the bed creaking softly beneath us. He breathes heavily against my ear, muttering out smothered curses, nibbling on my ear lobe.

This is crazy. I met this guy this afternoon, we've barely spoken at all, and now I'm letting him fuck me. Would I have thought it was weird if I'd just picked him up in a bar? Met him at a concert? Is it weird to fuck a random stranger in a crowded dorm right after flesh-eating zombies nearly tore you apart? I don't know anything anymore.

Before I can get too worked up, he shudders, and it's over. My breath catches in my throat as the air floods out of my lungs, hanging somewhere between arousal and disappointment.

He sighs, and leans his forehead against the back of my head. "Sorry."

I shake my head. "It's fine. It's OK."

"They fed me so many drugs, my body's fucked up."

"It's OK, really." I shift as he pulls out of me, clenching my thighs together to try and stop his cum running everywhere. I didn't even have time to feel good. I wanted that rush and now the feeling of deflation is so great that I just feel dirty. I don't even know what to do. Do I just get up? Do I encourage him to keep going? He catches his breath against my back as I just lie in his bed, wondering what the fuck to do next.

I don't have to think for long. The dorm door flies open, hitting the wall with a resounding crack that sends a shockwave of movement through the sleeping figures around us.

Shit.

It's the fucking feeder who just stares at me. He's stalking across the dorm, moving fast. Heads raise from their beds as he moves, and my face flushes violently as all eyes follow him, coming to rest on Matt and I in his bed.

The feeder comes to a stop at the end of Matt's bed, his jaw ticking violently as his crimson eyes move from Matt to me.

"What's this?" He growls through gritted teeth

"Nothing," I mutter, hoping to god that if I keep my head

down and just don't look at anyone that this will all just turn out to have been a bad dream.

"What's this?" He asks again. His hands aren't in his pockets, they're balled into fists at his side.

"Nothing!" I adjust my clothes, flinching as my panties become wet and cold as cum continues to run out of me.

The feeder's nostrils flare, and his eyes are positively flaming now.

"Get up." He orders.

Matt sits up beside me. "Hey, man, we were just -"

"Get the fuck up." His accent just makes him sound even scarier.

"And go where?" I hiss at him, very aware of the eyes of everyone else in the dorm boring into my flushed face. I sit up, my cheeks burning with shame.

"Shower, now." The feeder jerks his head over his shoulder in the direction of the door. Matt rises from the bed and the feeder points a finger at him. "Not you. Just her."

"Fuck you." I clutch the sheet to my chest like it'll somehow ward him off. "I'm not going anywhere."

With a roar that sends me stock-still with shock, the feeder lunges at me. Before I can scream or shriek or even draw breath, he's thrown me over his shoulder, stalking the length of the dorm.

"Put me down!" I hammer at his back. "What the fuck are you doing? Put me down!"

Everyone's up now, watching this whole situation unfold in front of them. The feeder keeps carrying me out into the night, across the yard to the shower block, ignoring my blows to his back and my shouted protests. Even the other feeders regard us with curiosity and confusion.

Who the fuck is this guy?

He slams open the door to the shower block, and in the shower room he unceremoniously puts me on my feet. I stumble a little, backing away from him against the cool tiled wall.

"What the fuck is your problem?"

Goddamn he's terrifying. His eyes are bright red, his shoulders heaving as he breathes through gritted teeth.

"Wash. Now." His voice is an angry snarl, echoing off the bare walls.

"I'm not showering in front of you."

"Suddenly got standards on who's allowed to see you naked, ey?"

My hand shoots out, nothing but instinct driving me, and I slap him hard across the face. "How *dare* you."

The slap barely moved his head at all, and his mouth curls into a cruel grin. "Get your fucking clothes off right now and wash that filth off you."

"Or what?" I counter, hands on my hips.

His hands slam against the wall either side of me, and I suppress a shriek. There's no way I'm letting this guy know I'm scared of him. I stick my chin out defiantly as he leers down at me.

"You wash right now, or I go back and divest your little boyfriend of his head."

I gasp, shrinking away from him as much as I can. "You fucking psycho. You're not allowed to do that."

"Try me." He yanks on the tap beside us, and a stream of water cascades down onto the floor. He takes a few steps back from me, crossing his arms over his chest. "Now. Clothes off. Wash."

I glare at him for a moment, before stripping off my sticky clothes and throwing them at his feet. I want to turn my back to him to shield my body from him, but the idea of turning my back to this unhinged asshole makes me shiver. No way am I taking my eyes off him.

I wash myself under his gaze, lathering myself up with soap twice over just to make sure I'm clean enough for him. I shut the water off, and brattily raise my eyebrows at him as I squeeze the water from my hair.

"And? Am I clean enough?"

He tilts his head, looking me up and down. He inhales through his nose, huffing out a heavy breath through his mouth, and his eyes meet mine. My mouth runs a little dry as I wonder if he was the creepy asshole that sniffed me out the other night, and the thought makes heat rise in my cheeks.

"Well?"

He runs his tongue over his teeth, pausing to probe the tip of one of his fangs. "Much better."

"Great." I run my fingers through my hair. "As long as you're happy."

"What's your name?"

The question takes me by surprise. "Wh-what?" They never ask us our names. We're numbers, nothing but numbers. I don't even know if they know our names at all.

"Your name." He says it slowly, still staring at my face.

I scoff, tearing a towel from the wall. "Like you care."

"I asked you your name."

I shrug, not meeting his eyes as I dry my hair with the towel. "Bloodbag 4211487."

Suddenly there's a hand on my arm, and he's towering over me, those red eyes blazing.

"I asked you... Your fucking name." His voice is low, every word dripping out of him with vicious intent.

"Juliet," I reply, trying to jerk my arm out of his grasp, but it's like iron.

"Juliet." He repeats it slowly, and tilts his head ever so slightly.

"Happy now?" I wrench my arm again, but he still won't let me go. "You want me to ask yours? Is this your idea of a meet cute?"

The corner of his mouth twitches, almost like he's going to grin. It's just a split second, but it's enough to reveal something almost human about him. It makes me uncomfortable in the weirdest way.

"My name is Silas. Silas King."

"Great to meet you, Silas." My voiced is edged with irritation. "Now, am I allowed to get dressed or is there anything else you desperately need to know while I'm naked?"

This time he does grin, almost as though he's going to chuckle, and he releases me. Leaning back against the shower wall, he watches me with narrowed eyes as I rub myself down with the towel.

"That... interaction."

I tilt my head with a sigh, meeting his eyes. "What about it?"

"It was consensual, yeah?"

"What do you care?"

His face darkens. "I don't approve of rape."

"You don't approve of rape?" I scoff, unable to suppress my laugh. "That's rich coming from the guy who just forced me to strip and shower for him."

"That's different." The predatorial tone in his voice makes the hair on the back of my neck stand up.

I shake my head, pushing away the shivers and uneasiness that his goddamn voice sends through me. "Sure it is. Twisted feeder logic, huh? Pin us down and take our blood but draw the line at rape. How fucking noble of you." I stalk across the wet room and grab my clothes from the floor, and when I spin back to face him he's right behind me.

"Was it consensual?" His intense gaze threatens to swallow me up. "Because if it wasn't-"

"Oh my god, yes, yes," I say quickly, not wanting him to race back into that dorm and actually tear Matt's head off. "I wanted it, OK?"

His expression becomes unreadable, and my stomach does that weird drop thing, like I've just gone over the top of a roller-coaster. His eyes move over my face slowly.

"If anyone hurts you," he says slowly, "let me know. I'll deal with them." His gaze drops to my lips. "Will you do that, Juliet?"

"No." I pull the tank top and my panties back on, recoiling for just a second as the cold, soaked fabric touches my skin. "I don't need your help. I don't need you calling me by my name. I need you to stop staring at me all the damn time."

I throw the wet towel at his feet and storm out of the shower room. He doesn't follow me, thank god. The moon hangs heavy in the sky as I cross the yard back to the dorm, the crickets singing loudly in the warm night. It's a stupidly idyllic scene for how pissed off I feel.

The feeder at the door lets me in, and I rush back to my bed. Matt sits up as I approach, asking if I'm OK, did they hurt me? But I ignore him, I can't even look at his face. I just climb into my bed and pull the sheets up over my head.

My whole body is shaking with anger and embarrassment.

Silas King.

What a fucking asshole.

I clench my eyes shut, hoping and praying I can fall asleep and pretend this whole fucked up world doesn't exist for a few hours. I just want it all to go away.

I HAVEN'T BEEN able to look at Matt.

The few times he's tried to talk to me, I've kept my eyes fixed on the floor and mumbled an excuse to just leave. The shame of that night is so burned into my brain it makes me feel sick every time I think about it. Everyone in the dorm knows what happened and it was so excruciatingly awkward. Gina has been like a bulldog, staring down anyone who made a quip about that night. It's been the week from hell.

But today I'm finally on garden duty, and that makes me happy. Movement and sunshine and fresh air, even if that air is humid and thick. It's exactly what I need.

Unfortunately, Matt is on the garden team as well.

I try not to think about how close he is, focusing on my work instead. I set about weeding, crawling around on my knees in the dirt, plucking one dandelion after another from the garden bed, when someone kneels beside me. I look up and meet Matt's eyes.

"Hey," he says weakly. "Please talk to me."

I sigh, my shoulders slumping as I go back to the weeding. "I don't think there's a whole lot to say."

"I shouldn't have done that the other night, I'm sorry." He hangs his head, and the remorse on his face makes me ache a little.

"I wanted to," I assure him, giving him a weak smile when his eyes lift back to meet mine. "I did. It's been years since I slept with anyone."

He gives a bitter laugh. "That just makes me feel worse. You finally get laid, and it's by someone like me." He shakes his head quickly when he sees me open my mouth to speak. "No no, come on, sorry, I don't want to make you feel bad. You don't need to pity me." He rubs his hands together and looks me over. "Did that feeder hurt you?"

"No, he just made me shower." And asked me my name. Aggressively. It was weirdly humanizing, knowing his name and him knowing mine. I don't like it. I prefer the distance.

Matt sits back on the grass, his arms resting on his raised knees. "I'm really sorry about that night," he says softly, tearing apart a blade of grass in his fingertips. "It was just about as fucked up as it can get."

I look over at him, rocking back onto my knees. "You said your body was screwed because of the drugs?"

He nods. "They fed me viagra, and a whole bunch of other shit, just constantly, so I'd be, you know, able to get all these women pregnant." He looks out across the garden. "So now, even when I'm really turned on, even when I'm with someone who's real hot, my body just..." His gaze moves back to me and he shrugs helplessly. "I hate it. I really like you, you know, as much as I can when I just met you. I wanted to make you feel good, and then it was just over. And then..."

"Yeah, it wasn't great." I spot Silas standing over near the garden shed, his arms crossed over his chest as he watches us. "That feeder is a fucking psycho."

Matt looks over his shoulder. "Sure is." He turns back to face me and gives me a small smile. "I like you, Juliet. I really do. And I'd like to, I don't know, I mean... Maybe we could get to know each other a little, I'd like to at least be your friend."

I return his smile. "I'd like that too. I'm sorry I didn't talk to you, I was just so embarrassed."

"I totally get that, I felt so bad." He reaches over and takes my hand. "This whole situation is so fucked up."

"Yes it is." I sigh.

"You felt good though." His thumb brushes over my knuckles. "You felt really good."

"So did you," I reply, clasping his fingers a little tighter. I feel a twinge at lying, it hadn't really been long enough for me to decide if it was good. But Matt's sweet, and gentle, and he seems to want to get to know me. I hate the glimmer of hope this conversation is igniting inside me. That I'm now thinking that maybe we can find a way to be together, somewhere quiet, where we can take our time, as unlikely as that seems.

The shiver that breaks out over my shoulders tells me Silas is still watching from a distance, and I pull Matt to his feet quickly.

"Come on," I say, grabbing a wheelbarrow and pushing it down the hill, "let's go for a walk." I just know Silas's eyes are following me, like the fucking stalker he is. I just pray he doesn't follow me right now, because I can't take his gaze on me for one more second.

"Where are we going?" Matt asks as we cross the sunny stretch of grass.

"Away from the feeders, away from everyone else." I smile over my shoulder at him. "I come down here sometimes, just to get away. If I grab a wheelbarrow no one asks me any questions."

Matt chuckles. "Clever."

"It's hard to get alone time here." I push the wheelbarrow towards the compost pile. "I miss being alone."

"I was alone a lot at the farm," Matt says, perching on the wooden edge of one of the raised garden beds. "If I wasn't... down in one of the bedrooms with a woman, I was up in my room, alone."

I regard him with sympathy, squinting at him in the bright sunshine. "Did you have a family before all this started?"

He sighs, nodding. "Yeah, hadn't even been married a year when all this started." He leans his elbows on his knees, and I sit down beside him. "She died pretty quick, she was a nurse so she was one of the first in our town to get infected."

"I'm sorry."

"And you?"

"My parents were the first to die in our town," I reply, looking down at my hands. "My mom was a teacher, and she caught it off a student. Took it home to my dad, and they died the next day."

Matt exhales heavily. "I'm so sorry."

I nod. "And then my brother died two weeks later, and that was that. Family gone." I flick my nails together and sigh. "My college was an emergency response center for like 2 months. When the National Guard left, the feeders came. And they brought me here." I turn to look at him, trying to smile. "Why didn't they keep you at the breeding farm?"

He shifts a little, and a flush rises on his cheeks. "Because, well, because of my... issues."

"Oh shit," I say quickly, looking away. "I'm sorry, fuck, it's none of my business."

"No, no, it's OK." He grabs my hand, turning me back to face him. "Really. Don't be sorry. You just wanted to know."

"I'm sorry they did that to you." I hold on to his hand. "You really have 25 kids?"

He laughs bitterly. "Yeah I do, maybe even more, the feeders weren't always clear on what happened, you know, after. I only ever saw two of them, the others, they had the moms moved real fast to other colonies. It's a weird feeling, you know?" He puts his other hand on mine. "I always wanted to be a dad, have kids, have a family. And now I have a bunch of kids, a whole lot of women were pregnant with *my* kid, and I never got to do any of the things a dad does."

I don't want to say sorry anymore, because it's useless. We're all sorry, we've all lost people we loved. Not one person in this colony has been spared that. We're all united in grief and loss, and it's the worst thing to bind you to other people. So instead of saying sorry, I lean against Matt and welcome his arms around me.

"Goddamn it's hot," he says after a while.

I look around to check that no one's watching us, and then get to my feet. "Come on," I say, holding on to his hand. "I want to show you something."

He chuckles but says nothing, letting me drag him across the lawn towards the tree line. I check one more time over my shoulder to make sure no one has seen us, and then break into a run through the trees.

We wind our way through the foliage, twigs crunching underfoot as we go. It's cool down here, and after a few minutes I hear the bubbling of the stream that runs through the ambling tree roots.

"Hey, this is real pretty." Matt looks up and down the sun-dappled glade, over the water that's rushing past us. "Do you come down here often?"

I kick off my flip-flops and walk into the cool water. "Whenever I get the chance, which isn't very often."

"That's a shame." He kicks his shoes off and follows me into the water. He stands in front of me and smiles sheepishly. "So, I kind of realized I didn't even kiss you before we, you know."

"No, I guess you didn't." I gaze up at him. "Did you still want to kiss me after I didn't talk to you for a whole week?"

"Yeah, I do." His hand brushes over my shoulder. "I like you, a lot. You're not like anyone else I've met, in a really long time."

I give a half-hearted laugh. "I'd want to hope you don't know too many women who get dragged kicking and screaming from your bed and then ghost you for a week."

Matt laughs out loud, and my stomach does a little flip.

"See? I said you were funny." He places two fingers under my chin, tilting my head back.

"Nope, just cynical." My voice had been reduced to something barely above a breath as my eyes dip to his lips and I wait for him to kiss me.

"Cynical, maybe." He smiles. "But pretty cute too."

He lowers his mouth to mine to place a tender kiss on my lips.

My eyes flutter closed as his arm moves around my waist, drawing me closer and deepening the kiss. I put my arms around his neck, and even though it feels so nice, an ache unfurls inside me. I miss being touched. I miss being held. Matt kissing me just brings that all crashing down, so much more than anything that happened in his bed that night.

I'm lonely. I'm never alone, but I never touch anyone. No one ever touches me like this. I'm so fucking starved. We have sunshine and fresh air and food but we don't have *life*. We don't have hugs and jokes and date nights, movies and candlelit dinners where one of us tries way too hard.

No wonder I was willing to let Matt fuck me the afternoon

I met him. I'm aching, I'm dying for this, for another person to touch me, to stroke my hair, maybe rub my back and trail kisses over my neck.

Matt laughs softly when we part, his arms staying around my waist, holding me close. "You're a good kisser."

"So are you," I reply, leaning my head against his shoulder. "I miss kissing."

"Me too. I miss waking up with someone in my bed. Christ, I even miss cooking. Just putting music on and cooking together."

I sigh, because I miss that too. *Life.* So much of it I didn't even get to experience, and being in Matt's arms makes that all feel so much more unfair.

The drone of the siren sounds in the distance, and we're both instantly on alert, Matt's arms holding me tightly for a second as he looks down at me with pure panic etched in his eyes.

"Oh shit," he mutters, and we both break into a run through the trees to head back to the garden.

Not again.

The feeders are ushering everyone back into the buildings, and I see Gina looking around wildly, her hands clutched to her mouth. She spots me running and raises a hand.

"Juliet!" She calls, even as a feeder shoves her forward to keep moving.

"I'm coming! It's OK!"

Feeders sprint past the fence line, guns hanging at their sides. I see Silas with an enormous rifle in his hand, headed for the observation tower. His eyes move to me for a moment, and they're bright red. His face softens for a split second, into something like relief, before hardening back into that mask as he keeps moving.

"Another attack already?" Matt says as we're hurried back to the dorm.

I shake my head. "This hasn't happened in years." Fear freezes my veins. What could this mean? Are the Afflicted getting stronger? Are there just more of them now? I don't know what to think.

The feeders are as anxious as we are, I can see the fear in their faces. Even though the virus isn't deadly for them, they'll still be fucked. The siren wails on and on overhead.

We're almost at the dorm when an explosion tears through the fence at the western end of the compound. I cry out and grab on to Matt. Everyone around us is screaming, and we all watch in terror as a horde of Afflicted begin to flood through the fence. There must be at least 100 of them.

We're fucked. We're going to die now. I'm going to die just like Kaden did, just like my parents, like Matt's wife. It's all over now.

Gunfire erupts, and Matt and I sprint for the nearest building, one of the administration buildings I think. We try the door, but it's locked.

"Fuck." Matt pulls me along behind him as we run for the next building, which is the shower block. That door is locked too. "Goddammit!"

The dorm is too close to the advancing horde of Afflicted, so there's no point trying for there. We can hear them now that the siren has been shut off, their sickening shrieks and groans getting closer, punctuated by gunfire.

"In here!" I pull him into an alcove between the shower block and a storage building. It's hardly good cover, but we can at least attempt to hide and ride this out. I claw onto some tiny hint of optimism, even as dread fills me. We crawl to the very back of the space, behind some black plastic boxes and sit against the wall. Obviously I'm still breathing but my chest is so tight I just feel like I'm suffocating, like I'm drowning in dread that continues to build as gunfire erupts close by. I cover my ears with my hands, and Matt puts an arm around me, some small gesture of comfort even as it feels like death is crawling closer and closer. I bury my face in his shoulder to find he's trembling just as much as I am.

Loud shouts pursue a figure that races past us, the high-pitched buzz of bullets whirring past it matching the sound the figure is making. I hold my breath, hoping it didn't see us, didn't smell us, but with a scream it pounces on the black boxes.

I've never seen one of the Afflicted up close like this before. Its skin is a weird ruddy color, like it has a fever. Blood runs from its eyes. It has no hair, not even any eyebrows. Its mouth hangs open as it looks around, sniffing for us. I clasp my hand to my mouth, stopping myself from crying out and burrowing further under Matt's arm like he's armor.

A bullet smashes into the side of its skull, sending blood and fragments of bone flying. It collapses out of view, but another one comes running from the other direction, sniffing and shrieking, smelling the blood of the one that just exploded in front of us. It has a better view of us, its bloody eyes spotting us immediately. It throws itself onto the black boxes with a shriek, and I scream as its hands flail towards us.

Matt tries to haul me away, but the Afflicted gets a hold of my ankle and starts pulling me towards it. I grab on to Matt's hand, kicking out with my other foot, striking it in the face, but it keeps pulling. Its mottled teeth snap together loudly, its fangs inches from my leg.

I'm going to die, it's going to bite me.

Suddenly there's gunfire, right in front us, echoing off the tin roof above us. The Afflicted doesn't even have time to screech, collapsing soundlessly on my legs, completely limp as its blood cascades over me. I lift my head to meet Silas's blazing red eyes.

His gun remains aimed at the Afflicted for a moment, stepping forward cautiously.

"Don't move." His voice is so low I barely hear the words, but I see him mouth the words, and is he fucking crazy? I don't think I can move. I'm frozen in place. He moves to my side, nudging the Afflicted with his foot. My heart is in my throat. But it doesn't move. It's very clearly dead.

Silas pushes his gun to the side, and hauls the dead creature off my legs like it's nothing. He backs out of the alcove, looking left and right as he takes his weapon back in his hand, then gestures for me and Matt to follow him.

"Come on," he says in a low voice.

I wobble to my feet holding on to Matt, and we stay ducked down as we run after Silas. He takes us to a small green wooden building, throwing open the door and standing aside, his eyes scanning the compound as we go through the door.

He leans in and points to a chemical shower in the corner of the room. "Wash her down," he says to Matt, "and make sure none of the blood gets into her eyes or nose. Put the clothes in there." He points to a yellow biohazard bin on the other side of the room. He slams the door shut and the metallic lock clicks into place behind him.

I'm shaking so badly I can't take my clothes off, so Matt has to do it for me. I stand under the shower, and clench my eyes shut, terrified some of the blood will make its way into my body. I start to cry as the water runs over me, and I slump against the wall.

"It's OK, you're OK," Matt says, over and over. He must be in shock too. His voice is almost vacant. Finally the water runs clear, and I sob with relief that I can't taste blood, or see it, or smell it. Matt turns to get a towel from a steel trolley, and rubs me until my skin is raw. "You're OK." It's all he says, robotically, over and over until his voice seems to give out.

I wrap the towel around myself and sink onto a chair. There's more gunfire in the distance. Matt sits on the floor under the window, his legs stretched out in front of him. I can't stop fucking shaking. I was so sure I was going to die. And I would have, if it wasn't for... for Silas.

He saved me because I'm his food, it's no different to a farmer saving a cow from drowning even when they know it'll be a cheeseburger in a week. Of course he saved me. I'm an asset, something he needs.

"You OK?" Matt asks after a while.

"Yeah," I say, goosebumps breaking out across my skin. My jaw is chattering. "Just cold." Cold? In shock? Both?

Matt crawls across the floor and checks the steel trolley, finding a set of blue scrubs packed up in plastic. "Here," he says, tearing the packaging open.

I pull the scrubs on, which are a little big, but at least I'm not shivering naked in a towel anymore. I crawl down onto the floor next to Matt, and he puts his arm around me. I'm so numb the gunfire doesn't even make me flinch anymore. We just sit and wait, holding each other.

I DON'T KNOW how long we sit there, it must be at least two hours.

The screams, shouts and gunfire die down. There's a rushing sound, like flames, and after a while I can smell smoke and something else, something awful. I remain slumped against Matt, my back starting to hurt from sitting on the hard ground, but too scared to move. Footfalls pass the window, shouted commands. Feeders calling for medi packs, stretchers, more fuel.

Matt hasn't said a word. We're both silent, waiting to be told it's safe to come out.

I hear engines starting, and there's the metallic sound of a saw somewhere off in the distance.

The door opens, and Silas looks into the building, glancing around the door to find our spot on the floor. He drops to his knees, and I eye him warily. His uniform is splattered with blood, his hands covered in all kinds of carnage, and his face is full of concern.

"You alright?" He's only looking at me.

"Is it over?"

"It's over."

I nod. "Good."

Silas's brow furrows, his jaw tensing as though he wants to say more. Instead, he gets to his feet, gesturing for us to follow.

My legs feel stiff as we walk across the compound, from sitting curled up against Matt for so long. The feeders are building up bonfires at the far end of the compound, and tractors with large buckets are picking up the bleeding remains of the Afflicted which are scattered everywhere.

Silas escorts us back to the dorm. Matt goes ahead and opens the door, waiting for me to follow him.

I pause and turn to Silas. He's looking down at me with those rusty red eyes, and his face is almost sad.

"Thank you for saving me."

"Any time." His hand moves a little at his side, like he's moving to touch me, but he doesn't. "I told you I'd look out for you, didn't I?"

I scoff, shaking my head. I don't know what to say. He doesn't mean anything by it. I'm desperate for humanity in a vampire, in a fucking feeder. He doesn't care about me. It doesn't matter that he's looking at me with concern right now. He's a predator, and I'm his food.

Without another word I follow Matt into the dorm, and stop myself from looking over my shoulder to see if Silas is still there, watching me.

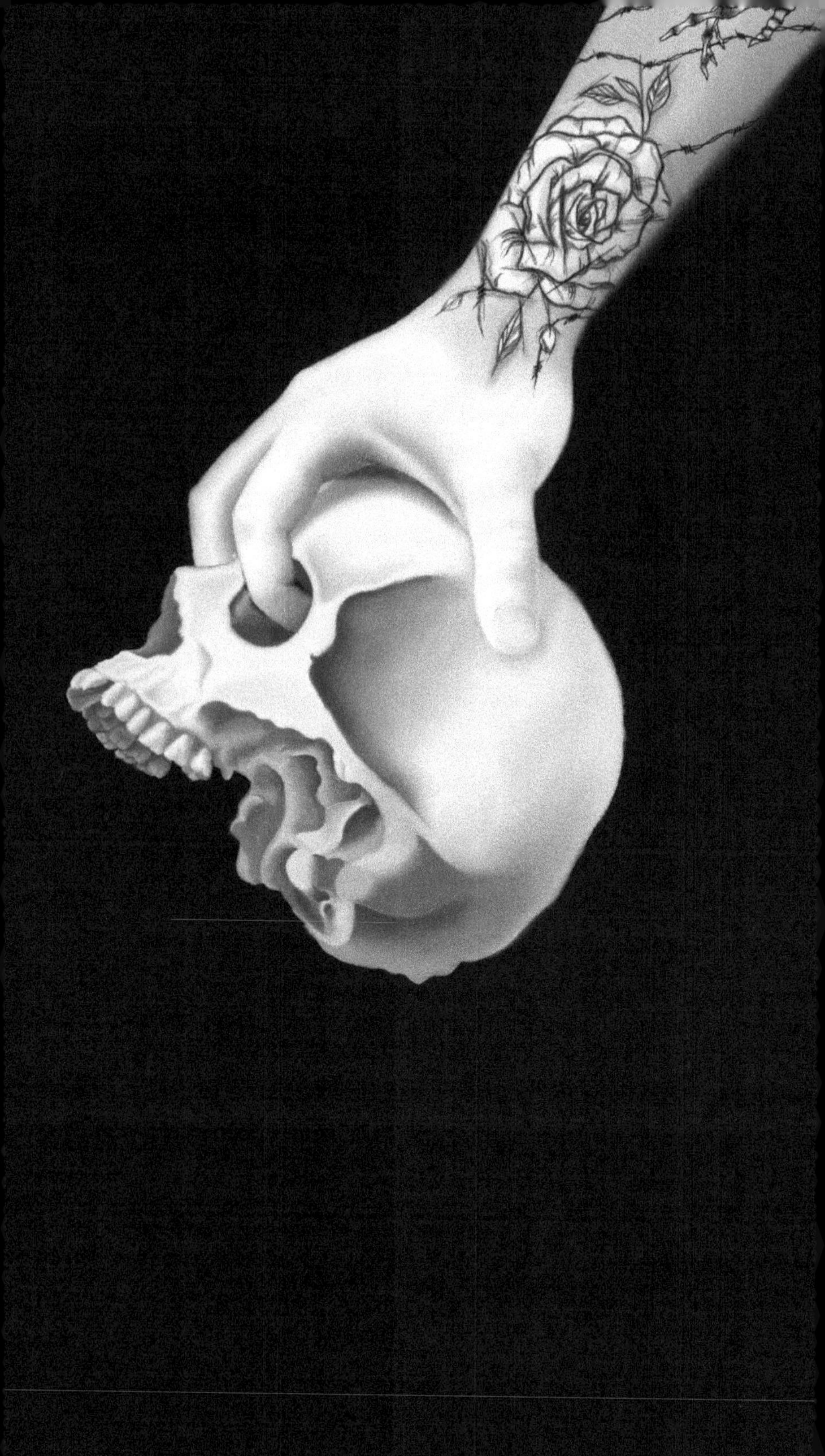

SILAS

THE SMELL of burning bodies is unlike any other I've ever smelled in my life, and when your sense of smell is heightened, it's even worse. Like the foulest barbecue you've ever experienced. The Afflicted smell especially bad. It makes my stomach churn.

The bonfires burn high, and that makes me uneasy. There were a lot this time. Too fucking many. We've gotten reports that there are more of them now. Some of the neighboring colonies were attacked and weren't able to defend themselves. Huge losses of human life, more infected vamps, and now more Afflicted.

I jam my hands into my pockets, walking around the bonfires. My hands curl into fists as I think of that Afflicted almost clawing its way into her, almost biting her.

Juliet. It's a name that suits her, as pretty as her face. Those freckles, the pouty, rosy lips, the long blonde hair. She looks like a painting, like something that's just walked out of a classic play. And her body, well there are enough fantasies of what I'd do to that body of hers floating around in my head to keep me awake for a century.

I shake my head at myself as I make my way to the officer's

hall. *Fucking fool.* I'm obsessed with a woman who cannot stand the sight of me. The way she looked at me after I'd saved her, after she thanked me for saving her - even in that moment of gratitude, she still looked at me as though I was nothing but a predator. I can't blame her. She hates the vamps, and why wouldn't she? What reason have I given her to want to trust me?

That doesn't make me any less obsessed.

Braun and Kaleb are sitting at the table in the officer's hall, a carafe of fresh blood sitting between them. They raise their glasses to me as I walk in.

"Evening!" Braun smiles widely, his teeth lined purple-red. "Smells incredible out there doesn't it?"

"Yeah, like a barbecue full of rotten fish, just lovely," I reply, picking up the carafe and filling a glass. "What do we have tonight, gentlemen?"

"A+, and a very good year." Kaleb picks up the empty blood bag and reads the label. "Aged 24 years apparently, female, 4211487."

My mouth goes dry. It's Juliet's blood. My musings over how she tastes are about to be answered, and the anticipation rushes into my lungs like acid. I pause with the glass at my lips, and just the coppery scent hitting the back of my throat is enough to have me biting back a groan.

"Not to your taste?" Kaleb asks, swirling the glass in his hand like he's consuming a fine cognac. "She tastes great to me."

"I'd like to get it fresher than this, though." Braun's hacking laugh is sickening, but Kaleb seems to enjoy the joke and joins in. *Idiots.*

I roll my eyes, taking a swig of the cool blood. Oh fuck. *Fuck.* Even though it's not fresh, even though it's barely tepid and accompanied by the maniacal cackling of two absolute tossers - all I can think about in that moment is Juliet. She tastes incredible. Sweet and spicy, with almost a hint of vanilla, how is that even possible? She runs down my throat and sets every single vein in my body alight.

Kaleb bursts out laughing, slapping his thigh. "Oh yeah, he likes that one, look at his eyes!"

Braun smirks at me, leaning back in his chair. "I told you. Imagine getting that fresh." His eyes sweep over my groin, making my skin crawl. "Imagine having *her* fresh. She's pretty darn cute."

"Which one is she?" Kaleb asks, taking another sip of her blood. I have to restrain myself so I don't knock the glass out of his hand.

Braun lets out a low whistle. "That one with the blonde hair and all the freckles. A real fresh Georgia peach that one. Her ass is a little small, but for the rest of her, I could live with it."

"Oh yeah, she is hot." Kaleb gives me a lascivious grin. "I like watching her shower. Those tits are-" He puts two fingers and his thumb to his mouth, puffing them away with an exaggerated kissing sound.

I down the rest of Juliet's blood in one gulp, electric sweetness burning across my tongue and soothing the boiling rage I feel at their words. "Good night, gentlemen."

Braun's disgusting, hacking laugh bursts from between his blood-lined lips again. "Yeah, we know what you need to go do now." He rubs a hand across his crotch. "Got a feeling I'll be doing the same."

Amidst their jibes and guffaws, I leave the hall. God, they're disgusting. Feral and animalistic, everything that's wrong with the vamps, everything that made the humans call us feeders in the first place.

And both are absolutely right. I'm so hard right now I feel

like I'm going to lose my fucking mind. Juliet's blood is magical. I knew it would be. Her smell is intoxicating, like the sweetest perfume I've ever smelled. That night when I smelled her getting herself off, it took all my willpower not to drag her out of her bed and straight into mine, like some fucking caveman.

But coupling her scent with the taste of her blood, I don't even know how to resist anymore. Goddammit. This is bad.

I walk along the line of cabins, taking the two steps up into mine in one stride, and slam the door behind me. My body is on edge, my fangs digging into my lips, my chest heaving. I don't need to breathe anymore, but arousal still has the same effect on me as it did when I was human. My heart is hammering in my chest, and I tear my clothes off, heading straight for the shower. I need relief from this.

I turn on the taps, and as I lick my lips I find a small speck of her there, in the corner of my mouth. I slam a fist into the wall as my cock twitches. *Fuck.*

Under the warm water, I hold onto her taste as I fist my cock. I feel her blooming on my tongue, imagining her in here with me. I pump myself, picturing her against the wall, legs wrapped around my hips as I sink into her. I can practically hear her crying out for me. I can almost feel that cunt clenching around me as I bite her, sinking my fangs into that soft neck.

I brace myself against the shower wall as I keep jerking myself off, imagining her bent over in front of me, screaming my name as I fuck her from behind.

I wonder if her pussy tastes as good as her blood. I bet it does. Of course it does.

I groan as I release, my cock pulsing in my hand, spilling hot jets of cum down the shower wall. Fuck what I wouldn't give to have her in here with me. I press my hands flat against the shower wall, wishing it would somehow help. I need to calm down. She's not for me. I can't have her.

And I'm instantly filled with fury as I think of her in bed with that fucker, that useless impotent fuck head from the breeding farm. Smelling him on her was torture. Carrying her over my shoulder and smelling *him* - no. His life was in danger. I meant it when I said I'd tear his head off.

But she wants him. Not me.

I shove myself off the tiles and shut the water off. What the fuck is wrong with me?

I haven't been interested in a human in years. I had no reason to be. They were food, something we had to protect but maintain a distance from. Sure, I'm still a man. I still noticed when someone was attractive. But Juliet has me entranced. She's different.

No she isn't. I try to reason with myself. *She's a pretty bloodbag with nice legs and fantastic tits and a cunt that smells like heaven and blood to match. You're like a fucking teenager, get a grip.*

But I can't convince myself that she's nothing and no one. I can't convince myself that this is nothing but a teenage crush. I can't even lie to myself.

Fuck's sakes.

I dry myself off, determined to sleep. It's been a few days and I should really rest. But the tension won't let me go. This is going to drive me insane. I make a mental note to check every bag of blood before I drink, to make sure it's not hers. Or maybe, to make sure it is hers, and no one else gets to taste her.

Bloodbag 4211487.

I pull on a pair of sweatpants and head outside, down the steps of my cabin and to the one three doors down. I knock on the door, waiting a moment before I hear movement on the other side. The door opens to reveal a short vamp with shoulder-length red hair and big, rust-brown eyes. She grins as she takes in my appearance.

"Well hey there." Her eyes take me in hungrily. "You need something, Silas?"

"You know I do, Sam." I lean on the door frame, looking her up and down. She's dressed in tiny white shorts and a thin white tank top, her nipples peaking under the fabric. "You busy?"

"For you, I'll make time." She grabs the waistband of my pants and pulls me inside. The door falls closed as she slams me against it, her mouth wandering over my chest. I rake my hands through her hair as her fangs drag along my skin.

Fucking Sam is always fun. Thank god we both got a promotion, because being buried in her ass is the perfect relief from any pent-up tension. She's crazy, a lot older than me but just as strong. She's put me through a wall before.

Sam jumps into my arms, kissing me ferociously as I carry her to the bed.

"No, over there." She shakes her head, pointing to the desk. "I want you to bend me over it."

"So bossy." I nip at her lips as she grins at me. But I take her to the desk, spinning her around once she's on her feet and slamming her down on its surface. "Now, are you going to keep your hands there like a good girl?"

"Only if you finish in my ass." She arches back against me as I slide a hand into her shorts.

"I'd love to." I bite her earlobe as I tear her shorts down her legs. I push down my sweatpants and sink into her. She's a lot shorter than me, so I have to grip her hips to lift her up to me, but that just makes her so much tighter.

She cries out, clawing into the desk and leaving big gaping scratch marks in the wood. We've destroyed three beds, two desks and fourteen chairs together. Not to mention that wall.

"Harder," she moans.

I pound into her, and a choked gasp leaves her throat.

"Greedy little slut, always wanting it harder. You want me to fuck your ass this hard too?"

"Oh god, yes." She braces her hands against the desk, trying to straighten up, but I grab the back of her head and slam her back down. I curl my hand around the back of her neck, squeezing hard as I hiss in a breath.

"Only good girls get it in the ass. Now stay fucking down."

"I fucking hate you," she says over a breathless laugh. "You feel too good."

I hook a hand under her knee, forcing it up onto the desk so I sink even deeper into her, and she yelps.

"*Fuck.*" She hisses. "You're too fucking big."

I'm suddenly overcome with the sensation of Juliet's blood running down my throat, and I feel myself become impossibly harder inside Sam's cunt. Fuck, this was meant to make me feel better. This was meant to relieve my tension, not make it worse.

Sam clenches around me as she comes. Her fingers curl around the corner of the desk, which comes apart in her hands in a shower of wood chips as she screams. "Fuck, *fuck.*"

She trembles and pants with anticipation as I bite open my wrist, coating my cock in my blood. I drip blood down between the creamy cheeks of her ass, and she shudders. I push the blunt head of my cock to her puckered entrance, and she whimpers as I ease myself into her.

"Silas, you're going to break me."

"Good." I slam into her, and she screams. The other vamps will hear us but I don't care. They'll have heard us before.

Fucking hell, her ass is so tight. I thank 20-year-old Silas who thought it would be a good idea to get a cock piercing, because right now the dragging pressure of that metal bar is so fucking good I can't see straight. She reaches back for me, and I curl my fingers around her wrist, forcing her arm against her back.

"Yeah." Her voice is barely audible over my own moans, over the sound of the desk creaking under us. "Oh god, yeah."

I close my eyes, my body tensing with heat as my climax builds. And suddenly it's Juliet's arms under my hands, her screams and whimpers meeting my ears. It's Juliet coated in my blood. The vision is so vivid, like daylight searing itself onto the backs of my eyelids.

My whole body ripples with release as I roar, coming so hard I'm sure I've crushed Sam's bones to dust in my hands. I'm gasping for air I don't need, my blood on fire. Holy fuck. Holy shitting fuck.

But Sam just laughs, slumping on the desk as I pull out of her.

"Jesus," she murmurs, "that was incredible." Her ass is covered in blood and cum and sweat, and when I look down at myself I don't look much better. It always looks like a massacre when vamps fuck.

"You OK?" I ask as she turns around, perching on the edge of the scratched up, splintered desk.

She pushes the hair from her sweaty face with the back of her hand. "Yeah, why?"

"That was, it was intense."

She grins and reaches out, running her fingers down my chest. "Silas, you're always intense. Not many men fuck the way you do."

"And what way is that?" I ask, pulling up my sweatpants.

"Like you want to own me or kill me."

Her words make me pause for a moment, and when I meet her eyes, she tilts her head.

"Something wrong?"

I shake my head quickly. "No, I'm fine. Always am after we're done."

"Well, you know, anytime." She watches me leave, giving me a lascivious smile as I pause at the door. "Good seeing you, Silas."

"You too, Sam."

I head back to my cabin, the night air cooling the sweat on my skin. *Like you want to own me or kill me.* Sam can't know the impact those words had on me. The feelings I've fought for years. The feelings my maker tried to persuade me weren't real.

I stand under my shower, washing the blood, cum and Sam's scent off me. When I close my eyes, letting the hot water cascade over my face, the specter of Juliet returns almost instantly. Her arm around my waist, her cheek resting gently against my back. *That was incredible, Silas.* Just the thought of her saying my name sends volts of pleasure down my spine, and I'm hard again.

Then it's her hand stroking my length, her fingers flicking over my cock ring, her hot breath against my neck as I come with her name on my lips.

Fuck.

This girl has me in a chokehold.

This is really fucking bad.

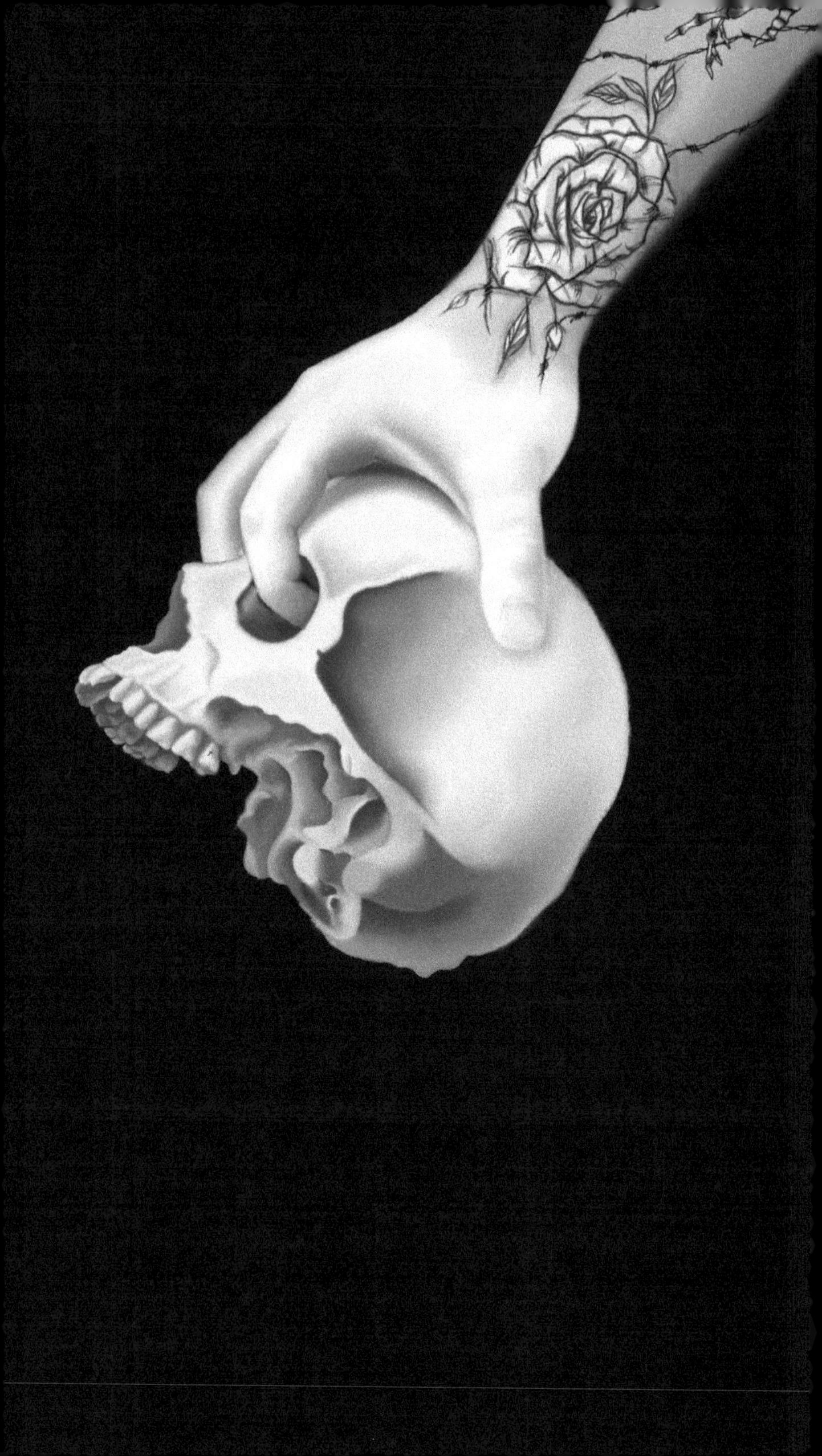

I MAKE a conscious effort to avoid seeing Juliet for a week or so. The few times I catch her scent, I immediately turn in the opposite direction. We're busy anyway, rebuilding after the attack, reinstalling security systems and fixing the perimeters. There's plenty to keep my mind occupied, which is perfect, because the minute it wanders, it wanders straight to the shiny blonde hair and freckled skin that haunts my fucking dreams.

I take Sam up on her offer, and while she's surprised by my frequent visits, she certainly doesn't complain. She loves the fucking as much as I do. She has to apply for another new bed, and gets asked why she keeps breaking them. We decide to avoid that from now on. And then put another hole in her wall.

But even Sam can't keep my mind off everything. As busy as I've been, and as satisfied as I am, there still comes that time, in the deep of the night, where all I can think about is Juliet. I imagine threading my fingers through that golden hair, pulling her head back as I fuck her, sinking my fangs into that soft neck while she moans.

Every night I'm a mess. Why, fucking *why* does this woman have me in this state? I don't get it. Some nights it makes me angry. I don't want to feel this way. I try to push it away. I go to the gym every night and take my frustrations out on a boxing bag. But as soon as I'm alone in my bed, nothing but the soft darkness around me, she's there. And I surrender to it, every single time.

I'm climbing down from the observation tower one evening, just as the sky is starting to turn orange, and someone calls to me. I look up to see Braun heading for me, his hand raised in greeting.

"Silas, I need you to help me out, man."

"What do you need?" I ask, jumping down from the last rung of the ladder.

"I'm meant to be on shower duty but the trucks have just come in and I need to go check the supplies." He jerks his thumb over his shoulder in the direction of the shower block. "Can you go watch the bloodbags get cleaned up for me?"

"Yeah, not a problem."

He turns on his heel and hurries across the compound. "Thanks!" He calls over his shoulder.

I walk over to the shower block, gazing up at the orange sky above. The air is a little cooler than it has been, not stifling hot. I wonder what the air in London is like now. I haven't been there in over 12 years. It's all destroyed now anyway, nothing to see anymore.

My family's graves are there somewhere. My little brother and sister, my sweet mother. I wonder if my father fought to protect them to the bitter end. If he'd spent his days saying "I knew it, I knew this would happen." If he blamed me. If he told them that this was exactly why I was kept away from them. My throat constricts as I remember his last words to me. *You're a monster. You ruin everything. You always have.*

I push open the service door to the shower block, into the side room with the one way mirror. The humans are filing in, bottles of shampoos and bars of soap in their hands. The water starts flowing as I take a seat on the blue office chair, spinning back and forth absently, not really watching what's happening on the other side of that mirror. What are they going to do? Throw soap? So much of this is ridiculous.

I cast a casual glance over the naked bodies, in the steamy room. All sizes, all ages, tattoos, scars and stretch marks. I always liked bodies, from an artistic stand-point. Every single one is unique, and fascinating, and deeply beautiful in its own way. I miss those life art classes.

And then a figure on the left hand side of the room raises lithe arms to run their fingers through long blonde hair, and my stomach is instantly filled with a whirlwind. I lean forward, the chair creaking loudly at the sudden movement.

It's Juliet. Of course it is. Water runs down those long legs, soap suds going with it. She lathers up her hands, running them over her breasts, her eyes closed as she tips her head back slightly under the cascading shower. I'm fucking jealous of that water, that soap that glides delicately down her skin, between her breasts, over her ass. *Get a fucking grip, Silas. Jesus fuck.*

She turns so she's facing the mirror, giving me a full view of her body. She curls her fingers against her scalp, washing her hair, her eyes still closed. A small smile ghosts across her full lips, her face relaxed. Maybe she's imagined herself off into another world, one where she's just come in from a day at the beach, salty and heated from the sun.

My grip on the armrest tightens as I imagine how she'd feel right now. How warm and slippery she'd be, how soft and supple her body would be, that gentle smile against my cheek. She'd feel fucking magical.

I know I shouldn't look. I should keep my eyes on that relaxed face. I shouldn't fucking look. It's not like I haven't seen her naked before. But that was different. When I was in the shower room with her, I was too incandescent with rage to notice her body. I was too consumed with needing his scent off her to focus on the peachy tan of her nipples, or the curve of her small, firm ass.

But now, with nothing else to distract me, my gaze wanders down her body, between her legs. There's a light scattering of curly hair, and between the lips of her cunt, I can see the barest tip of a rosy pink clit. It's all I can do to lick my lips, imagining pushing that pussy apart, finding that clit swollen and aching for my tongue.

I shouldn't have fucking looked. All I want to do right now is smash my way through the mirror and seize her in my arms.

My illusions are shattered instantly when *he* appears at her side. Matt. Limp-dick twat. The petty voice in my head snorts. *His dick isn't even that big.* I'm such a fucking shit.

Her eyes open and she looks up at him, smiling. He leans down and plants a furtive kiss on her lips, and her eyes sparkle. She looks so happy. He's grinning down at her, looking around the room at the others who all have their backs turned, busy getting themselves clean.

He puts an arm around her waist, backing her into the wall. He kisses her deeply, pressing his hips against her. Her arms wind around his neck.

There's a loud snap as the plastic armrest gives way under my grip. Fuck. I'm destroying half the compound because of this woman.

I lean forward and hit the alarm button, letting it whir for a split second. All the humans jump, gazing around the room with panicked eyes, like deer caught in headlights, trying to figure out what just happened.

All except for Juliet. Her stormy eyes are fixed on the mirror. Glaring. Like she knows. She knows it was me, and that I'm jealous. I reason with myself that I did that because of the rules. I broke up a fraternization that isn't allowed. It wasn't *just* jealousy.

They all get back to washing and finishing up, and I can see the irritation on her face as she does. She's not relaxed anymore, her whole body tense with fury. I'm an asshole. She was having a nice time, she was happy.

I'm a selfish prick.

He looks down at her, his lips moving, and she gives him a strained smile, nodding. Her eyes flash back over to the mirror, and if looks could kill I'd be disembowelled right now. She hates me.

I lean back in the broken chair, watching them all shut the water off. They move to the next room to dry and dress, and I leave the observation room to wait outside for them. They all file past, barely acknowledging me, heading back to their dorm. Like sheep. They know the drill.

Juliet storms past me, her scent even sharper now that she's freshly washed. So much of that delicious skin is on display, dressed in tiny shorts and a tank top that barely covers her stomach. It makes my mouth water. Suddenly she spins on her heel and fronts up to me, so we're almost chest to chest.

"What the fuck is your problem?" She hisses.

"I don't know what you're talking about."

"You jealous?" She asks, her voice low.

"You know the rules." I tower over her, enjoying this power play far too much. "What was going on in there isn't allowed."

She smiles bitterly, nodding. "Sure, that's exactly what's going on here." She looks me up and down, her nose wrinkling. "I bet you feeders can't even get it up, you're all bloodless and dead, right?" She's practically touching me now, her heartbeat thundering barely an inch from me. "Can you get hard, Silas?"

If she wants to play this game, I'm more than up for it. I grin down at her. "You think about that a lot, do you?"

Her eyebrows flicker upwards in surprise before a look of disgust crosses her face. "Fuck you."

"Well, that would be the idea, wouldn't it?" I'm so close to her now that her scent is overwhelming. I look her up and down before meeting her furious gaze again. "And yes, I can get hard. Maybe even hard enough to make you scream."

She steps forward and slaps me, her open palm slamming into my cheek. I saw it coming a mile off, and I grab a hold of her wrist, yanking her flush against my body. She lets out a surprised yelp, blinking up at me before her face sets back into that beautiful, stormy fury.

"Let go of me!"

I inhale her scent deeply, exhaling through my gritted teeth. "This is the second time you've slapped me. I'm starting to think that's a bit of a kink of yours."

She bucks in my grasp, pressing her scantily clad body against my chest. "I said, let *go*."

I lower my mouth to her ear, snapping my teeth just shy of her earlobe. "Keep doing that and I'll definitely be hard."

She shoves against my chest with an outraged gasp, and I finally let her go. Her shoulders are heaving, and her eyes are blazing with fury.

"Don't fucking look at me, don't look at me, don't think about me, nothing, OK? I am *nothing* to you. Just another bloodbag."

Matt appears at her back, and he takes her hand. "What's going on?"

"Nothing, it's fine," Juliet replies, and stalks off towards the dorm.

I watch her go. The other vamps turn to look at me questioningly, and I shrug. "Bloodbags, ey? So emotional."

They all chuckle, nod, murmur their agreement, before dispersing.

The night continues on, uneventfully. When I go to Sam's cabin once my shift is over, I don't wait for her to open the door. I throw it almost off its hinges, before I pin her down on the bed and fuck her until she can't even scream anymore.

AFTER ALMOST TWO weeks of rain, the garden team is outside again, working in the sunshine. They're all in good spirits, and I traipse around aimlessly, just watching them.

I walk along the repaired perimeter fence, and I'm grateful there haven't been any more attacks. They're always exhausting, the fighting and the repairs afterwards. And the fear that one of those Afflicted will get a bite in on us. I've seen firsthand what it can do. It's an ugly, painful thing, and I never want to experience that myself.

I wander down the hill towards the tree line, listening to the humans laugh and chatter. Nothing changes much from childhood - give humans a pile of dirt, the ability to grow something, and some sunshine, and they're happy. I remember feeling that way, those summer days as a child. All those years ago now, when my parents bought that little house with the garden on the outskirts of London. Etching pictures in the sandbox while Harriet spun her ribbons through the warm summer air.

I spot a wheelbarrow abandoned next to the compost pile, and look back up towards the garden. Juliet had taken off with that, but I can't see her anywhere now. Her loverboy is scheduled for donation today, so she hasn't gone anywhere with him.

I move closer to the tree line, wondering if she's headed in there. I can't see her. I keep walking, moving under the shade of the canopy. Birds sing to each other from the boughs of the trees, and the ground underfoot is soft from all the rain.

After a minute or so I can hear water, rushing loudly. Then splashing. I move quietly towards the sound, and come upon a stream, swollen from the plentiful rainfall.

Juliet is lying in the depths, water up to her neck, her clothes on a nearby rock. Her eyes are closed, the sunshine breaking through the trees glimmering on the bubbling water around her. She's smiling.

I keep moving towards her, silently, just watching her. She's so fucking beautiful. Goddammit, I should leave. I should just let her have this moment, but she's like a magnet. I stop at the water's edge, and because she hasn't heard my advance she's just lying there, totally relaxed.

I look over her naked body in the water, the sunlight playing across her freckled skin. She's stunning. She's perfect. She shifts a little, her thighs opening ever so slightly, and the sight is enough to almost bring me to my knees.

Her eyes flutter open, widening as soon as she sees me. With a scream, she scrambles out of the water to clutch her wet clothes to her body.

"What the fuck is wrong with you?"

"I didn't know where you'd gone." I keep my eyes fixed on hers, knowing my willpower can only get me so far. If I think too much about that cool, wet skin and how fucking good she'd feel right now, I'll drag her off and bury my mouth between those thighs. "I came to find you."

"Well, you found me, well done you."

I shrug. "I had no idea you'd be paddling about naked out here on your own."

"It's hot." She glares at me. "I wanted to cool off, and be alone for a minute."

"Well, I'm sorry I ruined that for you."

"No you're not."

I can't help but laugh, because no. I'm not sorry at all. I got to see her naked body spread out in sun-dappled water while she lay there with a half-drunk-on-happiness smile on her face. That smile is etched on my memory now.

"What's funny?" She asks, her voice full of sass.

"You."

"I had no idea you could even laugh, shouldn't you be skulking around threatening to tear someone's head off?"

"I only do that on Fridays."

Her eyes narrow, trying to measure what I just said. "Did you just make a joke?"

"You'd be amazed what we feeders can do."

"Oh sure, get hard enough to make me scream, I remember." She frowns at me, tilting her head. "Why haven't I seen you here before? You're not new, are you?"

"I was on gate duty, for two years. Just got a promotion."

Her eyebrows raise in faux delight. "Oh, congratulations. Can you turn around now so I can get dressed?"

I exhale heavily and rub the back of my neck. "I don't know about that. I should really keep a close eye on you."

Her glare becomes lethal. "Turn around."

With a chuckle I turn my back to her. "You've been here since the beginning, is that right?"

"Yes." The abrupt tone of her voice tells me in no uncertain terms she won't elaborate on that matter. "You can turn around now."

When I turn back to face her, she's standing there with a hand on one hip, her long hair dripping water onto the ground around her feet. Her white shirt clings to her wet skin, showing me every single curve and swell of her body. *Beautiful.* I huff out a breath and she cocks an eyebrow.

"Like what you see?"

I raise my eyes back to her face. "What gave you that impression?"

"You, ogling my tits."

I laugh out loud. "You're really not afraid of me, are you?"

"You like your women afraid, Silas?" Her nose pulls up into a sneer. "Does that turn you on?"

I run my tongue over my teeth. "Fear smells incredible, you know. Tastes great too."

Her face betrays the barest hint of surprise at my words, but she quickly pulls that nonchalant mask back into place and clears her throat. "Whatever. I know you like what you see, because you stare at me all the damn time." She tosses her hair, arching her back so her tits strain the fabric on her shirt. *Fucking tease.* "Must be hard though, seeing something you like and not being able to do anything about it."

"What does it matter to you?" I cross my arms over my chest. "You and what's-his-name are happy, aren't you?"

The split second of hesitation before she smiles and nods is all I need to confirm what I thought. He isn't satisfying her. He can't be.

"Of course." She gives me a little shrug, her voice just a little too high-pitched.

"You like me looking at you?"

"No." She snaps, far too fast. She rolls her eyes. "I just... You know, you saved my life. I'm grateful for that. But that's all." Her eyes move back to me, and she looks me up and down. "You're British, right?"

"I am. I was born in London."

"How old are you?"

"In human years or vamp years?"

She shrugs. "Either, both, whatever."

"I was turned 28 years ago, when I was 25. So, I'm 53 I suppose."

"Old." Her nose wrinkles again, making the freckles dance across her face.

I chuckle. "Yes, I suppose I am old to someone your age."

"How did you end up in the states?"

"For someone who wanted me to act like you're nothing and no one, you sure are asking a lot of questions."

She sighs and storms through the stream, passing me to go back to the garden.

"I came over here with my maker," I say when she's right next to me, and she stops, looking up at me. "She got tired of London, so I came here with her."

"And where is she now?"

"Dead."

The answer makes her face drop a little. "Afflicted?"

"Mmm." I nod. "Begged me to kill her, so I did."

"Oh Jesus." She flinches a little, and moves to keep walking, hesitating as she looks back up at me. Goddammit, those eyes. "Why did you save my life?"

"Because it's my duty to protect you." I hold her gaze, and her cheeks flush a little. "I told you. I want to look after you."

"No feeder has ever wanted to look after me."

"I guess they don't see what I do."

Her eyebrows flicker upwards, and she drops her gaze to the floor, the sweet flush of her cheeks rising higher and higher. "No one sees us. We're just food."

"No, you're not." I'm aching to reach out and touch her, run my fingers down the curve of that bare shoulder.

"Yes, I am." She tilts her head as though she's going to look at me again, but her shoulders slump with a sigh. "Please don't talk to me like this."

"Like what?" The urge to touch her is almost causing me pain.

She shakes her head. "I'm sorry you had to kill your maker," she says softly before walking away from me across the soft leaves, the sound of her footsteps swallowed by the rain-soaked ground.

As I watch her go, my mind wanders to Margot. Beautiful Margot, with wild black hair and big blue eyes. My maker. The one who taught me everything. Who I'd loved to the point of obsession. Who'd lain in my arms, begging for death as blood poured from her eyes. After 200 years of life, she'd been taken by this fucking virus.

I sigh, kicking a pebble into the bubbling stream. Most days my humanity is just a ghost, hanging in the background. I learned to suppress all those human emotions years ago. I let go of them. I became a monster. A killer.

But watching this human woman walk away from me, I feel humanity pooling in my chest, all those things I've ignored for years rushing over me again.

Fuck it all to hell.

IT'S BARELY dawn when I open my eyes, to find Matt in my bed, kissing my neck.

"Good morning, babe," he whispers.

I smile and wrap my arms around him, and he kisses me. "Is everyone still asleep?" I ask.

"Yeah, still snoring." He grins and reaches down to pull my panties off. I lift my legs to help him, and the movement pushes his cock against me. I gasp a little, feeling that same rush of anticipation like I do every time.

These past couple of months have been so nice. I feel like a person again, even if I am herded into a dorm with 40 other people. Matt is sweet and attentive, and the sex is slowly getting better as his body recovers from all those drugs they fed him.

I'm grateful for those depo shots, because we fuck a lot. Gina asked one of the feeders for ear plugs the other day, and for a moment I wondered if it was because of Matt and I. I was too embarrassed to ask.

Matt grinds into me, and I moan into his shoulder. "Is that good?" He asks me.

"Mmm." I tip my head back on the pillow. "So good."

He keeps thrusting, and I wrap my legs around his waist to take him in deeper. My bed creaks softly, but I kind of don't care right now. I want to coast into the morning on this high. It's draining day for me again. I need a good start.

Matt groans softly against my neck, his breath washing over me as he gasps. "Oh fuck," he says.

No, don't come yet. Please don't come yet. This feels too good. I put my legs back down, hoping the change in angle will delay things, but it just makes me tighter for him. Matt groans loudly, and shudders as goosebumps break out over his shoulders. He goes still on top of me, and I suppress a sigh.

He can't help it. We've had some really good times lately. He tries really hard, and he's so sweet to me. I just have to understand. I nuzzle into him, nudging him with my nose until he's facing me, and I kiss him deeply.

"Sorry," he says softly.

"Please don't apologize." I kiss him again. "That was nice."

"I want it to be more than nice," he says, rolling us onto our sides together, his arms firmly around me. "My wife and I used to have hours long sessions, you know, just fucking all night. And now I can't do that anymore, and I hate it."

I don't know how to respond and just sigh instead, nuzzling into his chest. He's mentioned it a few times, how good sex was with his wife, and I know he doesn't mean anything by it, but it makes me feel awkward. I don't want to know about how great sex was with his wife while he's naked between my legs. But I don't want to upset him. It's been years since I even considered letting anyone in, letting someone care and caring for them in return, and I don't want to ruin this by being too demanding.

Footsteps start to sound outside, and I hold on to Matt tighter, wanting to draw out these last few moments in his arms before the day begins. "Draining Day," I say with a groan.

Matt kisses the top of my head. "It's OK, it'll be over before you know it. And just think, you get to shower beforehand."

I roll my eyes. "Yeah, what a bonus, huh?"

"A shower, and a steak, and those fucking awful milk-shakes," Matt teases, rolling me on to my back and kissing my neck. "You're a lucky, lucky girl."

My giggle is cut off as the dorm doors fly open. Silas and another feeder walk in, waking people for their draining. I tense as Silas's eyes fix on me in bed with Matt. I quickly adjust my clothes before getting to my feet to retrieve my towel and fresh clothes from my locker.

I haven't seen Silas all that much since that day he caught me in the stream. I felt a little sorry for him that day. I know the bond between a feeder and their maker is intense, and he'd feel that loss deeply. Especially because he had to kill her. The thought makes my heart hurt. I'm not an ogre.

But then I reminded myself that we've all had terrible things happen to us because of the vamps and their medical experiments. They brought this on themselves, and all of us right along with them.

I try not to meet his eyes as I walk past him, intensely aware of his proximity and his size, and that goddamn stare of his. I can practically feel the pressure of it on the side of my face.

The sky is still pale pink as we walk to the shower block, and I tip my head back to look at it, breathing in the fresh morning air. The extreme heat of summer is slowly passing as we head into Fall, the days are still hot but the mornings are glorious. I feel a little giddy, the morning with Matt just setting me on edge. It's good, but unfulfilling. I hate myself for wanting more.

We head into the shower block, and the other feeder who was in the dorm is ushering us in. That means Silas is probably watching us from the mirror. Heat prickles across my skin as I remember the way he looked at me at the stream. He liked what he saw, I know he did. My cheeks burn as I think of him looking at me with that same lust in his eyes as I shower.

I strip off, placing my pajamas and my fresh clothes in a locker. I head into the shower room with the others, and they all take the shower heads closest to the door. There's only 10 of us today, a mercifully small group which means when I cross the room, I have this side practically all to myself. I can almost pretend I'm alone for once.

The hot water is already flowing, and it's so soothing as it runs over my shoulders. I turn into it, face on, and tiny needles of water strike my nipples. I'm still a little turned on, my elusive orgasm hovering between my thighs. Lathering my hands in soap and running them over my body doesn't help.

I look over at the mirror. Is he in there, looking me over and wishing he could touch me? Is he relieved Matt isn't here with me today?

The thought of him watching me has heat swirling in my belly that I damn well know shouldn't be there. But I find myself running my soapy hand over my breasts, pinching my nipple gently between my fingers.

I run the other hand down my stomach, teasing my finger-tips over the lips of my pussy. My mouth opens a little bit, a silent gasp as my eyes stay on that mirror. One finger slips over the tip of my clit, and the moan that bursts from my lips brings me violently to my senses. *What the fuck am I doing?*

I rinse off quickly, wrapping myself in my towel and heading into the other room to get dressed. The others follow me, talking amongst themselves but I can't focus on anything they say because my cheeks are burning, but not with lust. Just a weird sense of shame.

The feeder leads us to the cafeteria, across the yard that's quiet but for early morning birdsong. A cool breeze catches the droplets of water running down my arms, dripping from my hair.

I get my tray of breakfast, piled with eggs, a small bowl of supplements and the usual big glass of orange juice. I sit down on one of the metal benches, knowing I should eat the eggs but also feeling so tired of them. I push them around with a fork, dreading the day.

"Not hungry?" The deep voice behind me sends shivers down my spine, and Silas sits down beside me, straddling the bench. His eyes are blazing red, and he runs a tattooed hand over his mouth before gesturing to the food in front of me. "You should eat."

"I will."

"Good." He looks me up and down. "You smell great."

"Fuck off." I hiss, shoving a forkful of eggs in my mouth. But he doesn't move, just stays next to me, watching me eat. "Why are your eyes so red?" I shift my head to look into those glowing crimson eyes. "Smoke too much weed?"

"Sign of arousal."

The word makes my stomach clench. "Arousal?"

He leans closer to me, bracing an enormous hand on the table. "I just had to watch a girl getting herself off in the shower, so excuse me for being a little worked up."

My eyes drop to the table, and I chide myself for being so stupid. What the fuck am I actually doing? Taunting him like this? I wouldn't stand a chance against him. If he wanted to drag me off and have his way with me, he could.

I shrug, trying desperately to appear nonchalant. "I was just showering. I wasn't... doing that."

He cocks an eyebrow. "You trying to tell me something?"

I scoff, trying not to think about how close his groin is to my thigh. "Definitely not."

He leans right against my ear. "You should be careful. Might give me the wrong idea."

It doesn't feel like a threat. It feels like flirting. And that should make me uncomfortable, because he freaks me out. He's a feeder, a blood-sucking monster. I don't want him anywhere near me. I turn to glare at him.

"I'd like to finish my breakfast if you don't mind. Do you have somewhere else to be?"

Those blazing red eyes move over my face again. "Yeah. I do." He gets up and leans over me. "Thanks for the show." He turns on his heel and I shiver, not watching him as he walks away.

Fucking creep.

I manage to choke down most of those god-awful eggs before we're herded into the clinic. I take my place in the dentist chair, staring up at the ceiling. One of the feeders comes in, going through the motions, but then she asks me something and I have to ask her to repeat the question because they've never asked me anything like this before.

"I asked if you could be pregnant," she says, staring at me sternly.

I shake my head. "N - no, of course not. You give me the shots and -"

"Are you currently sexually active?"

Fucking son of a bitch. I grit my teeth together, determined to tear Silas's eyes out the next time I see him.

"Yeah, I am."

"I don't need to tell you that it's not allowed." She sighs heavily, draping her arms over one another. "Have you had any symptoms? Any indication that you might be?"

My mind races, trying to think. I didn't want to eat the eggs this morning, but that was because I hate them. Not because I was sick. Have I been more tired? Are my breasts sore?

The feeder waits patiently, and I stutter out a response, something like, *I don't think so.*

"Best to be sure." She retrieves a plastic strip with a pink cap on it from the drawer in front of her, and my stomach lurches. *Oh god. Oh fuck.* If I'm pregnant they'll haul me away to a breeding farm. It'll break Matt's heart. They'll take our baby away from me when it's weaned, and I'll never see them again. I'll never see Matt again.

My eyes sting with tears as I'm escorted to a bathroom to take the test. She leaves me alone, the cubicle door slamming shut behind me sounding like a gavel, determining my fate. My hands are shaking so bad as I try to pee on it and not all over my hand. *Please be negative. Please please please.*

I put the pink cap back on, and watch as the dye travels through the strip. One pink line glows. Just one. *Please just stay like that.*

There's a sharp rap on the door, and I nearly drop the test.

"If you're done, you can come out." The feeder says.

I clutch the test in my sweaty hand, as though I can somehow control it if I squeeze hard enough. Back behind the blue curtain, she holds out her hand, placing the strip that's about to decide my fate on the metal trolley, casting a quick glance up at the clock.

She fills out some paperwork as the second hand glides past the numbers, counting down the minutes until I find out whether or not I'm truly fucked. I clasp my hands over my stomach, protectively, out of nothing other than instinct. If there's a little person in there, I need to keep them safe from all of this shit.

After three minutes, which feel like years, the feeder looks at the test and gives a brief nod. "Negative. Good."

I nearly collapse with relief. Thank god. Thank everything. Tears spring to my eyes again.

She administers the depo shot, and if she notices my emotions she doesn't say anything. She just goes about her business, and then puts the needle in my arm. My blood runs into the bag, as it always does.

The curtain pushes aside, and I half expect Silas to saunter in. But when I look, it's another feeder, a really big one. He has long reddish hair, pulled back from his face. His eyes are bright red, and he leers at me as I sit in the chair.

"I thought I smelled you," he says, licking his lips. He takes my chart from the cart. "42 1 1 487. Your blood is incredible, did you know?"

"I had no idea."

He picks up the depo needle, and twirls it in his fingers. "Did you know that vamps can get humans pregnant?"

I balk a little. "No."

He nods, putting the needle back down. "Yeah. It can happen. The baby isn't immortal, but it will live a much longer life than a bloodbag."

"Great." I just want him to go away. I want them all to go away. But when I look up at him he's leering at me.

"I got to taste some of your exquisite blood the other day," he says, grinning widely. "It had us all very excited, I gotta tell you." He leans down over me, caging me in, and terror twists my lungs. "We all had to go and see to ourselves to relieve the tension. Especially Silas." He laughs, and the other feeder shifts in her chair. "Oh yeah, you should have seen his eyes."

"OK that's enough," the other feeder says. "Braun, out."

"Oh come on, Simpson, we're just having a little fun." He reaches out and runs his fingers down my cheek, laughing again when I flinch.

"Braun, I said out," she orders sternly. "This isn't appropriate."

He straightens up and grins. "I'll be seeing you later," he says, before leaving the cubicle.

My hands tremble, and I turn my face away from the feeder so she doesn't see the tears in my eyes. I almost wish it had been Silas who walked in. With him there's a boundary, there's a line he won't cross. Whatever his deal is, he seems to at least not want to hurt me.

But these other feeders, they're an unknown quantity. And these attacks from the Afflicted seem to have everyone on edge, and scared people - well, I know exactly how people react when they're afraid.

I just want Matt now, I want to crawl into his arms and cry. I need comfort, and I won't get it here.

Finally, the draining is done and I choke down that fucking donut and some of the milkshake. Nausea washes over me, and the feeder wants me to stay put because I'm so pale. I can't stop shaking and I just want out of there.

She leaves to check about getting me some medication, I don't listen to her so I don't know what for, it doesn't matter anyway. I keep looking out the window, not looking back as the curtain opens. They'll just give me whatever, I have no say.

"You alright?"

My head snaps around to look at Silas, and rage curdles my mouth. "Did you tell them I could be pregnant?"

"Are you?" His tone is strained, his shoulders tensing.

"No, of course not. Y'all force contraception on us, remember?"

"Contraception isn't 100% effective, you're a big girl, surely I don't need to tell you that." He crosses his arms over his chest, and he looks almost concerned as he raises his eyebrows. "You do not want these vamps in here if they take blood from you and you're pregnant. They will tear you into bloody ribbons, Juliet."

The way he says my name sends a shiver down my spine, slow and deliberate. I don't like it.

"Well I'm not, so lucky me, huh?" I rub my eyes violently, as though I can push the tears back in and ignore them.

"Yeah, very lucky. The breeding centers are run mainly by humans for a reason." His face darkens a little. "The vamps that work there have special training. For the rest of them, it's too much."

"What do you care?"

He lunges at me, leaning over me in the chair. "I don't know," he snarls, "I don't know why I should care." He seems to see my widened eyes, and his face softens, his head dropping a little.

"Get the hell away from me," I hiss, pushing him away so I can get out of the chair. I spin around to face him, and god fucking dammit he's tall, and broad, and so big he's almost suffocating me in this cubicle. "I don't know what you've told yourself about me, but you're wrong, OK? I'm just a bloodbag, I'm *nothing*."

Before I know what's happening, he has me by the throat, pushing me back against the wall. He bares his fangs and snarls in my face.

"*You're not nothing*." His eyes move over my face, almost desperately. "You are *not* nothing."

I suck in a breath, and he loosens the grip of his enormous hand. His eyes drop to the floor, his head dipping towards mine until our foreheads are almost touching.

"You're not nothing," he murmurs, and his fingertips brush along the skin behind my ear. He lifts his eyes, and gazes at me. "I can't have you talking about yourself that way."

"Why?" I ask the question even as he moves closer, the way he's looking at me makes me hurt in a way I haven't hurt in years. I recognise it, because I've seen it in my own face so many times.

He's in pain. He's lonely.

I hate that I can sense it, that I can see, and that I feel sorry for him. I hate every single one of these fucking feeders, and yet I find myself raising my hand to touch him. But before I make it to his face, before I reach out and touch that face that keeps inching closer to mine, I let my hand drop.

"Let me go," I say.

His eyes bore into mine, his hand staying right around the base of my throat.

"Silas, let me go."

He sighs, his head dropping as he lets me go and steps away from me.

"I'm nothing to you." I begin to back towards the curtain, watching as he tucks his hands into his pockets, his eyes still locked on the floor. "I don't know what you think you see in me, but I'm not what you're looking for. I don't *want* to be what you're looking for."

He nods. "I know."

"I want you to leave me alone." I try to keep my tone measured, and not betray how fucking shaken I am after everything that happened in the last hour. "I want you to stay away from me. I want you to stop staring at me. I want you to pretend I don't exist."

"OK." His eyes stay fixed on the floor.

I don't know what else to say. He's unmoving, just staring at the floor. I back out of the cubicle, and as soon as the curtain falls closed, I hurry out of the clinic and across the yard. I know I need to slow down after losing all that blood, but I push through the dizziness and break into a jog. I need to find Matt.

He's working on a garden bed, raking straw across the soil, and when he spots me he raises his hand in a wave. Just the sight of him has me in tears again. He balks a little, dropping his rake and rushing towards me.

"Babe, what's wrong?" He asks as I collapse in his arms. "Did something happen?"

I try to speak but my throat is too tight, so I just hold on to him, shaking my head. "I'm OK," I finally manage to squeak. "I'm OK, they made me do - do a t-test."

"What test?"

"A preg-pregnancy -" I start crying harder as I think of what would be happening right now if that test had been positive.

Matt's eyes widen and he clasps my face in his hands. "Are you pregnant?"

I shake my head. "No, no, no. I'm not."

His face crumples almost into an expression of disappointment, and he clasps me to him. I get it. Some small part of him wants that life he hoped for with his wife, the family and kids and a swing set in the yard. We both want normality. I can't blame him for it.

"I was so scared," I whisper.

"I bet you were." He kisses my forehead. "I'm so sorry, babe. You poor thing."

"I was so relieved." I wipe my tears away with the back of my hand. "I was so relieved when it was negative. They would have taken me away, and I'd have to give up the baby and -" I bite my lip, determined not to cry anymore. I'm not pregnant. I'm not being hauled away.

And Silas will hopefully get the message, and stay the fuck away from me.

EXCEPT I CAN'T CONTROL my dreams.

Silas can invade those. I wake up shuddering violently, my thighs clenched together as my orgasm rolls through me. The feeling of his body subsides slowly, those enormous arms crushing me in them as he ground into me. I clutch on to my pillow, panting.

It's still dark, no sign of dawn. It must be the middle of the night. I raise my head and look around. Everyone's asleep.

I half-expect to see Silas standing at the end of my bed, sniffing me out as I get off. But he's not there.

I haven't seen him in two weeks. I don't know where he's gone, or if he's even gone anywhere. Maybe he's just doing a great job avoiding me. I hate that I've noticed his absence. And I've had sex dreams about him three fucking times now.

And in my dreams, he's good. Really good.

I roll on to my back and sigh. It's just frustration. Matt is still really trying, but it's just... not satisfying. I try to show him how to touch me, how I like it, but he gets sensitive about it. Like I think he doesn't know what he's doing. I've never had a steady boyfriend before. I've never been in a long-term relationship, I don't know how to navigate this shit.

I was 19 when they herded me in here. Still a kid. I still feel like that 19 year old girl. Inexperienced, caged, unable to grow or thrive. Maybe I'm being immature. Maybe I'm expecting too much of him. If I let him take the lead, maybe Matt will feel better. Maybe he just needs to feel like a man to heal. I don't know.

I close my eyes, and Silas's face swims before me. My body reacts instantly, retreating back into that dream world where Silas was driving into me, making me scream. I take a deep, shuddering breath, trying to calm down. I'm just frustrated. I am. That's all. I'm trying to process it, and it's not like there's a lot of attractive men around. It's not that I want Silas. I'm just frustrated. I'm frustrated. That's all.

How many more times do I need to tell myself that's all until I stop feeling guilty?

Matt shifts in the bed next to me, and my stomach does a flip, like he knows what I'm thinking. Oh god, what if I made noise while I was sleeping. My lungs clench in terror as I wonder if *I said Silas's name.* I cover my face with my hands. *Shit.*

I don't have much more time to wonder as the alarm starts to whir above us. Everyone starts up in their beds, clutching blankets to themselves. Matt throws back his blanket and leaps over in my bed, clutching on my hands.

"Here we go again," he says.

We all sit quietly, waiting. There's nothing else for us to do but wait, as always.

"You OK?" Matt asks quietly. He seems to sense my tension, and strokes my knuckles with his thumb. "Sorry, dumb question."

There's an explosion nearby, and everyone scatters to the floor, carried by a chorus of screams. Matt and I huddle by my bed, his arms around me. I'm starting to wonder where the

Afflicted are getting these weapons from. They're sure as hell well-armed for a horde of mindless, virulent vampires.

Footsteps thunder past the dorm, and we hear shouting. Another explosion sounds, close enough to shake dust from the iron rafters above. Something hits the wall behind us, it sounds like gravel being kicked up, but it could also be bullets.

Matt and I scooch into the center of the dorm, away from the potential bullets. A few others do the same, and we all take cover there, just trying to breathe. Trying not to be consumed by terror.

It goes quiet suddenly, the alarm and the gunfire stopping simultaneously. For a moment, I'm seized by panic. If the Afflicted have overpowered the feeders, we're fucked. Then I hear that terrible, droning sound of the Afflicted as they wail, and they're really fucking close.

No one is firing on them. The feeders have abandoned us. There are probably too many of them, so they left us to our fate.

I clutch on to Matt's hand, and his eyes are wide with panic as he looks at me.

"Why aren't they shooting?" He asks. "Why the fuck-"

The dorm doors fly open, and Afflicted pour in.

I can't scream, I can't make any noise at all. I shuffle backwards from the shrieking, groaning figures. They descend on the people closest to the door. They don't stand a chance. It's all over for them.

Matt's scrambling alongside me, and I look around frantically for Gina. The Afflicted are tearing through those poor people, and the screaming is fucking awful. Something hot is running down my cheeks, and I figure it's tears, but I'm too fucking terrified by what's going on in front of me to even register whether I'm crying.

We're going to die.

This is it.

I turn to Matt and grab on to his hands. We're about to die. I don't know what else to say to him. He strokes my cheek, wiping away the tears.

"I love you," I blurt out. I don't even know if I do, but right now it feels like the best thing to say, the only thing to say.

"I love you too." He puts his arms around me. "I'm sorry. I'm so sorry."

We hold on to each other, knowing those will be the last words we say to each other. I don't even feel anything. It's like I floated away already. I clench my eyes shut as I nuzzle into Matt's chest, wondering what it will feel like to die.

It can't be that bad, right? Warmth and white light. It'll be OK.

All of a sudden the sounds around us change, and the dorm is lit up with an explosion of flames. The Afflicted shriek and wail, and I peek over Matt's shoulder to see the dorm doors burning. People scramble across the floor towards us, coughing and retching as the room fills with smoke.

Bullets ping off the walls and ceiling, and I cower against the bed next to me, terrified of being hit by a ricochet.

The Afflicted become quieter and quieter, and then feeders are advancing, killing every last Afflicted as they move into the dorm. My heart does a weird little flip as I spot Silas, handgun drawn and pointed at the screeching creatures on the floor. He fires without compunction, and finally all that's left is the sound of flames crackling and the folks around us crying.

"Are you OK?" Matt asks, holding my face in his hands.

I nod, clutching on to his arms, and suddenly I'm sobbing as all the adrenaline wears off. I can't stop shaking, I'm so scared. He helps me to my feet as the feeders direct us out of the dorm. Outside, a large part of the compound is burning, and feeders are running around with guns and flamethrowers, dealing with the last of the Afflicted as they lie on the ground.

Smoke grazes down my throat, and I cough. Matt is at my back, rubbing me soothingly.

"It's OK, we're OK." He keeps saying it over and over, and then suddenly hands are on us, shoving us towards the yard.

"Line up!" A feeder yells, and we all form a shivering, coughing, sobbing line on the grass. The flames illuminate wide, terrified eyes, faces covered in soot. My jaw is chattering, and I can't control my hands, so I jam them against my body with my arms.

Feeders begin to make their way down the line, looking us over. I'm too numb to realize what the fuck they're doing, until one of them steps back, raises a gun and fires. I jump back from my place in the line, and now I'm shaking so violently I can barely stand.

They move down the line again, pulling out someone's arm. I hear protests, garbled insistence of "It's fine! It's just a -" The words are cut off as another gunshot rings across the lawn.

Some of us were bitten. They're Afflicted now, carrying this horrible fucking disease that would kill them slowly, that would infect their blood and make them useless to the vamps. I try to tell myself that it's mercy, it's kindness. If they didn't kill them now, they'd be choking on their blood as it filled their lungs.

This is a good thing.

But as another shot echoes through the night, only a few people away from me, I'm so terrified I can't think. I'm going to faint.

The feeders stop in front of me, and a hand reaches out, unclenching my arms from across my chest.

"Come on now," a voice says, and I look up into a pair of rusty red eyes.

It's Silas. His hands are warm, and his face is soft as he gazes at me.

"It's alright," he says quietly. "Let me look you over."

I shake my head. "They didn't get anywhere near me, it-it was -th-they were... They weren't..."

I'm hyperventilating, my chest hurts as my lungs graze against my ribs. Silas's hands hold me tighter, and he's saying something but the roaring in my ears is so loud I can't hear anything.

I collapse in on myself, and Silas catches me.

"Hey!" He exclaims, his arms around me. "Hey, it's alright, Juliet, I've got you."

My feet leave the ground, and I'm in his arms, my head bouncing gently against his chest as he carries me off some-where. Everything is blurry and distant, and I don't have it in me to fight. All I'm aware of is Silas murmuring, "I've got you. I've got you." Over and over again.

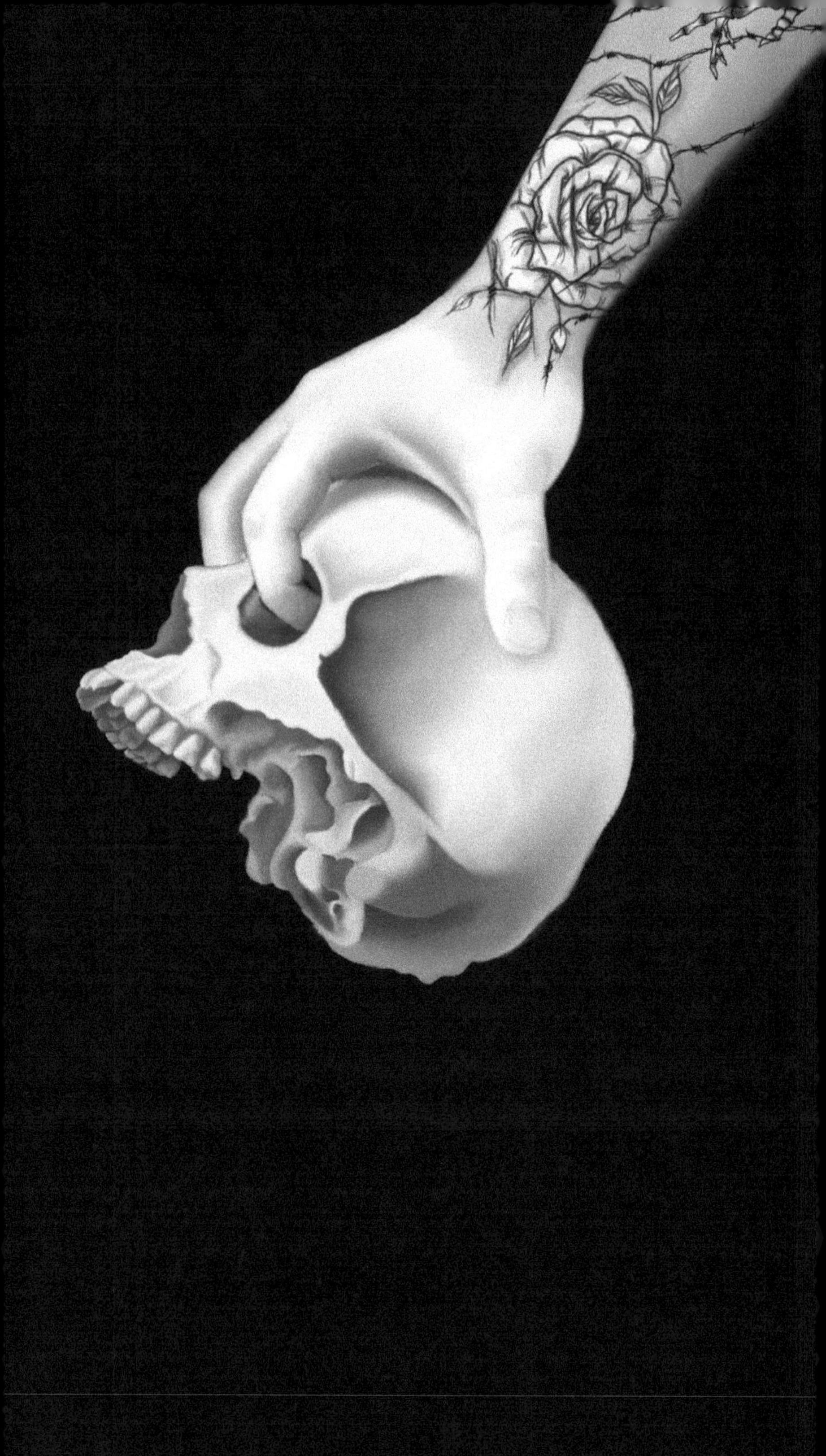

"FIFTEEN DEAD." Sam throws a file across the table, papers scattering onto the floor. She slams a fist into the table, throwing herself back into a creaky swivel chair. "What the fuck is going on?"

We all exchange glances, which infuriates Sam even more.

"Well?" Her eyes move from one to the next, her hands spread. "Hmm? Well? I thought we have patrols, and guards on the gate, and fucking security cameras? Maybe a fucking alarm or two? You want to tell me a horde like that didn't trigger *anything?*"

Goldman clears his throat and steps forward. "They didn't trigger the alarms," he says slowly. "I don't know how, but it seems they disabled them. Or something did."

"You mean to tell me the Afflicted have suddenly become hacking experts?" Sam laughs out loud, getting out of her chair so suddenly it tips onto the floor behind her. Her gaze is venomous as it's cast over us. "I have to go and explain this fucking failure to the higher ups now, and it's my fucking ass on the line. So thanks for that. Now, if you'd all be so kind and go and do your fucking jobs, and see how the fuck this could happen."

She storms out of the room, slamming the door with such force it cracks clean up the middle.

Goldman laughs nervously, and I clap him on the shoulder. "I'd shut the fuck up, man. She has excellent hearing."

The laughter immediately stops, and Goldman swallows hard.

"How the fuck could this happen?" Wallace, one of the older vamps, shakes his head. "Those alarms, I mean, can they even be hacked?"

Goldman nods. "Yeah, of course, with the right equipment."

"If someone hacked those alarms, that means the Afflicted have company. Company that wants us dead." All eyes in the room turn to me. "Either it's rival vamps that are after the bloodbags, or it's humans trying to take us out."

Wallace guffaws. "Come on, humans? You think they'd be able to control the zombies like that? Enough to target an attack?"

I shrug, aware of the soot clinging to my skin. "I have no idea, but something's going on, and until we know what it is, this compound isn't safe." I roll my shoulders and sigh. "Goldman, put extra patrols on the gate, and another lookout on the obs tower. If anyone else is coming towards us, I want to know about it sooner rather than later."

Goldman nods and hurries out of the room, the broken door creaking loudly.

"Fifteen dead." Wallace echoes Sam's words. "That's a big loss. Wonder if they'll send us any more expended bags from the breeding farm."

I'm not prepared for how much his words have my hackles rising, and my face must betray my emotions too readily, because Wallace's eyebrows shoot up in surprise.

"You good, man?" He asks.

I huff out a breath and nod, rubbing the back of my neck. "Yeah, think I'm just a little worn out." I wave him off as he starts to talk again. "I should check sick bay. There's a few bloodbags there."

"I'll go and see how the dorm relocation is going," Wallace calls after me as I leave.

The air is heavy with smoke and death, the edges of the horizon coloring orange as dawn begins to break. This was bad, the worst hit we've had since the early days of the affliction. My shoulders shudder a little as I recall the relief I felt when I realized Juliet was OK. No bites, no blood on her.

Of course, she's the reason I want to go to the sick bay. She's there with two or three others, all shaken more than anything. They'll be fine. She'll be fine. But I need to reassure myself that she's alright.

The harsh overhead lights in the medical block flicker as the generators stutter and struggle. The grid is being tested, for any sign of intrusion, any sign of where they could have been hacked. Uneasiness snakes its way down my back. I don't fucking like this.

I pass two curtained bays, where the humans are sleeping peacefully. I round the corner into the third one, and Juliet's head jerks in my direction. Her eyes are filled with fear, and she shrinks in on herself on the bed.

I stop at the foot of her bed, giving her a smile. "How we doing?"

She gives a small, shaky nod. "Y-yeah, better. They gave me something, to calm me down."

"Good, I'm glad. They're just setting up a new dorm in one of the other buildings, and then you'll be able to go and get some proper rest." I want to move to her bedside, sit beside her, fuck I want to take her hand and try and soothe the tremors that won't stop reverberating through her body. But her eyes are like a deer's, caught in headlights, and I'm worried that if I get closer to her she'll faint again.

"Is everyone OK?" She asks, her voice high-pitched, as though her throat is swollen. "Did you see Gina? I couldn't find her, and-"

"Gina?" *Gina, Gina, which one is Gina, fuck I only know them by numbers.* "The lady with the curly hair?"

Juliet bites her lip and nods shakily.

"Yes, she's fine, safely ensconced in the new dorm." I hope I sound reassuring.

She looks away, brushing the hair out of her face, and shivers. "I was so... So s-scared."

"I know."

"Are we safe here?" She asks in a small voice. Her stormy eyes land on me, her jaw chattering. "I w-want you to t-tell me the tru-truth. Are we s-safe here?"

I lean on the bed frame. "I promise you we're doing everything we can to keep you all safe. Really."

"That sounds like a company response." She sits up, her hands clasped to her chest. "I want to know. P-please. What's going on?"

I don't want to lie to her, but I don't want to scare her with half-truths. We don't know what's going on. We don't know how this happened.

"There just seems to be more Afflicted than normal around right now," I say. "Maybe a neighboring colony got attacked and they're making their way past us. I don't know. But whatever it is, we will keep you safe."

She sniffles, drawing her knees up against her chest and wrapping her arms around them. "How many people died?"

"Too many."

My answer seems to surprise her, and those pretty eyebrows dart up in her face. "You almost sound sorry."

"I am sorry. I don't want to see anyone die if they don't have to."

She cocks her head, regarding me critically before turning her gaze to the curtains. "I'm tired. I should try and sleep."

"Do that." I take a step back from the bed. "It'll be alright." I watch as she huddles back down into the bed, and it's not until she pulls the sheet up over her head that I step out of the cubicle.

I hate leaving her there, shivering and alone, scared down to her bones. She should be tucked up in a warm bed... Yes, with me. I groan at myself. I want to take her in my arms and soothe those fears, kiss her mouth until she forgets how scared she is.

Surrendering to those thoughts is a bad idea. A really fucking bad idea. This isn't the time.

I know I should go and help the others, I should see what else needs to be done. But the past few hours have caught up with me suddenly, and now I just want to be alone. I want to wash all this soot off me.

I head to my cabin, the horrid stench of smoke pursuing me. I shut the door behind me, stripping off my clothes just inside the threshold so I don't drag all this dirt and grime into the room. I drop the clothes on the floor and head straight for the shower.

I consider jerking off for a moment, because of course thinking about Juliet and holding her in my bed has got me hard. But instead I blast myself with cold water, hoping to chase away the arousal. It helps - not much, just a tiny bit.

I dry off and head back into my bedroom. There's a dragging sound behind me, and I turn around to see Sam forcing open the door which is catching on my discarded clothes.

"Open this fucking door, right now." She barks.

I roll my eyes and rush over, waving her away. "Just back

up for a second, hold on." I push the door closed before Sam obliterates it and leaves me with no door. I kick the clothes out of the way and Sam shoves her way in with considerable force, pushing me aside. She slams the door behind her, her eyes roving up and down my naked body.

"Did you know I was coming?" She asks, her eyes blazing bright red with fury and desire.

"You need something, Sam?"

"I need to be fucked." She advances on me and grabs a hold of my mostly-hard cock. "I just got a fucking railing from the boss that I did not enjoy, so now I'd like one I will enjoy." She pumps me roughly a few times, and I clench my molars together as I harden in her hand. "Get on the bed."

She releases me to do her bidding, and I lie on my back, watching as she sheds her clothes. Once she's naked she climbs onto the bed, straddling me. Without much preamble, she lowers herself onto my cock with a gasp.

"Oh fuck." Her head falls back, and she rolls her hips. "Yeah, oh fuck, I need this."

She fucks me freely for herself, rolling and grinding in that way that feels good for women but doesn't do much for me. I tuck my hands behind my head, watching her and enjoying the feeling of her hot, wet pussy around my throbbing cock. I need more to get off, but seeing her get off is fun too.

I reach out to press my thumb to her clit, and her lips shake as a needy little moan escapes her. When I pinch her clit between my thumb and finger, she bucks on me, her fingers scrabbling at my stomach.

"Fuck, fuck," she moans, and her pussy clenches around me as she comes. She shudders for a moment, gasping for breath before she starts moving again.

"Still need more, huh?"

She bites her lips, nodding, her eyes fluttering closed.

"Yeah, fuck, I need more." She grabs onto my shoulders and pulls me into a sitting position, her hips jerking harder against me now. Her eyes meet mine, her rosy lips parted as she gasps and moans. "I need more."

"What else do you need?" I ask, raking my fangs along her jawline. "Be a good little slut and tell me how you want to be fucked."

She groans at my words. "Oh fuck, Silas." She protests as I hold her still, trying to move and keep chasing the orgasm she so desperately needs. "I need to come."

With considerable force I push her off me and flat onto the bed. She's writhing and running her fingers through my hair as I press my mouth to her wet pussy. My tongue drags over her clit, and she half-laughs, half-sobs.

"Oh fuck, Silas, please." She's never been like this before, so needy and raw. It's the closest I've ever seen her to vulnerability. Instead of drawing it out and torturing her some more, I suck on her clit, lashing it with my tongue. I grind my achingly hard cock into the bed, and Sam's cries become high-pitched as she comes again, so wet she's dripping down my lips.

She's barely finished crying out, her body still shaking, when I rise over her, flipping her onto her stomach and pushing my cock inside her. Now I need to come. I need relief. I need to fucking relieve the tension from imagining holding Juliet's shivering frame in my bed.

I grip Sam's hair, pulling her head back and kissing her neck. She sighs, turning her mouth towards me, kissing me hungrily, our lips and fangs and tongues clashing. I groan into her mouth as I pump my release into her still-quivering cunt.

"Oh fuck," she sighs against my mouth. "Fuck. Thank you. I needed that. Holy fuck."

"Happy to help," I say with a laugh, pulling out of her. I roll onto my back, and Sam surprises me by snuggling up under my arm. I look down at her, and her face is twisted with sadness. "Hey, what's wrong?"

She sniffles and shakes her head, flicking her hair out of her face with her fingertips. "I'm being fucking stupid," she says, burying her face into my chest. "You just made me come so hard I'm emotional now, that's all."

I laugh and stroke her hair. "It's alright, today was a shit day."

"Yes it was." She looks up at me, and traces a finger along my lower lip. "You're a great fuck, Silas."

"So are you."

Her mouth quirks into a crooked smile. "You know, you've never told me what you were. Before."

I tuck a hand behind my head and stare at the ceiling. "I was... in security. Alarm systems and CCTV, boring shit like that."

"Oh, right." Sam runs a hand over my chest. "My father owned a plantation."

My head jerks to look down at her. "Like, a slave plantation?"

She nods. "Yep. We were rich as fuck. And then the slaves started getting sick, this weird illness started spreading. And one night, one of them broke into my room. She tore out my throat, but she panicked and gave me her blood to turn me." Sam shrugs. "I helped the slaves murder my whole family. Retribution I guess."

I huff out a breath. "Holy shit."

"Yeah." Sam extricates herself from my embrace and sits up on the bed. "I should let you get some rest." She gives me a small smile, and shakes her head. "Sorry for going all girl on you."

I sit up, resting on my hands. "Come on, we're friends, right? You can talk to me. That's not going all girl on me."

"Friends huh?" She lets out a little laugh. "Friends with benefits, I guess."

"Exactly."

With a nod she gets up off the bed, and pulls on her clothes. "That girl, the one who fainted."

"What about her?" I hope I sound nonchalant.

"You like her, don't you?"

I laugh incredulously, stretching on the bed. "Like her? A bloodbag?"

"I see how you look at her." Sam lifts an eyebrow. "You get that possessive glint in your eye whenever she passes you by."

"Sam, come on." I sit up, throwing my legs over the edge of the bed. "She's pretty, for a human. That's all. So I look at her, and?"

Sam's mouth quirks. "Have you ever heard the expression, thou doth protest too much?"

"I'm not protesting anything." I hold my hands up. "Nothing's going on."

Sam's lips set in a hard line, and with a nod she pushes out the door.

I lie back on the bed, staring at the ceiling as it starts to reflect the orange light of morning.

Others are starting to notice. Sam has eagle eyes, she sees everything. But it's only a matter of time before someone else notices me watching Juliet's every move, sees the look on my face as my eyes follow her.

I have to be careful. I have to stop being stupid. I have to let this go.

But I'm obsessed. Even now, with Sam's taste on my tongue, the second I conjure up the image of that blonde head of hair on the pillow beside me, I'm hard again.

"WE DESERVE ANSWERS!" The cry from the back of the dorm is met with angry shouts of agreement, fists waved in the air, nodding heads.

The red-headed vamp raises her hands for quiet. "I know you're all anxious!" She's barely audible over the angry crowd in front of her. "I know you're all scared."

"Fucking right we are!" Matt yells, clasping on to my hand.

The new dorm is much bigger than the old one, more space for the angry voices asking for an explanation as to what's happening, why this happened, why fifteen people are now dead, to echo off the walls. I was in such bad shock I had to stay in sick bay for two days, and I still can barely eat or sleep a week later.

"Listen, please, I can assure you, you're all safe," the vamp says, and she's met with boos and cynical laughs.

"What are you doing to keep us safe?" One of the younger men demands. "You keep saying we're safe, we're safe, but last week those zombies made it all the fucking way in here!"

"We don't know what happened," the vamp says. "It was a failure of the alarm system, but we're increasing security and it won't happen again."

"How do you know?" Matt bellows, and everyone gets louder again. "We want to fucking know what you're doing!"

"Everything we can!" The vamp calls.

"Tell that to all the people who died!" Gina clutches a hand to her mouth, tears running down her cheeks. The woman beside her puts an arm around her shoulders, and the crowd quietens a little. "We've all lost enough!" Gina's voice cracks, her lips quivering. "I don't feel like sitting here waiting to be torn to shreds if it's all the same to you."

"I promise you, we will protect you all." The red-headed vamp looks almost sad as she looks down at Gina. "I know this was frightening, but I assure you, we've upped our security and it won't happen again."

Gina begins to cry, and the anger in the room dissipates to weariness. Everyone disbands, walking back to their beds. I feel sick. I wobble back to my bed, collapsing onto it heavily. Matt sits down beside me, holding my hand.

"I'd ask if you're OK, but that seems like a stupid thing to ask right now."

I huff out a laugh. "Yeah, I'm not OK, so..." I look up at him and shrug. "I hate this. It's all scary. I feel like something really bad is going to happen."

Matt pulls me close and strokes my hair. "I'm sorry."

"It's not your fault." I sniffle, trying not to start crying again. I don't know what else to say. I don't want to live like this anymore, but I don't want to die. I want some kind of promise that my life can be normal, that there's some light at the end of this blood-soaked tunnel, but I can't see one. I can't think about it too much, because it's just too depressing.

Matt's still looking at me with concern and an air of hopelessness. I get to my feet quickly, pulling my hand from his.

"I just need to go to the bathroom," I say, and head for the door where the red-headed vamp is still talking to the guards.

They all turn to look at me as I approach. "I need the bathroom."

They wave me out the door impatiently, and I step out into the floodlit compound. A light drizzle is falling from the dark sky, and I pad across the damp path to the bathroom block.

"You OK?"

The voice from the shadow of the building startles me, and I stumble back a few steps.

Silas steps out into the light, running a hand through his hair in the increasing rain. "You OK?" He asks again. "I didn't mean to scare you."

I shake my head. "I'm fine. I dunno. I don't feel anything anymore."

Silas winces, rubbing the back of his neck. "I'm so sorry."

"You shot people," I say, and my voice is so hollow that it almost has its own echo, drumming through my skull as I look at Silas's pained expression. "You shot them, right in front of us. You executed them."

"Juliet-"

"And you know the worst part?" I think I'm smiling. I'm so numb. So fucking numb. "I actually thought to myself that y'all were doing them a favor. That you were being kind. Because they'd die anyway, right?"

Silas takes a step towards me, the rusty eyes lit up in the harsh glow of the floodlights. "We have to protect you all."

"Y'all keep saying that.." My teeth are chattering now. "You say it, over and over, and I know all of that."

"I know it's cold comfort."

"Yeah, you can say that again." I tip my head up to the rain, droplets landing on my lashes. "What do you call this feeling? Where you want to live, but you don't, and you don't want to die, not really, but you don't want to live anymore?" An almost hysterical giggle leaves my lips as I meet Silas's gaze. "What do

I call that?" I hiccup out a sob over the laughter. "I don't want to live like this, but thinking I was going - I was going t-to d-die... L-like-" I cut off as my chest begins to burn.

Silas's brow furrows and he steps closer to me, putting his hands on my arms. "Juliet, I need you to breathe, or you're going to pass out."

"Maybe I want to pass out." I clutch a hand to my throat, which feels like it's closing up. "Maybe I want-"

Silas has me off the ground and in his arms before I can protest, before I can even register what's happening. Then I'm in the shower block, and I'm under warm water.

I wrap my arms around myself, trying to breathe. Silas is standing next to me, not touching me, his hand braced against the shower wall, frowning. We just stare at each other for a while, as we both get soaked in the warm water. Droplets run from his hair, down his face. He just stays there, looking at me. After a while, he gives me a little smile.

"Alright?"

I nod, water running into my mouth as I suck in jerky breaths. "Maybe? I don't know?"

"Well you'll be warm at least." He holds up a hand. "I'll be right back. I'll get you some clean clothes and a towel."

"Why do you care?" My voice cracks, frayed at the edges with weariness. Silas frowns at me. "Why?" I demand. "Why do you care so fucking much? No one else does."

He opens his mouth then purses his lips, his eyes searching the floor then lifting back to mine. "I just do, alright? You deserve better than all this."

I want to laugh in his face, I want to sneer at him. I want to believe he's lying. Maybe I even want to believe he's just doing this because he sees me as nothing more than a piece of ass. Believing he actually cares hurts too much. The way he's looking at me, those rusty eyes filled with compassion and concern, they're too much. It's all too much to have someone like him look at me in a way no one has ever looked at me in my life.

"Will you hold me?" I murmur, and he visibly flinches.

"What did you say?" He asks, moving closer to me.

"I-I... Never mind." I cover my face with my hands, shivering despite the warm water. I don't even know why I asked him that.

I gasp as his arms move around me. I don't look up at him, just lean into him, trembling.

"It's alright, Jules," he murmurs. "I've got you, OK? It's alright."

Jules. He called me Jules. No one's called me Jules in years.

"What's going on here?" A woman's voice snaps across the bathroom, and I jerk with panic, burying my face in his chest. Silas keeps his arms around me.

"She collapsed," he says, his voice commanding. "I needed to get her warm, I was worried she'd go into shock."

The woman makes a sound of contempt. "This looks like more than treatment for shock, King."

"I can let her go if you want her to hit her head, Simpson." The way he emphasizes the other vamp's name is like a whip of authority, and footsteps retreat quickly.

Silas notches his fingers under my chin and tips my head back to look up at him. He smiles at me. "Come on now, let's get you dried off and warm, yeah? You need to sleep."

He ushers me into the locker room, and just as he hands me a towel, Matt comes in. He looks us up and down with confusion, and shakes his head.

"What the fuck is going on here?" He asks, moving to my side and putting his arms around me. "Are you OK, babe?"

"I'm fine, I just - I nearly collapsed and Silas caught me."

Matt is staring daggers at Silas, who holds his gaze. It's like being caught between two bulldogs who want to tear each other apart over me. Matt pulls me a little closer to him, and Silas's eyes flicker down to me for a moment.

"She needs to be kept warm," he says, looking back at Matt. "Clean clothes, and a warm bed."

"I know how to keep her warm, don't you worry," Matt snaps.

Silas quirks an eyebrow, and tucks his hands into his pockets. "Perfect." He backs off with a nod. "It's probably obvious to say this, but don't try to keep her warm by fucking her."

"Fuck off," Matt growls.

Silas's eyes blaze, and his mouth curls into a cruel grin. "Not that we'd need to worry about her working up a sweat in 10 seconds I suppose." He turns on his heel as Matt yells obscenities after him, calling him an asshole. He's so angry he's shaking.

I falter a little, and Matt quickly turns to look down at me.

"Babe? You OK?"

I nod. "I'm just tired, and I'm getting cold."

"Of course sorry, come on, let's get these wet clothes off you." He helps me get undressed, and rubs me all over with the towel until my skin is pink. He pulls sweatpants and a tank top from one of the lockers, and I shuffle them on, starting to shiver again.

"Did that guy touch you?" Matt asks quietly, his voice dripping with anger.

I frown at him. "Yeah he did, but I wanted him to."

Matt's eyes widen. "You *wanted* him to?"

I shake my head adamantly. "No, not like that. I mean, he didn't touch me without my permission. He was just helping me. He was being nice."

"Nice?" Matt scoffs. "Nice? These feeders aren't *nice*,

Juliet. They're monsters. I don't want that guy coming anywhere near you."

I'm too exhausted to argue. I just nod and let Matt take me back to the dorm. But I can't get Silas's voice out of my head.

It's alright, Jules. I've got you. It's alright, Jules. I've got you. I've got you.

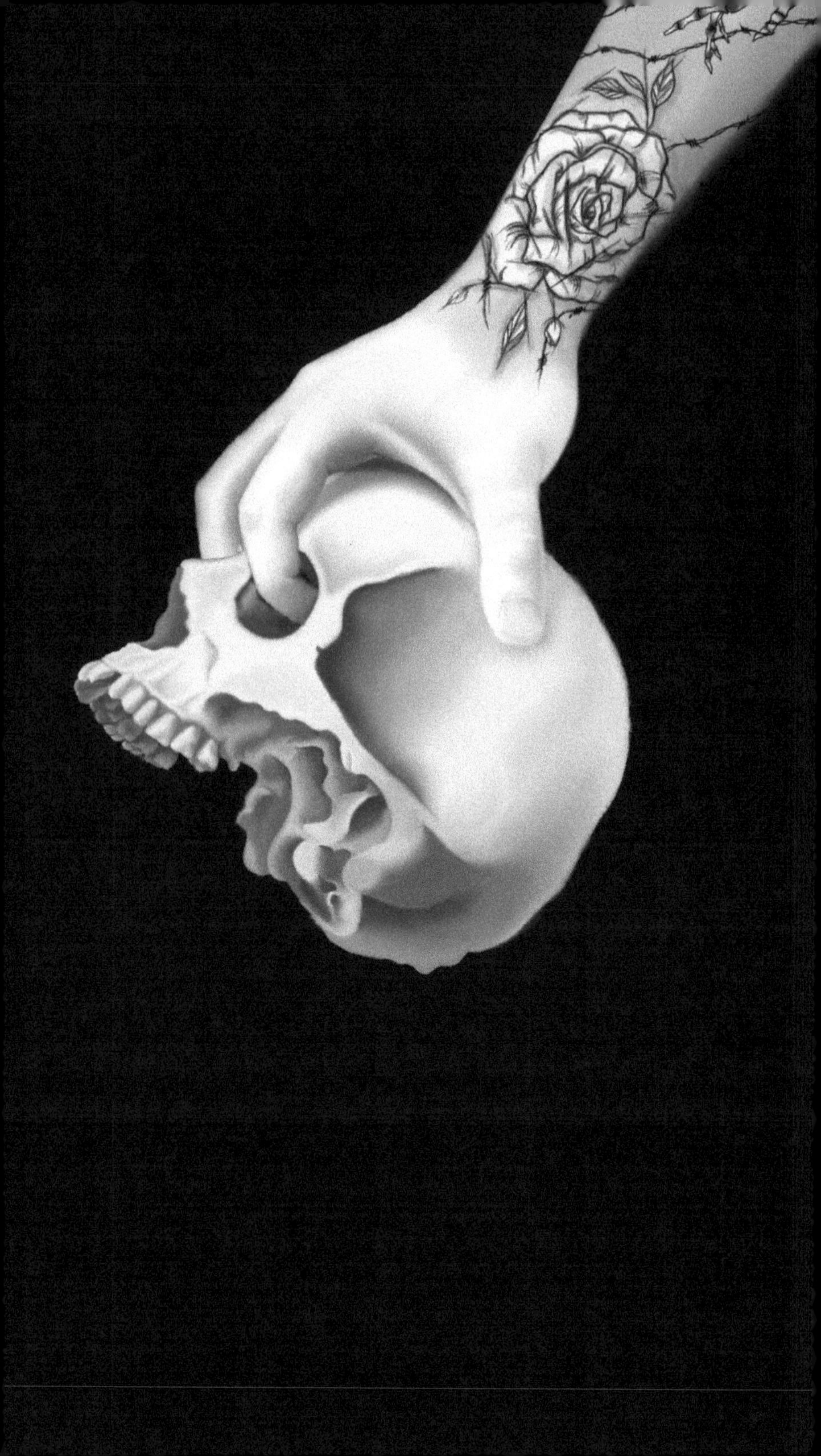

THE PUNCHING BAG groans and creaks as I pound my fists into it. The chain clatters, threatening to come loose from the metal bolt in the ceiling. But I keep punching it, imagining it's that useless, limp-dicked fuck's face.

Fuck that guy. Fuck him and his limp dick. Fuck him that he gets to touch her and I don't.

The punching bag comes loose from its chain with one last right hook, and goes flying across the gym. I stand there, shoulders heaving, sweat running down my chest. She was in my arms. She wanted me to hold her.

She wanted *me*.

She wanted me.

I run a hand over my face, gritting my teeth and overcome with frustration. He's touching her right now, he's touching what's... What's...

"Mine," I mutter to myself. I catch sight of myself in the mirror on the wall, chest still heaving, and I want to smash my fucking reflection into next week. "You fucking idiot."

The door to the gym flies open, and I growl over my shoulder.

"Fuck off."

"How come you're in such a charming mood?" Sam is standing in the doorway, arms crossed over her chest.

"Long story." I turn to face her, and she looks me up and down before casting a glance past me at the punching bag that's lying in the corner.

"Well something's gotten you mad," she says, quirking an eyebrow. "Or someone."

"I'm really not in the mood to explain right now, Sam, so if you have something to say, just fucking say it, alright?"

"Fine," she snaps. "You're needed in the office, they found something on the surveillance cameras and they want you to have a look. It would appear someone tampered with the grid." She turns on her heel and storms back out into the night.

I wipe my face and chest down with a towel before pulling a black t-shirt over my head. *You stupid fucking idiot.* The one time she asks me to hold her, and I'm acting like I own her.

The worst part of it is, I fucking want to. I want her to be *mine.* I don't want anyone else touching her. I don't want anyone else to so much as fucking think of her.

I can hear Margot laughing, chiding me, finding my obsessive nature sweet. "You have an addictive personality," she'd say indulgently, stroking my hair. "And addiction to love is no different."

I'm addicted to Juliet, and that one embrace was my first fucking hit.

I snarl as I stalk out into the yard, headed for the office block. I run a hand through my sweat soaked hair as the evening breeze washes over me. The office block is lit up, vamps arguing loudly inside. I push through the door and all eyes turn to me.

"Finally," Anderson says, throwing his hands up. "Come and look at this, King. This doesn't look normal."

I cross the room, the vamps making space for me to pass.

Anderson leans back in his chair, gesturing widely to the computer screen. I lean one hand on the desk as Anderson hits play on the surveillance footage.

At first it's just static, and the only movement is the lights flickering.

"What?" I ask after a minute.

Anderson holds up a hand. "Just wait."

As I keep watching, a figure in a black hoodie emerges from the shadows of one of the buildings. The figure runs in a crouch through the lit-up areas, coming to a stop at the edge of the fenceline. They pause, turning to continue.

They stop short and take two hurried steps backwards.

In the next frame they're gone. The timestamp in the corner has jumped 10 minutes.

I shake my head, squinting at the screen. "What the fuck?" I grab the mouse and rewind the footage. But it happens again, the figure is there, obviously startled by something - or someone - and in the next frame, it's like they've disappeared into thin air.

I look down at Anderson, who pinches the bridge of his nose.

"This isn't good, is it?" He asks.

I look across the room at Sam, who's standing in the corner with her arms crossed over her chest.

"You said there was evidence that the grid had been tampered with?"

She nods. "One of the generators was disconnected from the outer wires. The Afflicted would have been able to cross that initial alarm line unnoticed."

I turn to look back at the screen, playing the video twice over. I don't know what I'm expecting. Do I think it'll suddenly change? That the fucking Houdini in the video won't suddenly vanish into thin air?

"Wait a second." I replay the video, leaning close to the screen, looking at the bottom corner. "There." I point. "There's someone there. You can see the top of someone's head."

Everyone leans over my shoulder, watching as the figure stumbles and the curve of a head covered in hair comes into view, before the image flashes back to the empty yard.

"Great, and then they disappear too." Anderson slams an open palm against the table and sucks on his fangs. "This isn't possible, though, is it? Someone's tampered with the security footage."

I straighten up and cross my arms over my chest. "Yeah, someone's deleted a timeframe here, but there'd be evidence of that in the files. You can't delete these frames without there being a trail."

Sam scoffs. "You sure about that?"

"Sure. Whoever did this, they didn't do a good job. Leaving this footage, that's just a rudimentary cut job. They'll have left a trail somewhere."

Anderson rises to his feet and points at me. "You go through those files then and let me know what you find. You know what you're looking for, and we need to know what happened here." He shakes his head. "Why the fuck would anyone want Afflicted to flood the compound?"

"Revolutionaries," Sam says, moving closer to the desk, her hands on her hips. "They want to take out the vamps no matter what. Boston's been having troubles with them. They'll even use a volatile force like the Afflicted, because the end goal is taking all of us out."

I cast a glance over her face, and she shrugs.

"We'll lay new trip lines, I'll help rig them up tomorrow," I say, not sure if even that will be enough. I have to believe it'll help, but this isn't good. If someone inside is working on this... I don't even know where to begin looking. Humans? Who can roam free without a vamp noticing?

I look around the room at my colleagues, and they're either very good actors, or all genuinely freaked the fuck out.

Something bad is coming. I can feel it.

THE SUN BEATS down on us as I test the newly laid trip lines. The alarm whirs as one of the other vamps steps on the sensor buried in the ground. Another one walks a little further, and the motion sensor secured to the tree sends a silent alarm to the smart watch on my wrist. The other vamps look down at their wrists, and I know it's tripped the entire alarm system.

I rub a hand along my neck, humidity sending sweat running down my back. The horizon is heavy and black with an approaching storm.

"Braun, the battery banks are full, right?"

Braun looks up from his laptop and nods, rubbing beads of sweat from his top lip with the collar of his shirt. "Sure are."

"Good." I gesture at the gathering storm. "Last thing we need is to get caught in a power outage with a new system laid."

He shakes his head, hissing out a breath. "Fucking humans, getting brazen like that. I mean, where the fuck do they get off, huh?"

I lean back against the tree I'm sitting under and sigh. "Captives tend to revolt, Braun. I'm surprised it took them this long."

"Captives?" Braun laughs out loud. "They have it good! Three meals a day and a warm bed, that's more than I damn well had growing up. You're too young to remember the Great

Depression, well I'm not. These humans would be begging to be in a facility like this back in those days."

"I hardly think that's the same thing." I meet his skeptical gaze. "Or maybe it is, in a way. You were the victim of a greedy government, and these humans are the victims of irresponsible vampires."

"Victims?" Braun lets out a hacking laugh. "Irresponsible? This all happened because vamps wanted to protect the humans, remember? Those experiments were run so we wouldn't need as much blood. They couldn't have known it would go wrong."

"The vamps thought they could outsmart science and created something they couldn't control."

Braun throws his hands up, spittle bursting from his lips as he laughs out loud. "You got this all wrong, King. The vamps who did all this, they're heroes. They tried to make the world a better place."

"You have a funny idea of heroism." I gesture around vaguely with my hand. "This? It's just existing. It's not *living*."

"And you got a funny idea of living." Braun plucks a stone from the ground and throws it across the grass. "This here, it's heaven. We got everything we need."

"Maybe you should ask the humans if they feel the same way about your supposed heaven."

"You're a philosophical son of a bitch, King."

"Art majors are required to take philosophy," I reply, and instantly feel a little sick that I revealed something personal about myself.

Braun instantly jumps on this tid-bit, leering at me. "An *art* major, huh? Fancy. Let me guess, you grew up in some country manor out in the countryside, with butlers and maids."

I shift uncomfortably. "No, nothing like that."

"You always did strike me as a rich kid," he says, leaning

back on his hands on the grass. "That accent, and the way you look at us all like we smell bad or something."

I roll my eyes, slamming my laptop shut and rising to my feet. "Maybe you just need a shower, mate." I head back to the truck as Braun's laughter follows me.

A country manor. Hardly. My heart wrenches in my chest as memory overcomes me, and I'm thrown back in time to the last day I was ever in my family home, the sweet terrace house in London with the oak tree in the yard. The last time I saw my parents. My mother's tears, my father's face twisted with terror. Telling my siblings to get upstairs, to not come anywhere near me. My little sister crying for me, my brother's ashen face as he'd pulled her up the steps behind him.

I'd begged to be accepted. I'd begged them to see that it was a good thing. That I was a better person. That my life was coming together. I'd stood in my childhood home, and begged the people who were supposed to love me more than anything in the world to just accept who I was now.

You're a monster. You ruin everything. You always have.

Thunder rumbles in the distance. The crew starts to head back in from laying the perimeter wires, packing the supplies back into the trucks. I climb into the driver's seat, throwing the laptop onto the passenger seat. I stare out the windshield at the approaching storm, and my mind drifts to Juliet.

Because of course it does. I haven't seen her in a few days, and I keep trying to convince myself that's a good thing. Because I should stay away from her. This can't go anywhere. This can't lead any place.

I told myself over and over again that her wanting me to hold her was just fear. But as I look in the rear view mirror and see Braun pissing against a tree, I know it wasn't that. She'd never ask Braun, or Crawley, or Sam to hold her.

No, those grey eyes looked up at me with longing. I make her feel safe.

I gun the engine, leaving Braun to piss against the tree and catch a ride back with one of the other patrols. I drive along the perimeter line, testing the sensors, and every single one throws up an alert. The system is working.

The sun is starting to lose its fight with the approaching storm as I make my way back to the compound. The gate guards wave me through, and once I park the truck, I head to the obs tower. They're putting up fresh barbed wire along the fenceline as I pass, and the sight has me pausing to watch for a moment. This is how we live our lives now, surrounded by barbed wire and heavy gates. Sure, there's a garden, and a forest, and a stream hidden away in the trees.

But we're locked up.

Boston had turned into a giant walled city, and living there had been hell. I'd been allocated a tiny apartment, barely the size of a regular bedroom, and worked in a factory for 12 hours a day. After living a completely unfettered life of freedom with Margot for so many years, the transition had been a hard one. They'd seized all of her assets, which was easy since I'd been on my own. Margot had always rejected the idea of her own coven, she was too much of a loner. I didn't mind, I was incredibly possessive of her. The occasional orgy was one thing - sharing her with someone else full time was not an option.

It wasn't until the Affliction hit that she began to take in other vamps, letting them live with us to keep them safe. A decision that ultimately cost her her life.

After two years of that misery, mourning Margot and dealing with nights of crippling loneliness in my tiny apartment, the call went out that Milledgeville needed guards. The country compounds had been set up in the early days of the Affliction, a way to keep humans out of the big cities where the

Afflicted had more places to hide, and more opportunity to attack. They had expanded, and needed more guards. I jumped at the chance.

Being out in the countryside and away from a city that had essentially turned into a giant industrial complex was better, infinitely better. But watching the guards wind out large rolls of barbed wire now reminds me that we're all just prisoners, in our own way.

Braun's right. That philosophy degree really does seem to be coming into play more and more.

The obs tower is buzzing with activity, screens lit up, vamps talking over each other as they try to decipher all the incoming data. Lightning flashes in the navy sky, and I just hope the grid stays stable and the power doesn't go out. I look at some readings over the shoulders of my colleagues, and the sensors are all up. Everything looks as it should. If any Afflicted head our way, we'll know about it.

Satisfied everything is as it should be and not wanting to be in a room of arguing vamps any longer, I climb back down the ladder. A few raindrops have started peppering the ground, the wind picking up as it drags the storm in over us.

I cross the yard, turn a corner, and am hit with Juliet's scent the split second before she runs straight into me.

"Shit, sorry." I grab on to her so I don't knock her to the ground, and she inhales sharply, her wide eyes fixed on me.

"Hi," she says softly. "Are you alright?"

"Yeah, of course, I'm fine. You?"

She nods, and I realize I still have a hold of her. But I don't let go.

"I was out checking the perimeter, making sure the sensors are all where they should be."

"Oh. OK." The look she's giving me is hard to read and it's going to drive me insane. Is she frightened? Relieved? She's trembling ever so slightly under my hands, and I know I should let her go. But she feels so fucking nice, her warmth against my palms, and I don't want to move an inch.

"I told you I was going to keep you safe, didn't I?" I smile down at her.

"Hey!"

This fucking guy. I lift my eyes at the same time that Juliet jumps a little and casts a glance over her shoulder. Her stupid fucking boyfriend comes charging towards us, his features twisted with fury. Juliet backs away from me quickly, dropping her head, and rage leeches into my bones.

"You OK, babe?" He barks, and I want to backhand that fucking tone right out of his mouth.

"She's fine," I say.

"I didn't fucking ask you." He doesn't look at me as he snarls out the words through gritted teeth, putting a possessive arm around Juliet's shoulders. "Babe, are you OK?'

She nods, her eyes fixed on the ground. "I'm fine, we were just talking."

"Well you don't need to talk to him, you talk to me." His voice is cloyingly saccharine.

"She can talk to whoever she fucking well wants to, mate." I cross my arms over my chest. "If she wants to talk to me, she can."

His head snaps towards me. "Actually, according to your own little fucking rules, you're not allowed to touch her, and you're not supposed to fraternize with us, remember?" His mouth curls into a grin as Juliet's head drops further, her hair completely covering her face. "You're supposed to stay right the fuck away from her, *mate*. So how about you do that, huh?"

"If she wants me to stay away from her, she'll tell me. But the rules?" I take a step closer to him, and the certainty in his face falters just a little. "I've never much been one to follow the rules. So if you think some fucking by-line is going to stop me from talking to her, then you've got another thing coming."

"King?" Anderson's voice sounds behind me, and Matt's face lights up with triumphant delight. "King, can I talk to you for a minute?"

"We won't keep you," Matt drawls, herding Juliet away from us.

I grit my teeth and turn to face my boss, who's eyeing me wearily. He tilts his head in the direction of his office, turning on his heel as I begin to follow him.

"Close the door," he says once we're in his office, heading for the chair behind his desk. He loves to deliver a bollocking from the comfort of his leather chair, and I know I'm in for a bollocking. He heard every word I just said.

"Is something wrong, sir?" I try to keep my tone light.

He steeples his fingers in front of him and sighs. "You want to tell me what's going on with that girl?"

"What girl?"

"Don't play with me, King." Anderson doesn't raise his voice, he just keeps his expectant gaze fixed on me. "I asked you a question, and I'd like an answer."

"The answer is nothing." I shrug. "Nothing's going on."

"Uh-huh. Is that why Simpson found you showering with her?"

Those fucking words send a mental image straight into my brain, and this is definitely *not the fucking time.* "We weren't showering together." Fuck, I wish that had been the case. "She nearly collapsed, she was shaking and going into shock. A hot shower seemed like a quick way to warm her up."

"Right, and the fact you had your arms around her?"

Fuck you, Simpson, you fucking snake. I roll my shoulders, setting my jaw to stop any unwise words tumbling out. "I was holding her up. I told Simpson as much. She nearly collapsed. If she'd fallen and hit her head-"

"King, I asked what's going on." Anderson leans on his desk, his eyebrows raised. "Now, I want you to tell me what's going on, not argue semantics. I just heard you tell that bloodbag out there that you didn't care about the rules."

"The guy's a maggot."

"A what?" Anderson rises to his feet.. "I gotta tell you, King, this sounds a lot like two fellas ruffling their feathers in front of the female."

I laugh out loud. "You think I'm trying to show off to a bloodbag, sir?"

"Listen here, son, the way you're talking to that guy and the way you're talking to me now, it sounds like jealousy."

"I am *not* jealous of that fucking guy." I am. I'm so jealous I can't think. I'm so jealous I annihilated a fucking punching bag imagining it was his face. The thought of him touching my girl, putting his grubby fucking hands on that body that he can't even please - I'm so jealous I can barely fucking *see*. But I can't admit that to my boss. "I'm simply trying to look after the humans. I take this responsibility seriously. Blokes like Braun, they see them as nothing but a blood supply. I see them as people, like we should."

"Not like a piece of ass?"

My rage is so incandescent for a second I can practically smell it, ashen and scorching straight down to my lungs. I want to jump across the table and claw his fucking eyes out. I want to rip his fucking tongue out. *Piece of ass*. That's my fucking girl he's talking about.

"With all due respect, sir, you're way outta line." I'm almost proud of myself for swallowing down all that rage. "I've not touched a human, not once. I've never given you reason to doubt me. I've never given you reason not to trust me."

Anderson cocks an eyebrow. "No, I suppose you haven't. But that doesn't change the fact that you need to watch yourself."

"I am *watching* myself, sir."

We stare at each other for a moment, as though daring the other to make a wrong move. Instead we both just watch, until Anderson dips his head.

"Alright, King, you take it easy on yourself. You're a good officer. Keep it that way."

Keep it that way. The words pursue me through the rain, all the way back to my cabin. They're a thinly veiled threat.

I've heard what happens to vamps who break the rules before. Stripped down, chained up with silver, and injected with ever-increasing doses of silver nitrate. Eventually you're nothing but a heap on the floor, screaming and begging for the pain to stop. They starve you of blood. They starve you of light. They leave you there to rot until you're a ragged corpse. Then they feed you. And then they start it all again.

It doesn't happen often. The very idea of it is so monstrous that no one dares bend the rules.

But I'll bend the rules. I'll bend them till they break and shatter around me. And if I crawl out of this a withered corpse on bloody hands, then so be it.

SINCE THE ATTACK, things have been different. Everyone is much quieter, more aloof, less smiley. Not even sunshine can cheer us up.

The feeders have been busy laying new alarm lines, rigging up new security cameras, putting reinforced metal bar locks on the dorm doors. There are bars on all the windows now, not just the dorms. The doors are locked while we eat. Armed guards stand at the door while we shower. I feel less and less like that free range chicken, and more like a battery hen. It's only a matter of time before they won't let us out anymore.

I stare at the bowl of ice cream on the table in front of me, watching as it melts slowly. They're giving us better food, trying to distract us and cheer us up. Like we're toddlers who'll be sated with a bowl of chocolate ice cream.

Matt puts a hand on my leg, and when I look up at him, he smiles at me.

"You OK?" He asks.

I nod, shoving my spoon into my bowl and pushing it away. "Yeah, just not hungry,"

Gina eyes me from across the table with all the concern of a worried mother. "Sweetie, you've barely eaten in days."

I shrug. "I'm not hungry."

I can practically feel that she and Matt exchange a glance, but I don't lift my gaze until I sense movement at the door. I look up, and Silas walks into the cafeteria. His eyes land on me straight away, and where a few months ago I'd have hated that he's looking at me, the way his face melts as he looks at me just makes me want to cry. He looks so worried. He looks like he really cares.

Matt's arm is instantly around my shoulders, and I drop my eyes back to the table. He told me he didn't want Silas around me, and I need to respect that. I know that.

"That fucking guy," Matt mumbles.

"He's just worried," I say quietly.

Suddenly there's a shout, and something smashes at the other end of the room. We all crane our necks to see what's going on, and two of the men at the far table have gotten to their feet and are hurling the bowls of ice cream against the walls.

The feeders are yelling at them to stop, but the men keep going.

"You think you can buy us off with fucking ice cream?" One of them yells, throwing another bowl at the window, which smashes around the metal bars that now sit against it. "We're all here at the mercy of those fucking zombies and you're here feeding us fucking ice cream?"

Silas approaches them with out-stretched hands as more feeders rush into the cafeteria behind him.

"Hey man," Silas says, "I know you're frightened, but we're doing everything we can."

Matt scoffs, rising to his feet. "Fuck you, you fucking freak!"

Gina eyes him with alarm, and I try to pull him back down onto the bench.

"Matt, shut up," I say urgently, but Matt shakes me off, rounding the table to join the men who are throwing bowls.

"You fucking freaks are leaving us out here like lambs to the slaughter," Matt says, and more people get up from their tables, agreeing and sweeping bowls off the tables.

Silas watches Matt approach, and his gaze is lethal.

"Everyone needs to calm down!" The red-headed feeder climbs up on a chair, her hands held up. "We told you all, we're going to protect you!"

Someone hurls a bowl directly at her, and she jerks out of the way. Suddenly it's like the room explodes, and everyone is throwing everything they can at the feeders. Everyone is yelling at the same time, a symphony of fury and anguish that's so loud I cover my ears with my hands.

Matt rushes at Silas, who bares his fangs.

He's going to fucking kill him.

I try to fight my way across the room, feeders grabbing humans and wrestling them to the ground. By the time I reach Matt and Silas, Matt is against the wall with Silas's arm pressed against his throat.

I grab Silas's shoulder, and his head snaps around to look at me.

"Stop!" I plead. "Please stop! Don't hurt him!"

Silas's eyes are blazing red, but his face changes as he looks at me. I wrap my hands around his arm, trying to pull him away from Matt.

"Please, Silas." I shake my head. "Please, don't hurt him."

He sucks in a breath when I say his name.

Matt looks back and forth from Silas to me, then gunshots have us all ducking. A feeder has an assault rifle in their hands, and is firing at the ceiling. They're probably blanks, but the sound has me instantly on the floor with my hands over my head. Someone is over me, shielding me with their body, and I turn my head, expecting to see Matt's face.

But it's Silas, covering me, arms caging me in as he looks around the room. "Stay down," he barks at me as the gunfire continues.

I huddle underneath him, clutching my hands to my mouth to stop myself from screaming.

Finally the gunfire stops. There's shouted commands of "get up" and "move", and I peer out from underneath Silas to see feeders hauling people to their feet, shoving them out the door. The two men who started it all are being held against the wall next to the doors.

Silas gets up into a crouch and pulls me into a sitting position. He clutches my face in his hands and looks me over.

"Are you OK? Did I hurt you?" He runs a hand over my head.

"I'm fine, you didn't hurt me."

He gives me a weak smile, stroking my cheek gently. "Good."

He's thrown to the ground and away from me as Matt starts pounding his fists into him. "I told you to stay the fuck away from her!" Matt's voice is shrill with fury, his fists flying.

"Matt, stop!" I try to pull him away, even though I know Silas doesn't need any help. But one of Matt's punches misses, and his elbow smashes into my cheek bone as he pulls his arm back to lay into Silas again. I'm thrown flat on my back, cloudy white stars floating in my vision.

I'm aware of Matt over me, asking if I'm OK, saying sorry over and over again. I blink rapidly, trying to focus through the throbbing pain in my face.

"I'm OK," I murmur, letting him help me up. "I'm OK, I'm fine."

"I never meant to hurt you," Matt says, clutching me to his chest. "I'm so sorry."

I lean into him, my head feeling fuzzy. "It's OK, really."

Silas is standing next to us, his face dark with anger. He wants to kill Matt, I can see it in his eyes. But he says nothing, backing away from us as other feeders herd us out of the cafeteria and into the yard.

It's getting dark, and we're all ordered to stay there on the grass.

The red-headed vamp stands at the cafeteria doors, pulling a handgun from her waistband. The two men who started the mini riot are dragged out and thrown to their knees in front of her.

"You all want to riot?" She asks loudly. "You all want to start throwing things and acting like fucking barbarians? When we're doing everything we can to protect you?" She's livid. She's so angry, she's shaking. "So you all know, this is how we deal with rioters."

The crowd cries out as she points her gun at the back of the head of one of the men. I want to cover my face, I don't want to see it, but I'm frozen in place.

The man's face explodes in a shower of blood and bones, brain matter flinging across the ground. The gunshot is drowned out by the screams around me.

The other man is on his back, crawling away from her, his lips moving as he probably begs for his life and promises to never do it again. The vamp advances on him, and shoots him square in the forehead. He goes limp, stretched out on the dusty ground.

The red-head turns to us, pointing her gun in the air. "Anyone else?" She shouts.

We all fall silent but for the soft sounds of people crying. She looks at us all, eyebrows raised, red eyes blazing.

"This is how we treat rioters." She points the gun at the bloody corpse at her feet. "If you want to end up like them, then you do what they just did. We will not tolerate any unrest. Do I make myself clear?"

She's answered with nothing but silence. She exhales heavily, tucking her gun away, and waves a hand towards us. "Get them into the dorms," she orders.

"See?" Matt whispers to me as we walk. "I told you. They're monsters. These feeders are all fucking monsters."

THE NEXT FEW days pass in a bit of a blur. We get up, we eat, we're allowed to walk around a little. Gardening duty is strictly regulated, with small teams under tight supervision going down one at a time. If the last attack changed the mood of the compound, then the riot totally obliterated it. The delicate trust that existed between us and the feeders, no matter how precarious it sometimes felt, it was at least there.

Now there are two fresh graves in the cemetery and a whole lot of dark looks in the feeders' direction. Everyone is on edge, constantly waiting for the other side to strike the first blow.

It's exhausting.

I almost forget about draining. But then it's Monday morning, and I'm called out of bed just after dawn and ushered into the shower. I stand under the hot water, my arms hugged around myself, wondering if Silas is watching me through the mirror.

I squeeze my eyes shut as I remember the look on his face as he held me during the riot. The relief when he saw I wasn't hurt. The fury in his eyes when Matt hurt me. Sure, it was an accident. But to a man like Silas, I doubt that matters.

Why do I like him?

I open my eyes, blinking away droplets of water as they cling to my lashes. It's the first time I've admitted to myself that I might actually like Silas. It's such a strange feeling. I've never felt close to a feeder before - why would I? But with him, it's different. He feels safe.

But Matt made it pretty clear he doesn't want Silas anywhere near me. I shudder to think what would have happened if I hadn't intervened. Matt was out for blood, but Silas is the one with the strength to take it.

We all go through the motions, drying off and getting dressed, heading to the cafeteria for a stale breakfast barely anyone chokes down. Like sheep, lost in a new field, we head for the clinic. No one talks. Hardly anyone even looks up.

This sucks.

But my heart damn near leaps out of my chest when, instead of the usual vamps who deal with us in the clinic, Silas pushes through the blue curtain.

"Hello there." He smiles at me, even though his eyes darken when he looks at my black eye, that's still a really unique shade of purple.

"Hi. You on medic duty now?"

"Only for our VIPs."

"And I'm one of those?" I laugh. "Well, you can tell them the turndown service sucks."

"I'll pass that on." He sits beside me, raising his eyes to gaze at me with a small smile as he fastens the tourniquet around my arm. "You OK?"

I nod, suppressing a gasp as he taps the vein in my arm. His hands are really warm.

"You know, I never apologized."

"For?" He asks, without looking up.

"That day outside the shower block, when I said you're cold and bloodless."

Silas chuckles low in his throat. "Small scratch now." He inserts the needle, and I barely feel it. He looks up at me with an almost wicked grin. "Sorry I said I'd get hard enough to make you scream."

I laugh out loud, and it feels like weights are rolling off my shoulders. "You did say that."

"I did."

"Are you actually sorry you said it?" I purse my lips and look him up and down. "Something tells me that when a man like you says something like that to a woman, he means it."

He draws down his eyebrows, faux anger dancing across his face even though he can't stop grinning. "Are you asking if I can walk the walk, as well as talk the talk?"

My cheeks flush with heat, I'm sure I'm bright red. "I mean... I didn't mean..."

He leans closer. "Are you asking what I'm like in bed?"

"Oh god, no." I shake my head, hoping he doesn't see me clenching my thighs together. "No, sorry, I was, I was joking."

He laughs, and holy shit is he gorgeous when he does that. "I know, just like getting a rise out of you."

"Well, you certainly did that." I exhale heavily and relax into the seat. "But you also made me laugh, so thank you."

He gives me a nod, leaning back in the chair, his long legs stretch out in front of him. I marvel once again at just how tall he is, he seems to just go on forever.

"Are you tattooed all over?"

Instantly that grin is back, full of swagger and sass. He runs his tongue over his teeth, and I can just feel the innuendo coming.

"Trying to get me naked now?"

I roll my eyes, trying to mask just how much I'm enjoying

myself. "Yeah, absolutely. You've seen mine, time for me to see yours, right?"

"Well, if you insist." He starts to unbutton his khaki shirt, laughing and flashing his fangs when I shriek and cover my eyes. "Since you're so curious, I'm nothing but ink from the waist up."

"Well, except for that pretty face." I gesture with my hand, and he raises his eyebrows, clearly pleased with what I just said.

"You think I'm pretty, do you?"

I roll my eyes. "Stop it, you own a mirror right?"

"Oh well, thanks a lot." He crosses his arms over his chest. "Glad you think I'm pretty."

"So you're ink from the waist up. What about from the waist down?" Jesus, what is wrong with me? Why am I flirting with him? I have a boyfriend. This is so wrong. I quickly shake my head, hoping that the question I just asked somehow melts into the ether and he forgets about it.

Instead, the universe sends me a distraction in the form of a loud boom that has everyone in the clinic screaming. We're tied down with tubes in our arms, it's not like we can run.

"Hey now, you're OK, I've got you," Silas says, standing over me, his hands gently squeezing my shoulders. "It's just a weapons test, really it's alright."

"A weapons test?" I realize sweat has broken out on my upper lip, and I've grabbed onto his arm with the hand that isn't strapped down. "What do you mean?"

"Just new charges on the perimeter, they sound scarier than they are, really."

I gasp for air, focusing on his eyes, on the color. They're more brown than red, a really pretty rust color. He smiles softly, one thumb stroking down the side of my neck. My whole body relaxes at the touch, and I sigh, trying to regulate my breathing.

"Like a flash-bang, right?"

Silas laughs. "Yes, just like that." His thumb runs up the side of my throat again, back down again, his eyes still fixed on mine. "It's alright. You're safe. I promise."

"My dad was a cop." The words bubble out of me. "He taught me how to shoot. I-I used to be really good. I was never scared of how loud it was."

Silas nods. "Well, I know never to cross you then. You and all this sass, *and* a gun? No thanks."

I burst out into nervous giggles, and the sound is a little wobbly, tinged with hysteria. "They'd probably just bounce straight off you."

Silas laughs out loud, his whole face lit up, and if I was standing up my knees would go wobbly. God, this is all starting to mess with my head. I'm going crazy, because looking at him right now I'm convinced Silas is the most beautiful man I've ever seen in my life. I lift my hand, my fingertips barely brushing his jawline, and he freezes.

"Why do you make me feel like this?"

His Adam's apple races up and down his throat, the tattoos on his neck shifting. "Feel like what?"

I shrug. "Safe."

The curtain gets thrown back, and Silas quickly straightens up, increasing the distance between us in an instant. Another feeder steps into the cubicle, jerking his thumb over his shoulder as he looks down at Silas.

"The obs tower needs you, come on."

"Yeah, no worries, I'll just finish up here and then I'll be along."

The feeder nods and turns on his heel, walking away without closing the curtain. Silas looks down at my arm, hesitating for a moment before he starts removing the needle, pressing cotton wool to the vein.

"Here, keep pressure on it for me." He keeps his eyes down, his fingers lingering, even as I push mine underneath his to keep the gauze in place. His fingers brush over mine gently, and shivers run down my spine. "He..." He clears his throat. "He's nice to you, isn't he?"

"Who? Matt?"

He nods, his eyes still fixed downwards.

"Yeah, he is."

"Good." He removes his hand from mine, getting a roll of tape and securing the gauze over the puncture in my arm.

My hand feels cold now that his is gone, and I feel so stupid for wishing he'd touch me again. He rises to his feet, tucking his hands into his pockets.

"I'm glad I make you feel safe. You deserve that." Before I can answer him, he strides out of the cubicle, leaving me alone and wondering what the hell just happened.

"YOU OK, BABY?" Matt asks me as we clear our plates after dinner.

I sigh heavily. "You've asked me that about fourteen times already."

"Sorry." He leans against the wall next to me, running a hand through his hair. "You just seem really distracted tonight."

"Can you blame me? It hasn't exactly been fun around here." I sound way harsher than I intended to, and I meet his eyes with a shrug. "I'm sorry. I didn't mean to snap. I'm just... worn out."

He reaches out and rubs my shoulder. "You're tense, that's all. I get it."

I don't want to discuss my tension anymore, I don't want to tell Matt about Silas being nice to me and making me feel safe. I don't need the argument again. Instead I just give him a weak smile and nod.

Matt looks over his shoulder, then leans down close to me, grinning. "I know just what you need," he mutters.

"And what's that?"

"Come on." He grabs my hand, leading me out of the cafeteria while everyone finishes cleaning up.

"Where are we going?"

"You'll see." He nods at the feeders at the door, who barely acknowledge us. We walk down the steps, but instead of heading back towards the dorm, Matt turns left and starts walking faster.

"Matt." I giggle nervously, glancing over my shoulder. "Where are you taking me?"

He doesn't answer, guiding me around the side of the cafeteria, heading for the shower block. We reach an alcove at the far end of the building, and he pulls me into it, pushing me back against the wall.

"What are you doing?" I laugh breathlessly as he kisses my neck. "Babe, they'll be looking for us."

"Shhh." He pushes my top up over my breasts, and lowers his mouth to my right nipple, sucking hard.

I gasp, and rake my hands through his hair. "Matt, someone will see us." But even as I protest, I push my shorts and panties off. Matt follows suit, kicking his sweatpants away, lifting me up around his waist.

The wall at my back is rough, digging into my skin, but as soon as Matt sinks into me I don't even care, the discomfort melting away into pleasure. This position is so much better than being flat on my back in a tiny bed. His thrusts nudge against my clit like this, and it feels so good I dig my fingers into his shoulders. I've been dying for this release, just wanting to forget the last few days and have that rush.

Matt grins at me, breathing heavy. "Does that feel good?"

"Yeah, you feel so good."

"I bet he does."

The voice makes us both jump, and Matt and I both look over to see the big feeder with the reddish hair standing a few feet away. He's leaning against the wall, his arms crossed over his chest. He looks us up and down, his fangs glinting as he grins.

"Oh please don't stop on my account," he says, "the lady seemed to be enjoying that."

I unfurl my legs from around Matt's waist, and we both move to pick up our clothes.

"We were just heading back to the dorm," I say quietly.

The feeder laughs. "Yeah, I can see that's exactly where you were headed." He takes a step closer to us, his hands clasped behind his back. "Hmm, now, what am I going to do with the two of you?"

I quickly pull my shorts back on, shoving my panties into my pocket, and I suppress a shriek as the feeder rushes at me. He leers down at me, his red eyes glowing bright crimson.

"I'll take those, if you don't mind," he says, retrieving my panties from my shorts, and raising them to his nose. His eyes flutter closed as he inhales deeply, and my stomach contorts into a knot of ice.

Matt's just standing there, almost... almost casually. Panic whirs inside me. Why isn't he doing anything?

"Goddamn, girl," the feeder says with a sigh, "that sweet pussy of yours smells incredible." He looks back down at me, and lifts a hand to my face. "I'd have a lot of fun with you, little one."

I slap his hand away. "Don't fucking touch me."

He moves so fast I don't even see it, but suddenly I'm against the wall, his huge hand wrapped around my throat. He bears down on me, his lips pulled back to reveal his fangs.

"Matt," I say weakly as the feeder's hand presses the air from my windpipe, "call for help."

Matt looks around and gives the vamp a nod. "I'll keep watch out here."

The air is knocked out of my lungs. Matt's gaze sweeps over me, so indifferent it's almost cold. I shake my head weakly. This isn't happening.

"Matt," I plead, tears stinging my eyes. "Matt, call for help."

He leans back against the wall, hands in his pockets, eyes scanning the yard.

The feeder turns back to me, and lowers his lips to my cheek. "Now, sweet thing, you and me are going to have some fun." He releases my throat and I try to scream, but his hand smashes into my temple, and my vision goes fuzzy.

The ground moves closer, and then my head is swaying back and forth against his back. He's got me over his shoulder. He's carrying me off somewhere.

"You keep watch," he says. He keeps walking, his hand moving into my shorts. He pushes a finger inside me roughly, and I don't even have the presence of mind to flinch. It's like I'm watching it happen to someone else, like I'm walking behind this enormous man with an inert figure slung over his shoulder, dragging her off.

He withdraws his finger, and there's a disgusting sucking sound. "Delicious," he drawls.

A door scrapes on concrete, and slams shut heavily behind us. Then I'm flat on the floor, and there's concrete against my ass. My shorts are gone. I can't coordinate my limbs. They're made of stone, they belong to someone else. I open my eyes, pain shooting through my temple.

Through the haze, I can see the feeder undoing his belt.

"Oh, you and I are going to have a great fucking time," he says.

I can't scream.

He lunges at me.

I black out.

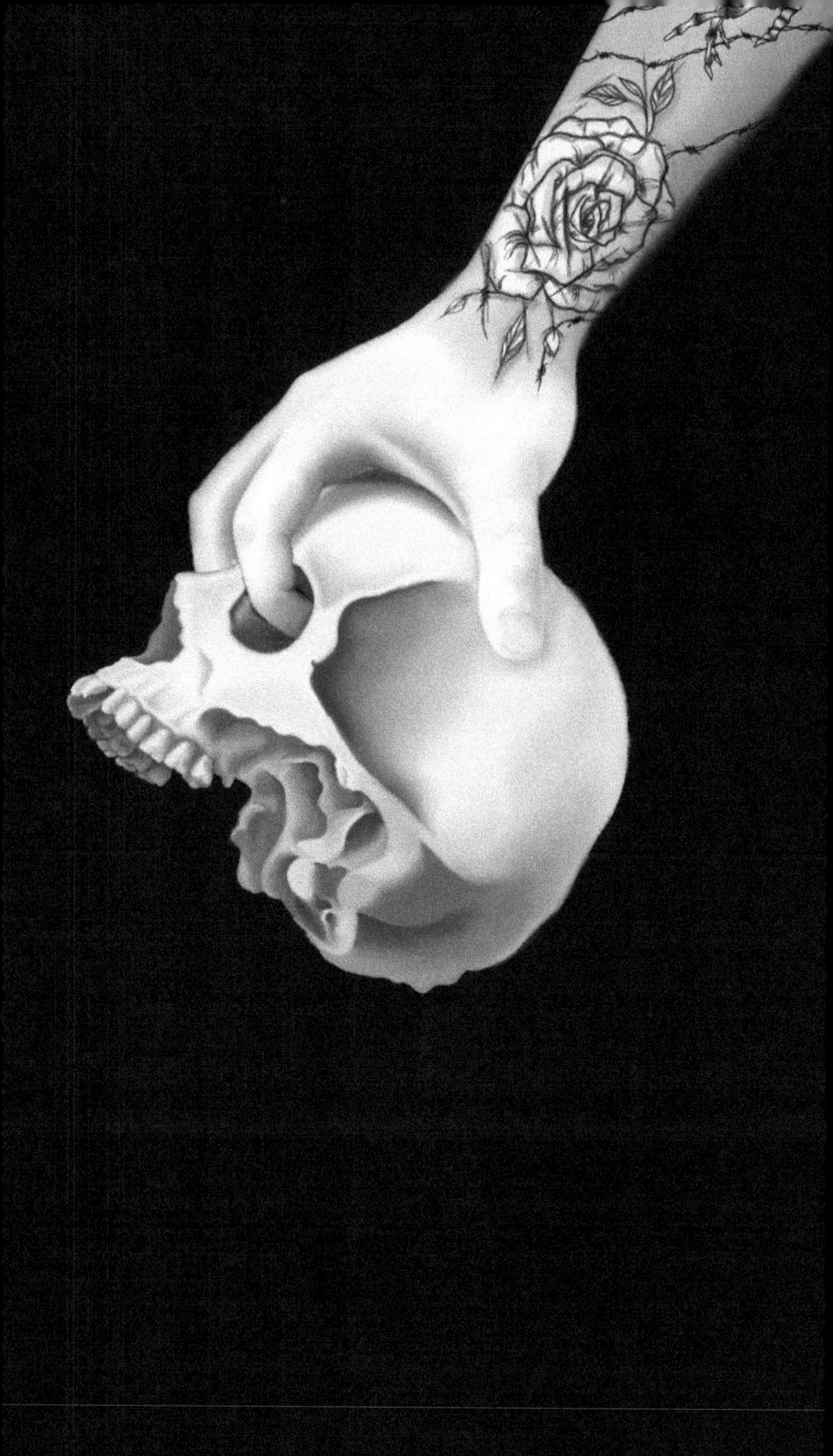

THE NIGHT IS COOL, but not unpleasant. I amble along the path, in the direction of my cabin. The past few days have been a nightmare. Sam's execution-style scare tactics caused a massive uproar with the higher-ups, but she didn't get the discipline I expected. I think they're secretly glad she did what she did. The humans rising up against us is the last thing they want, and they sure as hell don't want any more of them to die.

I think back on my conversation with Braun, about living versus existing, gazing around the compound. I wonder how Margot would have handled all of this, had she survived. She was a free spirit, wandering the world whenever she got bored. She'd be in one place for a few months and then decide somewhere else was more enticing.

I was the only constant in her life at the end. I was the only one she wanted around all the time. I never thought I'd feel the way I did about her ever again.

And yet I do. Do I fucking ever.

Juliet's face as she laughed in the clinic, the raise of her eyebrows as she - yes, she was. She was *flirting with me.* I try to keep reminding myself that she doesn't want me, that she's with someone else, that she's in love. But some tiny voice at the back of my head won't let me believe that.

Holding her face in my hands, checking her over after the riot, I was so flooded with relief that I couldn't think. Seeing her eyes fixed on me, not afraid but grateful I was there. Grateful *I'd* protected her. The brush of her fingertips against my jaw, telling me I made her feel safe.

Mine. Mine. Mine. The word keeps humming through my blood, hit after hit of need for something more.

Last night I nearly went to see Sam, hoping that fucking would get my mind off it all. It's a plan Margot would certainly approve of. Sex was always her answer to a downward mood, to those days when the grief for my humanity became too much.

"On your knees, *mon cher*," she'd say, and by the time I'd eaten her through several orgasms, I was so filled with desire I'd forgotten all my sadness. But I'm a fool. I know there's no way fucking Sam will abate my need for Juliet.

Not one iota.

Movement catches my attention up ahead, and I see a human standing by one of the storage buildings. He's pacing back and forth in a slow gait, arms crossed over his chest. He looks almost bored. He lifts his head to gaze at the sky, and jumps a little as he notices me. As I get closer, I realize it's Juliet's useless boyfriend. I look over towards the dorm, and see the lights on, streaming from the windows.

"Hey," I call out, and he takes two stumbling steps backwards before giving his shoulders a shake. "What are you doing out here?"

He shrugs, the exaggerated nonchalance making me grind my teeth together.

"Nothing, man. Just hanging out."

"You should be in the dorm," I say, drawing closer.

"You should chill out, I'm not hurting anyone." He gives me

a smarmy smile that makes me want to put a fist through his face. "Just enjoying the nice weather."

"Get yourself back to the dorm, right now."

He sneers at me. "What are you gonna do, huh? You want another fight?"

"Get fucking over yourself," I snap, and then I smell it. I smell *her*. Is it just her scent on him? I step closer to him. "Where's Juliet?"

"What's it to you?"

I seize him by the collar and slam him against the wall. "Where the fuck is she?"

He slaps at my hands. "Get your fucking hands off me!"

"Tell me where the fuck she is right now."

I hear a grunt from behind the door of the storage shed, and his eyes flicker to it for a second. He lifts his hands, surrendering. "Hey man, he said he wasn't going to hurt her, he just wanted to have a little fun. She was up for it."

I drop him and spin to the door, damn near tearing it off its hinges. The sight on the other side of it sends rage so violent through me that bloodlust sends my vision red.

Braun's bare ass is between the peaks of Juliet's knees, and her blood is running on the floor as Braun feeds from her.

Her hands lie limp on the floor beside her.

Braun turns and smiles at me, continuing to thrust into her. "Hey man, you want a turn?" Blood trails down his chin as he laughs.

I'm not entirely sure what happens next, because the bloodlust takes over for a moment. One second I'm in the doorway, then suddenly I'm standing there with Braun's head in my hand, dangling from my fist by his hair. The other half of him lies at the far end of the room, bleeding out onto the cold concrete floor.

His face is still frozen into that disgusting sneer. He didn't even have time to be startled.

I scoop Juliet's inert figure up in my arms. She's ice cold, her skin almost blanched white. I lower my mouth to her neck - I know it's risky, but I need to do something - and run my tongue over the puncture wounds Braun left behind. The electric thrill of her blood hazes over me for a split second, but I take a deep breath to steady myself.

The punctures close over, but it's not enough to just stop her bleeding. She needs blood, now, or she's going to die.

I storm across the yard towards the clinic, unsurprised to find her traitorous fucking boyfriend has disappeared. The clinic is all dark, of course, but I let myself in and move to the cubicles. I place her on a gurney and run down to the supply chamber.

I pull out three bags of her blood and head back, setting up the needles, guiding them carefully into her veins.

Her lips are grey. Fuck.

I get the blood flowing into her, and wrap her in a warm blanket. I feel for a pulse. It's weak, but it's there.

"Come on, Juliet," I say, taking her hand. "Come on, don't you die on me."

I see blood on my sleeve, and look down at myself, realizing I'm covered in what's left of Braun. No time to think about that now. Her hand is so fucking cold, so small and limp.

I rub her arms and legs, trying to get the blood moving. "Come on, you don't die today."

I'm going to have a lot of explaining to do, but I don't really care. Red seeps at the edges of my vision as I think of Braun, violating her, fucking raping her on the floor. I'm going to shred the rest of him when I can.

And her boyfriend stood watch. Her boyfriend fucking

stood by and let that happen. He didn't call for help. He just stood there. *Useless. Fucking. Fuck.*

I decide right then and there he's going to die. I don't know when. I don't know how.

But I'm going to tear that limp-dicked fuck's throat out. I'm going to roast his heart and eat it. Fucking fucker.

Juliet's lips blush with pink, and her chest shudders as she breathes. I take her hand, and it's not ice cold anymore. Not warm yet, but not icy with the promise of death either.

The minutes tick by, and she slowly gets warmer. After an hour, I change the bag of blood and give her a second. More explaining, but I still don't care. We're meant to keep the humans alive - this is part of that.

After two agonizing hours, she opens her eyes.

"Wh-what happened?" Her voice is so small, and she squints at me in the harsh light of the fluorescent bulbs overhead.

I lean forward and stroke her forehead, without thinking. "You're alright. I've got you."

She tries to shift on the bed and winces, her eyes widening with realization and memory. Her eyes clench shut, and she puts a hand to her face. "Oh my god," she says with a sob, "that feeder, he - he..."

"I know, I know."

She tries to curl into a ball, away from me, but the needle and tubes are in the way. "Where is he?" She asks, not looking at me.

"He's gone."

Her breathing is still shallow. She closes her eyes. "Did you kill him?"

"Yes." I lean back in the chair. She doesn't want me too close. I can't blame her. She has no reason to trust me. "He's dead."

"Where's Matt?" Her breath catches in her throat, and she coughs.

"Here, let me get you some water." I retrieve a bottle of water from a shelf in the hallway, and when I walk back in, Juliet is sobbing quietly. I sit down beside her, unsure of what to do. How do I comfort her after what just happened?

She turns to look at me, then down at her arm, her eyes following the tubing up to the bag of blood that's slowly filtering back into her body. "Won't you get in trouble?"

I shrug, opening the bottle of water and holding it out for her. "I don't care."

She tries to sit up, but her eyes flutter and she sighs.

"Can I..." I trail off as I shift closer to her. "I can help you sit up. Is that OK?"

She eyes me hesitantly, then gives a short nod. I put a hand under the base of her neck, and help her up slowly. Her eyes stay on me as I hold the water bottle to her lips, and she takes a small sip. She chokes a little, and coughs.

"Steady now," I say softly, and offer her a little more. She takes one more small sip, then shakes her head.

"Where's Matt?" She asks again.

"He was outside, standing guard," I say, and I instantly regret it when I see the tears well up in her eyes again. I shouldn't upset her any more than she already is.

"He - he didn't call for help," she says, and covers her eyes with her hand. "He just let it happen. He *helped* him."

The red begins to seep at the edges of my vision again, and I resist the urge to reach out and take her hand as she weeps. Fucking bastard.

He's dead.

I hear footsteps in the corridor, and suddenly Sam is standing there in her uniform. She looks down at Juliet on the bed, and back at me.

"What's going on here?" She asks.

I rise to my feet. "Braun assaulted her."

Sam's eyebrows shoot up. "I guess that's why he's now in two pieces in the storage building?"

"That would be why, yes."

"Right, OK." Sam looks down at Juliet. "Is she OK?"

"She'll be fine," I reply. "I've given her 2 units of blood, she'll be alright."

Sam sighs and shakes her head as her eyes meet mine. "They're not going to like this, Silas."

"I don't really give much of a fuck."

She scoffs, and gives me a lopsided smile. "Don't I know it." She casts another look down at Juliet and shakes her head. "Lucky for her you came along, huh?"

"I suppose so."

Sam chews her lip for a moment, before clasping her hands behind her back. "I'm going to need you to report to me in the morning, Silas."

"Understood." I look down at Juliet in the bed. She's still trying to curl up, as small as she can, covering her face with her hands. Sam's footsteps retreat, and we're alone again.

She asked me to hold her once. That day, after the attack. She asked me to hold her in my arms. She's told me that I make her feel safe. But she hadn't just been raped by a fucking vampire. She's probably terrified of me now.

And yet...

"Jules," I murmur, sitting down beside her. "Jules, it's OK. I'm here."

She reaches behind her blindly, as though searching for something. I put my hand over hers, and she clutches onto it.

"Don't leave me," she whispers. "Please don't leave me."

Relief so sweet I can taste it floods me.

"I'm not going anywhere." I reach out to stroke her fingers

as her body shakes. She's crying. "I'm right here. No one's going to hurt you."

"How could he do that?" She buries her face in the pillow, her cries becoming louder. "How could he do that?"

I have to touch her. If I don't, I'll go out into the night and find that bastard. I'll tear him to pieces. She needs me right now. I have to stay with her.

I lean over her, stroking her hair gently, still holding her hand. "Jules, I'm here."

She rolls over tentatively, wincing, and she gazes up at me. I reach out and brush the tears away from her cheeks, smiling at her.

"I'll kill anyone who hurts you."

"You promise?" She asks in a tiny voice.

"I swear to you."

She tucks my hand under her chin, curling herself around my arm. "Stay with me?"

I brush the hair from her forehead as I smile down at her. "Always."

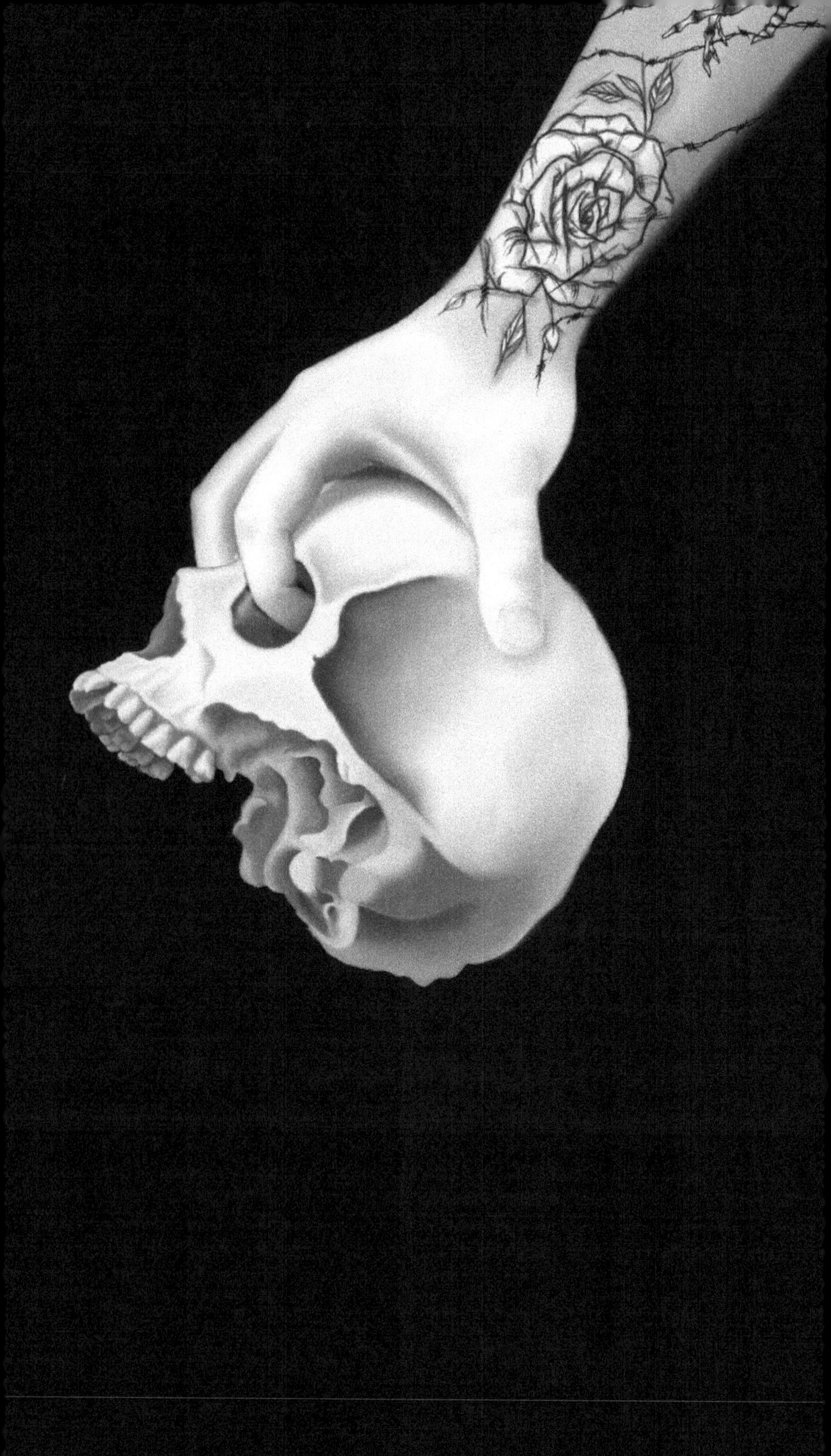

"YOU BETTER HAVE A DAMNED good explanation for this, King." Anderson's veins are popping at his temples, his jaw clenched so hard I half expect him to crack some teeth. "A dead officer and blood reserves being used on a human?"

"Braun was assaulting a human," I reply, my hands clasped behind my back.

"And whose word do we have for that? Yours?" Anderson waves vaguely at me.

I fix him with a mild glare. "Questioning my integrity again, are we, sir?"

"Considering you just tore a fellow officer's head off, I think it's probably warranted."

"Braun assaulted a human. He had her on the ground, where he was raping her, and feeding off her." I need to take a deep breath before continuing, because holy fuck the fury burns down my ribs and has my heart contracting painfully. "She's lucky I got there when I did, and that I acted as fast as I did. Because otherwise, she'd be dead."

Anderson huffs out a breath and rises to his feet. "Well, Braun *is* dead, so-"

"I don't know how you think rapists should be dealt with,

but in my book, execution's rather appropriate." Rage prickles at my palms, and I rub them together behind my back, trying to get a handle on my anger. I need to at least try and give a front of being reasonable.

Anderson leans back on his desk, crossing his arms over his chest. "It looked very much like bloodlust, and that's a problem when you're one of my senior officers."

"It wasn't bloodlust." It's a lie. I blacked right the fuck out. "I felt compelled to protect an innocent woman."

"I looked at your file," Anderson says, and a chill runs down my spine. "I saw your... history."

"My history, sir?" I roll my shoulders, biting back the gnawing shame that overwhelms me. "Everyone has a history."

"And yours is rather colorful isn't it, King?"

I clench my molars together. "That was a long time ago."

"It still makes you susceptible to episodes of bloodlust," he insists. "Past heavy drug use has an effect on the brain, and even in a state of immortality it can be dangerous."

"It *wasn't* bloodlust." I scoff out a laugh. "I can't believe I've been hauled in here when Braun lured off a human and was feeding on her, fucking *raping* her, but I'm in here like the naughty schoolboy who's going to get a ruler on the knuckles?"

"Watch your tone," Anderson snaps.

"You fucking watch your tone." I take a deep breath. Trying to look reasonable isn't working out so well. "Look, I'm sorry. But I have a very personal aversion to rape, and what Braun was doing is not just against our rules, but against society's laws in general."

"Yes, thank you, King, I'm aware of that," Anderson says with a roll of his eyes.

"Great, so why am I here?"

"Because you need to answer for what you did." He raises his eyebrows. "This can't just be ignored."

"What can't be ignored?" I cross my arms over my chest, and his face settles into a displeased frown. "The fact that I protected a human? Sir, we just had a fucking riot, because the humans don't trust us, and you want it getting out that vamps who look out for them get disciplined for it?"

Anderson looks instantly flustered, straightening up and lifting a finger to point it in my direction. "Now, I never said-"

"What do you think they'll do if they find out you let vamps rape them with no consequences?"

"Well I never said..." he trails off, rubbing his chin. "You do have a point."

I sense an in, a dangerous path I could go down right now. It's stupid. But the idea won't let me go, and it has me spilling words out before I can tamp them down again with some sense of self-preservation.

"Sir, look, we need these bloodbags, and if they're unhappy, and distrusting, it'll make everything around here worse." I throw my hands up, trying to appear amicable. "I dunno, maybe if they see me being friendly with this girl, maybe if they see me trying to look after her, get to know her as a person, the tide will turn."

Anderson considers my words for a moment, pursing his lips as his eyes wander across the ceiling. "So you mean sort of like, being friendly with a bloodbag in the name of good PR?"

"Yeah, if you wanna call it that." I huff out a little laugh. "I mean, she's gonna talk isn't she? Tell everyone how nice I am, how understanding. How I protected her when I didn't have to. And suddenly, we're not bloodthirsty monsters that blow their heads off at the first sign of trouble."

I'm throwing Sam firmly under the bus right now, but my words have their intended effect. Anderson draws up his eyebrows and puffs out a breath.

"Yeah, Ferris surely didn't do us any favors with that little display."

I suck on my teeth and nod. I'm a fucking traitor. "No, she didn't. But we have an opportunity to avoid an even bigger PR disaster right now.

"So what, you and this girl, you spend time together, make it look good?" Anderson rubs his chin. "You think that'll be enough?"

I shrug, letting my chest relax, because I think my plan has bloody well worked. "Yeah, I think so. Look, none of them are looking for much are they? They just want to feel like we're not a threat. Scared and unhappy, they're no good to us. But halfway trusting us? Yeah. I think it'll be enough."

Anderson nods. "You're right, you're right." He approaches me and claps me on the shoulder. "We need to try and move forward as a colony. You did the right thing."

"Thank you, sir."

"You're a good man, King."

I'm far from a good man. Because right now all I want to do is find Juliet's boyfriend and rip out his entrails. I want to hear him screaming as he dies.

I consider for a moment telling Anderson about Matt's involvement in Juliet's assault, but then I stop myself. Because something slips into place. Something that I hadn't thought of before. Something that was staring me in the face. Maybe I'm remembering it wrong. Maybe my mind is playing tricks on me. But something he said, something about what happened that evening...

Anderson is looking at me expectantly. "Everything alright?"

I nod quickly, giving him a smile. "Sure, yeah, thank you sir. Just want to go and check those surveillance camera files again."

"Oh of course, very good." He walks around his desk and waves me off as he sits down. "Go on ahead, and let me know if you find anything."

"Absolutely, sir." I rush out of the office and down the hallway.

I'm a fool. How didn't I see it before?

The cramped filing office is empty when I walk in. I cross the room to the desk and flip open the laptop that's sitting on it. I pull up the file of the night of the attack, waiting for the figure to come into frame. I tap my foot on the ground, not wanting to fast forward the footage in case I miss something.

Then the figure in the black hoodie appears. It looks like a man, broad shoulders, large hands. He keeps his head down.

Then he looks up, and jumps. Takes two stumbling steps backwards. The frame flashes and he's gone. I rewind and watch again, those stumbling steps backwards. There's a crack, and I've smashed the mouse under my hand.

The figure in the black hoodie is Matt. He reacts to whoever sprung him at the perimeter fence exactly the same way he reacted to me busting him outside the storage shed. I have to take a few steadying breaths to stop myself from storming out there and grabbing him now.

I pull up Matt's file, trying to find anything that would indicate he knew what he was doing. He has to have had some idea about electronics and generators to pull this off. I remember Sam's words about the revolutionaries, and I wonder for a moment whether Matt's transfer here was on purpose.

I skim the file, and find the words I expected to see - "Engineering degree." He worked as a mechanic but for sports promoters, dealing with complicated high-performance vehicles. He'd know what he was looking at when cutting wires. This was him.

I rewind the surveillance footage again, focusing this time

on the head that comes into view at the bottom of the screen. It's barely a flash, but I pause to see the wiry hair on top of that head. It's all black and white, so I can't see the color.

But I know it's red. I know what that hair feels like, because it was in my hand when I tore Braun's head off.

I don't even bother checking the code on the surveillance footage for Braun's signature. I know it's there, the fucking fool was too stupid to cover his tracks well. He deleted that footage, because he was the one who caught Matt.

I slam my fist into the desk, shattering the surface. That fucking dick has a counter over his head now. He's going to die.

I'll need to bide my time on that for now. Juliet needs me.

I cross the yard back to the clinic, which is busy as humans are brought in for harvesting. I pass them all, headed back to the room where I left Juliet that morning. She's lying in bed, gazing out the window as I open her door. As soon as her eyes land on me, they light up, and she gives me a small smile.

"Hi," she says, trying to sit up.

"Hi." I sit down at her side. "How are you feeling?"

"A little weak, but I'll be fine." She gives me a shy glance. "I was a little worried. That they'd, I don't know, take me out back and shoot me. Now that I won't be any good to them for a while."

I shake my head emphatically. "They wouldn't do that to you, I promise. I wouldn't let them."

She nods, tucking a strand of hair behind her ear. "Can... can you make sure Matt is kept away from me?"

"Of course."

"And can I be changed to the other dorm?" Her eyes are brimming with tears as she looks at me. "I don't want to sleep in a bed next to him anymore."

"I'll have him moved," I say, resisting the urge to reach out and take her hand. "You have friends in that dorm."

"Thank you." Her voice cracks, and she clutches a hand over her mouth. "I just wish I could understand why."

I think I know why. I'm sure I know exactly why. But until I hear it from him, I'm not going to say anything.

"I wish I could give you an explanation." I shake my head, rage filling my veins like lava. "All I know is that a guy like that, he's not worth the ground you spit on."

"Did I do something wrong?" She sounds so sad as she says it. I'm sure my heart is going to drop out of my body and shatter on the floor. "I mean, did I..."

"No, never." I lean over her on the bed, and she gazes up at me as tears begin to roll down her cheeks.

"You didn't deserve this," I say quietly, and stroke the tears away with my thumb. "I need you to know that." I know I shouldn't, I know this isn't the time, but I press a soft kiss to her forehead. She doesn't flinch, or tense. She lets out a small sob instead.

I want to take her out of here. I want to tell her that if she were mine, I'd kill anyone who so much as looked at her in a way I didn't like.I want to carry her to my cabin where I can care for her and murder anyone who touches her. I want to show her how a man who truly cares for her would treat her.

Instead I draw back from her and give her a smile. "I will always protect you."

"But why?" Her lip trembles. "I still don't understand."

"You don't need to understand, because it's beyond explaining. You just deserve to be looked after. And I want to do that, if you'll let me."

She sniffles and nods.

"Good." I stroke my hand over hers. "You're safe. Always. I promise."

"Thank you."

I give her slim fingers one last squeeze before I rise to my feet.

"I've got to go, but I'll be back to check on you soon." I move towards the door reluctantly.

"Silas." Every time she says my name it sends the best kind of chills down my spine.

"Yes?" I pause at the door, her grey eyes fixed on me.

"I just wanted you to know that I'm happy I'm not nothing to you." She shrugs, smiling a little shyly. "I don't know, it kind of felt important to say it. And I wanted you to know that you're not nothing to me. I'm glad you're my friend."

"HONEY, ARE YOU ALRIGHT?" Gina asks as we hang our freshly washed clothes on the line.

I nod, fighting the energetic breeze as it threatens to tear my tank top from my hands. "Yeah, I am." I bend to pick up a pair of shorts from my basket, and when I stand back up, Gina is still frowning at me. "I promise, I am, really."

"Something happened with Matt, didn't it?" Her eyes flicker over the bruises on my neck and chest that are still clearing up. "Did he do that?"

Sure, in a way. "No, that matter was dealt with." I avoid her eyes, continuing hanging up my clothes.

"So why are you and Matt not together anymore?" She asks, moving to my side. "I hate to pry, but you're so pale, you're barely eating, and I'm so worried about you sweetheart." She raises a hand to my face, cupping it gently, just like my Mom would have done. "Please talk to me."

My lip trembles, and I don't want to give in to the feeling, to the grief that keeps snapping at my heels everywhere I go. I blacked out when he raped me. I should be glad that happened, right? I should be glad I wasn't conscious for it. But somehow not knowing what he did, how he did it, just waking up knowing that he *had...*

I sniffle, trying to hold back my tears. "One of the vamps attacked me," I say quietly, and Gina inhales sharply. "He dragged me into a storage room, and... He..." I swallow hard, and Gina strokes my cheek.

"Oh my god, honey." She looks like she's going to cry. "Did they catch him? Did someone stop him?"

I nod, a sort of warm feeling breaking out as I think of Silas sitting next to me in the clinic all night, holding my hand and stroking my hair. "One of the other vamps, the tall one with the dark hair, and all the tattoos? He, well, he found... Us. And he killed the vamp that was..." I trail off, shaking my head.

Gina exhales heavily and gathers me in her arms. "Oh my god. Sweetheart. I'm so, so sorry."

"I'll be OK. Eventually." I laugh, a little bitterly. "I guess time heals all wounds, right?"

Gina draws back from me, her face twisted with anguish. "How did this even happen? None of the other feeders noticed?"

The lump in my throat stops me from answering. I just push myself into Gina's arms and let her hug me, and she soothes me with kind words as she strokes my hair. I just want my mom. I want my mom so bad. I try hard not to cry because crying is exhausting and I've done too much of it, but a few tears run down my cheeks.

"It's alright, sweetheart," Gina says softly. "We'll get you through this."

Suddenly she tenses, and turns us, pushing me behind her. She starts swearing in Spanish, and I look over her shoulder to see Matt crossing the yard towards us.

"You stay away from us!" Gina holds out an accusing finger. She has no idea what he did, but she obviously suspects enough to know that I don't want him anywhere near me. Matt's face is twisted with sadness, and he holds both hands up as gets closer.

"Please, I just want to talk to her." He looks past Gina, at me as I cling on to Gina's shoulders. "Juliet, babe, I'm sorry. Please, please talk to me."

I dig my face into Gina's back, and she waves her hands. "You fuck off." She turns to put an arm around me. "You leave her alone, the poor girl has been through enough."

"Please, I just want to talk."

"I don't want to talk to you!" My voice is shaking, my whole body trembling. I can't look at him. I can't look at the face of the man I thought cared about me, who let that feeder do *that* to me. "Just leave me alone!"

But he won't, walking closer still. Gina tries to steer me away, up the garden towards the feeders who are starting to move towards us, curious about what's going on.

"Juliet, you have to understand," he says, "this whole situation, I had to do what I had to do. This is important."

"Important?" My whole body goes tense with rage. "*Important*. He *raped* me. He nearly *killed* me. That's what *you* had to do, huh?"

Matt runs his hands over his head. "You don't get it, I never wanted that to happen. But I had no choice. Please, please, listen to me."

"No." Gina ushers me away. "No, I'm not listening to any more. She doesn't need to listen to you, *Hijo de puta*." She spits on the ground. "You don't come near her again."

She sweeps me up the hill back to the buildings, muttering and swearing under her breath. A feeder stops us when we reach him.

"Is there a problem?" He asks.

Gina nods, gesturing with a wave over her shoulder. "Just some asshole not taking the hint."

"As long as there's no trouble." His gaze turns to me. "The doctor wanted to see you once you were done with your chores, so why don't you go on ahead."

"I'll take her," Gina says quickly, her arm still around my shoulders as she guides me towards the clinic. "Do you want me to come in with you?"

I shake my head, wishing my breathing would steady itself. "No, no, it's fine, really. They probably just want to check my blood pressure again." I don't tell Gina about the emergency contraception they made me take while Silas wasn't there, or the gynecological exam I was subjected to. *Superficial scrapes, consistent with sexual assault.* That's what they'd said.

The words make me sag a little as I replay them in my head. As I relive that moment, when no one was there to hold my hand or soothe me.

No one except Silas.

Gina leaves me at the clinic doors, saying she'll wait outside but I wave her off, promising I'll be fine. I push inside, past the cubicles where humans are having their blood harvested. I go to the room with the blue door, which is open, the doctor sitting inside with a file open in front of her.

"Hi," I say, and she looks up, gesturing for me to sit down.

"How are you feeling?"

I sit down, nodding. "Not terrible. I'm still getting tired easy."

"Well, that's normal, make sure you keep eating well and tell the guards when you need to rest." She scribbles some things down in her file. "Any other problems? UTI or any bleeding?"

"No." I clench my teeth together to stop my jaw chattering.

I feel cold, even though the day is warm and sunlight is streaming in through the window.

"Good." She makes a few more scribbles before looking up at me. "I thought it might be a good idea for you to do some exercise, you know, start jogging and do some weights."

I frown at her. "What? Why?"

"Well, the thing we're concerned about after something like this is depression obviously, and exercise is a great way to produce endorphins. Not to mention it'll increase your appetite. You've lost a lot of weight, it's not good for you."

Lots of things aren't good for me here.

"Sure, sounds good." I fidget with my fingers as she writes down some more notes. I look out the window at the bright sun, at the trees waving in the breeze, and I feel like I'm stuck in some deep, dark hole.

We go through a few more basic checks of my blood pressure and temperature, and when she's finally satisfied I'm not going to collapse into a heap anytime soon, she sends me on my way.

When I get outside, Matt is waiting for me.

I tuck my arms across my body and put my head down, determined to just storm past him.

"Juliet, please," he says urgently, reaching out to grab my arm.

I fling his hand off me and keep walking.

"Juliet, talk to me, please."

"I don't want to talk to you." Why the fuck won't he just leave me alone? "I have nothing to say to you"

He grabs me, spinning me to look at him. "Babe, *please.*"

I shove against his chest, trying to get out of his grasp. "Let me go!"

"Juliet, stop it, you're making a scene!" He shakes me, his eyes wild. "Just shut up and let me talk to you."

"Fuck off!" I slap at him, trying to push him away, and then arms are around me, pulling me away from him. I spin straight into Silas's firm chest, looking up into his red eyes. He strokes a strand of hair out of my face.

"You OK?" He asks.

I nod, pressing my forehead against his chest, my whole body going soft with relief. "I just wanted to leave the clinic, and he... He just won't leave me alone."

"You've been given instructions, mate." Silas's tone is hard, authoritative. "I think you were told pretty clearly to stay away from her."

"I just want to try and explain-"

"I said," Silas interjects, his arm moving around my shoulders, "you are to stay away from her. You don't look at her, you don't talk to her, and you certainly don't fucking touch her. Have I made myself clear?"

"I just need to talk to her, goddammit!" Matt is shouting now, and I flinch.

"Right, you can go cool off." Silas calls to a guard nearby and orders them to take Matt away.

I don't listen to where they're taking him. I don't care. As long as it's away from me, I'm happy. I nuzzle into Silas and try to calm my breathing by focusing on his smell. He smells fresh and clean, like he's just had a shower. He smells a little like cologne, woody and musky. I like it, it's soothing. I keep my eyes closed, and focus on him and his warmth.

I realize after a few minutes it's gone quiet, Matt's shouts and protests can no longer be heard. I raise my head, looking straight into Silas's eyes. He smiles down at me, his arm still around my shoulders.

"He's gone now."

"Thank you. That just really shook me up. He-he wouldn't leave me alone. Kept saying he needed to explain."

"You don't need to listen to him anymore." Silas raises his eyebrows. "I'm sorry I didn't keep a better eye on you. But he won't be allowed near you. I'll see about getting him moved away permanently."

"Thank you." I laugh softly. "I'm surprised no one's told you off for touching me like this."

"I think they all know that you need a little extra care at the moment." He strokes a finger along my jaw. "We just want you to be alright."

"The doctor said I should work out, you know, for my mental health." I say with a sniffle.

"Good idea. I can take you to the gym with me if you like."

"You wanna be my personal trainer?" I ask with a small smile.

"Sure, anything you need that'll help." He brushes a soft kiss against my forehead. "Come on now, let's get you back to the dorm. You need to rest."

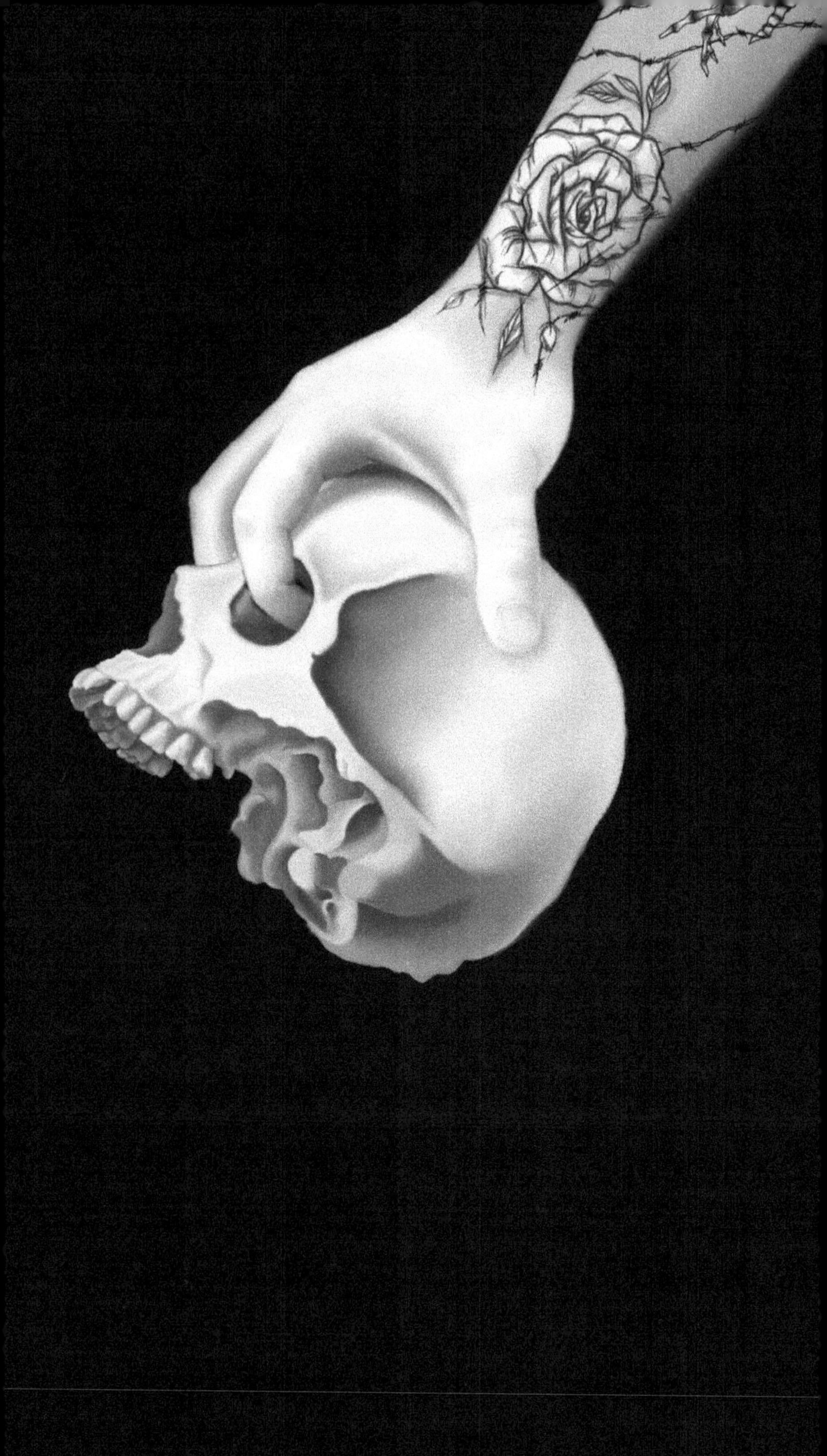

IT'S STARTING to get dark as I make my way to the makeshift holding cell that holds Juliet's ex-boyfriend. He ranted and raged for hours before he finally shut up. He's been calm for a while, so it's been deemed safe to let him out.

I volunteered to do it.

I unlock the door, throwing it open to find him sitting on the bed at the far end of the otherwise bare room.

"Evening, mate." I cross my arms over my chest, leaning against the door frame. "How are we tonight?"

"About fucking time," he snarls, scrambling to his feet. "I can't believe you left me in here all day."

"Just wanted to give you a chance to calm down."

He stalks towards me, glaring when I don't move out of his way. "So can I go?"

"I thought you and me could take a little walk, have a chat." I smile at him amicably.

"Why the fuck would I want to talk to you?" He says with a snort.

I look around me, then lean closer conspiratorially. "I know about what happened with Braun."

His eyebrows shoot up. "What the fuck are you talking about?"

"It's OK." I give him a wink. "I found the footage, I know what happened. Braun was less than careful, but I covered for you."

His face crinkles, considering what I'm saying for a moment before he relaxes. "So you know everything?"

"I've got a pretty good idea." I step aside from the door, waving him out. "Come on, stretch your legs, you must be feeling like shit after being in here all day."

He ambles out of the room into the evening light and takes a deep breath. "Thanks, man."

"No problem, mate." I start towards the gardens. "Come on, fewer prying ears down here."

He eyes me with distrust, so I give him my most dazzling wanker smile, pull out a cigarette case and offer him one.

"Go on, mate. You deserve it. Dealing with crazy women." I wink, holding the case closer to him. "Just don't tell anyone, ey?"

That does the trick, and with a snort he takes a cigarette and lets me light it for him.

"Crazy women is right," he says, watching me light my own cigarette. He falls into step beside me as we walk down the hill, the sky above us turning orange and purple.

Matt puffs out a cloud of smoke heavily. "You gotta know, I never meant for her to get hurt." He's looking at me, I can see it out of the corner of my eye. "But that feeder, he caught me."

"You were disconnecting the alarms, right?" I turn my head to look at him. "Your file says you have an engineering degree."

He dips his head. "Yeah, I know it's extreme, but the shit that Boston is hiding from you all, you know, it's bad."

"I believe that." I nod, taking a deep drag of my cigarette. "Boston don't give a shit about us."

"Look, I know some of you are on the up-and-up, alright?" He stops, and I do too, turning to face him. "I know not all of you are bad guys, but this." He gestures vaguely around the compound. "This needs to be stopped. There has to be a better way for us to co-exist than us being captives."

"You're right, there has to be." I slide my hands into my pockets, continuing to walk in the direction of one of the garden sheds. "Juliet's really not willing to listen to you on all this, is she?"

Matt sighs heavily. "No. I mean, I get it, she got hurt. It wasn't meant to be that way."

"How was it meant to be?" I kick a stone along the path. "I mean, maybe if you explain it to me, I can talk to her. Put in a good word, you know?"

"Yeah, she seems to like you a lot." His voice takes on a cynical edge, and I smile over at him.

"Girls with trauma always just want a big man to protect them." I hold his gaze, smirking, and after a moment he laughs.

"Yeah, you're right." He shrugs. "So that feeder-"

"Braun?"

"Yeah, Braun, right. He catches me. And I was convinced I was done for, like game over, you know? But he tells me, you know, your girlfriend, she's hot. That's all he wanted, I couldn't believe it."

I blow out a puff of smoke and shake my head. "That's seriously all he wanted?"

Matt holds out a spread hand towards me. "Right? Like, he's willing to give up his whole compound for some ass? It was fucking crazy."

I let out a low whistle. "Is she even that good?"

Matt laughs out loud. "Look, she tries. She's basically a virgin, has no idea how to get a guy off. But hey, she's easy on the eyes, and, well." He leans over and lowers his voice.

"Between you and me, she's tight as fuck. Like, I'm talking you have to work to get into her. So that's fun."

"Wow, really selling her there." I clap him on the shoulder. "So you told Braun all this?"

Matt throws his hands up, gazing into the darkening sky. "I agreed to help him get laid. I was meant to get her all warmed up for him, and then he'd have some fun with her. He told me he'd never hurt her, he just wanted his piece of ass, and everyone walks away happy."

I suck on my teeth. "You didn't think that maybe she'd be, I dunno, opposed to this plan?"

"Man, I panicked. And look, I'm a feminist and all that, I know consent is the thing." He rolls his eyes a little as he says it. "But, you know, she said she loved me, she'd rather that than have me dying, right?"

I rub my chin thoughtfully. "I mean, when you put it like that... But then why didn't you just talk to her about it? She strikes me as an easy lay, surely she'd have just done what you said?"

"You know, I think I was so freaked out by that feeder catching me, I just went with whatever." We reach the shed, and Matt turns to lean his back against the wall. "I never wanted her to get hurt. If I could just explain to her that we need to do things, you know, if we want shit to change, we need to make sacrifices."

"Of course, mate. I get that." I lean against the wall beside him. "Shame she's being so difficult, ey?"

He glances over at me. "So you think you can talk some sense into her?"

"You know, I think I can." I nod, taking a long drag on the cigarette, listening to it crackle. "Or I can deal with you myself, right now." I round on Matt, whose eyes widen.

He opens his mouth to scream, but my hand is already

around his throat, crushing his windpipe. I heave him through the door of the garden shed, slamming him into the wall and baring my fangs at him.

"You fucking limp-dick fuck." I press the still-burning cigarette into his eye, and his screams are smothered by my hand crushing his neck. He convulses and flails, but it's useless. "You know, ever since I saw that footage, I've been fantasizing about ways to make you suffer. To make you bleed and feel pain unlike any you've ever felt before."

His mouth snaps open and shut, whispered shrieks bursting from his lips. His tongue lolls around uselessly, his one good eye clenched shut as the other one smokes and steams.

"Unfortunately, *mate*, I don't have the time to make you suffer. But one thing I did want you to know, is that my girl was always thinking about me when you fucked her. The whole five seconds you managed." I laugh cruelly, enjoying this moment way more than I should. "And very soon, it'll be my cock in that tight little cunt, and I will make her scream in ways you could only ever dream of." I overcome my revulsion at touching his pathetic dick, clawing my hands around him and tearing that useless fucking appendage straight from his body.

The scream reverberates through his body, no sound coming from his mouth, his one eye flying open as blood flows down his legs. I shove his dick into his mouth, forcing it down his throat as far as I can manage. He collapses to the ground, legs kicking, hands flailing at his mouth as he tries to breathe. Red foam spills from between his lips, cascading down the sides of his face as the flapping of his hands becomes more frantic and uncoordinated.

I retrieve the molotov cocktail I'd hidden in here earlier, lighting the rag at the end of the bottle.

"Godspeed, mate. Have a great time roasting in hell."

I slam the bottle down next to him, the flames engulfing

him quickly. There's hay all over the shed, it's going to burn nicely. I take a cigarette from the case, leaning down to light it in the fire burning Matt's flesh from his bones, then leave him there, shutting the door behind me.

No feeders see me as I walk back to my cabin, and thank fuck because my hands are dripping blood, it's sprayed all over my clothes. I pause on my front porch, taking the last few drags of my cigarette. The fire alarm goes off just as I stamp the butt out under my boot.

I head straight to the bathroom, stripping off my clothes and dumping them on the floor. I'm not going out there. I just listen to the alarm drone as I wash the blood from my skin. By the time they find out someone was in that fire, it'll be impossible to tell how he died. And then I'll reveal what I know about the footage, how it all makes sense now. How he must have been planning another attack, a diversion, to distract us from another wave of Afflicted. Just one of the revolutionaries Sam was talking about. That Boston warned us about.

I wash the blood off my hands, running them over my face. There's a niggling feeling of shame in my chest, about how I talked about my girl. The things I said about her. Even just saying those words to gain that fucker's trust, and then to torture him - yeah, that felt like shit.

No one's ever going to talk about her like that again.

I'll make sure of it.

AS PREDICTED, charred human remains are found inside the shed. Burned beyond recognition. They can only identify him because there's only one human missing.

There's shock when I reveal to my colleagues that Braun was in on it, that he blackmailed this man into letting his girlfriend be raped. Outrage when I tell them I discovered who disarmed the perimeter alarms. And here he was, doing it again. Trying to create a distraction. Fucking bastard.

Matt's remains are thrown into a grave in the cemetery, covered with dirt and forgotten about. I go out one night under the light of the full moon to piss on it.

Petty? Sure.

But it made me feel a whole lot better.

What I didn't expect to see was Juliet fade away.

As the days wear on, she becomes paler and thinner. Her freckles stand out against the pallor of her skin. Her eyes are blank. She stops coming to the gym. She barely gets involved in gardening, which she always loved before. She doesn't sneak off to the stream anymore, which I try to convince myself is just because it's cooler now.

But that's not it.

She screamed when they told her Matt had died. Even amongst his betrayal, she still felt something for him. It wasn't all just erased.

On a stormy afternoon, I head across the yard as thunder rumbles overhead, and I spot Juliet sitting on a bench, knees pulled up to her chin. She's hugging her legs tightly, staring out at the falling rain.

I approach her slowly, making sure she can hear my footsteps.

"Hey," I say once I'm beside her. "What're you doing out here all on your own?"

"Just listening to the rain," she replies, her chin bouncing gently on her knees. "I like the rain."

I sit down on the bench, smiling. "So do I. But being English I suppose I don't have much choice there."

Her face softens into something that's not quite a smile, her eyes not meeting mine. "Do you miss it?"

"Not really. I mean, bits and pieces yeah. But England is just a lot of painful memories now." Shit, this isn't the conversation I should be having to try and cheer her up. "But anyway, that doesn't matter."

"I used to be a swimmer." Her lower lip trembles a little. "I like the water, I like the rain. That's why I go down to the stream. My mom, she..." She trails off, giving a small, sad laugh. "She wanted a water birth, but because she had twins she wasn't allowed to. So she always joked that I was mad I missed out on my water debut. That's why I spent so much of my life in the water." Her eyes are glistening with tears as she looks at me. "My hair was green when I was a kid, sun-bleached and green from chlorine. I was in the water all day."

"I bet you were a great swimmer."

She nods, her eyes drifting back to the falling rain that drums heavily on the tin roof above us. "I had a scholarship to college. A swimming scholarship. They said I'd make the Olympic team. I didn't want to do that though, I just wanted to do it to enjoy it." She smiles wistfully. "I really wanted to be an art teacher. I mean, I think I did. I always loved drawing. I was kind of good at it."

"I was an art major."

Her eyebrows shoot up as she looks at me. "Really?"

"Yep." I nod, looking out at the rain. "Drove my family crazy, my room always stank of oil paint, no tea towel in the house was safe from becoming a paint rag."

She chuckles a little, and I look back quickly to see that face, that face that isn't haunted by sadness. She tucks her hair behind her ear, and hugs her legs a little tighter. "Who's your favorite artist?"

I exhale heavily. "That's hard to say. I think Degas. I loved all those dressing room paintings, especially as a teenage boy. Gave me an excuse to look at tits without getting in trouble."

Juliet bursts out laughing. "I bet."

"And how about you?"

Her lips twitch. "I don't know. I think Jackson Pollock. Everyone says it's all just a mess, but I think it's beautiful. I like art where you can, I don't know, imagine yourself in it, you know? Like, what was that person thinking when they made that painting? What were they feeling? And you look at it and go, oh yeah. I get it. I've seen the world that way too."

My girl isn't just beautiful. She's smart too. I could listen to her talk like this forever. "And what did you like to draw?"

"I did a lot of still life, flowers and stuff. I liked doing roses, all those petals. I liked drawing people too, but I could never get the hands right."

I nod. "Hands aren't easy."

"What did you like to paint?" Her eyes are bright now, full of life and curiosity.

I give her a crooked grin. "I did a lot of life art."

"Oh, you really like tits, huh?"

I chuckle as she smiles from behind her fingers. "I've always liked bodies. Drawing them is fun, just how different we all look. Shapes and colors and all of that. I love it."

"So that's what you were before you were turned? An artist? Because I thought you were a doctor."

I regard her with a laugh. "A doctor? Me?"

"Yeah, you know, you're good with needles. You're the first vamp that hasn't completely destroyed my arm."

My mood plummets, my past coming crashing down on me. I look out at the falling rain, leaning my elbows on my knees. "No, not a doctor, though my dad would have loved that. He was a solicitor, and my mum was a music teacher at a very prestigious music conservatory in London."

"Oh wow." She lowers her knees, wrapping her legs into a pretzel. "That's so cool."

"Yeah it was. I just fell well short of their expectations."

"As an artist you fell short of their expectations?"

I clear my throat. I don't want to tell her the truth. I don't want to tell her what kind of a man I really was before Margot turned me, and saved me. But when I lift my eyes back to hers, and I see all that softness and vulnerability, I find myself talking before I can stop myself.

"I was a heroin addict."

I expect her to be shocked. I expect her to be repulsed. I expect her to jerk away from me.

Instead her brows knit together, and she reaches out to put a hand over mine. "Oh god, I'm sorry."

I'm frozen for a second, completely overwhelmed with disbelief. She isn't judging me. She isn't disgusted. She just wants to sit here and hold my hand. I swallow hard.

"Yeah, it wasn't great. University just introduced me to what my parents called, The Wrong Crowd. I thought the drugs made me a better artist, gave me a clearer vision of the world, or whatever the fuck I told myself. Instead, it just had me breaking into houses and made me a criminal." I rub my hands together. "That's how I got to know my way around alarms and security. Not the most honorable way I suppose."

"Addiction doesn't make you a bad person," she says softly. "Addiction fucks up your priorities. And look at you, you got clean, and now you wear a uniform and scare people with your British accent."

I smile at her. "My accent scares you?"

"No, not me. Just everyone else. I like your voice. It's nice." Her fingers stroke over mine, and the touch sends volts of pleasure down my spine. "Well, if you ever want to draw again, maybe we could draw together. I can show you just how badly I can fuck up a hand."

"Ah, but you can do an amazing rose, right?"

She smiles, nodding. "Well, you draw the hand and I'll draw the rose for it to hold."

I lace my fingers through hers, looking down at our joined hands. "Sounds good to me."

We sit there a while longer, just talking and laughing. Her cheeks flush pink. She looks so beautiful. When I finally leave her, I feel good, like maybe she's withstood the worst.

So when a few hours later the alarm gets raised that one of the humans is missing, I'm gripped with panic. It's Juliet. She didn't show up for dinner.

I run through the driving rain, into the forest. *Please no. Please no. Fuck, please no.*

She had a moment of clarity. A high. I've seen it before. I saw it in Harriet's face. After those fucking boys at school assaulted her.

Tears bite at my eyes. *No. NO.*

Harriet had smiled at me widely, assuring me she was fine. What those boys had done was done, she was over it.

My feet thump against the sodden ground, and I hear the crashing of the stream over the falling rain.

Please, no no. Fuck. Please. I don't know who I'm praying to. I sure as fuck don't believe in god. But I plead anyway.

My roar echoes off the trees around me as I see Juliet floating face down in the overflowing stream.

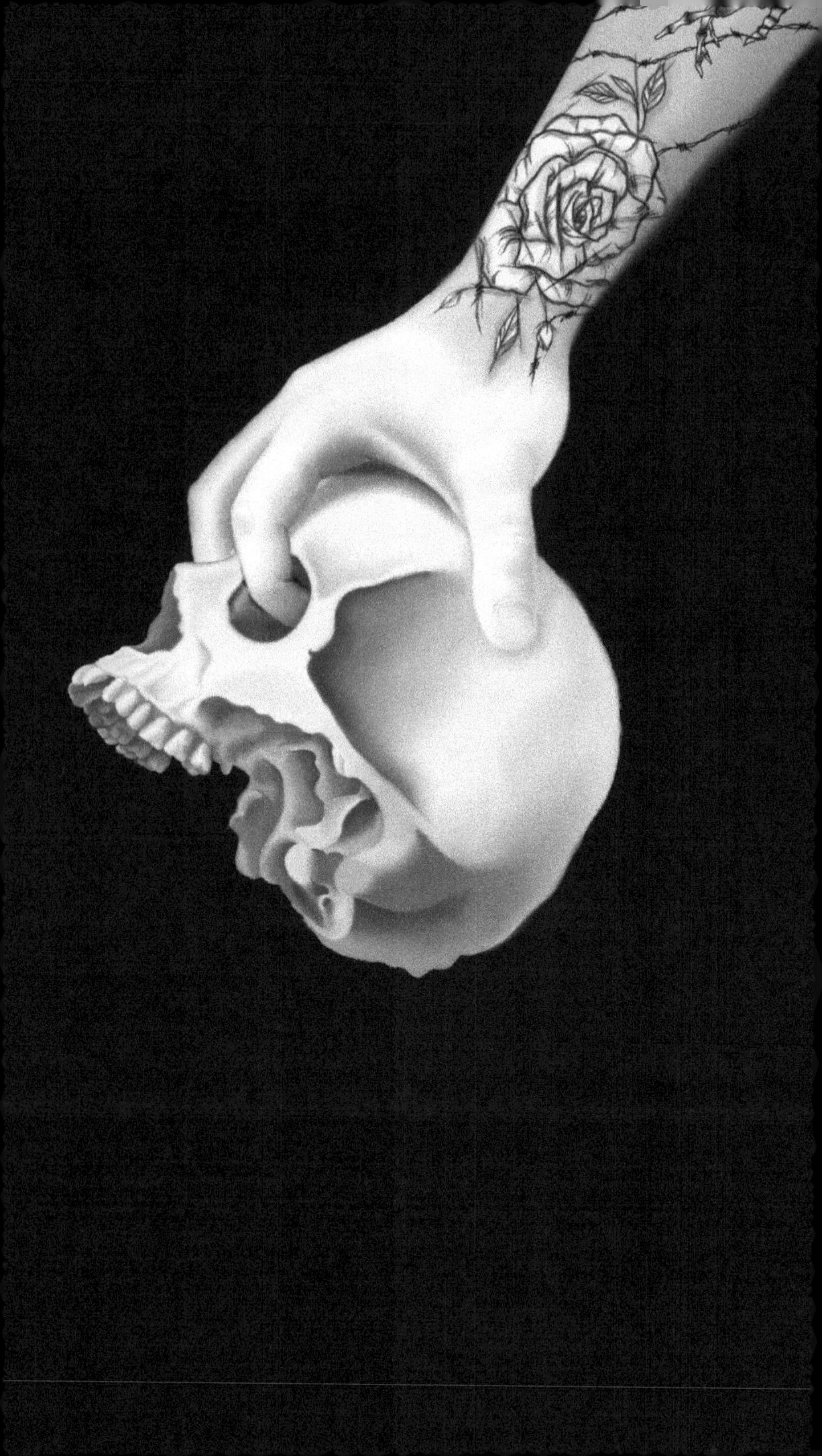

CHAPTER 20

SILAS

"SHE HAD AN ACCIDENT. She slipped and hit her head, and fell into the water."

Anderson regards me critically from behind his ridiculously large desk. "What the hell was she doing out there in a storm?"

I shrug, determined to keep my face neutral. "I don't know. I know she was a swimmer. With everything that happened she probably just wanted to have a moment to herself. Do something that made her happy."

"With everything that happened I think it's more likely she did this to herself." Anderson sighs, rubbing the back of his neck. "Poor kid. I had a daughter her age once, a long time ago."

"Right." My fingers are clenched together so hard they hurt. "And I doubt you'd want anyone to assume your daughter tried to end her own life just because she'd had a hard time recently."

Anderson exhales heavily. "Now come on, I know you have a bit of a jones for this girl, but King, you can't let that cloud your judgment."

"My judgment?" I scoff. "My judgment that tells me you'll take her off if there's even a hint of a mental health issue?"

"I never said I'd do that."

My shoulders jerk up in a defiant shrug. "So tell me you won't do that then."

He exhales heavily, caging his fingers in front of him. "King, we're not equipped to-"

"You know what this looks like to me?" I cut him off, leaning on the table, sneering down at him. "It looks to me like you just want to eliminate a problem. Girl gets raped on your watch and suddenly you have to take her off because she's mentally ill."

Anderson bares his fangs at me. "How fucking dare you."

"How fucking dare I? How fucking dare you hire officers with a known history of sexual assault."

"How the hell do you know about that?" He rises to his feet. "Those files aren't meant to be for you."

"The files you asked me to dig into? Those files?"

Anderson jerks an accusatory finger in my direction. "You were given strict instructions on what to look for, and staff history was not on that list."

"So you knew what our friend Braun had been up to then?" My vision starts to seep red. "You knew he'd spent 15 years in prison for raping three sixteen year old girls all the way back in the 50s?" I point a finger at the door. "You put all these people in danger having someone like that work for you."

Anderson's nostrils flare, the muscles in his jaw feathering wildly. But I'm not done. No one is taking Juliet off. No one's touching a hair on my girl's head.

"Now, if you think you're going to cover this up, you are sorely fucking mistaken. And don't think taking me out is going to end your problems either."

"You think I'm just going to kill anyone who opposes me?"

"Considering you'll kill off a human who simply slipped and fell in a fucking pond, I wouldn't put it past you." I throw a thumb drive on the desk. "I sent one just like that to Boston, minus the proof you knew about Braun. But there's one with that information in a safe place." I point my finger at him. "You threaten to end any more humans because of your sloppy morals, I'll send that one as well."

"This is blackmail, King."

I slam my fist into his ridiculous cherrywood desk. "This is ensuring we do everything we can to protect the people we're tasked with protecting."

I turn and storm from the office. I'm still in shock, I'm floating through clouds of misery and overwhelming rage. I'm furious with myself. I should have seen the signs. I lost my best friend this way, all those years ago. And I didn't see it in this girl I tell myself I care about. A laugh and pretty flushed cheeks made me think everything was fine. I left her sitting in the rain, and she went off to drown herself.

I growl out a breath through gritted teeth, raking my hand through my hair. How do I protect her? How do I bring her back from this awful precipice she's teetering on?

If they find out it was a suicide attempt, they'll take her off. They'll shoot her like an old dog. The thought has me stumbling, my hand slamming into the wall of the building beside me as I try to steady myself.

I won't let anyone hurt her. No one.

The rain is still falling as I make my way to the clinic, hurrying down the long hallway to her room. She's lying there, asleep, tubes in her nose. Her hands are curled slightly at her sides.

I sit beside her and hold her hand. I have to stop myself from clutching it to my chest.

She's been unconscious since I pulled her mostly-dead body from the water. I clench my eyes shut as I remember running back with her in my arms, screaming at her to stay alive. I wasn't going to let her die. I was so overcome I nearly forced my blood down her throat to turn her.

Because there's no fucking way I'm living without her.

But they found a pulse at the clinic. They brought her back from the cold brink of death, dragging her back into this hell she found herself in. Her skin went from dull grey to pale pink again, her body slowly taking in oxygen that she so desperately wanted to force out of it.

I told anyone who would listen that it had been an accident. If I said it often enough, I'd convince myself of it. Admitting to myself that she wanted to die, that her life was so hollow and barren that she no longer saw any value in it, was too much to bear.

"You'd better wake up, Jules," I whisper, brushing the backs of my fingers along her motionless hand. "I'm not losing you too."

There's movement behind me, footsteps in the hallway. Someone stops in the doorway, and sighs.

"I gotta stop catching the two of you like this," Sam says.

I don't turn around and look at her, I just keep holding Juliet's hand.

Sam walks into the room and sits down on the other side of Juliet's bed. She casts a cursory glance at the monitors telling me Juliet's heart is beating, that oxygen is flowing through her body.

"Lucky you found her, again." Sam's eyes narrow a little as she looks at me. "You OK?"

"I'm fine. Just brought back some memories."

"You wanna talk about it?"

"No," I say, shaking my head.

"OK, then I'll talk about it." Sam leans back in her chair, crossing her arms over her chest. "I remember reading about an attack, back when vamps first became public knowledge. It was all over the news, back in, what '96?"

My stomach twists, and uneasiness snakes down my back.

"An attack in London," Sam goes on. "Four friends, high school buddies, meeting up for a reunion. They were murdered right out the front of the pub as they left."

"People get murdered every day," I mutter. "It's a big city, it happens."

"They sure do, most of them don't have their heads torn off though. Most of them don't have their guts spilled all over the street while black cabs drive past." Sam crosses one leg over the other. "It stirred up a whole lot of fear. Humans had just found out that we existed, and then this attack happened."

"Bad timing I guess."

Sam snorts. "You can say that again. The media used it as a reason not to trust us. All the covens were furious."

I huff out a breath and meet her eyes. "What does this have to do with her?"

Sam raises her eyebrows. "I don't know, what does it have to do with her?" She taps a finger on her arm as she waits for me to respond. When all I do is glare at her, she goes on. "I had a look at your file."

"Good for you."

"Silas," she snaps. "I'm here as your friend. I'm here because I care about you. I know what it is to try and make the past right, trust me. My parents fucking owned *people* and I grew up thinking that was normal." She takes a deep breath, leaning her elbows on her knees. "What happened to that girl wasn't your fault."

"It was an accident."

"I don't mean her." Sam raises her joined hands to gesture to Juliet, and her eyes soften. "You can talk to me."

Memory crashes over me, and I feel sick. The numbness of

those days washes over me, the same helplessness I feel now as I stroke Juliet's hand, trying to anchor myself in her softness and her warmth.

"Harriet," I finally murmur.

"That was her?"

I sigh heavily. "I've never really talked about this. Only to my maker. It's... not easy."

Sam sits and waits patiently. My tongue feels heavy in my mouth, trying to find the words to describe all the pain I've been carrying for all these years. I press the heel of my hand to my eye, and inhale sharply.

"Harriet and I grew up together," I begin. "She was my neighbor, we were like two weeks apart in age. We were both weird kids, she was always dancing with these streamer ribbon things, and I was the awkward arty one. Hands always covered in paint, hiding in oversized jumpers."

Juliet's breathing changes slightly, like she's sighing softly, almost like she's listening, Her eyes remain closed.

I lean on the bed, gazing across at Sam. "We were best friends. All our lives. It was always Si and Harri. Always. We were inseparable."

"That's really sweet," Sam says softly.

I nod, swallowing hard, trying to dislodge the lump that's formed in my throat. "I never saw Harriet as anything but a sister. It was never a romantic thing. But one day she had her swan moment, you know, went from being an awkward gangly teenager to a young woman. And suddenly, all the boys wanted her. She was beautiful. Long coppery hair and big green eyes, they fucking panted after her every chance they got."

"Did that change your friendship?"

I shook my head. "No, she adored me. Nothing changed. It was all fine, until... Until..." I don't know if I can talk about that night. I take a deep breath. "There was a party. One of the snotty boys from the good side of town. She was invited, I wasn't."

"So she went alone?" Sam asks, clasping her hands together.

"She asked me to come with her, but I was a shitty little teenager, took it to offense. Told her to go and have fun with her new friends, like a right little dickhead." I clasp on to Juliet's warm hand, wishing I could somehow wrap it around myself. "So she went alone. Then she showed up to my place at 2am." I clench my eyes shut, remembering the pinging of the pebbles against my window, going downstairs to let her in. Her bruised face, her split lip, her eyes wide with terror. Her torn dress. She'd been so excited about that dress. It was red...

"Silas?" Sam asks after a while.

I clear my throat. "Four of the boys at that party had gotten her drunk. They'd dragged her into the bathroom, and they... They had their way with her. While everyone was just a few feet away, they raped her, for hours. When they finally let her go, she came stumbling down the street to my place. No one helped her along the way. They just let this bleeding, crying little girl run down the street, all on her own, in her torn-up dress."

Sam rubs a hand over her mouth. "Oh my god."

"She was so afraid to tell her mum, she was worried she'd get in trouble for drinking, can you imagine? As though it would somehow be her fault? I told her she hadn't deserved it. But..." Anger creeps into my veins, like acid, like lava. "When we told her mum, that was almost exactly what happened. I was so shocked. Everyone told her she had asked for it. That she'd given those boys the wrong idea."

"Oh my fucking god," Sam spits out. "Unbelievable."

"I was furious. I went to the police, all on my own, tried to make a report. But they did nothing. And those fucking boys, they told everyone in school what a slut Harriet was, how she'd wanted it, taken them all at once, just the most vile fucking lies."

Sam sucks on her teeth and shakes her head. "Poor kid." She sighs. "So what happened then?"

I look up at the ceiling, replaying that night in my head. Replaying every single second, the countdown to Harriet walking out my door into the night, for the very last time.

"It was a few months later," I say quietly. "She seemed to be doing OK. She'd come over for dinner, we'd watched some telly, then went upstairs to listen to the top 40. The number one song was one she loved, and her tape deck was broken. So I said I'd stay up with her and record it." I can't help but smile a little. "The Power of Love, by Huey Lewis and The News. She made me go to the cinema to see Back to The Future four times just so she could listen to that song."

Sam smiles sadly, but says nothing.

"So we stayed up, recorded the song and nearly carked it laughing, because my tape deck didn't have internal recording so we had to be quiet. In the background, you could hear us both giggling and trying to shut up." The lump in my throat is unbearable. "She was happy. She looked so beautiful. And then... Then she took that tape, and she kissed me, just a quick peck on the lips, which she'd never done before." I inhale through my nose. "I should have known, I should have seen the signs. Something was very wrong. But she seemed so happy."

"You were just a kid, you couldn't have known."

"But I should have seen past all the smiles, I should have fucking seen it." I grit my teeth, holding on to Juliet's hand to steady myself. "I went to bed, thinking all was fine. Then I woke up to screaming. My mum, and Harriet's mum, they were screaming and crying in the landing. I ran downstairs, every-thing was a blur. There was blue and red lights, an ambulance and police, all the neighbors were out gawking. And then there she was. On a fucking stretcher, her hand hanging out from under this horrible blue sheet they'd put over her."

Sam's face is weighed down by sadness. "She killed herself."

I nod, blinking rapidly. "Her mum found her hanging in the bathroom. No note, nothing. She just decided in that moment that she couldn't live with what had happened, and what those boys kept doing." I clear my throat, threading my fingers through Juliet's. "And then, there was a funeral, and flowers at the school, and teachers talking about the importance of asking for help. All those fuckers who'd believed the rumors, they lined up at her fucking funeral and cried, like she'd been their best friend, when she'd been *mine*." I swallow down the tears and misery on a heavy inhale, steadying myself. "And all I was left with was that tape, with her giggles behind her favorite song."

"I'm so sorry, Silas." Sam chews on her lip for a moment. "Those four men at the pub, all those years later. That was them, wasn't it?"

I run a tongue over the tip of one of my fangs. "About a year after I was turned, I saw one of them in the paper, he was becoming a barrister or something, had defended a big case straight out of college. I started tracking down the others, discovered they were all still friends because scum like to travel in packs apparently." I laugh bitterly. "Then they organized a little get together, sitting in the pub congratulating themselves on their amazing lives, their trophy wives and their mistresses, all while the girl they raped, the girl I fucking loved, was nothing but dust somewhere in a cemetery."

"I can't blame you for what you did." Sam shrugs. "I'd have done the same thing."

"Margot was so proud of me," I say with a laugh. "My

maker, she was thrilled. It was all over the news, right when vampires had come out. The perfect introduction, ey?" I scoff cynically. "No one ever knew it was me, but when they brought me down here I disclosed it all. Didn't feel right to be around humans when I'd killed them myself. I was expecting punishment, and all I got was understanding. They said they couldn't blame me for what happened."

"No sane person would. I think it's the power we all wish we had when we're helpless."

I smile at her wearily. "So now you know all about me, Sam."

"Explains why you're so attached to her." Sam's eyebrows twitch together for a second. "But you know that saving her won't change what happened to Harriet."

"Juliet didn't try to kill herself," I say again, seeing instantly in Sam's face that she doesn't believe me. "Juliet slipped and fell."

"Uh-huh." Sam runs a hand through her hair and sighs. "Silas look, you're an intense kinda guy, I can see that. I know that, and now I understand it. But this?" She gestures to my hand that's holding on to Juliet's. "This is going to land you both in trouble."

"I'm caring for someone, that's not going to land me in trouble."

"It will if you don't set yourself a boundary." She rises to her feet. "I get it, she's pretty. She's probably funny and smart and all the other things that have you gagging after her like a dog. But it's not OK. Jerk off, fuck me, do what you need to do. But this can't happen."

I don't say anything, looking back at Juliet. Sam stands there a moment longer, then stalks out of the room with a frustrated groan.

The monitors beep softly. Juliet continues to breathe

evenly, her brow twitching every now and then as though she's dreaming.

"You remind me of her, in a way," I say softly. "She always saw the beauty in things, the same way you do." I get to my feet, leaning over her to place a kiss against her forehead. "You have to wake up, Jules. You can only find beauty in things when you're alive." *Even if the world's gone to hell.*

WAKING up when you thought you'd died, when you'd intended to die, is a fucking trip.

I stare around the clinic room, deeply confused. My lungs ache. My eyes are burning, like there's broken glass inside my eyelids as I try to open them. There's a soft hissing noise, and a cold stream of air running into my nose. Plastic tubing sits against my face.

A warm hand is wrapped around mine, and when I blink and focus, Silas's rust-colored eyes are on my face.

"Jules?"

My eyes snap shut. *Jules.* I wish he wouldn't call me that. I love that he calls me that. It makes me feel a whole host of things I don't want to feel.

"Jules?" Soft fingers brush against my forehead.

"Go away." My voice is gravelly, barely audible. My throat feels like it has freezer burn, everything is cold and sharp. "I don't want to see you."

"Well that's too bad, because I'm right here." He's still leaning over me. He's not moving. If I open my eyes, I'll be looking right into that face, those eyes filled with concern and care, maybe even love? I don't know. I don't want to know. It hurts too damn much.

I shake my head. "Please don't look at me. I don't want you to."

"I want to." His lips brush against my cheek. "I'm so fucking glad I can look at you."

A tear bursts from between my lashes, running down my cheek and pooling against my face as it gets caught by the breathing tube. Why did I have to wake up? Why couldn't that water have snuffed me out?

"I don't want to live like this," I murmur.

"Jules, please look at me."

I take three deep breaths, then slowly open my eyes.

He's there, gazing at me, all the beauty of a thunderstorm, dark and ominous. But I'm not scared of him. I haven't been scared of him for a while. Even so, I can't handle the way he's looking at me. I can't take the twist in my stomach as I realize how badly I want him to take me into his arms.

"You found me, didn't you?" I ask, my voice cracking. "You knew where to look." He knows me. He *wants* to know me.

"I'll always find you, angel."

A little sob breaks from me, and he slides a hand behind my head, holding me close to him.

"I'll always find you," he murmurs again. "No one's going to hurt you, ever again."

"I just... I couldn't... When they told me about Matt, I just..." I trail off, and Silas tenses.

"Is that why you did it? Because you wanted to be with him?"

"*No.*" I shake my head against his shoulder as my throat swells shut. "I don't want this life, not like this, not anymore. There's nothing good, *nothing.*" My lungs ache too much to cry.

Silas exhales slowly, like he's relieved, and draws back so he can look down at me.

"I've been there, I have. I was sure there was nothing good left in the world." He strokes my cheeks, and the pain in his eyes is like a dagger to my gut. "I've been there, angel. And someone saved me. Even in this fucked up world, there's beauty. There's joy. Even if you have to dig for it."

My throat aches as I swallow. "How deep do I have to dig to find beauty in a world like this?"

He presses my hand to his chest. "Not far at all."

My lip trembles, and then the tears start falling, flowing down my cheeks. "I trusted him." I gasp for air, the cold rush in my nose catching at the back of my throat and making me cough. "I let him in, and I trusted him. I never wanted to let anyone close, I never wanted... And then he did that to me."

"I know, I know." He sits on the bed beside me, and I slump against him, the sobs tearing up my throat despite my aching lungs. He holds me close, stroking my hair, letting me cry.

"I hate that I'm glad he's dead." I clench my eyes shut. "That makes me a bad person, right?"

"No. It means he got what he deserved." His voice is like ice, but it doesn't scare me one bit. "You're not a bad person. Nothing about you is bad. You didn't deserve this. Any of it."

I sniffle, looking up at him. "Who saved you? You said someone saved you."

"I'll tell you all about her sometime."

"Are you going to save me?"

His eyes widen a little for a split second, then he frowns. He looks like he wants to speak, like he wants to say something, instead he sighs heavily, pressing a kiss to my temple before getting to his feet.

"I need to go, but... No one's going to hurt you, alright? I'm here. Even if I'm just a feeder, even if you hate me-"

"I don't hate you, Silas."

He sucks in a breath. "Thank you."

"I told you, I'm glad you're my friend."

"So am I, angel." He turns away, running a hand through his hair, shifting on his feet like a caged animal. "I need to go." He looks back at me with a brief smile. "I'll be back soon. I promise."

The doorway is a yawning chasm after he rushes through it. I want to ask him to come back. But more tears leak from the corners of my eyes, because I can't do that.

I can't ask for anything here.

AFTER THREE DAYS I'm allowed to leave the clinic and go back to the dorm. I'm not sure if I feel normal again, or if I'm just numb. My chest still aches a little, a scattering of bruises from the CPR along my sternum.

They're still worried about my weight, and my mental state. Every time a feeder comes near me, I flinch because I think they're going to come and get me, take me out back and shoot me. But Silas told me they wouldn't do that. He wouldn't let anyone hurt me.

Just as I have for months now, I feel his eyes on me. He's always in the background. It used to bother me. It gave me the chills. Now it's like a soft blanket I want to wrap myself up in. He makes me feel safe.

I'm off schedule for draining, because they want to get my weight up first. So I have even more time to be miserable.

Silas is waiting for me when I head out of the cafeteria after breakfast, three weeks after my little swim.

He's not wearing his usual khaki green uniform. Instead he's dressed in grey sweatpants and a tight black t-shirt. He's leaning against the wall of the opposite building, his rusty eyes fixed on me intently as I walk towards him.

"Morning," he says, a small grin twisting the corners of his mouth.

"Hey, you got the morning off?"

"Yeah, just wanted to see if you were up for a trip to the gym."

"The gym?" I raise an eyebrow. "I don't know if I feel like that."

"The doctor really wants you healthy." His smile is so fucking charming.

I gaze up at the bright blue sky, shielding my eyes with my hand. "It's such a beautiful day, why don't we go for a walk? I don't want to be inside more than I have to be."

He jerks his shoulders into a little shrug, tucking his hands into his pockets. "Of course. Let's go."

I kick off my flip-flops when we reach the grass, enjoying the feeling against my bare feet. Everything is warm and fresh, the sky above us littered with fluffy clouds. I breathe in deeply through my nose, becoming aware of Silas looking at me as we walk. I turn my head to gaze up at him. I can see his tattoos now, and my eyes wander down his arms, thick with muscle.

"Bones and roses," I say. "Do they mean anything or did you just think they looked good?"

He smiles, squinting in the sunlight. "I was 19 and thought they made me look tough."

"And who's she?" I point to the tattooed woman on his left bicep, bound with chains, her face twisted with ecstasy and her breasts very much on display. "Are those *nipple clamps*?" He stops so I can inspect her more closely, and he laughs out loud.

"That's Boudicca."

I raise my eyebrows incredulously. "As in, the celtic queen?"

Silas flashes that devastating smile again. "When I got her, I picked a name that I was fairly sure I would never associate with an ex-girlfriend. If I called her Jackie or Susan, those odds were decidedly not in my favor. So, she's Boudicca, and I'll never have my naked ex-girlfriend tattooed on my arm."

"Good plan." I look back at the tattoo, and smile. "Nice to meet you, Boudicca. You seem to be having a good time."

"Oh, she is." Silas's voice drops a little lower.

I try to ignore what that tone of voice does to me, and run my finger down his huge arm. "Were you always this jacked?"

He shrugs as we start to stroll again.

"I was a scrawny kid, so when I got older I wanted to be bigger. But..." He trails off, his face dropping a little. "Drugs aren't especially healthy. Wasn't until I got clean that I bulked up again."

"Right." We walk for a little while, skirting the edge of the forest. The garden is brimming with fruit and vegetables, ready for harvest. "My brother used to drag me to the gym with him."

"Oh, yeah? You said you're a twin."

I nod. "Well, I was."

"Did you look alike?"

"No." I smile a little. "I look like my dad, and my brother looked like my mom."

"Ah, they got one each, ey?" Silas plucks a peach from one of the trees and hands it to me. "Here, this one looks good."

It does, it's fat and glowing red. I sink my teeth into one side, making a big hole before I start peeling the skin away from the flesh. Silas watches me with raised eyebrows, grinning.

"Don't like the skin?"

I shake my head. "Nah, makes me gag."

"Mmm, can't say I've ever minded hairy things in my mouth."

A suppressed laugh grunts in my throat. "If that was an attempt at flirting you failed."

"Yeah, that sounded way better in my head," he says with a chuckle. He watches me finish peeling the peach, and I meet his eyes as I sink my teeth into the deep yellow flesh. "Good?"

"Mmmm." Juice runs down my chin as I nod. I rub it away with the back of my hand, very aware that Silas's eyes are fixed on my mouth. I lick my lips, and his shoulders tense visibly for a second. "Do you ever miss food?"

"Sometimes." God, his stare is so intense. "But usually no. Blood tastes amazing."

I wrinkle my nose. "Seriously? What does it taste like?"

"Depends on the blood. Everyone tastes a little different but it all tastes great."

"Have you ever had my blood?"

His chin dips a little, his chest expanding as he seems to hold in a heavy breath. "I have, as a matter of fact."

"And what do I taste like?"

His gaze sweeps up my arms, landing on my face, his eyes turning just a hint more red than they were before. "You taste like vanilla, with a hint of spice. Like some expensive coffee you buy in a wanker cafe. Comes in a cup that's far too small, just leaves you wanting more."

I huff out an embarrassed laugh. "That's one hell of a way to compliment a girl."

"Well, it's true."

I shrug lightly before lifting the peach to my lips and biting into it. I moan exaggeratedly and roll my eyes back in my head.

"Mmmm, you can keep my blood, this tastes so damn good."

"Might just have to lick that juice right off you and have a taste then."

We both freeze, staring at each other for a minute. I'm aware of peach juice running down my chin, my neck, into the collar of my shirt. Silas's eyes follow the trail of one of these droplets, and he does that thing with his lip again, drawing it through his teeth like he's imagining just what I taste like. Then he rolls his shoulders, running a hand over his mouth as he looks away, laughing lightly.

"Come on, let's keep walking." He gestures to the forest, then pauses. "Unless you don't want to go down here."

"There's another path." I pitch the peach seed into the garden. "It doesn't lead down to... There." I don't know if I can face the stream. Not yet.

We walk on in silence for a few minutes, birdsong ringing through the trees around us. The leaves are starting to turn yellow as Fall sets in.

"What was your brother's name?" Silas asks.

"Kaden," I reply. "My mom was an English teacher, our names were inspired by her favorite works. Kaden was named after a Polish philosopher she wrote a thesis on. I'll let you guess which one I was named after."

Silas chuckles. "What light through yonder window breaks?"

"'Tis me." I spread my hands and bob my knees into a little curtsey. "Good job."

"Were you and your brother close?"

I nod. "Sure were. He was my best friend. Everyone called us Raggedy Ann and Andy. We did everything together, until I went to college." I swallow hard. "He wanted to travel for a year before he started. I tried to talk him out of it, but..." I trail off. I wish I'd insisted. I wish I'd been able to convince him to come to UGA. He'd be trapped here with me, but at least he'd still be alive. I clear my throat, the sweetness of the peach sticking to my lips. "Did you have siblings?"

"I did, yeah." He looks up into the sun-dappled leaves. "A brother and a sister. I was the eldest. My mum had some trouble getting pregnant after she had me, so there was an age gap. I was 9 when my brother was born, and then 12 when she had my sister."

"So you weren't close?"

He frowns, his eyes grazing over the leafy ground. "They were adorable, and my little sister especially, she loved me. Had to carry her around everywhere. But then... things changed and I wasn't who my parents wanted around them."

"Sorry." I reach over to take his hand, then remember my hands are sticky and gross with peach juice, and pull back.

His head jerks in my direction, and his hand shoots out, his fingers entwining with mine.

So now I'm walking through the forest, holding hands with a vamp. Like that's a totally normal thing to do on a sunny Fall morning. His hand is huge, dwarfing mine, thick veins snaking across his knuckles.

We reach the end of the forest, the perimeter fence standing between us and an expanse of green fields. We stand there for a while, staring out at the world out there. I wonder what he's thinking. I wonder if he feels as trapped here as I do.

There's a faint mechanical whirring sound, and I look up to see a surveillance camera turning towards us. I instinctively step back, trying to pull my hand away from Silas's. They're watching us, and I don't want him getting in trouble.

But he doesn't let me go, and the resistance makes me stumble. My back hits a tree trunk, and Silas is crowded in front of me. I gasp as he gazes down at me. We're out of view of the camera, but if they turn it, if they go looking for us, they'll see us face to face like this, alone, out in the forest.

"Silas," I murmur. "You'll get in trouble."

He takes my hand, the one he's still holding, and lifts it, slowly, above my head. He pins it gently against the trunk of the tree, bringing his other hand to rest on my waist.

"Silas, what are you doing?"

His mouth inches closer to mine. The camera on the fence whirs, and my eyes flash up to it. It's turning towards us, slowly. But we'll be in view soon.

My eyes move back to Silas's. *Oh god.* Why is he so beautiful? Thank god I don't have to think to breathe, because I'd have stopped by now.

He dips his head until his lips are barely an inch from mine, pressing his body against me.

He's going to kiss me. Oh god, he's going to kiss me and the camera's going to catch us, and they'll send me away. They'll punish him. This isn't allowed. This isn't allowed, and yet my eyes flutter closed, waiting for him to crush my mouth with his, wondering what he's going to taste like.

With a sudden jerk I'm pulled away from the tree, and my eyes fly open. Silas drags me through the forest, away from the fence, away from the camera. I don't know what to think, my head's swimming. Maybe he wasn't going to kiss me. Maybe I imagined it.

He's not talking, just pulling me along behind him.

"Silas, stop." I try to yank my hand away, but his death grip doesn't budge. "What was that? Silas?"

"Sorry," he mutters, so I barely hear it.

"Sorry? For what? Did you not-"

He stops, rounding on me. "I'm sorry, alright? It won't happen again."

I keep walking, letting him drag me back to the compound. I can't understand the deflation I feel. Silas is my friend, did I really want him to kiss me? I grimace as I admit to myself that maybe I did. Some stupid desire to chase away everything that happened. I'm an idiot. I learned nothing from Matt.

Back at the compound, Silas takes me to the dorm, and leaves me there without another word. I watch his back as he disappears. For some stupid reason I start crying as I wash away the peach juice in the bathroom.

I crawl into my bed, and continue to cry. For Kaden, for Silas's baby brother and sister. And maybe a little bit for myself too.

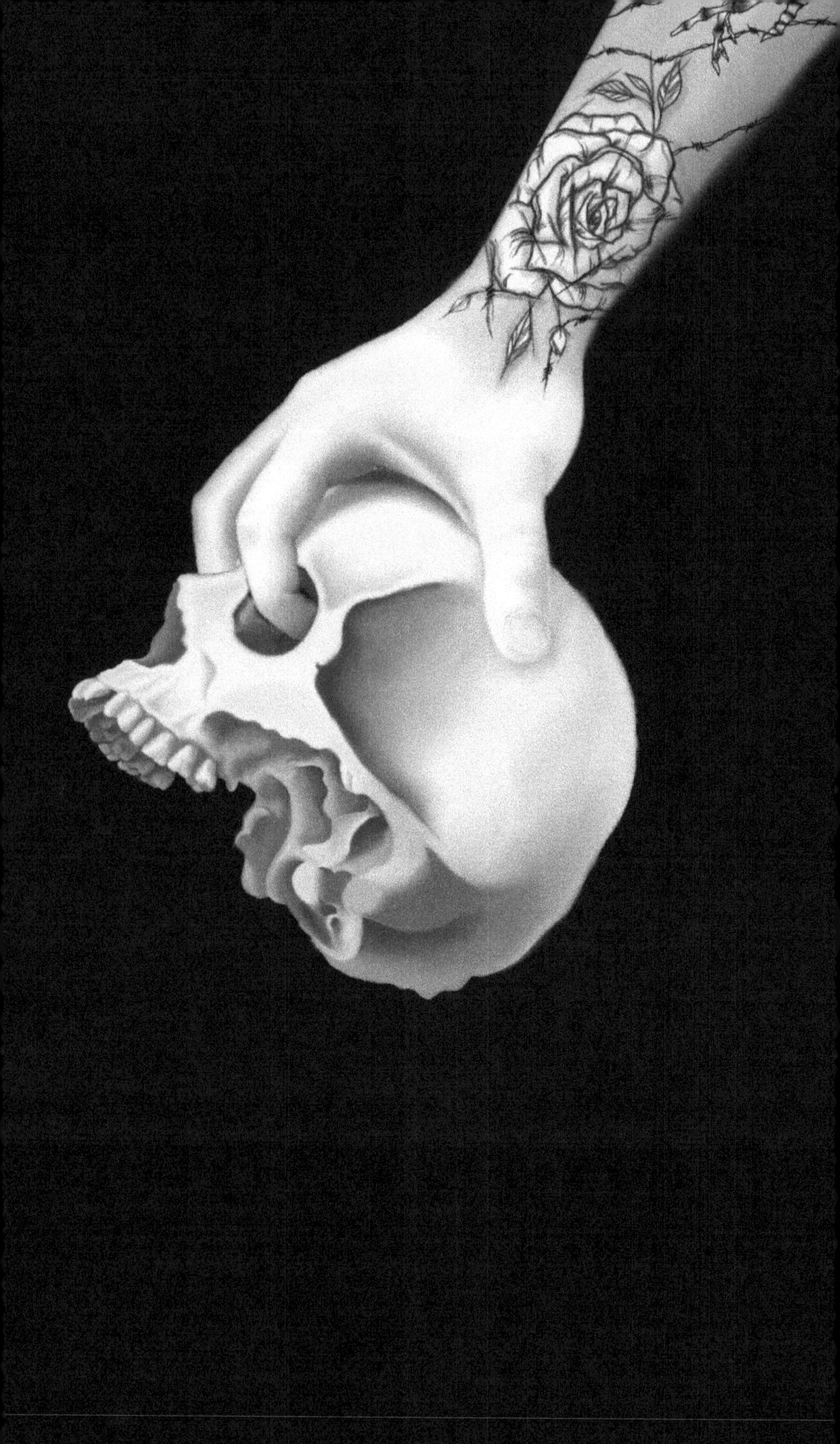

"YOU WANT TO DO *WHAT?*" Sam eyes me incredulously. "Please tell me you're joking."

"She's depressed, and needs a breather." The truck keys jangle in my hand. "Come on, what's she gonna do? Overpower me and run away?"

"If the other humans get wind of this there will be riots." Sam crosses her arms over her chest. "Absolutely not."

"Sam, seriously, I will sneak her out, no one will notice."

She cocks an eyebrow. "Why are you asking me? Why didn't you go ask your buddy Anderson?"

"You bloody know why." I tilt my head, giving her my most charming smile. "Come on, Sam."

"Don't use a sexy face on me, it won't work." She narrows her eyes, then rolls them, shaking her head. "For fuck's sakes."

I can't help but laugh, knowing that I've won. "Thanks Sam."

"Yeah yeah, go have fun." She waves her hand towards the door. "Just don't let anyone see, OK?"

"No problems." I hurry out of her office, heading down to the garden to look for Juliet. She should be down here some-where. I spot the blonde head of hair almost instantly. She's bent over a cucumber vine, plucking them and depositing them in a basket at her feet.

"Hi," I say as I approach, and she gives me a hesitant glance. I shouldn't be surprised, I haven't seen her since I almost kissed her in the forest two days before.

"Hi." She straightens up and brushes her hands together. "How are you?"

"Fancy going for a drive?" I hold up the truck keys.

She stares at me blankly. "A what?"

"A drive. I need to go to Savannah, they didn't send us enough needles with the last shipment, forgot about 20 boxes. Thought you might like to come with me."

She scoffs, shaking her head. "Yeah sure, they'll let me walk right out of here, huh?"

"Sure are. I've got boss approval and everything." My heart drops a little as I consider that maybe she doesn't want to be in a car with me after I backed her into a tree and pinned her there. Self-hatred seeps into my veins as my cock twitches at the memory.

She looks at me, her mouth quirking as she considers. "OK." She bends to pick up the basket, scooping it up and resting it on her hip. "I just gotta take these to the kitchen."

"Here, let me." I take the basket, and we walk to the kitchen together. I check the driveway before we walk out, and jerk my head. "Come on this is something of an incognito mission."

"So you are sneaking me out?" She shakes her head, smiling. But she climbs into the truck, keeping her head down.

I climb in, and gun the engine. I swing the truck towards the gate, waving to the guards. They already know I'm going, so there's no need to run any checks. The metal gate slides back slowly, and I drive out onto the road with a wave. We pass the guard compound, and turn left out onto the road.

I put my foot down, and the truck shoots forward on the smooth dirt.

"You can get up now." I look down at Juliet. "We're out of dodge, baby."

She laughs, sitting up and gazing out the window. "God this feels weird."

"I bet."

She winds down the window, leaning back against the leather seat as she takes a deep breath. Her hair flies about in the breeze, and I realize I'm not keeping my eyes ahead of me. I nearly miss the turn onto the sealed road, the old interstate, and Juliet's head jerks over as the tires squeal.

"Out of practice, Speed Racer?" She asks with a laugh.

"Just distracted."

"By?"

I can't look at her right now or we will crash. Because she's sitting there, one foot up on the dash, her hair blowing in the breeze.

"I think you know very well what by."

She scoffs. "By my skinny ass? I don't think so."

"Talking about your ass isn't helping."

"Arse." She mimicks my accent. "The way you say that. *Arse.*"

"Making fun of my accent now?" I shake my head as she giggles. "You bloody Americans, I tell you what."

"I happen to think your accent is very sexy." She pulls her feet up onto the seat, hugging her long legs to her chest.

"Oh, is that right?" I say with a laugh. "Yeah, you American girls did always love a British accent."

"Wait wait, can you say something for me?"

"I am not saying Bond, James Bond."

She laughs out loud, and fuck it's a beautiful sound. "How did you know I was going to ask you to say that?"

"Because that's what American girls always want you to say."

"It was worth a try." She chuckles to herself as she gazes back out the window. "And technically you did say it for me. Ha ha."

I shake my head, smiling. This feels too nice.

We drive on in silence for a while, enjoying the open space and the fresh warm air that's blowing in through the windows. We pass some small towns, abandoned gas stations. It's eerily fascinating, as though the world outside simply stagnated, holding its breath until the world returned to normal.

Not that that will ever happen.

"Can I ask you something?" She asks after a while.

I nod, keeping my eyes on the road. "Sure."

"And you don't have to answer this, it's none of my business. But... You said someone saved you once. Is that how you got clean? Is that what you meant?"

I exhale heavily, gripping the top of the steering wheel with one hand, letting the other drop to the seat beside me. "Well, that's a bit of a story."

"We have time." I can see her looking at me from out of the corner of my eye. "Savannah's still a ways off."

"That's true."

"Only if you want to tell me."

"I do." I genuinely do want to tell her. I shift in my seat. She's still looking at me, still waiting. "I told you, I was an addict. I used to break into big houses, when the owners were away on holidays. I was an expert at disarming alarm systems, so I was never caught. Made a fortune stealing shit, and it all went straight into my veins." I glance over at her. "Sure you want to hear this?"

She nods. "Mhmm."

"OK." I look back at the road and take a deep breath. "So

one day I broke into this house, on a huge property, surrounded by park land. Everything inside was *old.* Like, antique old. The windows are all covered in heavy velvet drapes, and the whole house smelled like gardenias. It was dark, and absolutely silent. It freaked me out, but I needed money, so I kept going." I exhale heavily. "And that's how I met my maker. Quite literally."

Juliet gasps a little. "Oh wow."

"Yeah. Margot had heard me coming a mile away, was waiting in her bedroom for me. I nearly fucking died when I walked in and there's this naked woman lying on the bed."

"Naked?" Juliet asks, laughing nervously. "Why was she-" She breaks off as I grin over at her. "You mean she…"

"She liked the look of me. Said she saw potential. I couldn't understand why this rich naked woman was coming on to me, when I'd literally broken into her house. Then I saw her fangs."

Juliet squeaks out a tiny gasp. "Does… I mean, did it hurt?"

"Getting bitten?" I shake my head. "No, not at all. Quite the contrary." I look over at her, and she bites her lip. "You've heard that it feels good, yeah?"

She nods slowly, clearing her throat as I move my gaze back to the road. "I'd heard that you can make it feel…"

"Pleasurable?" I don't look at her, because this topic probably isn't the one I should be broaching when I'm trying to not think about how close she is to me right now. "It's… yeah. An orgasm basically."

"But… how? I mean, it's a bite. How does it not hurt?"

"Venom." I gesture to my mouth with a wave of my hand. "It's in all our, um, bodily fluids. Saliva, blood… All the other ones."

She lets out a sweet, embarrassed giggle. "Oh god, OK."

"We can control its release, make a bite hurt, and leave

scars if we want to. But generally, it feels good for us to release the venom too. And *very* good for humans."

She puffs out a breath. "So, uh, how do you then, like, how do you get turned? I've never really found out how it works."

Change of subject, yes, that's good. I flex my hands around the steering wheel and try to wet my throat. "A lot like what the movies show, you get drained to the point of death, and then drink your maker's blood. A lot of it."

"And that doesn't hurt either?" She asks quietly.

"It's like... You know when you're going to sleep, and you have this really vivid dream while you're half-awake still, and it feels real?"

"And then your leg does that weird kick thing and you wake up?"

"Exactly like that. Except when you wake up, the kick is that you're immortal and thirsty as fuck for everything you can imagine." I smile over at her. "Everything. You want to drink and fuck and tear down a wall."

She smiles shyly. "Well that sounds pretty crazy. You die and then straight away want to do... that?"

"It's overwhelming, that's for sure." I look back out the windshield as we drive past the remnants of another abandoned town, its name long since lost as the sign is faded and cracked.

"Is that how you got big?" She reaches out and runs a hand down my bicep, and my cock fucking twitches again.

I clear my throat. "Yeah. Margot was old, turned during the French Revolution, so she passed those powers on to me. I was pretty scrawny from, well, poor life choices. But I woke up like this."

"No wonder she wanted to fuck you."

I nod, laughing. "Well, thanks. She did. For three days."

"Three *days?*" Juliet slumps back against the seat. "Jesus."

"It was like a fever dream. And then it sort of dawned on me, what it all meant." The deep feeling of dread sinks into my stomach, even all these years later. Juliet waits patiently for me to go on, gazing over at me as the breeze continues to snatch up strands of her golden hair and fling them about her freckled face. "I lost it. I ran away and hid in my flat for a week. Didn't see anyone or talk to anybody. It was stupid, Margot knew where I was the whole time."

"But she gave you space?"

"She did. She understood, I suppose."

"Did you, I mean, sorry if this is insensitive to ask." Juliet fidgets with her fingers. "Did you go through withdrawal? From the drugs?"

I exhale heavily, taking a gentle turn in the road as we pass a yellowing patch of forest. "It was odd. When you become a vamp, you sort of withdraw from everything. You get used to not needing food, and as much sleep, even air. I had the desire to shoot up, just to feel human, just to do something that made sense."

"I guess it didn't work?"

"Nope." I gaze over at her, those grey eyes looking at me with softness and understanding. "Eventually I ended up going home to my parents. I wanted to show them I was clean, and that maybe being a vamp was a good thing."

"How'd that go?"

I swallow hard, my throat feeling tight. "Bad."

She reaches over and threads her fingers through mine. "I'm sorry."

"It was a long time ago." I gently remove my hand from hers, not because I don't want to hold it anymore, but because the touch of that warm skin is too much. Feeling her pulse against my fingers - fuck.

"So then what happened?" She asks, wrapping her arms back around her legs.

I shrug, pushing down the visor as we change direction and the sun shines in my face. "I tried to be human. I met a girl, this cute little goth who worked in a record store in London. Vampires were slowly becoming public knowledge in some circles, and she was into it."

"What was her name?"

"Vivien."

"And what happened to her?"

I chew on the inside of my cheek for a second. "I killed her."

Juliet falls into silence, and it takes me a beat to get up the courage to look over at her. Her eyes are a little wide, filled with a mixture of fear and curiosity.

"It was an accident." The sick feeling of that night washes over me. "We were... we were having sex, and I bit her, just as I finished. That was a mistake."

"You took too much blood?" Juliet asks in a small voice.

I ripped her fucking throat out. "Something like that." I can't tell her the truth. It would horrify her. It still horrifies me, all these years later. There was so much blood... I blink away the image and the terror. "After that, I had to admit to myself that things weren't going to go back to the way they were. I wasn't the same person anymore. That life was over. So I went back to Margot."

We lapse into silence for a while, both caught up in our own thoughts. I think back on that day, when I went back to her. Her face when I walked in, the utter joy, love and concern in her eyes. She'd run me a bath, washed my hair, and held me as I mourned my old life.

"I know, *mon amour*," she'd murmured. "I know it is

painful. But you and I, we shall have the world. It is all there, for you and me."

"She died of the Affliction." Juliet's voice draws me back into the moment, back into the truck as the warm breeze floats through the open windows.

"Yeah she did. Four years ago."

"That must have been tough." She reaches over again to take my hand, but pulls it back. I love that she wants to touch me all the time. I hate that I feel the need to push her away.

After I nearly kissed her in the forest the other day, I know I need to be more careful. Touching her too much will drive me insane. I'm one hand-hold and lip bite away from pulling over the car and bending her over the hood.

Fucking STOP IT.

She seems to sense the shift in my demeanor, turning away from me so she's looking out the window. Her back is inches from my hand, her hair brushing over my arm as it waves about in the breeze.

The silence finally becomes too much, and I lean down to flick on the ancient iPod I have connected to the truck's stereo. Juliet nearly jumps out of her skin as Michael Jackson's Black or White comes on over the speakers at a volume neither of us expected. I quickly turn it down, and Juliet begins to giggle.

"Oh my god you have *music*?" She picks up the neon green iPod and turns it over in her hand. "I haven't seen one of these since I was a kid."

"Yeah, well it's the one thing I managed to hold on to, and by some miracle it still works." I chuckle as she continues to stare at it. "Back in the days before everyone had music on their phones."

She lets out a breathless little laugh, and puts the iPod back on the dash. "Yeah, those were the days huh?" She flexes her toes on the seat, then stretches her legs out in front of her. "This is an old song right?"

I lift a finger in her direction. "Ey, ey, watch yourself now."

I can sense the sass rolling off her as I catch sight of her grin.

"My *parents* used to listen to this music," she drawls softly.

I slam a hand to my chest and let out a strangled groan. "Brutal. Straight through the fucking heart, Monroe, Jesus."

She gasps, and my head snaps to look at her.

"You alright?"

She nods slowly. "You know my last name?"

Shit. Way to let her know you've been a creep and looked up her file.

I look back at the road. "Uh yeah. I looked you up. I was curious. Sorry."

"What does my file say?"

"It says your birthday is March 13. Born 1999." I smile over at her. She's still regarding me with that somewhat distrustful, incredulous look. "You were picked up from UGA and brought to the facility here. You were 19 years old at the time, in good health."

"They say that?" She scoffs. "I was in good health?"

"Yeah. The vamps are all about health."

"Yeah." Her entire mood has shifted. She curls up on the seat silently, and winds the window up. She stares out at the changing landscape, decaying buildings springing up either side of us as we approach Savannah.

"I didn't want to make you uncomfortable."

She waves a hand, not looking at me. "It doesn't matter."

"Well, it does."

"It's just a name, Silas."

No, it isn't. The protest dies on my tongue as she refuses to turn back around.

I want to explain to her why I looked her up. That I was desperate to know more. That my heart ached when I saw the picture attached to the file. The eyes wide with terror. The blurred fingerprints so obviously delivered by a trembling hand. Humans had known of our existence for all of her life - but to suddenly be a captive, to be tied down and harvested for blood, who could have foreseen that?

But I say nothing, leaving her alone with her thoughts.

"Juliet," I say softly as we approach the perimeter of the facility in Savannah. "When we get there, just stay in the truck, OK? Get in the back and lie down. There's a blanket for you to hide under. You'll be perfectly safe."

"Fine." She tucks her arms across her body, leaning her head against the seat in a way that makes the delicate veins on her neck stand out. My mouth waters at the sight.

I give myself a shake and focus on the road. As we get closer, Juliet climbs between the seats into the back, giving me the perfect view of her long legs and her ass as it passes my head. *Goddammit.*

"Silas?" The whisper comes from underneath the blanket in the back seat.

I cock my head. "Yeah?"

"Were you going to kiss me in the forest?"

My hands grip the steering wheel. The perimeter fence is in sight. This isn't the time for this conversation.

"I'm sorry about that."

She lets out an annoyed little grunt. "That's not an answer."

"Juliet-"

"Yes or no?"

I growl out a breath between gritted teeth. The guards up ahead spot me, lining up at the gate to prepare to let me in. "Yeah, maybe. I dunno."

"Yes you do."

"Juliet, not the fucking time. Now stay quiet."

"I would have let you."

I nearly tear the damn steering wheel from the dash. Blood roars through my body, remembering the feeling of her against me, pliant and wanting. Her hand pinned above her head, her eyes closed as she waited for me to kiss her. I can't tell her I wanted to do more than kiss her. I wanted to give in to every depraved fantasy I've had about her.

I breathe in and out heavily, steadying myself. I raise a hand in greeting to the other vamps who wave me in through the gate, completely unaware of the emotional and physical torment I'm going through right now. I jump down from the truck, slamming the door closed quickly. The blanket is covered in pheromone oil, so I'm sure it will throw off Juliet's scent, but I feel better knowing she's inside behind tinted glass all the same.

The vamps help me load up the supplies, bemoaning the growing number of Afflicted attacks and apologizing for the unnecessary trip. I make as much small talk as I can bear, the balls of my feet burning with the need to get her the fuck out of there. Maybe this was a bad idea.

But the vamps don't seem to notice my uneasiness, slapping me on the shoulder as I say I should head back before it gets too late, *don't want to get stuck out on these roads at the moment, haha.*

Finally I'm back in the truck, gunning the engine and heading out of the facility. Juliet stays in the backseat for a long time, until we're almost on the outskirts of Savannah, and I wonder if she's fallen asleep.

"You can come out now," I say in a low voice, not wanting to wake her.

The blanket shuffles and moves, and a long leg extends

between the seats, followed by a small ass and another leg. She flips around to plop down in the seat next to me, her hair sticking to her face. She's sweaty and smells *fantastic*. Her cheeks are all flushed and her lips are full.

Why the fuck does she look turned on?

"You OK?"

She nods, biting her lip. "I'm fine. Just... hot."

It takes my stupid brain a second to register what the fuck I did. I cast a glance into the back seat, at the blanket doused in pheromone oil. *My* pheromones.

You fucking idiot. It didn't even occur to me that while it would throw the guards off her scent, it would drive Juliet crazy.

"It's OK," I say quickly, trying not to focus on her thighs as she squeezes them together, her nipples that are peaking under her shit. *Shit. What the fuck have I done?* "It's the oil on the blanket, it's just going to heighten everything for you. Just breathe through it." *Yeah, just breathe through your erection, Silas.*

Juliet inhales sharply and nods. "Yeah, OK." She scrapes the heels of her hands along her thighs. "Can you put on the air, please? I need to cool down."

I flip on the air-conditioning, which throws up the scent of her arousal as the air bursts from the vents. Blood rushes to my cock, and I grasp the steering wheel hard to stop myself reaching over to grab her.

She snatches up a bottle of water from the dash and twists off the lid, gulping it down in three long bounces of her throat. Droplets run down her chin, and she licks her lips, trying to snatch them back up. This is bad. I'm an idiot. This was a bad idea.

I spot a sign up ahead, the white writing peeling off the green background, but still legible. *Ansom Lake.* I tear the steering wheel to the right and we fly down a corrugated dirt road.

"Where are we going?" Juliet asks, her voice still breathy and sexy.

"Somewhere to cool down."

It's only a short drive down the road, and the forest opens up to reveal a shimmering dark green lake. The tires screech to a halt as I pull up, and I realize as I kill the engine that we're both panting. Juliet looks over at me, her hands clenched between her thighs.

"What did you do to me?"

"I wanted to mask your scent," I say, waving to the back-seat. "It's basically concentrated vampire scent."

"Well y'all smell *real* good." She runs a hand over her flushed face, tipping her head back against the seat as she closes her eyes. Her chest rises and falls rapidly, her nipples still bunched up under the white fabric of her shirt. She turns her head and opens her eyes, gazing at me.

It would be so easy to have her right now. I could pull her onto my lap, tear those soaked panties aside and bury my cock in that pussy that's aching to be fucked right. I could pin her down and suck on her throbbing clit and not let her go til she's come on my mouth three times. I could soak my cock in all that arousal pooling between her legs and fuck her in the ass so she can't walk tomorrow. Right now, I can do what I want with her. She'd be open for anything, her body's so strung out on my scent.

And none of it would be because she wanted it. She's drugged out of her mind.

I throw open the truck door and climb down, sucking in heavy breaths of warm air.

The door on the other side opens, and Juliet clambers out, a little unsteady on her feet as she walks around to my side. She stops right in front of me, staring up at me. Her pupils are blown, sweat still beading on her forehead.

"Why don't you go for a swim?"

Her brows knit together as she looks at me. "A swim?"

"Sure. Get your mind off things. I'll keep watch."

She takes two steps back from me, then lifts her shirt. *Fuck.* She pulls it up over her head, and hands it to me. Her eyes stay fixed on me as she drops her shorts and her panties down her legs, picking them up with her foot. She hands those to me too, and the hit I get as her scent wafts up into my face - no drug is this good.

She stands completely naked in front of me, her hands at her sides. Her long blonde hair hangs over her shoulders, partially covering her breasts. She looks like an angel. My angel. *Maybe just once...*

But it wouldn't be once. It would be forever. If I taste this woman I know that she's the only thing I'll want for the rest of my life. I can't have her. I can't do that to her. I can't do that to myself.

"Go on." I tilt my head towards the water. "Go cool off. Swim. You said you were a good swimmer once." I give her a crooked smile.

The fog seems to lift a little, her face crinkling as she frowns. She looks over at the water, finally breaking the stare on me, and moves slowly towards it. I watch as she crosses the small sandy beach, a flicker of panic passing through me as she hesitates at the edge of the sparkling depths. Am I about to trigger an episode of PTSD? *Shit.* She hasn't been in the water since... That day. I take two steps forward, ready to grab her if I need to.

But after a moment, she wades in, her hands caressing the water's surface as it meets her fingertips. Her legs are almost fully submerged by the time she lowers her body in, her hair spreading out behind her like some heavenly lilypad.

I lean my back against a tree, breathing a sigh of relief, watching her swim. She moves through the water swiftly, naturally. Like she's never left it. Her long arms glisten in the sunlight as they lift then plunge back into the depths, propelling her forward.

Gradually my own arousal sinks away, eking out of my bones miserably. I want her. I want to own her, to taste her and consume her. When I nearly kissed her in the forest, I had to stop myself because I know what kind of man I am once that boundary gets crossed.

Vivien's boyfriend discovered that. Painfully.

Margot used to laugh at me. "My little love addict," she'd tease, stroking my hair. She was right.

I'd fucked Vivien out the back of the record store where she worked, it was meant to be a casual thing. She had a boyfriend. She didn't want any more than that.

But I did.

Once I'd tasted her cunt, her blood, her mouth, I was done. I had to have her. I had to own her.

I'd hunted her boyfriend down, torn him to pieces and thrown him into a canal. Vivien thought he'd left town. I was there to comfort her. She accepted willingly. We lived in our little bubble of blood and fucking for three months, before I tore out her throat while I was still inside her.

By the time they found her boyfriend's body, she was already dead.

As I watch Juliet float through the water, like a nymph who's finally found her way home, I know within myself - this girl is too pure for me. I feel something for her I've never felt for anyone before, not even for Margot. In another life, maybe. But not here, not like this. And whatever she thinks she feels for me, it's nothing but fear. She's scared and alone.

That's all there is to it.

After an hour, the sun begins to bathe the forest in golden light, and Juliet comes out of the water. She shakes the droplets from her hair, and she's smiling widely.

"That was amazing," she says breathlessly. "Oh my god."

I return her smile. "You really are an amazing swimmer."

"Thanks." She tugs her clothes onto her wet body, giggling. "Hopefully I dry out by the time we get back."

I say nothing, just keep smiling at her.

On the ride home, I'm keenly aware of the fact that she keeps looking at me. Her face is soft and happy.

And I realize that I've just made her like me even more.

MY FORAY into the outside world has set something alight inside me. I'm like a new person. I'm eating more, I have more energy, my sleep is so much better. Gina can't stop complimenting my smile.

But something changed between Silas and I that day, and it dampens my mood every time I think about it too much.

I'd wanted him to fuck me so badly when I crawled out of that back seat. I'd lain under that blanket, my mind boiling with desire, thinking about him and all the ways I wanted him to have his way with me. I'd nearly crawled straight into his lap. I'd nearly leaned over and unzipped him, aching to touch him in any way possible.

Thank god he'd sent me into the water. It had been cold, but comforting, like coming home. And it brought me to my senses. As those pheromones wore off, I'd begun to see clearly. I'd relaxed, and all that brainless desire had worn off.

And I realized I really did want him to fuck me.

But he's been avoiding me. I still feel his eyes on me, lingering in the background as always. Making sure no one hurts me. But he stays away. He doesn't come too close.

It makes me sad, and then bad weather sets in. The early

warm days of Fall pass us by, and we head into October. It rains almost every day and it becomes unseasonably cold. We're forced to spend more time inside, and the boredom is mind-crushing.

I spend a lot of time sitting undercover, wrapped up in a thick sweater as I watch the leaves change and fall. I wish I had pencils and paper so I could draw. I trace the shape of each leaf in my mind, the arching fingers of the branches on the trees.

Halloween comes around, with no celebration or fanfare. I'd always thought Halloween was kind of dumb, just an excuse to make yourself sick on candy and toilet-paper the neighbor's tree. But I loved the decorations. My Mom used to make our porch look so pretty. Not with cobwebs and skeletons, but beautiful harvest-themed wreaths made herself, and big jack-o-lanterns my dad would drill intricate patterns into. I loved it.

Then we roll into November, and it gets so cold I'm convinced it's going to snow. Maybe we'll have a white Christmas this year. Another holiday we don't celebrate anymore. Something else to remind me just what I miss about my old life.

On this especially cold morning, just a few days shy of Thanksgiving, I sit with my hands tucked into my sleeves, my sweater pulled up around my chin, watching the rain pelt down from the dark sky. I wait for it to turn to sleet any second now.

"Hello, stranger."

I look over my shoulder in the direction of the voice, and straight into Silas's eyes. I stretch my legs down off the bench, turning towards him.

"Well, hello. I thought you didn't like me anymore." I give him a crooked smile. "You haven't talked to me in a long time."

He looks sheepish, sweeping the dark hair from his fore-head with his tattooed hand.

"Sorry about that." He holds up a black duffel bag, his chest puffing a little, as though he's really proud. "But I have something I think might cheer you up."

I raise an eyebrow. "And what is that?"

"Come with me and you'll find out."

I don't ask any more questions, too relieved to be back in his presence to care what that black bag holds. I follow him across the yard, scurrying through the pouring rain. We head past the kitchen and an administration block, around some storage sheds and straight for a line of neat yellow and white cabins.

"Are you taking me to your place?" I ask with a giggle.

He grins over his shoulder at me. "You got somewhere better to be?"

I pad up the steps behind him, and he opens the door to a cute little room. There's a big bed in the middle, and an armchair in front of an enclosed metal fireplace. A desk with a big chair is on the opposite wall, beside which stands a bookshelf filled with books.

I peel off my wet sweater, and walk over to the bookshelf. "You like to read?"

"Yeah, always have. I guess you have too, daughter of an english teacher and all."

"That's for sure. Books as presents, for every birthday." I gesture to the shelf. "Mind if I take a look?"

He waves me over. "Course not. Go ahead."

I look over the spines, reading off the titles, some I know, some I've never heard of. On one of the shelves lies a faded polaroid picture, underneath an old cassette tape. I can't make out much of it, but it looks like a very young Silas with a pretty redhead. They're both laughing. On the cassette tape, in black pen, are the words "For Harri", along with two uneven little hearts.

"Who's this in the picture?" I ask.

A beat, a moment's hesitation in which the air becomes somehow heavier. I turn to look at him, and his eyes are fixed downwards.

"She was my best friend growing up." His voice is a little strained, and the small twitch of his jaw tells me that maybe I shouldn't push this, not when we just tenuously found our way back to each other. Instead, I walk to his side and look over everything he's spread out on the desk.

"You got art supplies?" I gaze up at him in awe. "How did you manage that?"

"I put in a special request to one of the family centers," he replies. "They sent me some things, excess stock apparently."

I laugh, reaching down to flip open a notebook, running my fingers over the heavy paper. "This is amazing." I smile up at him. "Are we going to draw together?"

"Well the weather's shit and I don't feel like going to the gym, so why not?"

Without thinking, I throw my arms around Silas and grab him in a tight hug.

"Oh my god, thank you!" I realize as he tenses that maybe that was a bad idea, not after we were panting over each other in a truck a few weeks ago. I quickly let him go and take a step back. "Sorry, I'm just excited."

"It's OK." He gives me that devastating smile again, and unbuttons his khaki shirt, peeling it down his arms. He's wearing a tight white t-shirt underneath which makes his tanned skin look even darker. He runs a hand through his damp hair, raking it back over his head and he looks good enough to eat.

He catches me staring at him, his eyes moving down to my lips.

"I wanted to apologize," he says slowly. "For what happened, in the truck."

"You don't need to apologize for that."

"I didn't want to make you uncomfortable."

I shake my head quickly. "You didn't. I was confused for a minute, but that was all."

"Me too." His eyes move back up my face to meet mine. "They want us to spend time together, the higher-ups. They think it's good PR. Make the humans trust us again."

"Good PR?"

"Yeah. They think it's good we're... friends."

"Friends, huh?"

"Yes, friends." His tongue nudges against one of his fangs, as though he's contemplating the word. His eyes flash down to my lips for a split second, and I think he's going to move closer to me. But then he breaks away from my gaze to look down at the desk, picking up a notepad and a box of pencils, handing them to me. "Here, sit where you like."

"I used to draw on my bed. Lying on my stomach, it was always the most comfortable."

His Adam's apple races up and down his throat as he swallows. "Make yourself at home then."

I lie down on his bed, flipping open the notepad in front of me and pulling a pencil out of the box. I gaze out the window at the trees that are waving in the wind that's sprung up, at the leaves that are falling, and put the tip of the pencil to the paper.

Silas turns the armchair so it's facing the bed, and sits down, throwing open the notepad on his knee. His pencil scratches across the paper, and he looks up at me sporadically, narrowing his eyes and tilting his head.

I sketch out the window frame, the drapes either side, and look over at him.

"Are you drawing me?" I ask after a while.

He smiles at his paper, his hand continuing to move. "What else would I draw?"

I lean up on my elbows as though trying to catch a glimpse. "Do I have clothes on?"

The corners of his mouth quirk. "You'll have to wait and see."

"Well you have seen me naked I guess." I look out the window, analyzing the shape and curve of the branches on the trees. "It's not a stretch for you to remember exactly what I look like."

"A refresher couldn't hurt," he mutters, still suppressing a grin.

I laugh and look at him with raised eyebrows. "Oh really? Well I'm scheduled for a shower tonight, maybe you can talk one of your buddies into swapping shifts."

"I might just have to do that." He keeps drawing, every now and then sweeping a thumb over the paper.

I carefully sketch out the trees outside, then begin to trace raindrops on the window pane even though it's covered by a roof and no raindrops are running down it. After a while he flips the notepad over towards me.

"What do you think?"

I stare at the picture. Not only is he *good*, he's drawn me. Lying in bed, face down. Hair trailing over my bare back, the barest hint of my ass peeking out over the sheets. There's a hand on my lower back, the owner out of frame. It's beautiful, so carefully done and the details so perfect, I can hardly believe he just threw that down on paper while I was lying here doodling trees.

I raise my eyes back to his.

"You're really good." My lips tremble a little as I smile. "Is that how you see me?"

He smiles, looking down at the picture. "I wish I could see you like this." He shakes his head and goes back to drawing.

"I did mean it."

He pauses his drawing and looks back up at me. "Mean what?"

"What I said in the truck. That I... You know, in the forest. I would have let you kiss me."

"Is that right?"

I nod. "I just didn't want you to get in trouble."

Goddamn his gaze is so intense. The rain patters loudly against the roof, as we look at each other, and after a while I shiver.

"You cold?" He asks, rising to his feet.

I sit up on my knees and rub my arms. "Yeah, a little."

He gets to his feet and turns to a set of drawers beside the bed, pulling out a black sweater.

"Here," he says, watching as I pull it on over my head. "It's probably gonna be enormous on you."

It is, the sleeves hang way over my hands, and it sits well below my ass. But it's warm, and it smells like him.

"Thanks." I gaze up at him. "Why didn't you talk to me for so long?"

He sighs heavily, frowning down at me. "I'm sorry. I didn't mean to hurt you."

"Then why?" My throat tightens a little, all the emotion I'd refused to acknowledge for the past few weeks welling up and making my eyes sting. "I thought you liked me."

"Oh, angel." He lifts a hand, jerking it back into a fist. With a frustrated sigh he runs a hand through his hair, and it's such a juxtaposition, this huge tattooed man standing over me, looking utterly lost and helpless for a moment. His jaw feathers as he looks back down at me, reaching out to stroke his thumb down my cheek. "I do like you, Juliet. I like you too much. And that's the problem."

I try to smile and not show my disappointment. "So you were trying to talk yourself out of it, huh?"

He huffs out a laugh, his perfect mouth turning up into another one of his devastating smiles, and heat tenses my stomach. "I couldn't even if I wanted to." His hand moves from my cheek, down my throat, until he's cupping my neck in his enormous warm hand. "And now you're here, sitting on my bed, wearing my clothes."

"It feels like a very girlfriend thing to be doing. Wearing your sweater."

A growl rumbles in his throat. "It looks good on you. I like it."

"Like I belong to you, huh?" I'm breathing a little harder now, and warmth is spreading between my thighs.

"If you belonged to me, angel, that sweater is the only thing you'd be wearing right now."

My breath hitches in my throat. "Is that so?"

"Mmmm." He leans on the bed, so he's almost face to face with me. "I'd peel these sweatpants down your legs. Get down to your panties."

"Oh really?" Why is my voice so damn squeaky? "You like having sex with clothes on?"

"I like delayed gratification." His eyes flicker down to my groin. "You're getting wet just thinking about it, aren't you?"

"No." I shake my head, trying to fight off the overwhelming desire rushing through me.

His mouth turns up into a devilish grin, bright red crimson seeping into his eyes. "Liar."

I swallow hard. "How do you know I'm lying?"

"Because I can smell you, angel."

Heat runs down my spine. I know this isn't allowed. I know he'll get in trouble. I don't know what they'll do to him, but it has to be bad. It has to be awful. But the way he's looking at me now, I can't resist playing further into this dangerous game.

"And then what?" My mouth is running dry. "Then what would you do, once you had my panties off?"

"Who says I'd take them off?" He leans closer. "I'd stroke your clit through them, feeling you get wetter and wetter for me. I'd almost make you come, have you trembling right here on my bed, almost at the edge. And then I'd stop."

"So you want to torture me, is that it?" I ask, trying to make my laugh sound nonchalant. My nipples are so hard they hurt. Every part of me is tense, listening to him talk like this.

"Not torture, angel. I just want you to beg. I want you to beg me to make you come. And once you're begging me, I'd tear those panties off, and I'd have those legs draped over my shoulders." He leans closer still, his breath hot as it passes the distance between us to wash over my lips. "I'd have your soaking wet cunt dripping down my lips."

I can't respond anymore. I'm one breath away from throwing myself at him. Instead I lean back on my hands, extending my legs out towards him. I shuffle down my sweatpants, just enough, just so he can see the tops of my panties.

"And then what?" I run a finger along my hip. "What would you do with your mouth then?"

A predatory haze sets over his face. I count out the seconds as his gaze follows the line of my finger.

"I'd suck that clit until you were screaming my name." His eyes rove over my body, his hands still planted on the bed. "I'd make you come until you couldn't take any more."

"And then?"

His eyes flicker up to mine, filled with lust. "Then I'd flip you over, push your head right down into the bed, and sink my cock into that soaked pussy. I'd hold you down while I fucked you hard, while you're screaming my name into the mattress."

I shift on the bed, desperate for him to touch me. If he

doesn't touch me soon, I'm going to touch myself, right here, on his bed, in front of him.

"Would you stop there?"

He growls, and it almost sounds like purring, deep in his throat. He licks his lips, shaking his head.

"I wouldn't stop til you begged me to." One corner of his mouth lifts in a grin. "I wouldn't stop til you were shaking, til you couldn't walk." He lowers his mouth to my ear, and my eyes slip shut. "I want to taste you, angel."

"I want that too." My breathing is so fast now I'm sure I'm going to pop a fucking lung. "No one's ever... I mean..."

"Bitten you?" He rakes his fangs against my pulse, and I bite my lip, shaking my head.

"No," I whimper. "No one's ever, ummm..." I gasp as his hand moves over the sweatshirt, over my nipples that are painfully hard under his touch. "Oh *fuck*. No one's ever gone down on me before."

He shackles my hands in his, whipping them up from behind me and flat on the bed. I'm pinned underneath him, gasping and hot and my whole body is *screaming* for him to fuck me.

"Poor angel," he murmurs against my throat. "No one's ever looked after this sweet cunt properly, have they?" He presses a leg between my thighs, I moan a little as I rock against him, trying to find some friction. His fang drags along my jawline, and the sudden sting of pain just turns me on even more. "You're fucking dangerous."

His words make me shiver. This is dangerous. This is stupid. But any sense I may have had goes right out the window when I find the right spot, grinding myself against his thigh. Heat rises through my core, rushing up my throat into my face. I exhale heavily around a moan, opening my eyes to find Silas gazing down at me.

"Is this what you want?"

I nod, licking my lips. "Yeah." My breath stutters in my lungs. "You do too, right?"

His mouth is at my throat again, moving down to nip at my collarbone. "What the fuck do you think?" The hard ridge of his cock presses against my hip. "Can you feel how crazy you make me?"

Tension drags at my shoulders, my whole body tense with arousal. I'm heat, and sweat, and nothing else as I squirm under him, chasing the climax that's clawing at my insides. He's that hard because of *me*, because he wants *me*.

"Such a pretty little fuckdoll." Silas grins down at me. "You're going to make yourself come all over my leg, aren't you?"

What did he just call me? I don't actually fucking care, because the explosion of heat between my thighs goes fucking volcanic. Sure, I love being called a fuckdoll, why not?

"Say that again."

"You want me to call you my little fuckdoll?" He lets out a breathy chuckle as I moan. "My dirty girl likes names, hmm?" He cages me in, breathing heavy against my ear. "You're going to come for me, get yourself nice and wet for me, angel. Such a fucking needy girl."

"Silas," I say with a gasp, grinding myself harder against him. He's groaning softly now too, exhaling through gritted teeth.

If he can make me come with just his goddamn *thigh* and some dirty talk, what the hell is he going to do when he's eating me out? When he's inside me? Wait, *when*? It's then I realize this is really going to happen, and I *want* it to happen. My whole body's soaring on euphoria, and I swallow back a choked scream.

"Kiss me," I plead, desperate to feel the warmth of his lips, to feel his tongue in my mouth. I'm going to come, my climax is cresting right there, and I begin to tremble as his mouth descends on mine.

I've barely tasted him, his tongue has barely touched mine, as the siren blares through the compound.

The rush of deflation is so great that my whole body feels cold as Silas rises off me, heading straight to the window. He looks out, side to side, before running to the desk and tearing open a drawer, pulling out a gun. Terror overtakes me, and I curl up into a ball, shaking, watching as he stalks back to the window.

"Fuck," he mutters as the siren continues to drone overhead. He turns back to me, holding out a hand. "Stay here. Lock the door. Hide in the bathroom, stay out of sight, do you understand?"

"OK."

He tears open the door.

"Silas!" My voice is cracking, and he pauses to look over his shoulder at me. "Please be careful."

He barely nods before he's out the door, the siren continuing to drone overhead. I rush to the door and flip the latch shut. He told me to hide in the bathroom. I turn the light off in the cabin, and huddle by the window. I know I should hide, he told me to, this is dangerous. But I can't bear not being able to see what's going on.

Feeders are running past the cabins, some of them armed. I can't hear what they're saying over the siren, but they look worried. There's a flash of light overhead, and then the ground quakes as an explosion rocks the cabin. I clap my hand over my mouth to stop myself crying out, and press myself harder against the wall.

I peer over the edge of the window frame. The sky seems to have gotten darker, and the rain is coming down in heavy sheets. The yard in front of the cabin is illuminated by the rotating orange light perched on top of the perimeter fence. Everything goes so oddly quiet.

Maybe it's over. Maybe it was nothing.

I lift up a little, craning my neck to see further out the window.

The whole cabin shakes as an explosion lights up the storage buildings nearby. I throw myself flat on the floor, covering my head as debris pings loudly against the windows and roof. I crawl across the cabin on my stomach, dragging myself to the bathroom door. I've almost reached it when I hear it.

That awful screeching cry of the Afflicted.

They're right outside the cabin.

I haul myself into the bathroom, pushing the door closed and turning the latch. I back into the corner, quivering, my arms wrapped around my legs. They're pounding on the cabin walls, groaning and screeching. I can see the shadows passing the frosted bathroom window, their nails trailing along the shiplap.

They're here. They're all the way in here already.

Please don't let me die here. Please don't let me die here all alone. I don't want to die alone. I'm crying, hot salty tears running down my cheeks and into my mouth. I'm gasping for breath, trying to stay quiet. And then it occurs to me that Gina might already be dead. That Silas might already be dead. My stomach is clenched in terror.

Please let them be OK. Please let them be OK.

The scratching and banging get louder, there's more of them. I cover my ears with my hands, biting my lip to stop myself sobbing. They're going to break down the door. They'll smell me in the bathroom, then they'll break that door down too. They'll eat me in the damn bathroom.

My skin is coursing with ice and electricity.

There's another explosion and I yelp, wishing I could somehow curl up into an even smaller ball. A high pitched squeal fills the air, making my eardrums ache, sending pain right down into my jaw. It makes me feel sick, my throat feels tight and I struggle to breathe.

As quickly as it starts, it's over, and the Afflicted outside are quiet. My head aches. I blink away the pain, stretching my mouth open to try and make that ache dissipate. What the hell was that? Why is it so quiet?

There's voices outside, deep and muffled. Heavy footsteps sound on the porch. There's banging against the door.

"Anyone in there?" A voice calls.

Is it a feeder? I crawl slowly across the floor.

"Hello?" More banging against the door, shadows moving past the bathroom window.

I open the bathroom door slowly, peering around to see if I can catch a glimpse of who it is through the windows.

I see two figures, wearing helmets and body armor. They're both holding assault rifles.

Across their chests there are two words emblazoned in white script.

National Guard.

I get to my feet, stepping out from behind the door and one of them spots me.

"Someone's in there," he says, gesturing to me. "Hey! Open the door!"

They're human. They might not know I am. I don't want them to shoot me.

"I'm human!" I raise my hands. "I'm human!"

He gestures urgently at the door. "Open up, we're here to he-"

I scream and drop to my feet as a bullet tears through the

man's head, piercing straight through his helmet and splattering the window with blood as it shatters. I drag myself under the bed as gunfire erupts, and something heavy slams into the door.

The guns stop quickly, and all I can hear is groaning. Blood seeps under the door, crawling across the floor slowly. There are two more brief shots, and everything goes quiet outside. I'm shaking so hard my head bounces against the floor.

Someone kicks in the door, and boots slam against the floor.

"Who's in here?" They drop down to look under the bed, and it's a feeder, peering at me. "You OK?" He asks gruffly.

I can't talk, my tongue is swollen in my mouth and my jaw is chattering. I try to nod, scraping my nails into the floor to pull myself out. As soon as I clear the bed, hands are on me, pulling me to my feet, hauling me out over the blood splatter and past the dead bodies on the porch.

There's four of them on the grass outside the cabin. All of them, in the same uniform. *National Guard.*

Littered amongst the bodies of the Afflicted, in their blue uniforms and their helmets, their huge weapons lying beside them on the ground.

I stumble a little, trying to make sense of it as panic and terror continue to whir through my head. The National Guard are here. The one at the window had been about to say they were here to help. They came to rescue us? At the same time as an Afflicted attack? Did they follow them here?

I can't comprehend what's happening.

We round the corner, past the destroyed storage buildings, and it's a war zone. There's dead people everywhere, the rain carrying their blood with it in sickening rivulets that spread around my feet. There's people crawling along the ground, obviously bitten by Afflicted.

Feeders walk around, and executing the bitten one by one.

I can't even comprehend this horror anymore. I let them drag me past it all, into the cafeteria where everyone is huddled, shaking and crying.

And all I can think about is Silas. All I can do is pray that he's alive.

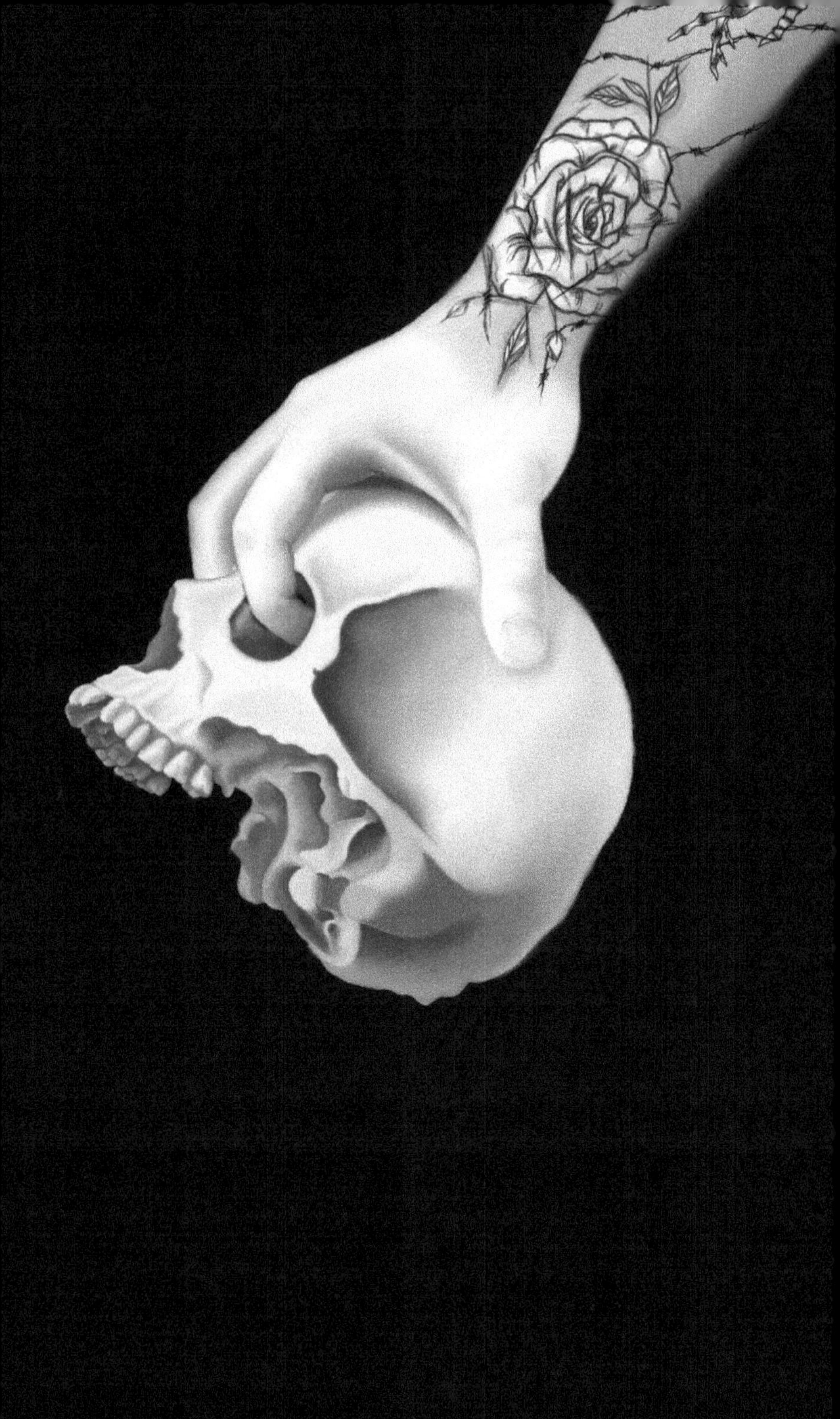

"FUCKING IDIOTS!" Anderson's chair goes flying across the room, notching a hole in the thin walls and sending the pinboard crashing to the floor, papers flying up like confetti. "Fucking humans! What the fuck are they thinking?"

I look around at my colleagues, many of them soaked in blood, their eyes bright crimson from the sudden sensory rush. There are dead humans everywhere, bleeding out into the ground, into the deep puddles forming around them as the rain continues to fall.

"Boston said they'd had reports of the National Guard mobilizing," Sam says, pushing aside the hair that hangs in her face in thick, blood-soaked ropes. "Looks like they're using the Afflicted now."

"To what end?" Anderson slams his fists into his desk, which groans as a huge crack splinters through its surface. "What are they hoping to achieve?"

"They're trying to eliminate us." The room goes quiet, and eyes turn to me. I shrug. "They're trying to kill off the vamps. They're sending in the Afflicted as decoys, and following them in to try and rescue as many humans as they can."

"The Afflicted killed 20 humans!" Anderson's finger darts

angrily towards the door. "Twenty, King. If the National Guard are trying to rescue them, then they're doing a bad fucking job."

"Collateral damage." I rub my hands together. They're soaked in blood, tight and cloying. "They kill many to save a few. They know they can't overpower us."

Anderson growls, exposing his fangs. "Fucking idiot humans." He punches the wall, creating a hole that goes straight through to the outside. Cool air rushes in. He's not going to have an office by the end of his tirade. "Go on and reinforce those perimeter fences. Set more alarms. Double the guards on the towers and gates. Get out!" He waves an angry hand in our direction, and we all hurry out.

"He's *pissed*," Crawley mutters under his breath.

"Can you blame him?" Sam snaps over her shoulder. "This is bad. We didn't have enough warning."

"I'll drive out and set perimeter alarms," I say. "Set them out 2 miles away. That's the max range on those sensors."

"Good." Sam shakes her head. "This is fucked."

Yes it is. There are dead everywhere. National Guard operatives blown to pieces all over the ground. Afflicted half-burned and torn apart. And humans. So many humans. Juliet's not among them though.

I storm through the rain towards the cafeteria. The humans were herded in there when we annihilated the National Guard. *Fools.* Using something as volatile as a herd of Afflicted to try and rescue humans. It's the stupidest thing I've ever heard.

And it isn't lost on me that they're trying to seize back control.

There was a brief uprising against vampires when they started doing genetic testing. Politicians whipped the public up into a mad fury, saying vamps were playing god, and that it would end badly. Some labs were burned down, vampire covens sought out and attacked.

But it was over pretty quickly when they discovered the HIV vaccine. Suddenly vamps were heroes. We were loved and admired. What amazing work we had done.

Then we got too fucking brazen for our own good.

I take the steps up into the cafeteria, crossing the porch and tearing the door open. I scan the room for the blonde hair, the freckled face. There are people everywhere, huddled in little groups on the ground. They're holding each other, trying to comfort each other. These people have no one. Even other humans are happy to sacrifice them now.

I spot her in a corner, and the relief sends my heart thumping against my ribcage. Her knees are drawn up under her chin, and Gina has an arm around her. They're both pale, tears tracking down their cheeks.

I cross the room and drop to my knees in front of her. Without a second's hesitation she throws her arms around my neck, sobbing into my shoulder.

"You're OK." Her voice is tight. "You're OK."

I wrap my arms around her, wishing I could somehow wrap her up and hide her away. "Thank god you're alive. Fuck, I was so scared." I stroke her hair, and I'm aware of the silence around us. People are watching, brows furrowed, leaning forward curiously as this human woman and a feeder hold each other in the cafeteria.

Juliet gazes up at me, her trembling breath washing across my face. I brush the tears out of her face.

"It's alright now, we're not going to let anything else happen to you." I try and give her a reassuring smile, but the relief that she's alive and safe has me shaking.

"I'm so sorry. I'm so fucking sorry."

"I'm just glad I was with you, before." Fresh tears stream down her cheeks. "At least, if something had happened-"

I clutch her to my chest, and a small gasp goes up from the people around us.

"Don't say that," I murmur into her hair. "Don't talk like that."

I hold her as she sobs, as Gina regards me with mild shock. No one knows what to think. Their eyes on me are making my hackles rise, I want to get Juliet out of here. I don't want anyone staring at her, or at me. I just want to be fucking alone with her.

At that moment, the other vamps come in and start telling the humans to return to the dorms. I take the opportunity to usher Juliet out, past the others. She doesn't protest as we head for one of the side buildings, the rain beating down on the tin roof.

I push through the door, into a storage room of some kind. As soon as the door closes behind us, I have her in my arms. She presses herself against me, frantic fingertips clawing at my neck.

"I was so afraid," she says, sobs hiccuping out of her. "I was so afraid something had happened to you."

"I got back to my cabin, and there was just blood every-where." I brush my hands over her head, cradling her against me, her forehead touching mine. "I panicked, angel. It took me so long to realize that it wasn't your blood."

She angles her head so our lips are even closer. I want to kiss her. I need to taste her. That brief touch of her tongue in my bed, that wasn't enough. I need to feel her under me again, watch that beautiful face as she comes undone for me. I need more, always more. My whole body is aching with need, with the elation of her being alive. I need to feel her heat and her breath, knowing it's just for me, that she's mine and no one else's.

Her hands wander up my back, pulling me closer. I lower my mouth to her neck, my lips lingering on her pulse, and she whimpers.

"Silas."

I'm shaking as her hands wander up and down my back, as her blood thunders against my mouth. I can't let go, not now, not when the other vamps are mobilizing outside and any moment someone will come and find us. But she's wrapping herself around me, the scent of her need and her want filling the space around us.I grip her jaw in my hand, tipping her head back, and a small moan leaves her lips.

"If you died, I'd die," I say, and her face crumples. "I don't want to live without you, not anymore."

She shakes her head, clenching her eyes shut, sending a fresh cascade of tears down her cheeks.

"Don't say that. Don't say that."

"I mean it." I lay my forehead against hers. "You're every-thing, angel."

"I can't say no to you anymore." She opens her eyes slowly and gazes up at me. "I can't. I don't want to."

"Juliet..." The thread's tearing. Who am I fucking kidding. It tore off when I had her under me on my bed. Watching her come, watching those sweet lips swell as she moaned - that thread of restraint that was wound so tightly around the man who'll scare her away, now it's gone. There's just me, *me,* ready to tear her clothes off and pin her down onto the floor just so I can hear my name fall from those quivering lips over and over again.

This isn't allowed. This isn't allowed. But not even the thought of being discovered and having my system poisoned by silver over and over is enough to deter me. Nothing is worse than every second that she isn't mine.

Her lips quiver as she looks up at me, her grey eyes wide.

"On your bed, I wanted you. I wanted you more than I've ever wanted anything in my life."

"I'm dying for you, angel." I stroke her shivering lower lip with my thumb.

She gasps, and her eyes snap shut. "Oh *god*." She presses her hands against my chest, her shoulders slumping as she begins to sob. "I can't... I can't..." She shakes her head as she begins to wail, a sound that pierces my dead heart.

I clutch her to my chest, and she thrashes, sobbing and howling.

"No, no, no, no." She chants it over and over.

"Jules, it's alright, I've got you."

"I can't - Oh *god,* they'll hurt you. They'll hurt you because of *me*." Her head tips back and she gazes at me, her eyes filled with tears and pain. "I can't be the reason you get hurt."

"You wouldn't be." I shake my head emphatically, trying to talk her out of it, trying to stop that defeat that's seeping into her eyes. "No, Jules, don't. Don't do this."

"If we do this, they'll hurt you."

"I don't care!"

"I do!" Her eyes are torn wide, bloodshot and glistening. "I was so scared today, so fucking scared that something had happened to you, that they'd killed you. I can't... I can't be the reason for that. I can't be the reason someone else dies."

I hold her face in my hands, wanting to yank her into me and crush these words with my mouth. "No one died because of you, nobody, none of that was your fault."

But it's useless. She closes her eyes, tears pouring down her face, over her lips, and she shakes her head. She's slipping away from me.

"Jules, Jules, listen to me, *listen to me.* Don't do this. Please."

She opens her eyes, and pulls me down to her. It happens

so quickly, a mere split second, but she's kissed me, pressing her salty lips to mine.

"I wanted it to be you," she murmurs. "I really did. But I can't lose anyone else. I can't do this again."

She pulls herself out of my arms and rushes out of the room. I'm so blindsided I let her go. Need flares in my blood, coursing through my arms. Her hands on my back, that was the tourniquet. Her lips on mine, that was the fucking needle.

I pound my fists into the wall, bellowing. Fuck this life. Fuck this place. Fuck this world that brought her to me when I couldn't fucking have her. Fuck all the pain and sadness that's threatening to take her away from me.

"*No.*" I growl it to the empty room. "*No. No. Fucking NO.*" My words are punctuated by more punches into the drywall.

I'm not letting her go.

Not now.

IF I WAS OBSESSED with her before, I'm a fucking criminal now.

I change shifts with other guards, playing an insane game of stalker hopscotch, moving across the compound so I can watch her wherever she is. The thought of anyone else watching her shower, seeing her skin, naked and wet, fills me with such blinding rage I smash my way through another four punching bags in two days. I'm barely keeping another episode of blood-lust at bay.

But I manage to have them all kept away from her. None of them care, none of them suspect my agenda. None of them know that she showers closer to the two-way mirror, as though she can sense I'm there. None of them know that I lean against that mirror and jack myself off, self-loathing coursing through me. I'm pathetic. I'm fucking gone for this girl.

But the scent of her skin is all I can smell. The brush of her lips is fucking branded on me forever. Sam gives me that knowing look every now and then, and she seems relieved that Juliet appears to be putting distance between the two of us. Sam thinks I'll get over it. Like some little stupid crush.

She has no idea.

The darkest parts of me whisper to me in the deep of the night, telling me to just take her. To drag her off into a corner somewhere. To suck on that sweet clit, to make her come on my cock, to cover that pretty freckled face in my cum so she knows who she belongs to. So she knows she's never saying no to me again. She'll never say no to me when she's come with my name falling from her lips.

I hate that part of myself.

No, when I'm finally inside her, it's because she's begging for me, because she can't go one more second without me. Because she's begging me to make her mine. And it won't take much longer.

In the meantime, her eyes still look for me. They're still filled with relief when they spot me. She knows I'm there. She wants me to watch over her. She needs me. My girl needs me so badly.

But I still need to attend to regular duties which take me away from her. Like another fucking supply run to Savannah. I consider asking to take her with me again, but after the National Guard stormed the compound, there's no way they'll let me take a human out.

So I spend the drive thinking far too hard and far too wide, trying to quantify and reason something that's beyond understanding. I look over at the seat beside me, and I see her blonde hair whipping around her face, I hear her laugh. I grip the steering wheel, thinking of her standing naked in front of me. *Fuck*, she wanted me. On my bed, she wanted me. If the attack hadn't happened, I'd have had her.

I groan as I think of the look on her sweet face as she ground herself against me. *Dirty girl*. She looks like an angel but holy shit, I can feel that there's something filthy and sinful hiding behind those grey eyes. She's begging to be unlocked and torn open.

I blast myself with cold air as I approach Savannah, because the last thing I need is to meet my colleagues with a bulging erection. By the time I wave to the gate guards, I've calmed down suitably. Discussing medical supplies is about as unsexy as it gets anyway.

I nod absently throughout the small talk, answer questions vaguely, keenly aware of the sinking sun and the urgency to get back to the compound. The other vamps are curious about the National Guard attack, looking at each other with concern. I repeat myself a few times, then suddenly one of them says something that snaps up my attention.

"What did you say?" I turn to the dark-haired vamp with a frown.

He shrugs. "I know, it caught us by surprise too. I mean, a whole human colony? It's been years since we broke them all up."

"Where is it?"

He gestures to the air over his head. "Up in Roanoke."

The vamp loading the last box onto the truck grunts. "I heard they got vamps working there as well."

"No way?" The dark-haired one raises his eyebrows. "Why the fuck would a vamp wanna live with humans?"

All the vamps chuckle. All except me.

"Wait, so you're saying there's a whole colony up there living without any vamp supervision?" I ask. The chuckles subside, and one of the other vamps nods.

"That's what we got told," she says, leaning back against the gate. "And with the National Guard regrouping, you gotta wonder, you know? How long is it gonna be like this?"

"You saying our days are numbered, Kowalski?" The vamp asks as he jumps down from the truck. "That's depressing."

"I don't think the Covens will let that happen." She tosses her short blonde bob. "But the humans can still try and fight back, right? Who knows what could happen."

Everyone laughs awkwardly. The attack made us all nervous. But I can't give that any more thought now, and I made my excuses to leave. I gun the engine and speed all the way back to the compound.

By the time I get back, the sun has almost slipped behind the horizon. I unload the supplies with two of the other vamps, and head to Sam's office to bring her the papers.

When I open the door, she's sitting behind her desk, her shirt open more than it should be while she's on duty. She watches me cross the room with blazing red eyes, and I can feel the heat rolling off her.

"Silas," she says in a low voice. "You got something for me?"

I throw the papers on to the desk. "Yeah, all delivered and accounted for."

"Fantastic." She runs a hand down her chest, into her open shirt. She gives me a smile, her eyes hooded with desire. "You look so good tonight."

I take a step back from the desk. "Thanks."

She lifts an eyebrow. "Thanks? Not, *Do you need something, Sam?* Because I do need something. I need something real bad."

"Not tonight, Sam." I turn to the door and she's in front of me in an instant.

"You haven't been to see me in a really long time. I'm so lonely." She puts a hand against my chest.

"I said, not tonight." I try to push past her, but she grabs me and spins me so my back is against the door. Her lips nip at my jawline.

"I need you to fuck me, Silas."

"No." I push her away, hard, and she stumbles, sneering at me.

"What's wrong, Silas? Pretty human got you sprung has she?"

"Fuck off." I turn to open the door, and Sam's hand slams against it, pushing it shut. She glares up at me, and I bare my fangs at her. "I said, fuck off."

"It is her, isn't it?"

"You don't know what you're talking about."

"Oh, I think I do." She grabs my crotch. "Maybe you just need to be cured of this little crush."

I shove her away from me. "Don't fucking touch me. If you're that desperate for vamp dick, go see Crawley, he's always up for it."

She hisses as I tear open the door. The cool night air rushes up my nose as I head for my cabin. The window is boarded up, the blood of the National Guard washed away.

Sam knows.

Of course she does. She's not stupid. She watches me like a hawk. Maybe she's jealous? It doesn't matter. Maybe I should have just fucked her to assuage any suspicions she might have had. Maybe I just made it worse. But I grit my teeth as I think of touching anyone but Juliet.

I can't do it. Not even to release the tension. I don't want to get off to anyone but her. I don't want to come inside anyone but her.

I head straight for the shower, then remember I have second shift on the dorms tonight. I douse myself in cold water to chase away the feeling of needing Juliet, of wanting her, and dress in a clean uniform. I retrieve a bottle of blood from the fridge, and down it. It's cold, which is disgusting, but the temperature helps me calm down.

I can't decide if I should be worried about Sam. I doubt she'd turn me in. She's jealous, not malicious. And even if she did, she has no proof. Nothing's happened.

Yet.

The time for my shift rolls around, and I walk out into the cool night. The compound is quiet, everyone is asleep or resting. The vamp at the door of the dorm gives me a nod as I approach.

"They're all out cold," he says with a smile. "Think they're a lot better behaved since the Guard came through." He laughs stupidly and I wanted to smash his face in.

Instead I just give him a tight smile. "Yep, no motivator like fear."

He waves off as he heads towards the cabins, and I take my spot by the door.

I can practically sense her inside. I can feel the smooth skin of her thighs under the sheet. She's not wearing much, I know that. I imagine that warm skin, naked against me. Fuck she'd feel amazing. I can practically smell her...

My senses go into overdrive. I *can* smell her. *Oh fuck.*

She's in the dorm getting herself off. Heat races through my veins.

I swallow hard, my hand gripping the door. She's in a dorm full of humans. I need to try and stay calm. I shouldn't go in there.

Then a little moan carries on the air, and I can't take it.

I move soundlessly, past all the others. Sleeping, snoring softly. I approach her bed, and she's lying on her stomach. Her body is jerking in tiny, barely perceptible movements. I can hear her blood thundering in her veins, and her smell. Oh, *fuck*, her smell. It's enough to bring me to my fucking knees. The thought of having that smell on my face, having her pussy pour her orgasm all over my fucking mouth. I grit my teeth to stop myself from groaning.

I stop beside her bed, just as she whimpers into her pillow. I lean over her, and put my hands either side of her.

She gasps, tossing her head to the side and looking over her shoulder with wide eyes. Her hair is sticking to the sweat on her face, her lips quivering.

I lean closer to her cheek. "Don't stop," I mutter.

Her eyes flutter closed, and she shifts a little, lifting her ass from the bed. She's so wet, I can hear her fingers in her pussy, I can hear her rubbing her clit. My mouth is fucking watering.

"That's a good girl," I whisper, putting my lips right up against her ear. "What are you thinking about?"

She quivers, tilting her head back and pressing her cheek against my mouth. "You."

This was a bad idea.

I push the sheet away, looking down between our bodies at her ass as she writhes on the bed. Humans fuck in here all the time, right? They don't get caught. No one's guarding the door. No one would know...

I put my hand between her legs, feeling her fingers working as she fucks herself, getting closer and closer.

"Silas," she whimpers, and my willpower shatters.

Juliet stops as I tear her panties down, planting her hands on the bed, panting. I'm about to unzip myself when there's movement in the corner of my eye, and someone lets out a muffled yelp. I look up into the face of the woman who sleeps in the bed beside Juliet.

Gina's eyes are wide with horror.

Fuck.

I hold out a hand, then bring a finger to my lips. "It's OK," I whisper urgently. "Nothing happened. She's alright. I thought she was sick."

"Sick?" Gina hisses.

"I'm fine." Juliet pushes herself up onto her elbows as I climb off the bed. "I promise. He didn't hurt me."

The person in the next bed begins to stir, and I quickly pull the sheet back over Juliet.

"What the fuck is happening?" Gina asks, swinging her legs over the edge of the bed.

"Nothing, nothing," Juliet says, pushing herself up into a sitting position. "It was just-"

"*He pulled down your underwear!*" Gina's voice is getting louder, and someone raises their head from their pillow.

I stalk to Gina's bed and grip her throat. Her eyes bug out as I push her back down onto her pillow. "*You didn't see a fucking thing, do you understand me?*"

She's spluttering, her lips moving but nothing but whistling breaths coming out of her.

"*Nothing happened,*" I snarl in her face. "You didn't see *anything,* do you understand?"

She nods, a frenzied jerking of her head as I squeeze her throat.

"*Not. A fucking. Word.*" I raise my eyebrows. "Now go to sleep." I release her and she rolls away from me, clutching the sheet over her head.

I turn back to Juliet, who's kneeling on her bed. Her head tips back to look up at me, her lips parted. I expected to see fear, resentment, shock.

But she's gazing at me, trembling, her hands clasped between her thighs. She's still a little breathless, and she pushes the hair from her face. And then she smiles at me.

Filth and sin. I fucking knew it. I walk to her side, reaching out to stroke her cheek.

"Get some sleep, angel."

She leans into my touch for a brief moment before she lies back down, on her stomach again, that delicious ass on display for me. Heat claws at my throat, and I back away before anyone else wakes up and I end up threatening the entire fucking dorm.

I head back outside, inhaling the cold night air through my nose. Fuck, I wish I had a cigarette. Something, anything, to try and take the edge off the need to have her in my fucking bloodstream.

That was idiotic. That was too stupid. I threatened a human because I got caught. *Nearly* got caught. Jesus fuck, what is wrong with me?

But she smelled so good. She *felt* so fucking good. She was so close, hot and slippery, that pussy screaming to be filled, just inches from me. I grit my teeth as I imagine watching my cum drip out of her.

I run a hand over my heated face, and decide that next time I'm going to pick my moment.

Next time, I'll find a way to get her alone.

THE FIRST SIGN that something weird is going on comes in the cafeteria. Someone bumps into me, making the coffee cup on my tray wobble, brown liquid dribbling over the edge. I turn towards them, muttering an apology out of habit, and I stop short when I see their face.

The man, Jeff I think his name is, looks terrified. His brown eyes are wide as he backs away from me.

"S-sorry," he stutters, sweat visibly beading on his forehead.

"No problem, it was an accident."

The others walk past me with their heads bent, avoiding looking at me, almost scurrying away from me. I shake my head, heading for a place near the window. When I sit down on the bench, the people nearby shuffle away from me.

What the fuck?

Gina sits down opposite me, and a few heads shoot up, eyes full of alarm. I meet her gaze, and she's frowning.

"What is going on?" I ask quietly.

"I was hoping you'd tell me," she replies, leaning across the table to take my hand.

"What do you mean?"

She clicks her tongue. "Come on now, I saw what that feeder was doing to you the other night."

"He wasn't *doing* anything to me."

Gina squeezes my hand, leaning forward, her brow furrowing with concern. "Baby, I know you're young and you want love, that's normal. We've all seen how close you and this vamp have become."

I yank my hand out of her grasp and cast a glance around the cafeteria. Eyes shoot down to plates, heads snapping away from me.

I look back at Gina, my jaw dropping. "Everyone's weird with me because of *Silas?*"

"They all think you're his favorite or his pet or something." Her eyes flicker from side to side, and she leans closer. "Some people are saying he's feeding off you."

I cough out a laugh. "Oh my god, this is ridiculous. Everyone knows they're not allowed to bite us."

"They're not allowed to have sex with us either." She reaches across the table to try and take my hand. "I *saw* him take off your panties. He was lying right on top of you."

I bury my hands in my lap, leaning back away from her. "You didn't see that, that's not what happened." I can't look at her as I lie. I cast my eyes down to the table, and I can feel her gaze burning into my face.

"*Pequeña*, what is going on?"

"Nothing."

She sighs heavily, throwing her hands in the air. "Baby, I can't help you if you won't talk to me. You'd think you'd have had enough bullshit with that other asshole."

"Silas is nothing like him," I snap, and when I look up at her, she's crossed her arms over her chest and is giving me that Mom look. *That* look. Like she knows. She knows exactly what's going on. "Silas cares about me, OK? He's my friend."

"A friend who wants to screw you in a dorm full of sleeping people?" She tilts her head. "Baby, he's not good for you. He's your goddamn prison warden."

"He's not like that. And he wasn't going to screw me."

"How can you let a predator like that touch you? After everything you've gone through."

"He is not a predator!"

"He *threatened* me." Gina emphasizes the word, and a few heads turn in our direction. "That's what you like, is it? A friend who chokes me out because I caught you two-"

"You didn't catch us!" I spring to my feet. "Nothing happened! Alright? Nothing!"

Gina leans back, shaking her head. I look around at all the staring eyes. There's looks of disbelief, fear... and disgust. They all think I'm some vamp whore. I can't take them all just staring at me. I can't take them all judging me like this.

I push out of the cafeteria, into the rain, mumbling something about needing fresh air to the vamp at the door. He doesn't stop me, and now I really am wondering if I have Officer's Whore privileges. For some stupid reason, the thought sends tears pricking at my eyes.

I dash them away as I head across the grass. It's a misty morning, and the damp clings to my cheeks, coating my throat as I breathe in deeply to try and stay composed. I walk down to the garden, my mind racing. The humans see me as a traitor? All because I'm friends with a vamp?

Friends.

Silas and I aren't just friends anymore. As much as I wanted to lie to Gina, as much as I've tried to convince myself it's not true, we want each other. We've been toeing a line that's loaded with 10,000 volts, waiting for the shock, like it's going to catch us by surprise. But even if we feel it now, we're both ignoring it. We're in too deep.

I tried so hard to push him away, so terrified I'd cause him to get caught, and hurt. But that night, the night he caught me, the thoughts of him and what I wanted him to do to me were too much. The shock I felt when he was suddenly lying over me, the thrill I felt when he touched me, when he pulled my panties down...

Just thinking about it now makes my stomach clench with desire.

I claw my hands through my hair. This is wrong. I'm not supposed to feel like this. I should be afraid of him. I should be repulsed by him. I shouldn't want to have anything to do with him. Gina said it herself- he's a predator, a monster.

But he's nothing like Matt. He's nothing like Braun. He's beautiful and dangerous and looks at me in a way no man has ever looked at me before.

I like him. I like him a *lot*.

I stop in the orchard, the trees around me bare of fruit and leaves. I tip my head up to the rain, taking a deep breath. A shiver runs down my back, a warm, familiar rush. That shock tingles at my fingertips.

"I know you're there."

Silas's footsteps move to my side. I open my eyes and turn my head towards him. Rain is pearling on his face, dripping from his hair. He gazes down at me, softness and darkness all at the same time.

"You alright?" He asks.

"No."

"What's wrong?"

I bite my lip, trying to decide what to ask first.

"That night you dragged me off to the shower, after you caught me with Matt. Why did you do that?"

He sighs, his eyes dipping to the floor. "Come on, we should get you out of the rain."

"Answer the question."

His gaze flashes back up to me. "Why do you think?"

I swallow hard. "You were jealous."

"Something like that."

"You could smell him on me."

"Yes."

"And you couldn't take it." I hug my arms around myself. "The others, they all think I'm yours too. Like I'm your pet."

He growls. "They have no idea. Fuck what they think."

"Yeah, fuck them." I tilt my head to give him a side glance. "Speaking of fucking..."

His gaze is pure lust and shadow as he looks back at me. "Speaking of fucking?"

"The other night, in the dorm... When you caught me..." The words hang in the air, sparks passing between us as we test that line.

His mouth shifts into a crooked grin. "I could smell you, getting yourself off."

My cheeks burn at the thought, and so does my clit. Holy fuck, the heat between my thighs almost takes my breath away as he gazes at me. I lick my lips, because suddenly everything feels hot and tight. He watches the sweep of my tongue, and his eyes start to change color.

"There was a night, when someone stood over my bed, and smelled me after I got myself off. Was that-"

My question is cut off as he grabs my arm, pulling me into one of the wooden work sheds at the edge of the garden. He slams the door behind us, and has me against the hard edge of a bench. I catch myself on my hands, breathing hard as I look up at him.

His arms cage me in place on either side of the bench, and his body is so agonizingly close. He's stunning and terrifying at the same time. He could snap me in two, split me in half, so easily.

Fuck, I hope he does.

"That was me, that night." His eyes wander over my face, his jaw ticking as though he's fighting some internal battle with himself. "And every night since. I'd stand over your bed, and smell you, and think of all the things I'd do to you if you were mine."

I raise a hand to reach out to him, but he jerks his head away from my touch, his eyes staying on my face.

"I need you to understand something about me," he says in a low voice. "I want you, so badly it fucking terrifies me. I've never wanted anyone as much as I want you."

I open my mouth to speak, to protest, to tell him that I want him to, but he seizes my chin.

"I want to fucking own you." His eyes drop to my lips as his thumb sweeps across them. "I want to own every fucking inch of you. I want to kill every man who's ever touched you before me. I want to fuck every trace of them out of you. Because I want you to be *mine.*"

My lip trembles under his touch, and his jaw sets. Self-loathing twists his face, his eyes filling with a sort of quiet yet furious defeat. He's expecting me to be disgusted by him. He's expecting me to shove him away, to run and tell him to never come near me again.

"And what if I want to be yours?"

It's like we both stop breathing for a second. I lift my hands to his face, stroking the backs of my fingers down his cheeks. His eyes flicker for a moment, and he exhales heavily.

"I want you, Silas." I cradle his face in my hands. "I knew the moment I got out of that lake. It wasn't just whatever you drugged that blanket up with. It was *you.* I've wanted you ever since. You're all I think about."

"I'm not a good man, Juliet."

"Was Matt a good man?" I shake my head. "You expect me to see nothing but a monster when I look at you. But I don't. I know that you'll never hurt me. You could have plenty of times. And you never did. I know you'll never hurt me. I trust that."

"I would never hurt you, angel." His arms move around my waist. "I swear it. I'd kill anyone who hurt you."

"I feel safe with you." I wrap my arms around his neck, leaning my body into his.

"I killed Matt."

The air rushes out of my lungs. I'd suspected. I'd wondered. It had all been too odd, too convenient. Now I understand the way he reacted when he'd held me in my hospital bed, guilt eating him up as he thought he'd driven me to do what I did. Not understanding that he was what was saving me.

He keeps his eyes on mine, watching me carefully.

"I killed him because of what he did to you." His hands on my back don't waver, still holding me to him. "He had to die. The way he talked about you, what he'd sacrificed you for... I couldn't let that go unpunished."

"The way he talked about me?"

His jaw feathers as he closes his eyes, seeming to take a steadying breath. When his eyes open again, they're blazing crimson.

"I'm not a good man, and I'll keep not being a good man if it means I can protect you." One of his hands runs up my spine, until it rests at the base of my skull, cradling my head as he leans over me. "Do you know how hard it is, watching you and not being allowed to touch you? Not being allowed to take what I want from you?"

"I wish you could." I pull him closer to me. "I'd let you do whatever you wanted to me."

His eyes flare. "Is that right?"

"I know you'd make me feel good."

"I'd make you feel so fucking good, angel." His lips graze mine.

I close my eyes, feeling a rush as his hand flexes on my back. I almost moan at the touch, and I feel his lips turn up in a smile.

"Silas," I murmur. "If you don't kiss me now, I'm going to go crazy."

His hand moves under my sweater, over my heated skin. "I like the idea of you going crazy. I bet you'd be a lot of fun crazy." His grip on the back of my head becomes firmer as he holds me in place. His body still has me pinned against the bench, and I gasp as his hand cups my breast. "I want you crazy. I want you fucking unraveled at the seams for me."

"Most guys tell me they'll be gentle," I say, sucking in a breath as he pinches my nipple hard.

"I'm not going to be gentle with you, angel." He chuckles darkly against my ear. "Because I can feel you're desperate to be destroyed."

My pussy is flooded with heat at his words, and I buckle a little in his grasp. "Silas, please."

In an instant he lifts me up and places me on the bench. His hips push my thighs apart, and I wrap myself around him as his hands hold my head. His mouth descends on me, and fire rushes through me because he's kissing me, he's finally kissing me. His fangs prick my lower lip, but the pain just turns me on even more. His tongue strokes inside my mouth and all of me opens up for him. All of me wants him, any way he wants me.

I'm melting against him. No one's ever kissed me like this before. The shock zaps through my veins, because the line we weren't meant to cross, we've stormed past it. There's no going back now. *This isn't allowed, this isn't allowed, this isn't allowed* - the words reverberate through my head over and over, but any sense I might have had, any self-control he had, it's been obliterated.

"What will they do to you?" I murmur as he releases my mouth.

He shakes his head. "I don't care."

"But-"

"If this is all we have, I don't care. If this is all the time we have together, I don't care." He kisses my neck, his fangs raking hard against my skin, and the pain makes my toes curl in the best fucking way. I yank at the buttons on his shirt, our fingers frantically fighting to get his clothes off.

He throws off the shirt and tugs my sweater off over my head. He cups my breast, lowering his mouth to my nipple. My heels drag up his legs as I moan, locking my legs around his waist. I'm trying to stay upright, catching myself on my hands, then my elbows as his body leans over me. I can't resist. I don't want to. His fangs brush against my nipple as he sucks hard, his other hand moving down over my stomach into my pants.

His groan echoes against my skin as his fingers stroke over my panties. "So wet for me, angel," he says, lifting his head. "This needy little cunt is so desperate to be fucked."

I move to shuffle my pants off, and Silas hooks his fingers into my waistband, tearing them down my legs. I'm lying on a bench in a garden shed, totally naked, in front of a vampire who looks like he's pondering which part of me to eat first. He runs his hands up my thighs, and I quiver under his touch.

"I want to see you too," I gasp, pushing myself up on my elbows. "I want to see all of you."

His belt buckle clinks as he flicks it open, and my breath catches a little as his dick springs free from his pants. He's huge - I already knew that. But his dick is *pierced*. Two metal balls adorn the blunt head, and he grins at me as my eyes meet his again.

"Makes it better for both of us, trust me."

I let out a breathless laugh, and he advances on me. He leans over me, his hands splayed over my breasts as his mouth moves over my stomach. His lips are soft, but every now then there's a sharp scratch of his fangs, and the combination sets me totally on edge. Who am I fucking kidding, I'm already on edge. I moan and writhe under his hands, under the hot breath washing across my skin. I can't tell if the thundering in my ears is my own blood roaring or the deafening rain on the roof.

"Are you going to bite me?"

He straightens up, running his hands down my body. "I haven't bitten anyone in years." His eyes meet mine. "I want to taste you, angel, but fuck if I do that now, I'll make you come harder than you've ever come in your life, and I want to feel you first."

His words make my heart race almost painfully against my rib cage. I exhale heavily around a moan as Silas presses himself to my entrance, but instead of pushing inside me, he teases my clit with the head of his cock. His piercing strikes me over and over again in just *that* way, and my thighs squeeze around his hips.

"Oh fuck, *fuck*, Silas, holy *shit*." I'm panting, my back arching off the bench as he continues to fuck my clit. "*Ah,* oh my god."

"That's it, angel. Fuck, I want to hear you."

My thighs begin to tremble, clenching either side of him, my orgasm building. "Don't stop," I moan. "Oh god, don't stop."

I look up at him, at his blazing red eyes, and cry out as my climax shatters through me. Silas barely gives me a second to catch my breath, running a hand up my back and pulling me upright. He looks down, his breathing hitched as he pushes his cock inside me. God, he's so *hard*. I whimper and moan as he pushes, more and more. Oh fuck, I still haven't taken all of him.

"You're too big," I gasp, and his grip on the back of my head tightens. His eyes meet mine, and he pulls out a little.

"You can take it, angel." He pushes my thighs further apart, keeping his eyes on me as he slides back inside me. This time, he pushes all the way in, and holy *fuck*. He kisses me, swallowing down the cry that leaves my lips. "OK?" He asks, gently biting my lower lip.

"Yeah." I'm more than OK. I'm so much more than OK right now, filled with him, his body so hot against mine.

"You should have told me to stop, angel." He groans as he thrusts into me.

"No, never." I press him closer with my thighs. "I need you." I whimper as he thrusts again, and his brow furrows as he pants against my lips.

"Am I hurting you?"

I growl as I nip at his lips. "Fuck me til I'm sore. Please."

That dark, threatening chuckle rumbles through his chest. "Such a dirty fuckdoll." He withdraws from me, pulling me down off the bench and spinning me around. He bends me over, running his hand down my back as I press my hands flat, looking over my shoulder at him.

When he does sink back into me, we both moan. I reach back for him, and he twists my arm so it's pressed against my back. *Oh fuck, yes.* I curl my other arm back so he can hold me down completely. With his other hand he grips my hair, winding it around his fist. I want to be at his mercy. I want him to fuck me and use my body and make me come.

I want to *feel like I'm his.*

He fucks me hard, hitting me so deep inside that it almost hurts. But when I breathe out, relaxing into the feeling and surrendering to him completely, it feels so fucking good. I close my eyes, opening up for him, letting him push into my body over and over again.

The line is miles away. There's no going back now.

And I don't ever want to.

"Fuck, so fucking tight," he murmurs as he slams into me, grasping my arms and pulling my hair. "*Fuck.*"

My toes curl, lifting me up against him, making me even tighter, and I feel my next climax building.

"Ohhh, god, Silas, I'm going to... *Oh god.*" My legs are trembling, and I can barely keep myself upright.

"Let go for me, angel, let that pussy come all over my cock." He hisses in a breath.

Even as wet as I am, there's still friction, and the drag of his piercing right against my g-spot - how can sex feel this good?

Silas is gasping and moaning, I've never been with a man who's given his pleasure a voice like this. It makes it all so much hotter, hearing just how much he's enjoying this. How much he's enjoying *me*. His grip on me doesn't release, not even a bit, and it makes me come even harder. My second climax crashes through me, and coming with him inside me, feeling the pulse of my body around his cock, heightens every single sensation.

Silas releases my hand, pulling me up against him by my hair. His fangs brush against my neck, like he's hesitating.

"Please," I murmur. "Do it, please."

With a groan, he strikes, just as he fills me again.

I knew the bite would feel good, he'd told me that. He'd said it would make me come. But I wasn't prepared for his bite to send the most violent orgasm I've ever experienced coursing through me. It peaks over my last climax, lighting up my whole body, sending it crashing and shattering, falling apart for him. He drinks down my blood, his tongue lapping it up in long, hot sweeps over my skin.

His fangs pull out of my neck, and he grinds into me as I

ride out the high, as I feel him tense against my back. I *feel* him come inside me, feel his heat fill me, spilling out of me. He groans out his release against my neck, turning my face towards his, kissing me so I taste the copper of my blood that's glazing his tongue.

He pants against my mouth, muttering out curses and praise, telling me how beautiful I am, how fucking sexy I am, how I was made for him. I settle into the euphoria, that post-fuck haze that makes my heart thump and my blood sweeten. His fingers are still tangled in my hair, his other hand wrapped around my throat, his cock still seated deep inside me. I feel utterly possessed and strangely whole, in a way I've never experienced before.

"Fucking hell, angel."

"Can we do that again?"

He laughs dangerously, pressing kisses down my throat. "My needy little fuckdoll."

I moan, rolling my hips on him.

"You like the names, don't you?" He growls against my skin.

"Yeah." He's still hard, and I rock my hips, bouncing myself on him. "I-I only like it from you. I don't - oh *fuck*." I whimper as he holds me still, wrapping his arms around my waist. "I don't want to stop."

"Me neither, but I need to." He withdraws from me, turning me around gently in his arms as I quiver. Blood lines his lips, and his eyes are still that blazing crimson. He strokes his fingers over my pulse, over the spot where he bit me, and inhales heavily. "I nearly bit you when I came, and..."

Bad memories. I wrap my arms around his waist, drawing him close to me. I nuzzle into his broad, warm chest, dark with tattoos. "I told you, I trust you."

He brushes his hands over my hair. "I know, angel."

Thunder rumbles overhead, and suddenly tears are biting at my eyes. I sniffle and Silas's whole body tenses, tipping my face up to his.

"What's wrong?" He raises his eyebrows, his fingertips running over my cheeks. "Jules, what's wrong?"

My lips tremble. "I want to stay with you. I want to *be* with you, and I can't be." I throw my arms around his neck, sobs bubbling up my throat. "I fucking hate this life. I hate this place. I hate that we can't be together."

He pulls back from me, taking my arms and removing them from around his neck. I panic for a moment, thinking he's pushing me away. But then he raises one hand to his mouth, tenderly kissing my palm. He repeats the action with my other hand, his soft lips pressing against my skin.

I start to cry harder.

His eyes are fading back to their normal rusty color when they meet mine again. "If you think I'm going to regret this, I won't. Even if that makes me selfish."

I shake my head, hot tears cascading down my cheeks. "You're not selfish. I don't regret it. I just want... I want more than what we have. More than just this."

"I know." He pulls me close to him, wrapping his huge arms around me. It's the safest I've ever felt in my life, skin to skin with a predator who could tear me to shreds.

"Maybe you could tell them I am your pet." I laugh cynically, brushing my tears away with the heel of my hand. "We're not really people are we? We're just bloodbags. What would it matter if-"

He cuts me off, punishing my mouth with a bruising kiss. "Don't say that," he mutters, shaking his head. "Don't fucking say that."

I let him hold me, slumping against him, taking in all the heat of his body and letting him warm me up. He keeps kissing me, hard but slow, and with each stroke of his tongue he claims another part of me. I'm his, forever, whatever that means. But even as he draws me back into that warm haze, even as I wrap myself around him and swear to never let him go, I know. I know that trouble lies ahead. I can feel the storm clouds crackling on the horizon.

We may have crossed the line - but reality is going to keep tugging us back, back, back. Until the shock finally catches up with us.

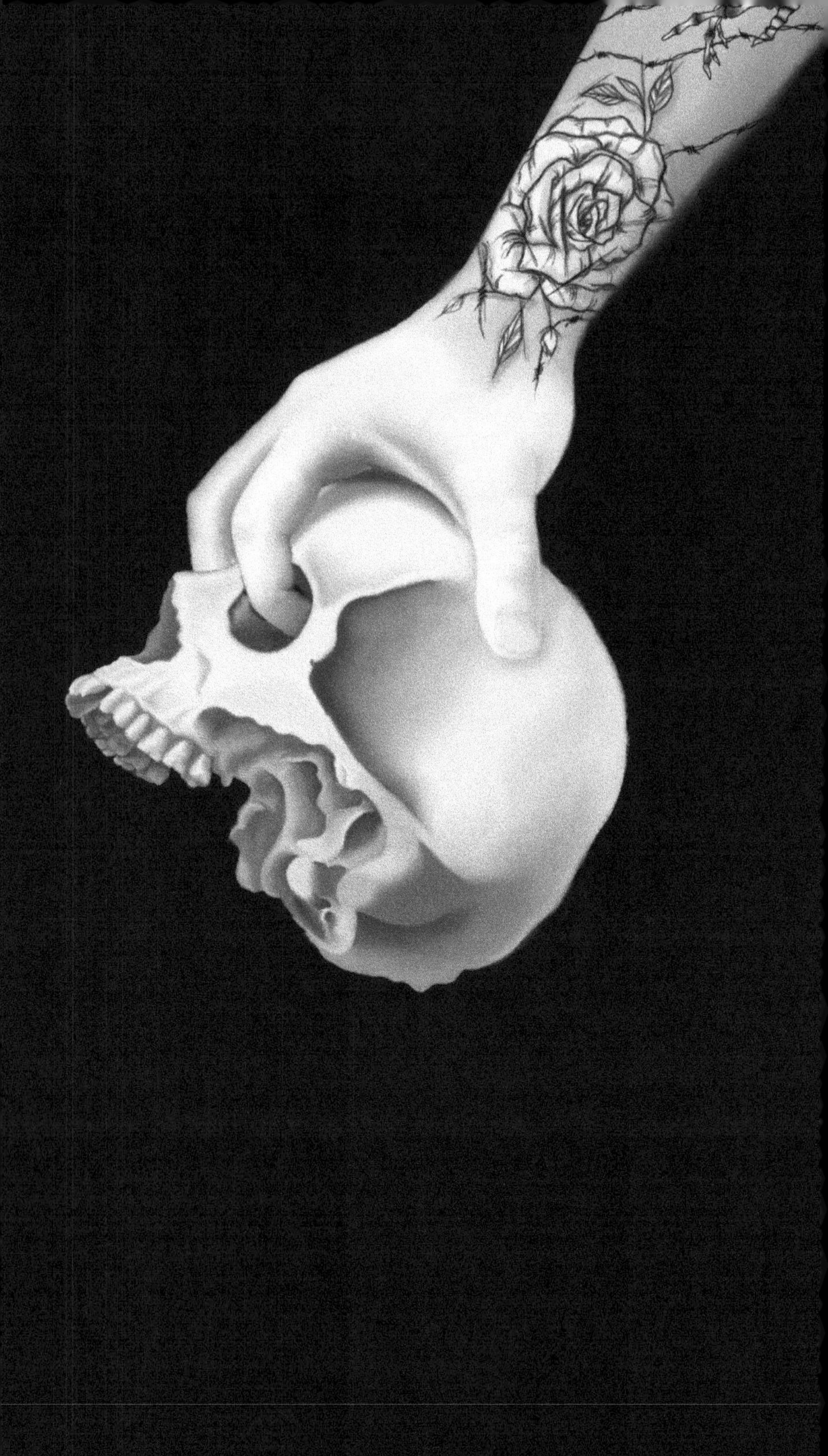

CHAPTER 26

SILAS

WATCHING a woman you've fucked performing her mundane daily chores is torture.

I stand at the edge of the garden as Juliet digs in the vegetable patch with the others, as they plant in preparation for harvest, and all I can focus on is the curve of her thighs, remembering what they felt like pressed around my hips. What her cunt felt like as I drove my cock into it. What her blood tasted like as it ran down my throat.

She was perfect. I'd known she would be, but she was even more than I thought. She was begging to be overpowered, to be fucked and worshipped. She's addictive in the most dangerous way possible. That one encounter has me needing more, I need to fill all of her, I need to mark all of her as mine.

Instead I have to stand here and watch as she works away, tending plants and tossing that blonde hair over her shoulder. It's tied up in a ponytail right now, and I imagine wrapping it around my fist, sinking into her.

Having her once didn't sate anything. It made everything even more acute.

Every now and then she looks up and catches my eye. She

gives me that slow smile, the freckles around her mouth dancing as she does. I have to clench my fists to stop myself charging across the yard and seizing her in my arms.

I can still feel the heat of her blood as it poured down my throat. The sweetest taste I've ever experienced. I want to wrap her up, hide her away, spend our days fucking and tasting each other.

I chew the inside of my cheek as I think of her crying. Hating this life. Wanting to be away from here. Wanting to be with me, just *me*.

How do I keep her safe?

"Silas!" Sam's voice rings across the garden, and I turn to see her waving me up towards her.

"What's up?" I haven't really spoken to her since she accosted me in her office, but if she feels awkward she doesn't let it show. Her face is neutral, almost friendly.

"Hey, a few of the sensors on the grid aren't showing up," she says, gesturing towards the front gate. "There's a major storm warning, and the last thing we need is an outage in the system."

"Uh, yeah of course, I'll drive out and check on them."

"How is she?" Her gaze remains level as my head snaps in her direction.

"What?"

She jerks her head down towards the garden. "The girl, is she doing better?"

"She's fine, why?"

Sam cocks an eyebrow. "You're acting weird, everything OK?"

Everything's fine, I just broke every rule we're meant to adhere to and not only did I bite a human, I fucked her and made her come a handful of times, no big deal.

"I'm fine, just worried about this storm, you know?" As if on cue, thunder rumbles in the distance.

"Yeah, well go on out and check these sensors, hopefully the grid holds up." She takes a step closer to me. "If the power goes out, maybe we can keep each other entertained."

I jam my hands in my pockets and back away from her. "I better go."

She lets out a little grunt as I turn away from her. I head straight for the office to get the truck keys and my laptop, my head swimming with thoughts of Juliet. Those filthy thoughts are mingled with the weight of the consequences of what I've done.

I should feel bad for violating my position. I'm her captor. She has no power here.

But I can't bring myself to sully what I feel for her. I haven't violated her. I haven't abused her. If anything she made it more than clear that she wants me. *Fuck me til I'm sore.* Fucking christ. My girl is filth and sin, just like I thought. She wants to be mine, she wants me to possess her.

I can't feel bad about that.

But if we get found out...

I hiss in a breath through gritted teeth as I turn back down towards the gardens instead of heading for the truck like I should. The horizon is thick with threatening black clouds, the air oppressive and thick.

You're an idiot, Silas. Turn around. Go back to the truck.

Like a true addict, I tell the voice to go fuck itself.

Juliet is emerging from a shed, brushing hay from her clothes, when I seize her around the waist, one hand clapped over her mouth. I drag her behind the building, out of sight of the others.

"Shhh, it's me." I nip at her earlobe, feeling the thump of

her racing pulse a mere inch from my lips. "I need to head out before the storm, come with me."

She shakes her head, her mouth still covered, a mumbled protest against my palm.

"I'm not taking no for an answer." I brush my hand over her breast, and she whimpers. "Come on."

I release her, taking her hand and pulling her along behind me.

"Silas, you're crazy," she hisses behind me, but she doesn't resist.

I pause at each corner, checking that the coast is clear before I pull her along. The compound is busy but everyone seems preoccupied, worried about the impending storm. They don't even notice us.

We reach the truck and I open the back door for Juliet.

"No sex blankets this time?" She giggles as I shove her in.

"Just keep your head down," I tell her, and slam the door shut. I climb into the driver's seat, and take a deep breath, looking over my shoulder at her curled up behind the passenger seat. She grins up at me, and I smile back. "Stay quiet, we'll be out of here in just a minute."

The guards at the gate are similarly preoccupied as the others in the compound, waving me out impatiently. The sun is still beating down, but the black clouds beckon in the rear view mirror as the storm draws closer. We clear the compound by a mile before I slow down and turn back to look at her.

"You can come out now."

She climbs over the back seat, but shocks the shit out of me by getting on her knees on the passenger seat and unzipping my trousers.

"How did I know you'd already be hard?" She says with a grin. She pushes my arm out of the way so she can put her face in my lap.

"*Fuck!*" I hiss out, spearing my fingers into her hair as her mouth descends on my cock. My head slams back against the headrest. "Such a dirty little slut, aren't you? Fuck, angel. So fucking greedy for my cock."

She moans, the sound vibrating through me and making me clench my molars together so I don't tear the steering wheel clean from the dash. The girl that was worried about not being able to take all of my cock yesterday is now taking me so deep, hollowing her cheeks as she bobs up and down. I shove her down onto me, and she moans again.

"You love having your mouth fucked, don't you?"

Her tongue swirls over my head, flicking at my piercing, and I don't know how I'm still managing to drive. I look down to watch that pretty head bobbing furiously, her hot wet mouth dragging me closer to the edge. I grip her hair and tilt her head so I can see those pink lips wrapped around me. Fuck, she's perfect. My dirty fuckdoll.

I stop the truck, pressing my foot down on the brake. I watch as she moves, as she sucks me hard. Tears pearl at the corners of her eyes, but she doesn't stop. I'm hitting the back of her throat, and she chokes a little but keeps going.

"Fuck, yeah, that's it. Don't stop. Don't fucking stop." I groan as my climax stabs through me, my stomach tensing before I exhale heavily and pump the hot streams of my release into her mouth. She bobs gently, swallowing and licking up everything I give her.

When she lifts her head, she's beaming, positively triumphant. I shake my head, smiling, and reach out to stroke her lips.

"You're full of surprises, aren't you?"

She nips at my thumb with a grin. "I couldn't stop thinking about you. I spent all night in that fucking bed all on my own, thinking of all the things I wanted to do with you."

I want to ask her what she did, how many times she made herself come thinking of me, but my foot is still on the brake and the truck is idling. I put my foot on the gas, the truck lurching forward towards the perimeter sensors.

"What are we doing out here?" She asks as we bounce across the field.

"There's a storm coming and the sensors are out," I reply, driving the short distance and bringing the truck to a stop. Without a word I jump down from the truck and round it, tearing her door open. The look on her face tells me she's ready for exactly what's coming.

I pull her down from her seat, spinning her around as I yank down her pants. I rut into her hard, and she squeals, scrambling against the seats of the truck.

"So wet and ready for me, aren't you?" I dig my fingers into her hips as she moans. "Dirty fuckdoll, this cunt is always desperate for me, isn't it?"

"Yeah," she gasps. "Fuck, yeah."

The sun beats down on us, sweat beading between us as I continue the relentless rhythm of my hips against hers. She's so wet and tight, and she cries out and moans, clawing into the truck seat.

"Stroke that clit, angel," I say, and she obeys immediately. "That's it, just like when you think of me at night."

"Oh fuck," she breathes, her back arching. I brace a hand against the frame of the truck, slamming into her, so wet she's dripping down my fucking balls. I want to bite her, I want the violent buzz of her blood flowing down my throat, but I hold back, wanting to be in the moment and feel her come on my dick.

And *fuck*, when she does, she's so tight I tumble right down after her, spilling and spilling inside her until I'm running right out of her. She slumps on the truck seat, sweaty and trembling.

I pull out to look at her glistening pussy, swollen and pink, and so fucking beautiful. An aftershock of her orgasm rushes through her, her hips jerking, and a rope of my cum drips out of her.

"Fucking perfect," I murmur, stroking her ass.

"Is this how you fix the sensors?" She grins over her shoulder at me.

"If it is, I hope they go out every single day."

With a heavy breath she pushes herself up, turning around as she pulls her pants up. "Me too." She wraps her arms around my neck and kisses me. I clutch her to me, tasting her perfect mouth. When she pulls back from me, she's giving me that slow smile again, the sun illuminating those big grey eyes, and she's the most perfect thing I've ever seen.

"If I'm ever too much, you tell me," I say, running my hands up her back.

She frowns. "Too much? You mean, like, during sex?"

"Yeah. I, uh, have some proclivities, and I don't want to hurt you. Mentally or physically."

She cocks an eyebrow and drapes her arms over my shoulders. "Proclivities? That sounds ominous."

"I like... things I probably shouldn't. Like, the word no."

Her face betrays the tiniest hint of shock.

"I don't mean like that," I say quickly. "I mean, I'd never do anything you didn't want. But I like the pleading. And the names."

"I happen to like being called your dirty slut." She nips at my lips. "Makes me feel special."

"Mmmm, I noticed." I curl my arms around her waist, pressing a kiss to her forehead. "I mean it though. We don't do anything you don't want to do."

She nuzzles into me with a happy sigh. "I love how sweet you are to me."

My lungs contract painfully at her words. I thought she was about to say something else. The leap my heart just took, *fuck*.

She seems to notice the tension in my body, and gazes up at me. "Are you OK?"

I smile and nod, stroking her hair back behind her ears. "Sure am, angel. I should get this done before the storm hits." I pull up my trousers, tucking myself away, her eyes still on my face. "Feels almost like tornado weather."

"Yeah it does." She watches as I pull the laptop from the truck, flipping it open on the seat. She wraps her arms around herself as she takes a few sidling steps away from the truck, and inhales deeply through her nose. "It smells so good out here."

"You smell better."

She giggles. "What was your maker like?"

My fingers pause on the keyboard for a moment. "Margot? What do you mean?"

"Like, what was she *like*? I mean, you loved her right?"

Love. There's that word again. "Yeah. Of course I did."

"So what did you love most about her?"

I keep typing for a moment as I think about Margot. I bring up the sensors that are out, testing the grid, remembering Margot's fingers running down my back. Her hands tangled in my hair. The sweet smell of gardenias that clung to her clothes. The clothes I buried my face in just to hold on to her scent as I lay in our apartment, howling after she'd begged me to kill her.

"Is this hard to talk about?" Juliet's voice is soft and hesitant.

"Sometimes." I reboot the system, the countdown timer telling me it will take five minutes. I turn to Juliet, who's leaning against the truck, regarding me sadly. "Margot was extraordinary. Strong, brutal, intelligent. She saw the world in a way, I don't know. I've never seen someone see the world with so much passion. She saw opportunity everywhere, discovery in everything, you know?"

"Was she beautiful?"

The question makes me wince. "She was so beautiful it hurt. Long black hair, this white skin, it was like ivory. And for some reason, her eyes never went red. They were blue, like a sapphire. She was amazing."

Juliet's head drops, and she clasps her arms tighter around her. "And you had to kill her?"

I clench my eyes shut for a moment. "Yeah. One of the other vamps, he came stumbling in, said he'd been ambushed. I didn't see the bite on his arm, I wasn't paying attention. And he fell on Margot, just attacked her. By the time I got him off her, it was too late. He'd bitten her."

"I'm so sorry," she murmurs.

"She begged me to kill her immediately. She didn't want to suffer." I clench my hands into fists, leaning back against the truck, staring at the ground. "But I refused. Said that maybe she was strong enough, that maybe she could survive it. I was selfish. I couldn't bring myself to do it."

"You're not selfish," Juliet says, looking over at me. "Killing someone you love, I mean, that would be a nightmare."

"I let her suffer though, for days." I swallow hard, misery clawing at the base of my throat. "I just... I couldn't do it. Then her eyes started bleeding, blood pouring out of her. She was so thin, her cheeks were hollow. Her eyes were dull black." The memory makes me shiver, sending icy rivulets down my spine. "She begged me, one last time. Said she couldn't do it. Couldn't live like that anymore. Told me to kill her, and be safe. That she loved me. And if I loved her, I'd do it."

Juliet watches me silently, waiting for the rest of the story.

"So I... I killed her." I can't verbalize how I did it. I can't talk about holding that beautiful head in my lap after I'd torn it from Margot's body. How I hadn't even been able to kiss her one last time, in case I became infected. How I'd sat with her, saying I'm sorry, I'm sorry, over and over.

Juliet shuffles closer and leans her head against my shoulder. "I'm so sorry, baby."

The word *baby* sends me reeling. I put my arm around Juliet's shoulder and tug her close to me. *She's too good for you. She's too good for you.* I try to shut that voice up, the dark specter that fights its way to the base of my skull. I'm not going to hurt her. I'm not going to ruin her.

I know I'm lying to myself.

The laptop blips as the timer ends, and the system alert pops up on the screen. I reluctantly release Juliet, who wanders across the field, gazing at the approaching storm. A breeze springs up as I check the system, finding two sensors that are still out.

"Fuck's sake," I mutter, slamming the laptop shut. "Come on, get in the truck, we need to drive."

"Where to?" She pads back to the truck, her long legs flexing as she climbs in.

"There's two sensors out and I need to see if they're damaged, maybe something dug them up." I gun the engine as the trees around us start to bend and sway in the wind. The sky is darkening, the sun beaming on the clouds making them appear almost black.

"That's one helluva of a storm," Juliet says. "Do you think we'll make it back before it hits?"

"Of course." I hope we do. Last thing I need is for this whole thing to be blown open because I was a fucking idiot and headed out with Juliet right in the middle of a superstorm. If we get locked out of the compound and they discover she's missing, we're fucked. *I'm* fucked.

As though she can sense what I'm thinking, Juliet reaches over and puts her hand over mine on the gear shift.

"You said that you'd get in trouble if they ever found out about us," she says slowly, her fingers grazing over my skin. "What will they do to you?"

"You don't need to know." I raise her hand to my lips, keeping my eyes on the field ahead. "I don't want you to worry about that."

"I'll worry anyway." She fidgets with her fingers. "I don't want anything bad to happen to you."

"It won't." *It fucking might.* I don't say that part out loud.

We pull up just shy of the tree line, and I kill the engine. The wind is rushing through the trees as we climb down out of the truck, and Juliet hugs her arms around herself. The temperature has dropped, clouds rushing across the sun, and the air is so sticky with humidity it feels like it's clinging to my face.

Thunder growls loudly as I flip the laptop open again, checking for the position of the first sensor.

"Silas!" Juliet is standing a few feet away from me, looking down at the ground. "Come and look at this."

I walk to her side, and there's a hole in the ground. Something has dug up the sensor. But the dig is clean, not the clawed scrabbling of an animal. The dirt taken from the hole lies nearby in a neat pile.

The wind roars above us, and my head snaps up.

"Juliet, get back in the truck," I growl.

"What's wrong?"

"Get back in the truck. We're not alone." There's a scent on the breeze, sharp like gunpowder. I can sense someone breathing nearby.

Juliet hurries back to the truck, but before she makes it a bullet whirs past me and hits the side door. She yelps and throws herself down on the ground. I back towards her, keeping my eyes on the forest.

"What's happening?" She cries as another bullet smacks into the black metal.

I don't answer, pushing her under the truck. "Stay down!" Another bullet crashes into the truck as I commando crawl around the other side, opening the door and pulling out the gun from under the dash. Juliet is shivering under the truck, hands clasped over her head.

I lift my head, looking over the hood back toward the forest, and a bullet pings off the bull bar of the truck. Who the fuck is this? I drop back down, leaning against the truck.

"Silas?" Juliet cries out as another bullet smashes one of the windows.

"Stay down, it's OK. It's OK." I scoot forward and lean around the front of the truck. I aim into the forest and fire. I don't like wasting bullets, but the way they're firing, they're either scared or well-armed. No one fires back.

The seconds tick by agonizingly, and I peer back around the truck. No movement.

"Stay here," I whisper to Juliet.

"Don't go out there," she replies urgently.

"I'll be right back. Stay down." I get to my feet slowly, peering over the hood of the truck. Still no movement, no more bullets.

I cross the open expanse between the truck and the forest, waiting for the bite of a bullet into my flesh. They can't kill me, but I wouldn't welcome the pain either way. But none come, and as I get closer to the trees, I can smell someone out here.

Sweat and fear, mixed with gunpowder and leather.

"Who's there?" I call, raising the gun. "Come out!"

There's a snap of twigs, shuffling footsteps.

"I said come out! I can hear you! I can fucking smell you!"

My eyes scan for movement, and then it comes, just inside the tree line.

A man rises to his feet, his hands raised. His skin is pale, his hands shaking. He's wearing a navy blue uniform and a bullet proof vest with the words, *National Guard* emblazoned across it.

"Don't shoot!" He calls. "Don't shoot!"

"Funny request from someone who just shot up my truck," I reply, keeping the gun trained on him. "What the fuck are you doing out here?"

"I was out here taking out your sensors." His honesty catches me a little off guard.

"How did you know where to look?"

He chuckles, spreading his hands. "Got the same tech you do. It wasn't hard to guess where you'd lay the lines."

"So why shoot at us?"

"You're a feeder, my friend." He shrugs. "It's not personal. Though she's human isn't she?"

"Juliet, you better still be under that truck!"

The man chuckles. "She's not."

"You could have killed her." I keep my eyes on him. "She's a human."

"Yeah, that would have been too bad, huh?"

Rage prickles at the back of my throat. "So, you're disrupting our alarms and trying to kill us, what else?"

The man seems to relax, confident I won't shoot him. He lowers his hands and still keeping them where I can see them, taking a few steps past the tree line.

"You feeders have gotta know it's all over now."

"Over?"

He sidles a little closer. " For you and your little human whores." His poisonous gaze lands on Juliet. "I'd hardly call her human anymore. Not when she's been sullied by a dirty fucking feeder like y-"

Juliet yelps as the gunshot rings echoes over the wind that continues to tear through the trees above us. The man's head snaps back as the bullet hits his forehead, skull and brain matter flying as his body crumples to the ground. I try desperately to blink away the red at the edges of my vision, breathing rapidly.

Juliet is at my back, fingers clawing into my shoulders. "Oh my god, Silas, what did you do?"

I don't answer, because the bloodlust flares again as I hear her thundering pulse, as I scent all her delicious fear. I snarl, and her eyes widen as I leer down at her.

"Silas?" She shrieks as I seize her in my arms. "Silas, what are you doing?"

I can feel that caged animal, that intrinsic dark shadow, clawing at my skull, trying to tear free. "Are you afraid of me?"

She twists herself out of my grasp, but we both know I've let her go. The scent of her fear becomes stronger and stronger as she backs away from me, sweet and bitter on the tip of my tongue. It makes my mouth water.

"Have you ever played catch and kiss, little rabbit?" I stalk after her slowly, matching each one of her stumbling footsteps.

"Silas, what's wrong with you?" She brushes the hair out of her face as the wind flings it about. "*Silas?*"

I bare my fangs at her. "Run," I command in a voice that isn't mine. "And believe me, when I catch you, I won't just kiss you." She shudders as I growl, echoing the thunder ringing through the clouds above us. "*Run.* I want to see if I can taste the fear in your blood."

Like a flash, she darts into the forest, long hair flailing out behind her. She has speed, certainly, but nothing compared to me. I match her every move as she weaves in and out of the trees. Rain begins to dot the ground, crashing down in heavy drops.

The darkness within me shrieks and snaps, tearing free of its cage as Juliet's fear becomes more and more potent. I gain on her easily, falling back to keep the game going, until her panting is so loud I can't stand it. I'm so fucking hard, if I don't have her now, I'm going to lose my mind.

I lunge at her, my arms locking around her waist, and shove her against the trunk of a towering tree. She's whimpering and panting, her head slamming back against my shoulder as she says my name and pleads with me.

"Not fast enough, little rabbit." I chuckle into her ear. "Now, what am I going to do with you?" I twist her arms behind her back, holding her to me with one hand as the other wraps around her throat. She sucks in a breath as I squeeze, her ribs contracting against my chest. "I could snap this pretty neck in half, you know."

Her answering moan sets the beast inside me feral. I release her neck as I nick her earlobe, eliciting a small shriek of surprise.

"You like that do you, filthy little whore?" I tear her shirt from her shoulder, scraping my fangs along her bare skin, and she cries out. "How bad do you want it to hurt?"

"M-more," she stutters.

"More?" I bite her shoulder, not releasing enough venom to make her come, but enough to send a wave of pleasure through her body.

I push down her pants, ripping her panties from her body and casting the scrap of fabric to the ground. I shove her against the tree, kick her legs apart, spearing two fingers inside her roughly. She tosses her head back, fighting the pressure of my hand on her arms.

"So wet, does my dirty little fuckdoll like being chased?"

"Oh, oh god." She quivers. Her scent is overwhelming, her blood thundering louder than the roaring wind.

"Are you afraid of me?" I breathe against her ear.

And my girl shakes her fucking head, turning her mouth towards me as she moans.

"N-no." She clenches her eyes shut as my fingers move from her pussy to her clit. "Let me touch you, I want to - *Ah*, oh Silas, *fuck*." She trembles against me. "I want to touch you too."

The feral beast inside me is so thrilled I almost let her go. She's not afraid. Filth and sin. But she slumps against me, letting out a low *Ohhh*, telling me she's almost there.

"You going to come for me, angel?"

"Silas, *please*." She lets out a strangled moan as I move my fingers away from her.

I spin her around, sinking to my knees and not caring that the ground is sodden with mud, that the rain is pelting down on us both or that the storm is well and truly setting in now. She yelps in surprise as I hoist her legs over my shoulders, burying my mouth in her swollen, needy pussy.

"*Silas*," she moans. "*Fuck, fuck*. Ohhh god."

The dark thing inside me bares its teeth, cackling with feral delight because no man has ever tasted this. No man has ever sucked this clit between his lips and heard those beautiful fucking moans echoing in his ears. Fools, all of them.

But thank fuck, because now this belongs to me. This sweet cunt is *mine*. I spear my tongue inside her, dragging it back over her clit, and she hisses out my name. Her hands rake through my hair, trembling, that orgasm she so desperately needs so close I can taste it. She's so goddamn wet. She needs to come, all over my face.

But I need something else. I need my filthy little fuckdoll to come harder than she ever has in her life, and she needs to do that with my cock buried inside her. The red haze is so strong now I can barely see, tasting her as she begins to shiver and moan. Just as she's about to tip over that edge, as her arousal begins to run down my chin, I stop, and she claws at the back of my head, trying to force my mouth back to her pussy.

"Don't stop, don't stop!" She almost sobs.

I hold her against the tree, rising to my feet and pushing down my trousers just enough to free my cock. I plunge inside her, and strike at the same time. Her cries are choked as she comes, shaking and moaning loudly as thunder growls overhead. She tastes like fear and love and sex and sin, hot and sweet, warming my throat and my veins as she crashes through me.

I keep drinking her down as I fuck her, as the white heat flaring at the base of my spine shoots through me, and her nails dig into my back as I fill her pussy up with my release. As her blood runs down my throat. The beast inside me falls silent, sated and full.

Through my heavy breath, through the rain cooling the back of my neck and the long sweeps of my tongue as I lick up her blood, the haze lifts.

And I panic.

I pull back instantly, and she slumps against me. Fuck. I lost control. I bit her, right as I came.

What the fuck have I done?

"Juliet?" I grasp her jaw in my hands, tipping back her head, expecting to see blood, expecting to see eyes blank with death. *You hurt her. You ruined her. You're a monster. You destroy everything.* The voice whispers poison in my ear.

But the panic dissipates, the whirring black blurring my vision clearing. I'm looking into a pair of grey eyes, a face of freckles that dance and shift around her pink lips as she pants and smiles at me. Her hand reaches up to stroke my cheek.

"Are you OK?" She asks.

I stare at her incredulously. "Am *I* OK?"

She nods. "You shot that guy, and then you kind of went, I don't know, crazy?"

I put her on her feet, and she wobbles, bracing her hands against my chest.

"That was bloodlust, killing can do that sometimes."

She sighs lightly. "So like, you want to chase someone?"

"Something like that. I'm - I'm sorry. I didn't want to scare you."

"Oh, you didn't scare me," she says, gazing up at me. "You just surprised me a little, that's all."

This girl. I regard her slack-jawed for a moment, before sweeping her into my arms. I clasp her to me, drinking in her scent, the taste of her blood as it buzzes on my tongue. I can't help but laugh. Accosted by a vamp in the middle of an episode of bloodlust, and my sinful, dirty girl is just *surprised*. I tip her head back and kiss her.

My girl. Mine. Mine. *Mine.*

She giggles against my lips, and licks her own as she pulls back from me. "I can taste myself," she says, her eyes sparkling with all that filth her angelic appearance keeps so well hidden.

The wind begins to howl above us, and a loud clap of thunder reminds me that we need to get back to the compound as quickly as possible.

"Come on, the storm's setting in. Let's go."

"What about the guy?" Juliet asks as she adjusts her clothes. "Do we just leave the body?"

I consider for a moment. "Yeah, no point dragging him back with us."

Juliet shivers on the way back to the truck, thoroughly soaked through. As I hold her trembling frame under my arm, as I remember the bullets flying past her, another burden of reality weighs down on me. Danger is coming at us from more and more corners. How much longer would the compound be safe?

How much longer would I be able to keep her safe from all of this?

As the truck bounces back towards the compound, as rain bursts against the windshield and through the shot-out window, it crashes down on me, as it has a million times before - I have no idea how to stop any of this.

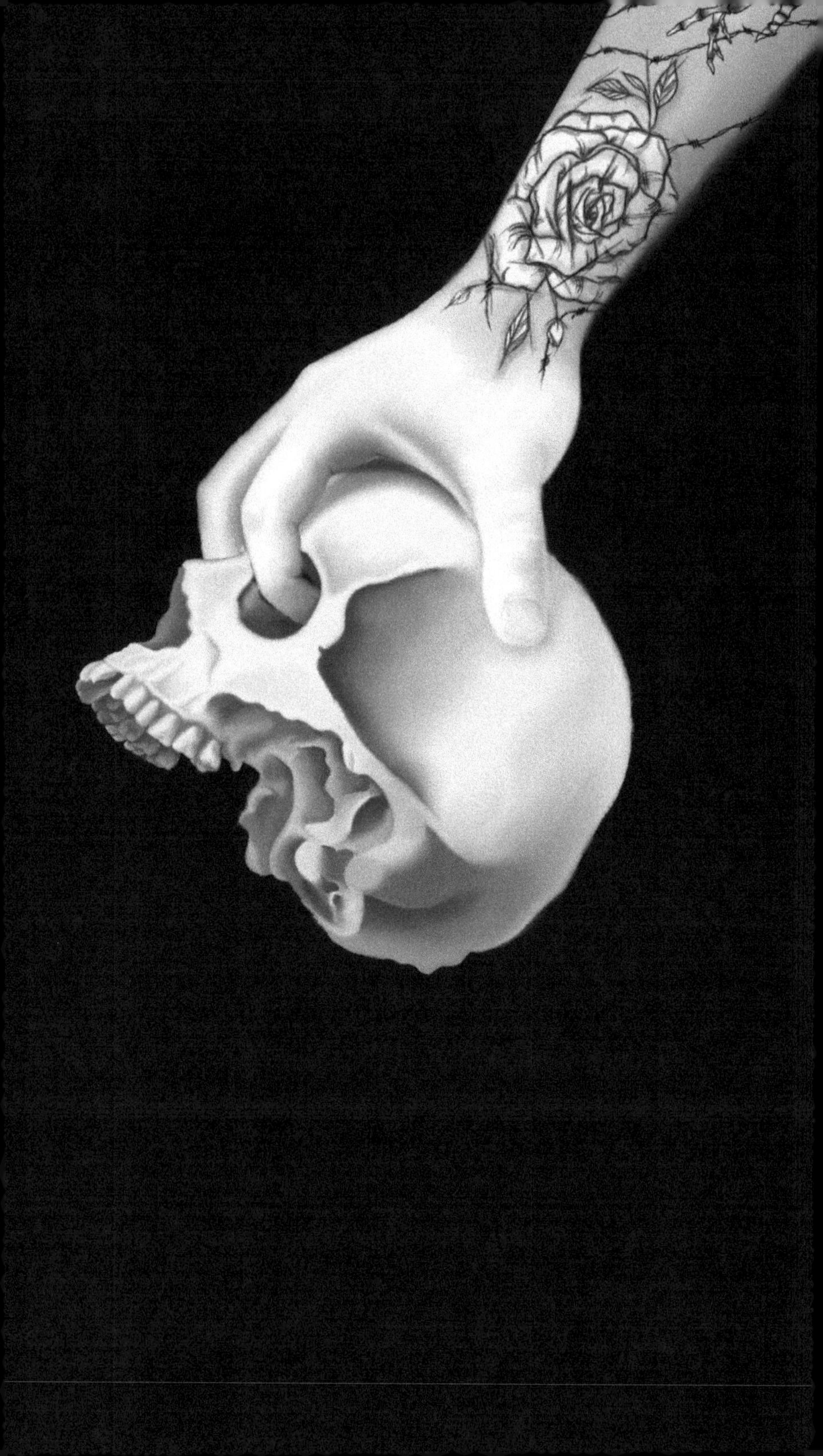

CHAPTER 27

SILAS

ANDERSON REGARDS me with raised eyebrows and an open mouth.

"The National fucking Guard is sabotaging our alarms?" He leans back in his creaking leather chair, steepling his fingers in front of his mouth. "And you said there was only one of them?"

"Yes, just the one, thankfully. He shot at us without a second's thought."

Anderson huffs out a breath, wincing as a crash of thunder sounds above us. "Jesus, this storm." His eyes move back to me. "What do you think? Can we keep the bloodbags safe out here?"

I consider my answer for a moment. I honestly don't think we can, I think we're in danger. I think we need to move to Savannah, we're too isolated out here. Where once being out on our own was considered safer, making us less of a concentrated target for attacks of Afflicted, things have changed now. Our weapons stores are finite.

But all I can think about is Juliet. In a large compound like Savannah, like Boston, I'll never see her. We won't have the freedoms we do here.

And it's with that singular, selfish thought in my head that I meet Anderson's gaze, and shrug.

"I don't think we'd have better chances elsewhere right now, if I'm honest. It's better if we wait to see what Boston says about it."

Anderson seems pleased with this answer, his lips pulled into an expression of approval as he nods. "Great, that's what I hoped to hear."

Rain batters the roof, and the wind howls through the cracks in the windows. Lightning flashes heavily beyond the blinds, and Anderson swivels in his chair to crack them with his finger, gazing outside.

"We'll be lucky if the power stays on," he mulls quietly.

"Well, fingers crossed, ey." I rise to my feet. "If that's all, sir."

"Yeah, thanks King."

I head for the door, my hand on the knob, when Anderson's voice stops me.

"King, just a question."

I half turn back towards him, looking over my shoulder at him. "What is it, sir?"

"You were out there alone, weren't you? Today, I mean?"

"Yes, sir. I was." I nod emphatically. Hopefully not too emphatically.

"You said Us." He narrows his eyes a little. "When you said the National Guard was shooting at you, you said Us. Who's Us?"

Fucking idiot. Fuck fuck fuck. I laugh lightly and shrug. "Sorry sir, bloody British slang, still creeps up on me every now and then."

Anderson's face instantly relaxes, and he laughs too. "Ah, got it." He dismisses me with a jovial wave of his fingers and a nod.

It shouldn't be a big deal, but as I head out into the raging storm, I berate myself over and over. Fucking misspeaking like that, slipping up - it can't happen. I have to be careful. Sneaking Juliet back into the compound in the midst of a massive storm was hard enough. They'd been frantically searching for her and I'd had to make up a story about her getting scared in the forest. Thankfully everyone was too busy to ask questions.

The lights overhead flicker and dim for a moment, like they're breathing, trying to stay alive in the raging storm. They brighten back up, only to flicker again as another gust of wind batters the compound. The sky is filled with one burst after another of lightning, threading its way through the dark clouds as they build above the compound.

A sheet of rain catches me as I head for my cabin, just as a deafening roar of thunder claps directly overhead. The compound is plunged into darkness. Glowing dots of flashlights begin to appear, and I head for the obs tower. Just as I reach the bottom of the stairs, Crawley is there, waving me away.

"It's all out, man. The storm knocked that network right out. We gotta go secure the gates and the bloodbags." He says something else which is drowned out by another growl of thunder directly above us, and he waves his hand, gesturing for me to follow him to the shower block.

Lightning continues to dance around us, sending shadows dancing along the walls, and I hate the fucking panic that begins to whir in my limbs. The compound is unprotected. If the power is out the alarms are out. I don't like this. And the National Guard are no doubt out looking for their man who never made it back...

Crawley throws open the shower block door, shining his flashlight inside. "Anyone in here?" He calls.

A few voices reply, peering into the tunnel of light, holding their hands up and blinking in response. Humans, some wrapped in towels, some half-dressed, walk towards us.

"Powers out," Crawley barks. "We're in lockdown conditions. Into the dorms and stay there."

They all nod their assent, and then the sweet scent hits me like a gut punch. Juliet's walking towards me, her damp hair hanging over her shoulder, dressed in a thin white shirt and tight leggings.

"You go ahead," I say to Crawley, "I'll check the rest of the building for stragglers."

"No problem." Crawley turns, telling the humans to follow him out into the stormy night.

Juliet's gaze lifts to mine as she passes me, and my hand shoots out to wrap around her arm, holding her still. Her eyes don't waver from mine as she waits. The others shuffle out, and we're alone, her grey eyes illuminated by the harsh glow of the flashlight.

"What are you doing?" She asks quietly

"I'm not leaving you in that dorm." I pull her closer to me. "All the power's out, and I don't trust them to keep you safe."

"You're crazy, they'll notice."

"Stay here." I raise my eyebrows, waiting for her to agree. "Stay here, and I'll be back in a minute."

Finally she nods, taking a seat on the bench. "Don't leave me here too long, I don't like the dark."

I give her a crooked smile, and quickly turn on my heel to head after Crawley. As I approach he's waving the humans into the dorm, looking like he's half-counting, but also too put off by the gusts of wind that keep battering us.

"All accounted for." I raise my voice to be heard over the storm. "Shower block's empty."

"Great!" He blinks the rain from his eyes. "Anderson's put out the order for everyone not on shift to stay inside."

"Right, no problems. Not much to be done anyway, ey?"

"Guess not!" Crawley shoves the door closed after the last human walks in and gives himself a shake, like an irritated terrier. "You go on ahead and get out of this rain, you had enough on your plate today."

"Thanks, man." I head off with a wave, checking over my shoulder that he's not watching as I detour to the shower block. *Fucking idiot.* The voice is back, chiding me, cursing me and my stupidity and my addiction to this woman. But I'll be damned if I leave her unprotected. I'd rather face Anderson's full fury and every sadistic punishment he can dole out than leave her out here.

I stick to the shadows, weaving my way back to find Juliet waiting where I left her, her arms wrapped around herself. Wordlessly, she gets to her feet and takes my hand, letting me guide her back to my cabin under the scant cover of darkness, an angry light show flickering through the sky.

But finally, we make it across the compound, to the dark line of cabins. The wind and thunder continue to rage, swallowing up all sound as I hurry Juliet up the stairs and through the door.

"You're crazy," she says as I shut the door. "They'll be looking for me."

"Crawley won't give a fuck, he shoved all the humans into the dorm and closed the door." I run a hand over my face, brushing away the rain. I can still see her, even in the darkness. She's soaked through and shivering lightly. "I'll get a fire going."

"Oh good, it's freezing in here."

There's shuffling sounds behind me, and her scent begins to fill the room.

"This storm is wild."

"Yeah it is." I stoke up the flames, the logs crackling loudly as they catch. When I turn back towards her, she's crept into my bed, her wet clothes discarded on the floor. The firelight catches the gold in her hair, and she smiles at me as I move towards her.

"You're all wet," she says in that sexy, breathy voice that drives me fucking crazy. "You should strip off."

I don't need to be told twice. I remove my clothes, relishing that look she gives me as her eyes move hungrily over my body. This is foolish. This is a bad idea. But I punch that voice down. No one will know. No one will come looking for her, not now.

She's mine, for as long as this storm rages.

And I'm going to take my fucking time with my girl.

I kneel at the end of the bed and pull the blanket down, so I can see her. She smiles and bites her lip as she gazes at me.

"Open your legs," I command, and she does, spreading them not quite wide enough for me to see all of her. But fuck that smell hits my senses, and my fangs suddenly feel ten inches longer. I growl at her. "Wider."

She lifts her hips and opens her thighs more, showing me what I want to see. Then she runs a hand down her stomach, pushing two fingers between the lips of her pussy, spreading them into a V so I can see her swollen clit.

"Better?" That fucking voice. That husky, dangerous voice. It makes me want to do all manner of things to her, right now and all at once.

But I'm taking my time. The rain battering the roof reminds me - I have time tonight.

"So much better, angel." I crawl towards her, and her scent spikes, hot and intoxicating. "Now, for what I want to do to you tonight, I need you to have a safe word, do you understand?"

Fear licks through the scent of her arousal, but that just makes me even harder.

"A safe word?" Her voice drops an octave, and she's as turned on by that flicker of fear as I am.

"Yes, angel. Because saying No or Stop, well…" I run my nose along her thigh, along the line of her veins where her heated blood thunders so close to my lips. "I told you I want to hear you beg, and plead. I meant it."

Her breath catches a little, her nipples peaking and a new rush of blood to her pussy telling me she's more than ready to beg and plead and ask me to stop, while not meaning it at all.

"*But…*" I press a kiss to her inner thigh, grazing her skin ever so slightly with my fangs. "You pick a safe word, and when you say it, everything stops. Instantly. No question."

"Red." She says it so quickly, almost urgently. My dirty little slut wants me to shut up and fuck her.

I chuckle against her skin, so hot and soft, the smell of soap still clinging to it. "Red? So original."

"I snuck books from my mom's office," she says over a gasp as I move my mouth over her stomach. "They were dirty books, or to a kid they were. And their safe word was red."

"Red. OK." I raise myself over her, looking down into that sweet angelic face. It'll be lashed in my cum by the end of the night. "Red, and everything stops, angel. Immediately. No questions as-"

"Oohhhhh my god stop being a gentleman and fuck me!" She closes her eyes, tipping her head back on the pillow, her throat so mouth-wateringly on display.

I huff out a laugh against her throat. "So fucking needy."

Her hips roll underneath me, pressing her wet heat against my dick. I let her do that some more, because holy fuck the anticipation of sinking into that hot pussy is making me drunk. But it's not enough for my girl, because she shoves against my shoulders to push me on my back. Of course I let her. There's no way she could move me unless I let her.

She scrambles on top of me almost clumsily, panting and crazed. She positions herself on top of me, reaching down to guide me inside her. I watch my dick disappear into her cunt, slowly as she adjusts to me at this angle.

"Fuck, you stretch so good for me, angel." I'm clasped so tight inside her it's like she'll never let me go.

"Oh *fuck*," she moans, circling her hips. She tips her head forward, her hair covering her face, like she's hiding. Has my girl gone shy on me? It's almost as though she's never done this before, as though she's never been in control.

"Fuck, angel, do you know how beautiful you look right now?" I caress her thighs, and she raises her chin just enough so I can see her face. I hiss in a breath as she carefully circles her hips again. "You feel so fucking good."

"Yeah?" Another movement back and forth, and a breathless moan.

I grip her hips, not moving her, still letting her lead. "Like a fucking dream. Find that spot, angel, find how it feels good for you."

The praise gives her renewed confidence, and she throws her hair over her shoulders. She leans back, one hand resting on my thigh, holding herself steady as she rocks herself back and forth. She finds that rhythm, that sensation that has sweat beading between our bodies.

She closes her eyes, losing herself in the moment, sinking into that feeling as she rides my cock.

I find myself rocking under her, meeting her movements, because fuck every single movement of her hips has my balls drawing up tighter and tighter. I'm going to fucking come. I've never come with a woman on top. I take three deep breaths, trying to hold off, because watching her like this is too good, it's fucking beautiful.

But I keep rising and rising, my stomach tensing under her hand. I press my thumb to her clit, and she moans, riding me harder as she finds the friction she needs.

"That's it, angel." I didn't want to come this fast, but I remind myself - I have time. Thunder crashes and wind howls through the roof, the storm continuing to rage as Juliet's orgasm tears through her, her cunt so tight around me that I don't even have a fucking choice but to come. Pumping her full of my cum, buried this deep inside her - I couldn't have imagined a better way to start the night.

She's panting, her breasts covered in sweat, glistening in the firelight. Her head is tipped back, the veins in her chest thrumming, tracing a delicious maze leading straight to her nipples. I can't resist. I can't hold back. I sit up and seize her nipple in my mouth, sinking my fangs into her silky skin. She screams, the sound drowned out by another clap of thunder, and her pussy damn near chokes another release out of my cock.

I swirl my tongue over her nipple, sealing the puncture marks, and she shivers. With a small moan she rises off me, onto her shaky knees and collapses onto her stomach on the bed.

Cute. She thinks we're done.

I trace kisses up her spine, over her ribcage. "You were amazing, angel." I roll her onto her back, licking the sweat from her jawline. Her hands are thrown over her head, her eyes closed, her chest pounding.

"I've never done that before," she murmurs.

"So many firsts with me, hmm?" I kiss her gently, her soft lips parting for me. "Lucky me." The taste of this mouth. *Fuck.*

"Silas," she says softly, nuzzling into me.

"Yes, angel?"

"Have you ever done a 69?"

I laugh out loud, and her head snaps to look up at me.

"What?" She sits up and indignantly pushes the hair out of her face. "Also you look really sexy when you laugh. I hate it." She pouts a little, and looks even more fucking adorable.

"You're the sweetest little thing to ever exist, do you know that?" I sit up, leaning on my hands in front of her, nudging the corners of her mouth with my lips. "Yes, angel, I have done a 69. I've done a whole host of things, anything you can imagine."

"Threesomes?"

I chuckle. "Threesomes, foursomes, orgies, all of it."

She sighs a little as I run a finger along her collarbone. "Have you ever had sex with a man?"

"Yes, angel." I follow the line of my finger by kissing along her chest.

"So you're bi?"

"I'm a vampire," I say with a grin, meeting her eyes. "We fuck everyone. But right now, I just want to fuck you." I pull her to me, wrapping her in my arms, putting her flat on the bed.

"Wh-what's your favorite thing to do?" She asks, a whimper bursting from her lips as I slide my dick inside her.

"My favorite thing to do is fuck this cunt, angel."

She shakes her head, her back bowing as I fuck her. "No, I mean, your favorite position."

"You'll need to guess." I lean up to maneuver her leg over my shoulder. She winces, but within a few strokes she's moaning and thrashing underneath me. She's beautiful, those lips parted in an O, fresh sweat bursting from her skin. The smell of her arousal is mixed with my own. Now she smells like mine. I want to fill her up til every vamp in this compound smells that she's mine. I want to scar her neck with puncture wounds so everyone can see I drank from her.

The thought makes the darkness at the base of my skull swell and swirl. Red prickles at the edges of my vision. I shouldn't give in to this. It's dangerous, a step too fucking far.

No. The voice tries to reason, but I'm too far fucking gone with desire now. I pull out of her roughly, her breathing choking a little. I seize her hips, pulling her up to my face, sinking my fangs into her labia and slashing two lines down the inside of her thigh.

She cries out, gasping and hissing. I didn't release any venom, I know that hurt. I know it's fucking agony. The dark thing inside me doesn't care. I admire my handiwork, two sharp lines, from the lips of her pussy. Blood drips from the gashes, and I lower my mouth. Now I release venom, just enough to heal, but little enough to leave a scar.

"Mine," I murmur against her skin.

"Yours."

My eyes skate up her body, meeting her gaze. Her mouth is open, and she's panting. She leans up on her elbows to see what I've done.

And she fucking smiles.

"You branded me?" She cocks an eyebrow.

I grin, running my lips along her thigh. "Yes, I did. And if anyone else ever fucking touches you, I'll rip their throat out."

"And what if I want to have a threesome?" She stretches her arms over her head, smiling. "What if I want to fuck another guy while you watch?"

I have her by the throat, baring my fangs at her. "Say that again."

She's not even a little scared, smiling lecherously. "What if I want one guy in my pussy and another in my mouth, and you watch while they have me?"

"You're a filthy little slut, but only for me, you understand?" I squeeze her throat, and she moans. "Say you understand."

"I understand."

I rise to my knees, and straddle her chest. Her eyes fly open, surprised, her gaze flickering down to my hard cock before she looks back up at me.

"Mouth, open." I pump myself, staving off the image of her

being with anyone else but me. "You want to think about other men?"

She shakes her head, her mouth obediently open, her tongue extending past those pretty swollen lips.

"You ever think about another man, I tear his head off. Clean off. You understand?" I clench my molars as my orgasm rises. "You ever, ever look at another man, I kill him, you get that?"

A small flicker of fear, enough to make me even harder. Her eyes are wide, her breathing rapid. She licks her lips, quickly opening her mouth again.

"You're mine, fucking *mine.*" I groan, and ropes of my cum fly across her face. She flinches, her eyes closing out of instinct, but her mouth staying beautifully open for me. One hot stream after another lashes her, until I'm leaning over her, panting, braced against the headboard.

A hand reaches up, stroking my jaw, and I turn my mouth into it, kissing her palm.

"My perfect girl," I murmur. "My perfect fucking girl."

She giggles softly, and I look down at her face. She licks the cum from her lips, stroking her thumb across her chin and pressing it into her mouth, her eyes on me the whole time. She hums appreciatively, smacking her lips.

"You're delicious."

I inhale through my gritted teeth. "Fuck, angel." I shake my head. "You look so good right now."

"Maybe you should let it dry on my face for good."

That grin. Maybe I should have a fucking safe word.

But that grin dissolves quickly as I roll onto my back and take her with me, directing her on top of my face.

"*Silas.*" She squirms, protesting with a shy little sigh as I clasp her thighs. "You just came inside me."

"So?" I drag my tongue over her clit, and she stutters out a curse as lightning illuminates the windows. She's backlit in the crackling flashes, like some sinful, fallen angel. *My* angel. I can taste both of us as I drive her back towards that edge, her body pulled taut.

She comes quickly, hands pressed to the wall as she shakes and moans. But I don't stop.

I keep sucking and licking, her protests swallowed by her moans and hissed breaths. She says *no, no, I can't,* and fuck that makes me even harder.

She comes again, and again, shaking and clawing at my head. With every lick, every climax that rips through her, she comes more and more undone for me, like a beautiful, ruined tapestry, falling to pieces and raveling back up into a pattern of my own creation. She tastes like mine, she smells like mine.

"Silas, *fuck.*" She sobs a little, her hands clasped to her face, her shoulders shaking. Her body quakes as her pussy contracts on my mouth one last time, and I finally release her. She slumps off me, aftershocks creeping up her spine as she flops face-down onto the bed.

I run my hands up her back, over the beads of sweat running down her skin, over the sun-kissed freckles.

"So beautiful," I murmur, bringing my lips down to her shoulder blades, tasting the scent of her arousal as it hits the back of my throat. "But we're still not done."

She whimpers, shaking her head against the bed. "I-I can't... I-"

"Shhh." I soothe her with a kiss to her neck, and she melts against me. "I want to try something."

She turns her head, her eyes hooded as she gazes at me. "What?"

I slice open my fingertip, a small bead of blood pooling at the cut. I press it to her lips, and her eyes slip closed as she licks it up.

"My blood will make you feel so much better, angel." Even as I say it, I can feel her body tense, the weariness washing off her. "I want you wide awake for what's next."

She moans, stretching underneath me like a cat. Her fingers claw and flex into the sheets as my blood courses through her, and it's better than any drug I've ever taken, knowing she's full of my cum, covered in my cum, and now has my blood inside her.

"Now, my dirty little whore is going to let me claim this ass," I murmur into her hair, and she shudders, gasping as she writhes away from me.

"Silas, I've never done - I've never done that."

"I know, which is why you're going to give it to me."

"Silas-"

I seize her chin, her eyes wide as she looks up at me. Her lips quiver under my thumb. "Is it no? Or is it red?"

Her eyes clear, and that defiant grin is back. Her body shifts under me, her ass pressing against my cock. Her breath hitches, and a smile creeps across that perfect fucking mouth.

"No."

"Good girl." I press a hard kiss to her lips. "Now get on your fucking knees."

She makes as though she wants to scramble off the bed, and I catch her thighs, pulling her back to me. I bite open my wrist, blood pouring down my arm.

"Silas, *no*." She thrashes, inhaling sharply as the hot drips of my blood run over her back and her ass. "Oh fuck, no, I've never done this. You're too big!"

I clasp onto my little wildcat's hips as she tries to move away from me, her protests and the fear that's spiking in her veins making me so hard I can barely see. I laugh viciously as she bucks and thrashes, leaning over her and squeezing my hand around her throat.

"You want to run? Because you know I can chase you."

She lets out a high-pitched gasp as I squeeze harder. "Silas-"

"Shut up," I growl in her ear. "You shut the fuck up now and take everything I give you."

She moans, her throat vibrating in my grip, and the dark thing inside me chuckles.

"That's my good little whore. You want my cock in your ass, don't you?"

She shakes her head wildly as I rub my cock in my blood. Everything is hot and wet, and when I press my cock to her ass, she goes rigid.

"No!" She sucks in a breath as my tip passes the first ring of muscle. Her breathing is ragged as I drop more blood onto myself, and push in further. "Shit, *shit*." She exhales over a moan, her head dropping between her shoulders.

"That's it, angel. Fuck you're taking me so good." I spread her ass with my hands, pushing a little harder. "Jesus fuck, Juliet. You're so tight." I stroke her back, her thighs, letting her take more of me, slowly, slowly.

I bottom out, and she lets out a guttural moan, arching as she throws her head back. I don't move for a while, letting her body stretch to me, letting her get used to this new sensation - this feeling only I've ever given her. She relaxes into me as I stroke her clit, her thighs trembling ever so slightly. When I finally do start to move, fucking that impossibly tight ass, she whimpers.

"I want you sore," I tell her. "I want you sore so you remember all day what it's like to have me buried this deep inside your ass." My girl moans. "Is that good?"

She nods, turning her head slightly so I can see her parted rosy lips as she pants. "Oh fuck, Silas, that's so good."

"Such a good girl, letting me fuck all your holes like this."

She cries out as I pound my cock into her ass, not holding back because my dirty little whore is coming apart so fucking beautifully for me. She won't be walking tomorrow. I'm sure of it. I'll fucking make sure of it. She begins to stroke her clit, fresh sweat glistening down the slope of her back. Her whimpers are high-pitched, pleas falling from her lips.

"Every part of you will be full of me by morning." I flex a hand into the hair at the base of her neck, and she moans as I tighten my grip. "You're marked by me, in every way."

"Yeah." Her voice is strained, her fingers rubbing her soaked clit as she chases her climax. I grab her hand, curling her arm behind her back. She protests incoherently, lost in her near-orgasm, her body pulsing and hot.

"That's mine, angel." I don't want anyone making her come but me.

And she does, screaming my name so loud I know someone will hear her, even over the raging storm. But the sound is so sweet I don't care, crashing down after her, coasting on the sweet sound of my girl saying my name. There's a deep pulse against my cock as I pump inside her.

There's nothing else in this moment, just her and me, her quivering skin and the feeling of goosebumps under my fingertips.

I gently pull out of her, lifting her back against me. She's shivering as my chest connects with her back, and she smells so goddamn good. I wrap my arms around her, knowing we're both covered in blood and sweat, and not giving a single fuck. It's us, mingled on each other's skin.

"You're so fucking sexy," I murmur against her ear. "You should see yourself when you're stretched around my cock. It's so fucking beautiful."

"I wanna see," she breathes, her head falling back against the crook of my neck. "I want to see you stretch me."

I chuckle, tracing kisses along her forehead. "Is that right?"

"Mhmm." She sighs, buckling a little in my grasp. "But not right now. I can't - I can't again."

I have no intention of being done, but right now I want to look after my girl. I want to clean her up and wash her down, wrap her in my arms and tell her all the ways she makes me feel whole. I kiss her tenderly, and her lips curl into a smile against my mouth.

She lets me lead her to the bathroom, lets me wash her while I tell her how beautiful she is, how well she did. It's just us in the dark, my voice and her happy sighs, our naked bodies against each other as the storm continues to rage overhead.

It feels blissful, and perfect, and much more contentment than a depraved fuck like me ever expected to feel again.

It feels like love.

The realization weighs down in my gut, tugging at the thread of my self-control that I fucking well know is already snapped and withered.

I love her.

I love her.

I love her.

I don't know what I thought I felt for her. I don't know what the fuck I thought was driving me on all these months when I watched her, when I stood over her while she slept, when I craved just the tiniest hint of her scent.

Can I love her in a world like this? How do I love her? How do I stop myself wanting to tear everything apart and burn this entire compound to the ground just so we can be together?

I don't know. And that leaves me numb.

"You're extraordinary," I whisper against her throat.

Her arms wrap around me. "So are you."

I sink my fangs into her neck, flooding her with venom and feeling her body react instantly. But she's quiet this time, not sending those cries out against the barraging storm, but keeping them here, between us, like a gift, just for me. She shudders and whimpers against my chest, her hips rocking through her orgasm. I swallow down her sweetness, and following that is a sensation so sharp that it almost has tears springing to my eyes. Because I can taste it in her.

She loves me too.

MY EYES SLIP open slowly as thunder growls overhead. A blast of wind peppers hail against the window pane, and rain continues to fall heavily, drumming on the roof. It's dark, the storm swallowing up the dawn.

And Silas's head is buried between my thighs. His hands hold me to him firmly, his tongue moving in lazily in long, soft strokes. I shift a little and moan, my whole body enveloped in a lovely sort of warmth, like I'm still half-dreaming.

My fingers rake through his hair, and he half-growls, half-purrs.

"Good morning," I murmur.

"Morning." The word is a hot breath against my skin, and then he goes back to licking my clit. Good fucking morning indeed.

My whole body aches, and there's a dull throb inside me. But it's so goddamn satisfying.

Silas took me back to bed after he cleaned me up, and I thought we'd stop and go to sleep.

I was wrong.

He praised me, telling me how well I did as I took him, as I came for him again and again. He told me how beautiful I was as he fucked me from behind. Then he called me a dirty whore while he fucked my mouth, hands in my hair and shoving me down onto him until I choked.

I loved every minute of it. I loved everything he did to me. I loved hearing the sounds he made because of what I was doing to him.

I love...

I shudder, pressing the heels of my hands to my eyes as my orgasm rises.

It bursts through me in a rush of heat and a clenching of my weary stomach muscles. "Oh fuck," I murmur, my whole body trembling. I groan as Silas keeps licking. "You're going to kill me if you keep making me come."

He sits up on his knees, grinning down on me, and I puff out a breath of relief.

"You looked so pretty sleeping, I couldn't resist."

I roll my eyes and laugh. "You're meant to wake me first, creep."

He cocks an eyebrow. "What happened to, *I'd let you do anything you wanted to me?*" He crawls over me, etching a trail of kisses from my navel, up my sternum.

My cheeks flush, because I love him using me any way he wants. It was so indescribably hot and wrong to beg him to stop, and feel him get harder. Fighting him, knowing there was no point - I shouldn't love that, should I? It's wrong.

But his lips find mine, kissing me sweetly, tenderly, and I know he cares. If I'd used my safe word, he'd have stopped. He's unlike anybody else I've ever been with. I trust him with my body and my pleasure in a way I never thought I would trust anyone, ever.

He props himself up on an elbow and gazes down at me, stroking a strand of hair out of my face. I must look a mess, all tousled and probably covered in love bites and maybe still some blood? But he's looking at me like I'm the most beautiful thing he's ever seen.

I don't know what to do with this feeling thumping in my chest. It's wild and dangerous, comforting and secure, all at the same time. I've never felt it before. And the way Silas is looking at me now, it's like he feels it too and I don't know what that's going to mean for either of us. I want to stay here with him, but every second that ticks past, I know the bubble of our storm-bound night is closer to bursting.

We can't be together. Not really.

"I need to get back to the dorm," I murmur. "You'll get in trouble."

Silas's face drops, and he sighs, brushing his fingers along my collarbone. "I know."

He doesn't move though. He just pulls me into his arms, holding me against his broad chest.

"Juliet." He clears his throat. "I want to tell you someth-"

A sharp rap on the door has me slamming a hand over my mouth to suppress a shriek of terror. Silas curses under his breath, and pulls me hastily from the bed, pointing to the bath-room. I scurry in, terrified. Oh fuck. They know. Someone knows. They'll smell me on him. They're going to hurt him. God what are they going to do with him?

I don't cower, I just stand frozen in the middle of the bath-room, listening, waiting for that handle to turn and a bunch of feeders to haul me out of here.

"Silas, we need you in the obs tower, right now." A woman's voice, sharp and commanding. It sounds like the redhead who's in charge or seems to be. Murderous bitch.

"Yeah, no worries, just let me get dressed."

A lecherous little giggle makes the hairs on the back of my neck stand up. "I mean, I prefer you like this, but yeah, prob-ably give the others a bit of a start."

"Yeah. I'll be right along." Silas's response is tight.

"Hope you weren't too lonely in here last night. It was such a crazy storm." *What the fuck is this bitch's deal?* I'm so consumed by jealousy over her talking to Silas - to *my vamp* - like this, that I have to stop myself storming out there.

I feel a rush of satisfaction as Silas sighs loudly.

"I'll be right along, if you let me get dressed."

"I can watch." *Bitch you better move on right now.* She laughs again, that fucking flirty laugh women do when they're not getting the reaction they want. "I mean, it's not like I haven't seen you naked before."

"Sam." Silas's voice is a deep rumble through the door. "Get lost. Now. I mean it. I'll be right along, if you just fucking let me close this door and let me get dressed."

"What's got you all wor-"

"*Fuck. Off.*" There's a startled yelp and the door slams. An indignant huff comes from the porch before thumping footsteps head down the steps and get lost in the rain.

After a few very tense heartbeats, the door opens, and Silas leans against the frame. He's in a pair of grey sweatpants, and his hair is a little mussed up. He gives me a smile, and all my anger dissolves instantly. He tucks his hands into his pockets and raises his eyebrows.

"You OK, angel?"

I nod, licking my lips because suddenly I feel completely dried out and also tired, maybe a little hungry?

"Yeah, I'm fine."

"I need to get up to the obs tower, I'll take you back to the dorm." His eyes drop to the floor as he says it, and my stomach sinks all over again. Back to the dorm. The fucking dorm, and my twin sized bed. Away from him.

"Who was that?" I ask, watching as he retrieves my clothes from the chair behind the desk.

"That was Officer Ferris." He doesn't look at me as he says it. "The redhead, you know, she's, well, I guess she's my direct superior."

"Sam?" I step closer to him, and he still doesn't look up at me. "You called her Sam. You and her, you-"

"Not for a while." His eyes snap to meet mine. "Not for a long while. I couldn't... I couldn't bear the thought of touching anyone but you."

I feel too goddamn smug at hearing him say that, at hearing those words come from this beautiful man. This man who only wants me.

I put my arms around his neck, the blanket dropping to my feet, and he inhales sharply as I press my naked body against him. I kiss the base of his throat.

"So, I'm yours then, right?" Another kiss, and he shivers, like he's trying to hold back from throwing me down on the floor and fucking me into next week. "Like, your girlfriend?"

He chuckles, threading his fingers into my hair. "You're jealous, I like that."

"I am jealous." I palm his hard cock through his sweatpants, and his grip on my head becomes almost aggressive. "I'm jealous, because you're mine."

"Oh, is that right?" He tips my head back, his eyes blazing as he looks down at me. "Maybe you should brand me too, huh?"

I shake my head. "No need, I already have." I stroke a hand down his bicep, over one of the tattoos that makes up his sleeve. "This, right here, that's my brand on you."

He looks down at the skeleton hand holding the red rose, and when he looks back at me his expression is one of almost... shock.

"You got that for me before you even knew it." I swallow hard as unexpected emotion wells up inside me.

"Because remember, you were going to draw the hand and I'd draw-"

"The rose." He finishes for me, his brows drawn down. "I remember."

I sniffle a little. "That was the last thought I had before I... Before I... In the stream. That I was sorry that I'd never get to draw with you."

Silas crushes my mouth with a kiss, wrapping me so tight in his arms that I think I'm going to melt straight into him.

I love him.

Tears spill down my cheeks. A few months ago I wanted to die. Now I want to live, but I can't, not the way I want to. I'm in love with a man I can never have, who can never have me.

"Don't cry, angel," he murmurs against my mouth as salt-water spills down between us. "It's alright. Don't cry."

But I do cry. I cry all the way back to the dorm, where he explains to the guard that I was sick and had to be isolated in case it was contagious. I cry as I leave his side, head down because I can't even kiss him goodbye, or *say* goodbye. I cry as I crawl into bed, pulling the blanket over my head as the others begin to stir.

Then I mercifully fall asleep, but I don't sleep peacefully. I dream of Silas slipping away from me, dragged down by grabbing, grasping hands, and voices that scream *Not allowed, not allowed,* over and over again.

I WAKE up to a quiet dorm. Light rain still patters against the roof, but the storm has mostly blown itself out. Silas must have told them to let me sleep.

I breathe out heavily, trying to erase the weight of my night-mares still bearing down on me. When I stretch my legs, they hit something solid at the end of the bed. I start up, pulling the blanket around me protectively, and find myself looking straight into the redhead's eyes.

"Hi." She smiles brightly, crinkling her nose. "You doing OK, hon?" She's pretty, tiny and petite with full lips. I can see why Silas slept with her. But the way she's looking at me makes me feel so fucking small. She's much shorter than me, but she could still tear me to pieces, and she's letting me know just that.

"Yeah, I'm fine."

"Silas said you were in the infirmary, some sort of suspected infection?" Her tone sends chills down my spine. Her smile isn't reaching her eyes.

"Uh, yeah, he just wanted to make sure I didn't get anyone else sick."

She tuts and shakes her head. "That man, so caring and considerate." She leans closer to me. "And kinda hot too, right?"

Oh Jesus shitting what the fuck? I hope my face doesn't betray the panic that's sending goosebumps down my legs. My veins are filled with ice.

"Uh I mean, I guess, he's... He's a nice guy."

"Oh, you can tell me, it's just us girls." She leans back on a hand, like she's my best friend who's come over for the gossip after my night with the hot guy on campus. "I know you two have sort of become friends, everyone can see he likes you a lot."

I shake my head quickly, casting my eyes down to the bed so I don't have to look at that smile that's starting to border on maniacal. "We're friends, that's all. He's nice to me. We under-stand each other."

"Oh, *do you?*"

Goddammit, why did I say that? I fidget with my fingers, wishing she would just go away. I have to keep the panic at bay or I'm going to fuck up, I'm going to give us away.

"It's just a friendship."

"Yeah, I know." She smoothes a hand over the sheets, still smiling that creepy smile. "The boss thinks it's good because of what I did."

"Oh, OK." Unease is making my throat swell shut.

"It's not as though I *like* killing people," she says, her fingers still running over the sheets. "But sometimes you have to make a point. Let people know who's in charge." She lifts her eyes to mine, and they're bright red. She tilts her head, looking me up and down. "I can see why he likes you. You're so cute."

"Thanks." Is my jaw chattering? God, I hope she can't see it.

"You smell good, too." She leans closer, and inhales. "Mmm. Almost like something I smelled in his cabin this morning. But that can't be, right?"

Oh fuuuuuuck. I swallow hard, opening my mouth to speak, but Sam laughs, tossing her head back.

"Good to have a little girl chat with you, hon." She rises to her feet, grinning, her fangs protruding over her bottom lip. "Let me know if you need anything. Always happy to help."

The door opens just as she heads down the aisle, and Silas steps in. Sam spreads her arms, almost skipping towards him. Silas stops short, his eyes darting from me back to her.

"Silas!" Her voice is fucking terrifying. "We were just talking about you!"

"Is that right?" He gives her a nod.

"Yeah, talking about how great it is that you're such good friends, weren't we, honey?" She looks over her shoulder at me, smiling a saccharine smile.

"That's right." I give Silas a smile that I hope looks genuine and doesn't betray how I'm really feeling.

"He needs to do a supply run to Savannah, just FYI." Sam gives me a wink, before tossing her red hair and breezing past Silas with a clap on his shoulder.

We both wait for her to leave, for the door to firmly swing shut before Silas keeps moving towards my bed.

"You get some rest?" He perches on the end of my bed, reaching out to take my hand.

"Yeah, I did." I give his fingers a squeeze, so intensely grateful that he's here and that crazy bitch is gone. "She was just here when I woke up and... I don't even know. It was so creepy."

Silas exhales harshly, and pulls me a little closer to him. "She's being fucking weird."

"Maybe she's jealous?"

He grunts out a laugh. "Yeah maybe, but she is right."

I frown. "About what?"

"The supply run. I need to go to Savannah tomorrow." His eyes start to change color, and I can practically feel the lust dripping off him as he smiles. "Fancy being busted out of here again?"

"You're crazy." I roll my eyes. "She's probably baiting you and she'll turn you in the second the truck leaves the gates."

"Nah, she wouldn't do that to me." His expression shifts, and he pulls me closer still, so that our legs are touching. "I need to be alone with you. I don't know how I'm going to go without..." He shakes his head, his eyes dropping to my chest. My nipples instantly harden under his gaze, goosebumps prickling down my arms, and he growls low in his throat. "Fuck, angel."

"Silas, we have to be careful," I say urgently, trying to

stamp down the desire that's coursing through me. This isn't the time, it isn't the place. But the way he's looking at me...

His hand creeps under the sheet, up my thigh, and his eyes meet mine as he slips a finger inside my panties. He groans softly as my lips part in a silent moan, his finger stroking my clit, then slipping inside me.

"Silas, they're right outside," I whisper, biting my lip as his fingers keep moving and probing. He pushes two fingers inside me, and I whimper, covering my mouth with my hand. He's insane. That creepy bitch is probably watching through a damn peephole or something. "You need to stop."

"Quiet, angel." His eyes stay fixed on my face as he works me into a frenzy, hot and wanting. He smiles as I pant, trying to stay still on the bed in case anyone looks in on us. "That's it, eyes on me. Fuck, you're so desperate, aren't you?"

"Mhmm." I nod, my body starting to shiver.

He leans closer, his thumb stroking my clit hard as his fingers crook against my g-spot, rubbing and pushing. "Are you sore?"

I nod again, keeping my lips pressed together to stop myself crying out. My answer seems to please him, his eyes wandering over my face.

"Can you still feel me inside you, angel?"

"Yes." My eyes slip closed, but fly open again almost instantly as he pinches my nipple hard.

"You stay right here with me," he commands in that low voice that almost has me come apart on his hand. "Fucking hell, I wish my cock was in your ass right now."

I moan at his words, the pressure in my belly too much, I can't keep quiet. I want him in my ass too, I want him to fuck my throbbing pussy, no matter how sore I am. I reach out and stroke him through his pants, and he hisses in a serrated breath.

"I need to feel that hot cunt on my cock," he murmurs. His

words unravel me completely, and I come hard on his fingers, swallowing down my cries. I'm sweating and shaking, my hand digging into his thigh with so much ferocity, I'm surprised I haven't shredded a hole into his uniform.

Silas withdraws his fingers slowly, raising them to his mouth and licking me off them as I watch. He looks me over and grins, shaking his head.

"Such a bad girl, making me crazy like this."

"We have to be more careful." I can barely speak, my breath rasping out of my lungs. "You can't do that here."

"So come on the supply run with me tomorrow."

I laugh, running a hand through my hair, and puffing out breaths through pursed lips. "Was that your plan? Make me come so I'll agree to this genuinely stupid plan?"

"It was, in fact." He inhales deeply through his nose. "You smell so good. If I don't have you again soon, I'm going to go insane."

I stroke my hand over his and sigh. "How is this going to go on? We can't... I mean, we can't be together."

"Don't think about that right now."

"Silas-"

"No." His jaw is tense, and he shakes his head. "Don't. Don't dwell on what can't be and just focus on what we can have."

"Even if it's just stolen moments in a truck on a supply run?"

"Whatever I can have." His tone is almost desperate, his eyes hardening as he gazes at me. "Whatever I have of you. I told you, if this is all I ever have, then it's enough."

"It isn't for me." The words slip out before I think about it, and my head drops. "Sorry. I just... I'm in my own head right now, I've never... I mean I've never had... I've never felt..." I don't know what I want to say, but I know it's bigger and heavier than anything I should say right now on a bed in a dorm, when he's just made me come on his hand.

But then his fingers are notched under my chin, forcing my head up to look at him, meeting those red eyes. He searches my face, and shakes his head.

"I never thought I'd feel this way again. And I'm so fucking angry that this is how we met. That this is our story. But if the world had to go to hell for me to find you, then let it be damned. It was worth it."

I inhale sharply. The warm, jagged feeling surrounding my heart right now drives tears into my eyes. "Do you mean..." I trail off because I don't know if I can handle him saying those words to me. It would hurt in the most beautiful way. I never expected love to hurt in this way. Instead, I shake my head, brushing a quick, dangerous kiss to his lips. "I'll come with you tomorrow."

"Good." He dips his head briefly to mine, our foreheads touching before he gets to his feet. "I'm sorry."

I raise my eyebrows. "For?"

He hesitates, shifting on his feet. "I've never been good at... talking about it. How I feel. But I want you to know that last night... That was me showing you." His eyes meet mine, and they're flooded with love and tenderness. His mouth curves into a brief grin as he huffs out a laugh. "It sounds incredibly trite, but, you know, I mean that. I may not be good at saying it, but I'll show you. Every day, in every way I can."

I nod, because the emotions putting pressure on my lungs right now are too much. I just nod, and watch him leave the dorm. And all I can think about for the rest of the day, as the rain keeps falling and the vamps assess the storm damage, is that the next day Silas and I will be alone again, for hours.

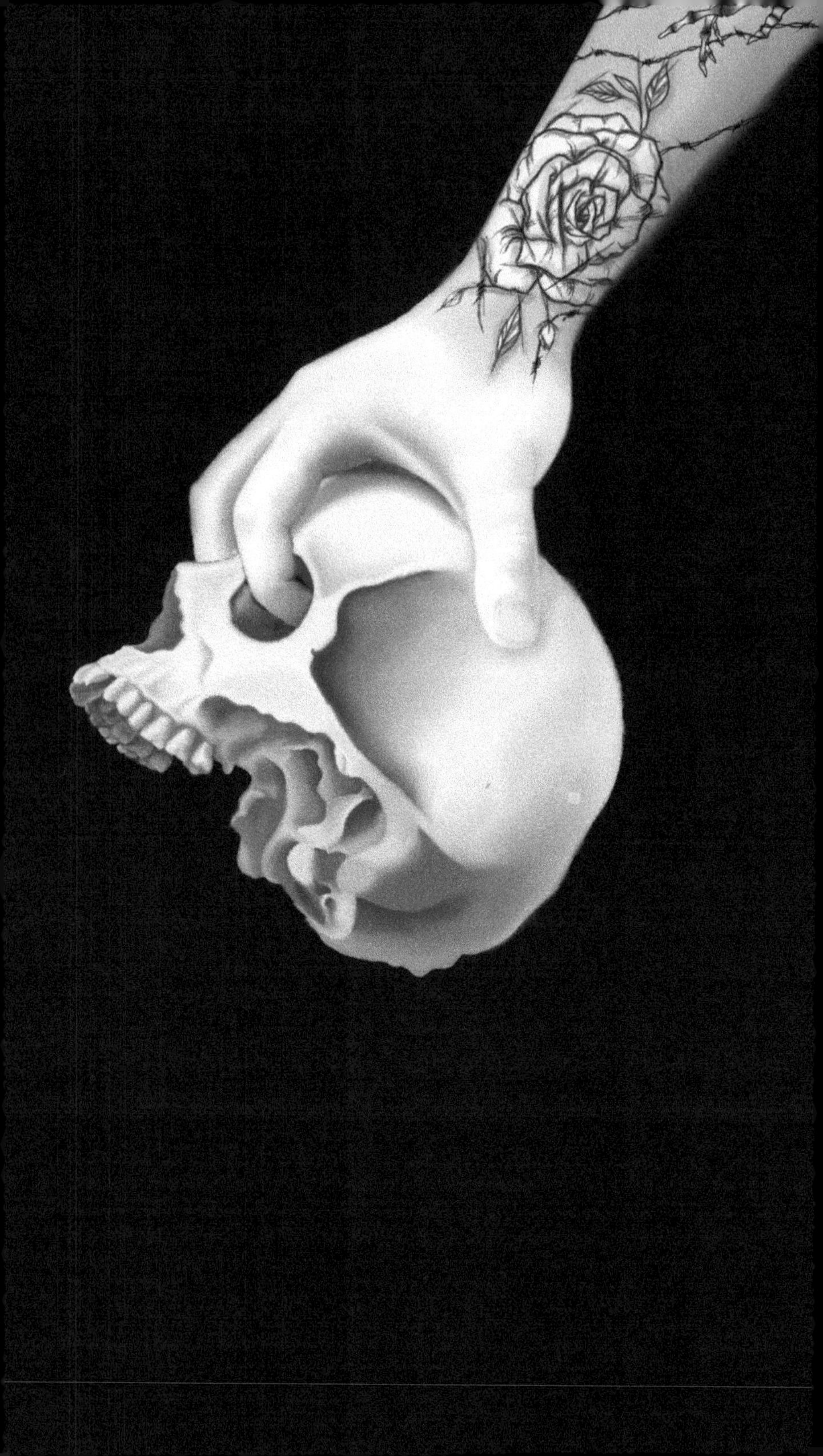

CONVOLUTED. That's the only word that comes to mind right now. It's how I feel. It describes pretty accurately the situation I find myself in. It lays down every single fucked up thing about my life. *Convoluted.*

I keep trying to strong-arm my way through the thoughts that plague me, trying to find a way forward. But there is no way forward. How can there be?

I lie in bed, watching the light change as dawn breaks. I'm going to get an early start over to Savannah, to have as much time with my girl as possible. The thought hurts. It's a tightening noose around my neck. I know that sooner or later, I'll fuck up. I know that sooner or later, I'll put a foot wrong. We'll be discovered.

What that will mean, I still don't know.

I surrender to thoughts I shouldn't. Thoughts of a future we'll never have. Being together, every day. Never needing to sneak around and say goodbye. I even imagine her pregnant, her belly round with my child. I never wanted children, and in a world like this it wouldn't be right to have one. But the thought of Juliet's swollen belly, knowing I put a baby in there, *my* baby, another piece of *me...*

Convoluted. I shove the blankets aside and get ready for the day. I'm determined to do exactly what I told her yesterday - focus on the now. Because I can never guarantee her anything else.

I find Juliet leaving the shower block, and usher her down the side of the buildings towards the trucks. She remains completely silent as I hide her in the backseat of the truck, as we go through the gate. The guard waves me through without a second glance, and I breathe a sigh of relief as the gate rolls shut in the rear view mirror.

There are trees down along the highway, and I maneuver carefully as we navigate our way from the compound. It's still in sight when Juliet's scent begins to fill the car, and I look in the backseat.

My heart nearly leaps straight out of my ribcage. She's lying on the backseat completely naked, her legs open, her fingers swirling over her clit. Her eyes meet mine and she grins. "The road, babe."

I tear my eyes away from her, and narrowly avoid hitting a tree that's down on the road. I hiss out a curse, and Juliet laughs breathily before letting out a moan.

"You should be careful," she says. "They can still see us from here."

I grit my teeth and growl out my frustration. "You're a fucking tease you know." I adjust the rear view mirror so I can see her cunt, wet and glistening as she fucks herself. "Get that cunt nice and wet for me, angel. I want to see you dripping for me."

The convoluted feeling is gone, replaced with the feral desire to fuck her senseless. Jesus fuck, what she does to me. I can hear how wet she is. I look in the mirror, and her thighs are shaking.

"Don't you dare come," I growl. "You stop before you come."

She's panting, her hips lifting off the seat. "Oh fuck, I need you inside me."

We're almost out of view of the compound. Another half mile, and I'll fuck her and fill her up. I'm so hard I can barely focus on the road. I take the turn, and count down the distance, the trees becoming thicker around us.

As soon as I know we're clear, the tires squeal as I pull off the side of the road. I've barely brought the car to a stop when Juliet is clambering over the seat and into my lap. She fumbles my trousers open, pulling out my cock and lowering herself onto me as she kisses me greedily.

We're nothing but teeth and tongues and moans, her sweat dripping down her back as she swings her hips on me.

She leans back against the steering wheel, giving me the perfect view of my dick slipping into her cunt over and over. It's mesmerizing, her body stretched out in front of me, her hands braced against the roof of the truck.

"Fuck you're perfect," I murmur, gripping her hips, forcing her further down onto me. Her tight heat envelops me down to the base of my cock, and she cries out. "Are you still sore, angel?"

"Yes." One hand runs down the flat plane of her stomach, and she flicks two fingers over her clit as she continues to ride me. "I never want to stop - *fuck* - stop being sore from you."

I roll her nipples between my fingers, causing her to gasp and thrash. "Good. I want to fuck you raw every day. Fill every single fucking hole with my cum every day."

Her high-pitched whimper fills the truck, and she slams herself down on me as her pussy contracts around me. I hold her hips steady as I pound myself into her, fucking her right through her orgasm. She moans my name and claws at me, faltering and pressing her tits to my chest.

"Bite me," she pleads breathily.

My balls draw up tight as I sink my fangs into her neck, and white heat explodes through me as she screams my name. I keep coming, and coming, riding one wave after another as her blood warms my throat and my cum fills her cunt.

The sun beats down on us through the windshield as she catches her breath. My mouth releases her neck reluctantly, but she stays on my lap, keeping me within her. She wraps her arms around my neck, and kisses me slowly. We stay like that for a long time, so long it starts to feel like some sort of dream, hot and euphoric. I never want it to end. I want to stay like this forever.

But finally, she lifts herself off me, slumping into the passenger seat. Her thighs are splayed, her skin flushed, her hair a tumble of glistening gold around her shoulders and over her breasts. My perfect, cum-soaked angel. She tips her head, her face filled with satisfaction as she gazes at me.

"How many times can we do that today?" She asks, stretching.

"As many times as possible."

She giggles and reaches back for her clothes.

"Uh-uh." I pull her back into the seat. "You stay like this."

"*Silas*." She regards me with wide eyes. "You want me to just sit here naked while you drive?"

"Yes. I want you on display for me. All day." I lean over and scrape my fangs along her jawline, making her shudder deliciously. "You sit there with your legs open like a good little whore, and let me touch you however I want."

"I could sit on your cock while you drive," she says against my lips with a grin.

"Don't tempt me." I tuck myself away even though I'm

hard again, and gun the engine. Juliet obediently sits next to me, watching me as I navigate back out onto the road. Her hair glints in the sunlight, and her scent is so strong in the warm air I have to pull over and fuck her twice more before we make it twenty miles from the compound. After the second time, with her sweaty hair bunched in my hand, my chest pressed to her back, she laughs breathlessly.

"We're never going to make it if we keep doing this."

"Well at least the vamps won't smell you," I mutter into her ear. "Soaked in me as you are."

"Good thing I get those depo shots, huh?" She giggles, clenching her thighs together as I pull out of her. "You'd have me pregnant in a second otherwise."

The image of her swollen belly that I conjured up in my bed this morning swims in my mind's eye. And the convoluted feeling comes back. I wipe a hand over my face, brushing away the sweat.

"It's not that easy for a vamp to get a human pregnant, actually." Why am I saying this? What the fuck does it matter? But the image won't let me go. That hard, round belly... Without thinking, I reach between her legs, pushing two fingers inside her as she squeaks, her body shuddering.

"Wh-what are you doing?"

"I don't want anything leaking out" I murmur, nibbling her on her earlobe. "I want you full of me, remember?"

She laughs, gasping as my fingers curl and push further. "You wanna get me pregnant, creep?"

"No." I don't. I really don't. But fuck, I want a lasting piece of me in her, something that binds us forever. "Just marking my property."

"Your *property?*" She screams as I sink my fangs into her shoulder, her pussy clenching my fingers, heat flooding both of us. When I release her, she's shaking, sweat beading and running down her back.

"R-red." She stutters. "Red, red. I can't... Oh fuck"

"It's OK, angel, I've got you." I pull her into my arms, stroking her inflamed skin gently, licking over the puncture holes in her shoulder. "You're so beautiful, you know that?"

She can't talk, she's trembling violently, her whole body overstimulated. I reach through the seats to the dash and retrieve a bottle of water.

"Here, you need to drink." I hold the bottle to her lips, and she sips it down carefully. "That's it, angel. I'm sorry I was too much for you. Are you OK?"

She slumps against me, nodding into the crook of my neck. "You were great, really. It was just... intense."

"That's alright, I've got you. What do you need from me right now?"

"Can you just hold me for a while?" Her finger brushes against my jawline, and sweetness shoots through me. "I just need you to hold me, please."

I sit back on the seat and pull her into my lap. She's limp, and warm, covered in sweat, curling up against me. I stroke her hair, relishing the feeling of her cheek pressed against my chest. This is where she belongs, where *we* belong.

"Do you want kids?" She asks me after a while in a small and tentative voice.

"No, I never wanted that for myself. You?"

She shakes her head against me. "No, I mean, I was only a kid myself when... yeah. It's never been something that seemed like it was possible. And I don't want to bring a kid into this world. But..." She trails off, and the air becomes heavy.

"But?"

She gazes up at me, her big grey eyes full of uncertainty. "It feels different with you. It's stupid, but with you I see a future. That's dumb, isn't it?"

"Not dumb at all, angel. That's normal when you…"

She raises an eyebrow. "You can say it, you know."

"I know. But it feels like it would be unfair." I plant a kiss on her cheek, and her eyes flutter closed. "To both of us." I feather my fingers down the ridges of her spine. "I'm glad you used your safeword."

She snuggles into me with a sigh. "I trust you."

Somehow that hurts more than if she'd just told me she loves me. Having her love, her trust, her whole fucking heart in my hands feels like a burden I don't deserve, and its one I certainly can't honor. She trusts me to keep her safe - and I do that how? In this fucked up world?

"Stop it," she murmurs.

"What?"

She brushes her lips against my throat. "You're worrying. I can feel it. You get all tense and grumpy and English."

I grunt out a laugh. "All English, ey?"

She smiles up at me, running her hand down my cheek. "My beautiful, grumpy Englishman."

"I thought I smile a lot for you."

"Mhmmm." Her eyes light up as she wraps her arms around my neck, drawing my mouth closer to hers. "You always smile for me."

"Because it's just for you, angel. You make me happy."

"Ditto." Her grin turns sassy. "That's from an old movie, right?" She shrieks as I swat her ass.

"You seem pretty happy to fuck an old man, you cheeky little bitch."

She laughs out loud, curling herself around me, and the moment feels so wholesome and normal that I could almost forget where we are and what we're meant to be doing.

Almost.

With a sigh, I press a kiss to her temple. "Alright you, we need to get moving."

"Dammit." She huffs out a warm breath against my chest, then sits up. "I'm getting dressed now though." She gives me that sassy grin again. "Can't risk us stopping *again*."

I nod, running my hand down her chest, splaying it gently over her stomach. The image of that swollen belly floats in front of me, and my fingers flex. "You need to get dressed and eat something. I need to be careful taking too much blood from you."

She climbs off me with a shrug, retrieving her clothes and pulling her tank top over her head. "They haven't drained me in months. It's really weird."

"Well they wanted you stronger, going to the gym and all that. Which you haven't been doing."

She shakes out her hair, giggling. "Because you've been working me out the last few days, in case you hadn't noticed."

"True. But we should start going again." I gesture to the front seat. "Now, eat. There's food in the bag there." I pull my clothes back on as she scrambles into the front, rifling through the bag. "I'd make you chips and eggs to get your weight up, but-"

"What and what?" She asks, apple in hand.

I let out a laugh, buttoning up my shirt. "Chips and eggs, with a big mug of milky tea. Meal of champions."

She wrinkles her adorable nose. "It sounds disgusting."

"Wait til I tell you about pie and liquor." I climb out of the truck and get into the driver's seat, and see her eyeing me out of the corner of my eye. When I turn to look at her, she almost looks sad. "What's wrong, angel?"

She shakes her head, sighing, looking down at the apple in her hand. "We both had lives, and we can't share them with each other. We can't... I can't take you home to meet my family, you can't fly me to England to meet yours." She swallows hard. "You've made it hard to accept that my life isn't normal. I tried not to care. All these years I tried not to care. But with you... I do."

"I hate that." I reach across and take her hand. Her slender fingers curl around mine, and her touch makes the ache worse. "I told you, I'd never regret this, and I won't. Ever. Because even if this hurts, it's worth it to me."

She dashes away a stray tear from her cheek and nods. "I don't regret it either. I never will. But I'll always wish for more. Because I want everything, but only because I want it with you."

The ache turns into a visceral pain. *Only because I want it with you.* I curl my hand around hers, hating god and the world and every other thing keeping me away from her, from the *everything* she wants. The pain sends red into the corners of my vision, and I have to swallow down the grief for the life I can't give her along with all the love my fractured soul will bear until we're nothing but dust.

With a final squeeze of her fingers, I let go and gun the engine of the truck. If she wonders at my silence, she doesn't say anything, just settles back into her seat and crunches her teeth into her apple.

We coast along the highway, the damage from the storm evident all around us. We pass towns that look like a tornado swept through them, the crumbling buildings now mostly collapsed. A car is overturned on the road ahead of us, and I'm surprised the storm became that strong.

Juliet squeaks suddenly, sitting up in her seat and tapping against her window. "Oh my god, Silas!"

I look out her window, and my stomach turns to ice. There's Afflicted out in a field in the distance, a huge horde of them. They're aimlessly roaming, but there's got to be at least 200 of them. I slam on the brakes, and we both stare out at them.

"Silas," Juliet whispers. "We can't keep going."

"They might have already gone through Savannah." I grab the radio, flipping the dial to Savannah's frequency, and give her a pointed look. "Stay quiet." She nods, wrapping her arms around her legs as she turns to look back out the window. "Savannah, do you read me?" Nothing but empty crackling answers. "Savannah, do you read?"

No response.

My smart watch pings at that moment. The perimeter alarm has been triggered.

Juliet eyes me with alarm. "Oh god, Silas."

I replace the radio and throw the truck into reverse, turning around the trees on the other side of the road before flooring the accelerator.

"They're going to find out, oh god." Juliet starts to cry,

"It's OK, we'll make it back, we'll beat them." The truck roars down the highway, and I'm sure the Afflicted have heard it, but I need to get back. I need to get her safe, and I need to hope to god that they don't see her when I get back.

"What are they going to do if they find out?" She hiccups as she tries to breathe through a sob. "What do they do?"

"I'm not going to tell you that."

"They're going to kill you, aren't they?" She's sobbing loudly now. "Oh my god, what will they do?"

"Don't worry about that now."

"I want to know!" She sounds like she's going to hyperventilate, panic tearing through her, and the smell of fear coming from her does nothing but shatter everything inside me over and over.

"Angel, please." I reach over to her, and she swats my hand away. "Please, you need to calm down."

"Tell me what they'll do!" She punches me in the arm, her voice a grief-stricken snarl. "I want to know what this is going to cost you! Fucking tell me!" She hits me again, sob after sob wracking through her chest.

"They'll poison me!" I shout at the windshield, at the sky, at the fucking injustice of it all. "They'll strap me down and poison me with silver."

"And that'll hurt, right?" She covers her face with her hands. "That'll hurt you? You're allergic to silver, aren't you?"

I swallow hard, my throat swelling shut. "Yes. It'll hurt."

"And they'll starve you?" Her voice is muffled. "They'll starve you and -"

"Yes, yes. It's... It's awful, alright. It's agony."

Juliet crumples against me, wailing, her hands clasping onto my arms. "I'm sorry, I'm so sorry."

My smart watch pings again, and I put my arm around her, drawing her close. "I told you, it was worth it. It was all worth it. I'd die for you, angel. Gladly. Every single fucking day."

We drive on in silence, her shivering frame under my arm. I kiss her hair, over and over, knowing with each passing mile that this will be the last time I touch her, the last time I hold her. But I had this. I had it. I had *her*.

Five miles out from the compound my watch pings once more, and Juliet burrows into me. "You can't leave me."

"Just get in the back, angel. We might have beaten them back." I know I'm lying to her, but I have to do it. I have to hope. We have to try. "Come on, it's OK." I give her a smile, and she throws herself at me. I slam the brakes, taking her in my arms as her soft lips devour my mouth. *One last kiss.* "Come on angel," I murmur, leaning my forehead against hers. "Get in the back. I need to get you safe."

"You were worth it, too." Her breath washes over my lips, and she climbs, sniffling, into the back seat.

I don't even feel dread as we get closer. I'm strangely calm. I knew this would happen. It was just a matter of time. I'd fuck up, and it would all go to hell.

You've ruined everything. You always have.

My father's last words to me echo through my head. Maybe I have always ruined everything. Maybe I let myself fall in love with a human because I have a sick need to destroy, to sabotage the people I care about, not to mention myself. All I've done now is left an already traumatized woman with more loss, and yet more trauma. No one to protect her.

Just as the compound comes into view, I almost veer the truck to the other side of the road, and speed off. But where do I go? I can't keep her safe out in the fucking wild. I can't leave her at the mercy of the Afflicted, and the National Guard, and who knows what else is out here.

I brace myself as I keep driving. But the sirens aren't going. The flashing lights on the fence are out. The truck gets closer, and the guards at the gate become visible. They're standing around, as normal. No frantic activity. Nothing unusual.

I pull up at the gate, ready for an inspection, ready to be told to get in quickly. Instead, they wave me through as the gate rolls back. I stupidly pause and roll down my window, one of the guards approaching.

"I had an alarm go off," I say, holding up my smart watch. "I got back as quickly as I could."

The guard laughs, waving his hand. "Yeah, scared the shit out of us too. But it was just a drill. Nothing to worry about. They should have told you that when you headed out."

Yeah they should have. *She* should have told me. Juliet was right, and I'm a fucking fool.

I drive into the compound, and park the truck. I climb down, checking for anyone nearby, but everything is clear.

When I open the back door, Juliet stumbles out, her face red and tear-streaked. She wraps her arms around my waist, still sobbing quietly.

"Oh god, oh god," she murmurs against me, shoulders shaking.

"It's all over, angel, we're OK." I tip her head back and plant a soft kiss on her lips. "We're safe." Maybe. Maybe we're safe.

I usher her back to the dorm, past the vamp standing guard at the door, who is completely uninterested in the crying human under my arm. Gina looks up with alarm as I guide Juliet back to her bed.

"What the hell?" Gina eyes me suspiciously, getting to her feet to take Juliet from me. "Where the hell have you been?"

"She needed to..." I trail off, out of lies, out of answers. "She's alright, just had a fright."

"Sure she did." Gina shakes her head and wraps Juliet in a hug so maternal it makes me miss my own mother. Just for a moment.

I give myself a shake and hurry from the dorm, heading across the yard to Sam's office. I tear open the door, to find Sam sitting at her desk, poring over some paperwork.

"Can I help you, Silas?" She doesn't look up. She was fucking expecting me.

"Yeah, you can tell me why I was out there with no warning that there was a fucking perimeter drill planned for today."

"Scared you, did it?" She still won't look up, still calmly looking over her.

"I rushed back because I thought there was an emergency." I stride across the room and slam my hands on the table, and she finally looks up at me. "I was out there, fucking stranded on my own and-"

"On your own?" She interjects, leaning back in her chair. "Were you now? On your own? You're in my office pitching a fit because you were out there on your own?"

She fucking knows. "Sam, don't ever pull a stunt like that on me again, do you hear me?"

"I'm not the one pulling stunts here."

I growl, my hands balling into fists. "I swear to god, if you ever do anything like that again-"

"You'll what?" Her eyebrows lift, and she swivels back and forth languidly in her chair. "What'll you do, Silas? Same thing you did to Braun?"

"Try me."

"Are you threatening a senior officer?" She leans on her elbows, tilting her chin up at me. "I'm going to give you some friendly advice. If you want people to cover your mistakes, don't threaten them."

I narrow my eyes. "My mistakes?"

"YOUR MISTAKES. Like the one I could smell in your cabin yesterday morning."

"I don't know what the fuck you're talking about."

"This conversation is over." She drops her gaze back to the paperwork in front of her, and waves me away. "You can go now."

"Sam-"

"I said, you can go."

I shove myself away from the desk and back out into the yard. Instead of heading to my cabin, I head for the gym. Once inside I tear off my shirt, casting it aside before laying into the punching bag with rage so acute I can smell it.

Sam knows. Of course she does. And today was just a little flex of power to let me know that she's watching. She'll use this to her advantage. I know she will.

As the punching bag goes flying across the gym, I realize I didn't tell them about the horde of Afflicted, or about Savannah not answering their radio. I should tell them. That horde was massive. I move towards the doors, scooping my shirt up from the floor, but as thunder rumbles overhead, I pause.

I chew the inside of my cheek for a moment, before throwing my shirt over my shoulder and heading back to my cabin, deciding to keep that information to myself for now.

It could very well be useful to me, maybe even sooner than I think.

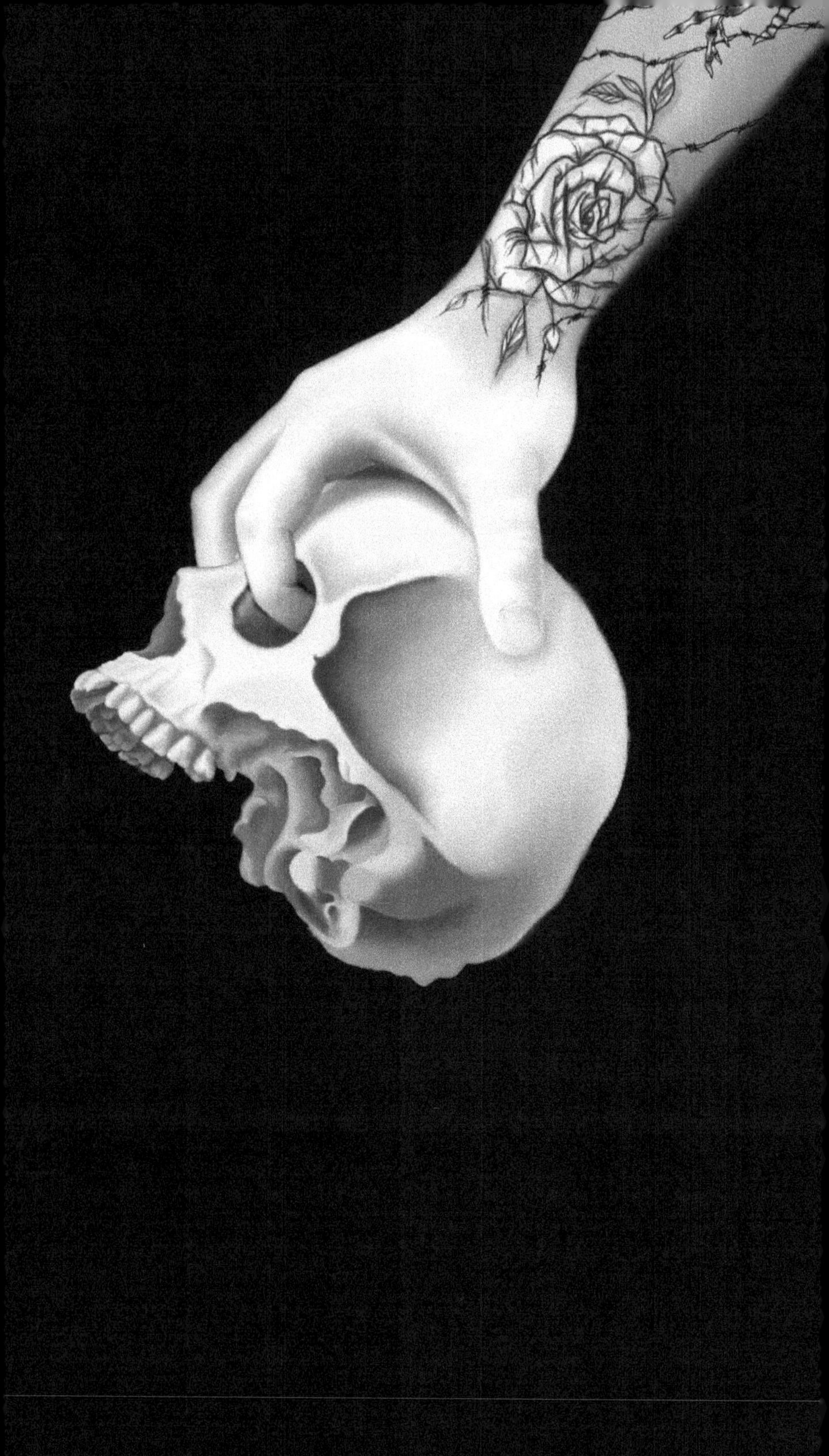

I KNOW I'm being watched. Logically, I know I should keep my distance from Juliet, to assuage any sort of suspicion. I know I'm being irresponsible, and I'm probably placing us both in danger. But none of that stops the need to see her from thumping in my chest. The need to be with my girl is too strong. I can't live without her. And I'm prepared for that need to be the addiction that finally kills me.

I tend to my duties, running checks on the perimeter, checking the positions of the security cameras. All the while thinking of nothing but Juliet, wondering where she is and what she's doing. It's been raining heavily all morning, so I know she's not in the garden. As I flick through each camera, I look for her, coming up empty until I reach the gym.

There she is, running on the treadmill. Her hair is wound up on top of her head in a messy bun, and she's wearing the tightest pair of white shorts I've ever seen, along with a crop top. *Holy shit.* I can practically smell her through the screen. She rubs a hand over the back of her neck, brushing away sweat, and I have to suppress a groan.

"Georgia Peach getting herself all sweaty, huh?"

I'm so entranced I didn't even hear Crawley enter the

office. I flick away the image of the gym and Juliet running quickly, clearing my throat.

"Yeah I guess so. She was told to work out by the doctor."

"She was, huh?" Crawley drops down into the chair beside me. "You seem pretty interested in her."

I shrug, keeping my eyes trained on the monitor. "She needed help. I gave it. End of."

"Hmm." Crawley leans back in his chair, gazing at the ceiling. "Anderson said you had the brilliant idea of running PR after what Braun did. Good excuse to spend time with her I guess."

"Well, it worked, didn't it? No more riots. Happy bloodbags. Job done."

Crawley strokes his chin thoughtfully. "Yeah, well done you." He inhales through his nose. "You know, there was a guy at the last compound I was stationed at, up near Roanoke. This young vamp, he fell in love with one of the bloodbags."

"Did he now?" I'm going to keep my voice perfectly even. "That's a bit stupid, innit?" This has nothing to do with me. Crawley's just talking. If I maintain the nonchalant tone, he won't suspect a thing.

"Yeah, pretty stupid." Crawley swivels back and forth lazily in the chair, eyes still focused upwards. "Sorta ended up bad for everybody."

"Oh yes? What happened?"

Crawley puffs out a breath. "They poisoned him, starved him, then put her in the room with him. After two weeks of no food, nothing was going to save her from him."

My blood runs cold. "He killed her then?"

"Sure did." Crawley gets to his feet and claps me on the shoulder. "I can still hear him screaming when he realized what he'd done. Shit like that, it never ends well."

"Well, the rules are there for a reason I suppose." I don't

meet his eyes, aware of his gaze fixed on the side of my face. "Break 'em, deal with the consequences."

"That's for sure."

When he doesn't move, I look up at him, praying he can't see the betrayal that has to be written all over my face.

"Did you need something, Crawley?"

"No, not a thing." He turns for the door. "Take care, King."

His parting words are heavy, and I begin to wonder just how many people know. I wonder if Anderson knows. I click the screen twice, bringing up the feed to the gym. Another click, and the screen goes black. I shake my head at myself, pushing away from the desk and heading out into the rain. If Anderson knew, I wouldn't be here anymore. I'd be either dead or stationed elsewhere, far away from Juliet.

The story Crawley just told me makes me shiver. The thought of hurting Juliet makes me sick. The very notion that they'd do that to her, to me, as punishment for merely wanting to be together - it's disgusting. I glare at the barbed wire as I pass it, once again cursing this fucking world we find ourselves in.

I head for the gym, barely acknowledging the humans that pass me as I head up the steps. Juliet is climbing down off the treadmill just as I walk in. I want to go to her side and take her in my arms, and the way her face lights up as she turns and sees me tells me she wants the same thing.

But we're not alone. Two men are still by the weights, finishing their sets. Juliet dips her head, then makes a bee-line for the ladies bathroom. Making sure the men are more concerned with their reps than with me, I follow her, and lock the door behind me.

Juliet is leaning against the counter, her face breaking into a smile as I stalk towards her.

"Hey there," she says breathily, moaning softly as I crush her mouth with mine.

"You OK?" I pull back from her, eyes searching her face.

She nods. "Yeah, I am. As long as you are, I am too."

I cradle her head, sinking my fingers into her hair. "I couldn't stop thinking about you all night."

"Me too." She leans her forehead against mine. "I had a dream you were in my bed, and you were rubbing my back. It was so nice." She kisses me again, her teeth catching my lip. "I just want your hands on me."

She fumbles with my buttons, pushing the shirt from my shoulders before dragging me against her. She plants tiny kisses along my collarbone, flooding my body with sweetness. When she gazes up at me with her big eyes, I know this is dangerous. I know we're behind a locked door, and it doesn't make me feel even a little better.

But something's wrong. I pull back, frowning at her, trying to place that smell.

"Silas?" She raises her eyebrow, shifting against the counter. The tiniest fluttering of her eyelids tells me that she's in pain.

I clasp her jaw in my hands. "Angel, what's wrong? Are you sore?"

"Not from you, really." Her lower lip wobbles, and her eyes shine with tears. "I'm fine, really. I just want you."

She kisses me again, but even as she does, she begins to cry. That smell, it's... sterile. Medicinal. Something acrid covering her scent.

"Angel, please, talk to me. What's happened?"

She takes a deep breath, her eyes clenching closed and a cascade of tears spilling over her lashes. "They did an examination."

"An examination?"

She tips her head back to look at me, and nods. "A gynecological exam. They said they need to see if... if I was OK."

Panic pools in the pit of my stomach. "They examined you internally?"

"Yeah. It was... It was so uncomfortable. I just wanted you, the whole time. I just wanted you to be there to hold my hand. I didn't understand why they were doing it, and they wouldn't tell me..." She trails off, wrapping her arms around my waist and crying softly.

The whirring feeling in my stomach won't stop. Why the fuck would they be examining her?

Her fingers claw at the back of my neck suddenly, and she draws me down to her, kissing me hungrily as she shoves a hand into my trousers.

"Juliet," I grit out against her mouth. "What are you doing?"

"I missed you, so much." She presses her face to the side of my neck as she tries to pump me with her hand. "I just, I need-"

"Juliet, stop." I pull her hand away from me gently, and she slumps against me, crying. "I'm right here, angel. Right here." I put her hand against my chest.

"I need to feel you," she murmurs, pressing a hand to her eye. "I just, I don't know what to do. I don't know... I don't know what's happening."

"You're upset, and you want to push it away." I encircle her with my arms, kissing her temple. "It's OK to be scared. It's over now. I'm here."

Three loud thumps against the door make us both jump, and I crush her against me.

"Out, right now." Sam's voice is sharp and clear. "Silas, I know you're in there."

Fuck. Juliet's wide eyes gaze up at me, more and more tears pouring over her lashes. She shakes her head, clasping my face in her hands.

"Silas-"

"It's OK." I stroke her hair, and place a kiss on her forehead.

"Silas!" Sam's voice is edged with irritation.

"Just give us a minute!" I bellow over my shoulder. She's so eager to see me suffer she can't even give me a second to get dressed.

Juliet is shaking so hard she can barely stay upright, leaning heavily on the counter as she watches me pull my shirt on and button it up. Loud sobs start to break from her throat, and by the time I unlock the bathroom door, she's near hysterical. Sam eyes us both as we step into the corridor, one hand on her hip.

"Had fun?" She cocks an eyebrow as she regards me with blatant disgust. "You really don't learn, do you?"

"Guess not." I put an arm around Juliet's shoulders as she covers her face with her hands. "I'm a bit dense that way."

"Evidently." Sam's gaze moves to Juliet. "She should go. We need to have a little talk."

I swallow hard as I press a kiss to the side of Juliet's head. "I told you, it was worth it, remember?"

"Go. Now." Sam's voice has dropped low.

"You're going to hurt him!" Juliet drops her hands from her face, her voice shrill as she continues to cry. "If you're going to hurt him, just kill us both!"

Sam rolls her eyes. "Oh, don't be so fucking dramatic."

"Fuck you!" Juliet hisses back, her arms locking around my waist. "You feeders are all the same."

Sam's eyes flame and she advances on us, and I step in front of Juliet.

"Hey now, you back the fuck off from her." I bare my fangs. "I swear to god-"

"Get her the fuck out of here right now, Silas." Sam's eyes flicker over my shoulder. "If she knows what's good for her, she'll go."

I turn to Juliet, and meet her eyes, cradling her jaw with my hands. "Go, alright? It'll be fine."

Her face is pulled into a defiant frown, and she shakes her head. "No, I'm not-"

I silence her with a kiss, ignoring the scoff that comes from Sam. There's no point hiding anything now. We've been discovered. It's all over. Sam's going to turn me in, and that will be the end of me.

"I'm sorry, angel." I murmur against Juliet's mouth. "But I need you to go now."

"I can't leave you." Her voice is strained, the words struggling to leave her throat.

"I need you to. Please."

"Will you two cut the theatrics?" Sam's arms are crossed over her chest, her booted foot tapping against the floor. "Get her out of here, now."

"Go. Now." My voice drops low, and Juliet squeezes my hands one last time before pushing past Sam and running out of the gym.

Sam's eyes stay fixed on me until the gym door slams home with a heavy thud. She rolls her eyes, leaning against the wall casually.

"Jesus, that was painful." She shakes her head as she gazes back at me."You two really got it bad for each other, don't you? Gonna change your name to Romeo?"

"What does it matter?" I shove my hands in my pockets. "You're going to turn me in."

"Am I?" Her coquettish tone sets my teeth on edge. "Now why would I want to do that?"

I scoff incredulously. "You are joking, aren't you? You've been waiting for this moment."

Sam pushes off the wall, tutting as she takes a few steps towards me. "Now, Silas, you think so little of me?" She looks me up and down, smirking. "I'm hurt."

"I don't fucking care."

She looks up at me, pursing her lips, and I can see in her eyes she's considering her next move. "You said I was your friend once."

"Yeah. Guess I was wrong."

"Oh no, honey. I'm the only friend you have here." She reaches out to touch my chest, eyes snapping up to mine when I jerk away from her hand. "I'm not going to turn you in."

"Why not?"

"Would you prefer it if I did?" When she's only answered with silence, she shrugs. "I'm not going to turn you in, because there's no point."

"So what do you want in return?" I know she wouldn't do this unless there was something in it for her. Why the fuck would she cover for me like this?

"I don't want a thing, Silas. I came here, as your friend. When I saw you'd cut the feed to the gym, I knew you'd made yet another mistake. So I came over here to stop you."

"Another mistake, ey?"

"Yeah, like the one you made the night of the storm, and the supply run to Savannah."

"You were baiting me."

Sam laughs lightly. "I was always very good at fishing, Silas. Fish are stupid. And so are men when they got a pretty girl in front of them."

"It's not like that," I snarl, feeling my rage building. "This isn't just some cheap lay, not like what you and me had."

"Ouch." Sam's nose wrinkles. "That wasn't called for."

"Fuck you."

"Maybe so, but either way, as your friend, I did come here to stop you from making a mistake."

"Juliet is not a mistake."

"She may not be, but coming inside her would be." Sam's face is infuriatingly neutral, her chin tipped up as a self-satisfied smile crosses her lips.

I recoil at her words. "What are - What do you mean, coming inside her would be?"

"I *thought* it would be a momentary thing, between the two of you." Sam rolls her shoulders, her gaze lazily moving back to the ceiling. "But that night you absconded with her to your cabin, when I could smell her practically dripping from your walls, I could see it wasn't going to end. You were just going to keep sleeping with her, no matter what."

Panic snakes its way up my back. "Yeah, she's mine, that's why."

"Mmmm, yours huh?"

"Yes."

"Well, not for much longer." Sam's icy gaze drops back to my face, and she tilts her head. "Did she tell you she got an exam this morning?"

"Yes."

"Did she tell you what kind of exam?"

"Yes." I growl, my hands balling into trembling fists. She's fucking enjoying this.

"And what do you think that was for?"

I lunge at Sam, slamming her against the wall. She almost moans as her back connects with the stone, her eyes bright red as she runs her tongue over her fangs.

"Pent up, honey? Did I interrupt before you got to finish?" She laughs in my face.

"Tell me what the fuck is going on or-"

"I got her transfer papers this morning." Her expression turns into one of defiant triumph, and my arm drops from her throat.

I blink stupidly, letting the words sink in. "Transfer? To where?"

"Charleston." The word rolls off Sam's tongue slowly, as though she's savoring how it tastes. "She's prime age."

My body reacts instantly to the grief and revulsion that wells up inside me. *Charleston.* The breeding farm. They're going to lock her in a room with a man jacked up on drugs, who'll rape her until she's pregnant. They'll force her to carry a baby that will be torn from her arms once she's done feeding it. And then they'll do it again. And again. And again...

Sam watches with detached curiosity as I stumble away from her, my back quickly connecting with the opposite wall in the tiny corridor.

"No." It's all I can say. It's the only word that's running on a loop in my head. "No. No. No."

"Yes, Silas." Sam takes a step towards me, clasping her hands in front of her. "Believe me, this will be for the best. Once she's gone, you can forget all about her."

"No." I shake my head, raising my hands to ward her off as she takes another step towards me. "No."

"Silas, she's not for you." She lifts her hands as though to touch me. "You'll be so much better off without her."

"Who ordered it?"

"That doesn't matter now." Sam's hands land on my shoulders. "What matters is that you need to get over this."

"It was you, wasn't it?" A white hot ember of rage runs up my spine, settling in the base of my skull as my vision goes red. "You ordered them to take her away, didn't you?" My hands aren't my own anymore. I curl both hands around Sam's throat and slam her into the wall. "You ordered them to take her away from me, didn't you?"

Sam's cool demeanor shatters ever so slightly, her eyes widening as she claws into my arms. "Silas, let me go."

"I want to hear you say it." I growl in her face. "I want to hear you say that you ordered them to take her away to be raped, over and over again. That you ordered them to tear her away from me."

"Silas, stop!" She pushes back against me with all her might, shoving me into the wall behind me.

But it's not enough, not nearly enough. The image of Juliet being forced away, the very idea of losing the woman I love more than anything I've loved in my life, gives me strength that Sam isn't prepared for. With every ounce of loss and grief I've been forced to endure driving through my veins, I pound Sam back across the corridor and into the drywall.

Her exclamation is caught by my hands landing around her throat again, crushing her neck in my hands. She squeaks, like a distraught animal, her eyes bugging out. She lands punches in my middle, too weak to deter me. Blood trickles from her nose as I squeeze harder and harder.

"No one takes her from me. No one." My vision flashes bright red, and with a twist of my hands and a loud crack, I wrench Sam's head from her body.

My shoulders are heaving, my fangs digging into my lower lip as her shocked, wide-eyed face stares back at me. Her body slumps down the wall, spilling blood on the ground, her fingers still twitching as her nerves register her body's final death.

Fuck, what have I done? My mind starts to race, trying to think what to do next. I take a deep breath, trying to calm down. I need to think logically.

It's late in the day, the gym will be empty until tomorrow

morning. I have that much time, and I need to use it now. I have to get us out of here.

I deposit Sam's body and her head in a cubicle in the bathroom, slamming the door behind me. The corridor's covered in blood, but it's not visible from the door. Unless an errant vamp gets nosy and sticks their head in here, no one will smell what's happened.

I look down at myself. I'm covered in blood. I hurry into the other bathroom, turning on the shower and stripping off my clothes. I bundle them up and throw them in with Sam's body once I'm clean.

I cross the gym, to the lockers, tearing them open until I find one containing a spare set of clothes. I leave the gym, closing the door securely behind me and casting a glance through the glass just to make sure the blood truly isn't visible from here. The compound is quiet, as preparations for dinner begin. The sun is low in the sky. I only have a few hours of daylight left.

I head straight to my cabin, pulling out a duffel bag from under my bed. I throw in a change of clothes and a bottle of blood before pulling on my sneakers. I cross the room to my desk, pulling out the gun from the drawer, then hesitating as I see the notepad I sketched Juliet in. I toss it in, before swiping the polaroid of Harriet and I along with the worn out cassette tape into the bag as well.

After leaving my cabin, I go straight to Sam's office. I check that no one has seen me before pulling the door closed behind me. Inside, I go straight to her computer. I click on "Perimeter" and disable all the sensors. The whole grid goes down without even alerting anyone.

I kill all the security cameras, and set the connection to the obs tower to go down in ten minutes. It's not much time, but I need to find Juliet now. Then I select the fence charges, and set them to go off in ten minutes as well. I open the drawer to Sam's desk and pull out the handgun she has stashed in there. I pull out a battery bank from the storage cupboard, and pluck the keys to one of the trucks from the wall.

Throwing the duffel bag over my shoulder, I head out of Sam's office. I look left and right, before sprinting across the grass to Juliet's dorm. The vamp at the door looks up at me and nods. "Hey man, they're all showering."

"Oh thanks."

I try not to walk too quickly towards the shower block, and as I approach, Juliet is coming towards me, her face red and puffy, her hair wet. Her eyes are fixed on the floor, she doesn't notice me, her shoulders trembling as she cries quietly.

When she's right in front of me, I reach out and brush her arm. She flinches, her hands flying to her mouth as her blood-shot eyes land on my face.

"What are you-"

"Is there anything in your locker that's important?" I ask, my fingers curling around her arm to draw her close.

She frowns, shaking her head. "What? Important?"

"Anything you wouldn't want to be without. Go and get it now, along with a change of clothes. Grab it, and come straight back here."

"Silas, what is this?"

"Trust me."

My words have the intended effect. Her mouth sets in a line, and she nods quickly, heading into the dorm. I try not to show how anxious I am, how fucking on edge I am, every second that she's out of my sight trickling by like an hour. We have seven minutes at most.

Crawley ambles past me, looking me up and down, frowning when he sees the battery bank in my hand. I hide the truck keys in my pocket and give him a smile.

"Alright mate?"

"Yeah, you?" He leans against a post, one hand in his pocket.

"Yeah all good, just had to get some things from a truck."

"Oh, OK." He nods. "And now you're just standing here with it all?"

I laugh, shrugging. "Sam told me to wait here, no idea why."

"Oh, right." Crawley nods. "She was looking for you."

"Well, she found me." I hold his gaze, even though I'm so fueled by anxiety I'm half-tempted to tear his head off too.

But Crawley pushes off the post and heads off with a wave of his hand. "Take care!"

"Yeah, you too!" I exhale heavily, relief flooding me as Juliet comes out of the dorm, a bundle of clothes rolled up in her arms. I head in her direction, and as I reach her side she turns tail, her eyes fixed downwards, and follows me wordlessly.

We round the dorm, across the open yard beside the obs tower, but I can hear raucous laughter drifting down, so I know they're distracted. We reach the truck, and Juliet climbs into the back seat as soon the door is open. She huddles down under the blanket, shivering lightly. She's scared. She has no idea what's happening. But her eyes flash to mine for a moment, and she gives me a weak smile.

She trusts me.

I slam the door, and quickly go to the garage, hauling out one generator and a solar pack, before thinking better of it and grabbing a second one. If this plan is going to work, I need to be able to drive a long distance. Two generators are better.

Once the generators are loaded onto the back, I know I'm down to maybe two minutes. I climb into the truck, and gun the engine.

"No matter what happens, stay down," I say to Juliet as I

turn the truck around and head for the gate. She doesn't answer, just stays silent in the back.

The gate guards all approach with raised hands as I drive up to them. I wind the window down, one hand in the duffel bag beside me.

"What's going on?" A guard asks me. "We don't have any runs scheduled."

I shrug, smiling amicably. "Ferris told me to head out and check a sensor."

"This late?" The guard looks over his shoulder, at the other vamps who all shrug and shake their heads. "She didn't tell us anything."

"Well, she just came to tell me they're down, so I better head out fast before I lose the light."

The guard rubs the back of his neck, considering my words for a moment. "I mean, I really can't let you out without clearance."

"If you don't let me out, Ferris is going to have your head," I say with a laugh.

"Just let me call her." He raises a hand and takes a step back from the truck.

"No need, mate!"

He stops at my words, his eyes widening for just a split second as I raise the gun into the window and fire straight into the middle of his face. His body is thrown backwards at the exact moment the fence charges all go off, the sound deafening. The gate clicks open as the perimeter power goes out, the vamps not noticing as they all scatter and run.

I put my foot down, the engine of the truck roaring as I barrel straight into the gate. The metal protests, but gives way, falling haphazardly to one side. The next gate is already opening, and there's a loud metallic scrape as the truck catches just the edge as I speed out into the open.

Juliet whimpers loudly as bullets hit the back of the truck.

"They'll stop in a minute, Jules, it's alright." The vamps won't waste the ammunition on a runaway truck. Sure enough, after about 30 seconds, the pinging stops.

"It's OK, angel," I say, reaching into the back seat. My hand is met with cool, steely fingers, wrapping around mine. "We're out. Just stay down for now, OK? Just until we're clear."

She does as I say, sniffling and crying softly. I try to come up with a plan, try to think what's next. The light is fading, and we won't make it all the way to where we need to go tonight.

Focus. Focus. Get away from the compound. Find shelter and keep her safe.

That's all I can do for now.

BY THE TIME Silas reaches for me, beckoning me out of the back seat with a soft, "Come on, angel," I've stopped crying, and mostly stopped shaking. I climb into the front seat, and Silas pulls me against him, one arm slung around my shoulders.

"Are you OK?" He keeps his eyes on the road, but his voice is so strained with worry.

"What happened back there?"

"Not now, angel." He brushes a kiss against my temple. "I'll tell you later, but not now."

"I thought she'd hurt you." I slump against him, relieved and scared in equal measure. "I was so sure she was going to drag you off somewhere, and they'd know and-"

"She won't be hurting anyone. Not anymore."

My head snaps up to look at his profile, his jaw ticking violently. "Did you kill her?"

He grinds his teeth for a second before giving me a terse nod. "Yes."

"What did she say to you? Was she going to turn you in?"

"Angel, I said not now." He squeezes my shoulders. "Not now. We need to drive and find some shelter, and then we can talk."

Then we can talk. My curiosity almost has me wanting to shake him, because what the hell happened back there? I look out at the road as it meets us, the light becoming deep golden as the sun begins to sink low over the horizon.

"Will they look for us?" I ask after a while, gently brushing my hand over his chest.

"I doubt it."

"You don't sound very sure of that."

He kisses my forehead, his fingers brushing lightly up and down the side of my neck, and any other questions I had melt away into irrelevance.

"Don't worry, Jules. I've got you, alright? Now, let me do the worrying."

I'm so overwhelmed with this feeling of freedom, this knowledge that he just busted me out, that he blew up half the compound if what I heard while hiding under that blanket was any indication. I snuggle up to him, breathing deeply as the evening breeze washes in through the window.

"I feel like I should be hysterical." I laugh softly. "I feel like I should be a mess after what just happened."

"It hasn't sunk in yet, that's all."

"Where are we going to go?"

Silas checks the rear view mirror, shifting in his seat. "We'll find somewhere, off the main roads, and bunker down there for the night. Then in the morning we'll keep driving."

"Where?"

"Roanoke. The vamps in Savannah mentioned a human colony up there. Living free of vampire rule, apparently."

I sit up, instantly alarmed. "A human colony? You want to take me-"

He hits the brakes, cutting off my words, and sweeps me into his arms. "*Us*, angel. I'm taking us to Roanoke." He kisses me urgently, his lips soft and warm. "I'm going to get us safe, and then we can be together, alright?" His eyes bore into mine, and I can't help but sigh.

"Alright."

His mouth shifts into a smile. "You said you trust me, didn't you?"

I nod emphatically. "I trust you, I do."

"Good." He kisses the tip of my nose, before turning back to the steering wheel. "Now, let's get off these roads so you can rest."

I have a million more questions, but I keep those for later. I can't help the sliver of dread that winds its way around my stomach at the mention of a human colony. Humans with no vamps - what does that mean for us? I'm not leaving Silas, not after what just happened, not after what he just did for us to be together.

A strange thought begins to spin around in my brain. I think back on the conversation we had about him being turned. He'd said it wasn't painful. It was like going to sleep and waking up a new person. That doesn't sound bad at all. I begin to wonder if he'd do that to me, if he'd be my maker so we could be together forever. The thought makes me uneasy, because I don't want to be a vamp. I want to be me. I want to be alive.

But I want to be with Silas too.

I startle awake to Silas's smiling face. I blink at him in the overhead light of the truck, realizing it's mostly dark outside. He's backlit and beautiful, reaching out to gently brush my cheek with his fingers.

"You fell asleep." He kisses my forehead and shifts me towards the door. "Come on, I found somewhere for the night."

I rub my bleary eyes, trying to focus on our surroundings in the semi-darkness. We're parked out front of a white farm-house. Thick vines have taken over one half of the crumbling facade, pulling windows from their frames. The porch is mostly sagging, the once-yellow door long since faded, the inset window smashed. It would have been a real sweet house back when folks lived here.

Silas flicks on a flashlight for my benefit, lighting the way across the overgrown yard. The porch creaks loudly under our weight, and Silas pushes the crooked door aside for me.

"I did a sweep," Silas says with a smile. "It's all clear inside. Just you and me."

"I like the sound of that." I follow him in, gazing up at the ceilings, at the dusty pictures hanging on the walls. Blue and white wallpaper peels from the walls, dotted with mildew. I can make out a wedding picture under a layer of dust, and a pair of boots stand by the stairs. A sign sits over what I guess was once the dining room, thick cobwebs hanging from it. *Eat Pray Love.*

It all makes me shiver. People lived here. People who had lives, people who bought cheesy signs for their home and loved them, people who were married and loved each other. And now Silas and I stand in the wreckage of all those lost lives, in the stark glow of a flashlight, seeking shelter in what was once more than likely a happy home.

Silas gives my hand a squeeze, and leads me past the stairs into the lounge room. An old dusty couch stands to one side, an armchair on its back behind a smashed coffee table. I snap my gaze down to the floor when the flashlight washes over the bloody hand marks streaked across the wall, long since imprinted into a dark rusty banner.

"I wonder who lived here," I murmur, sitting on the floor in front of the couch while Silas makes quick work of the wrecked furniture, moving it aside to reveal a fireplace. He doesn't respond, just sets about building a fire with logs he must have retrieved from outside while I was sleeping. "Is that a good idea?"

He looks over his shoulder at me, and I gesture to the fireplace.

"Smoke. The National Guard, or the Afflicted, what if they notice the smoke?"

Silas shrugs and goes back to his work. "I doubt they'll have drones out at night, it's almost pointless." He strikes a match, lighting cotton wool that looks like it's soaked in accelerant, and drops it into the kindling where it lights up with a loud snapping. "And the Afflicted are too brainless to notice something like smoke at night. Too busy seeking out blood."

My shoulders sag as what we've done begins to weigh down on me.

"What happened back there?" I ask as Silas moves across the floor to sit beside me.

He opens his backpack and pulls out a white bottle, shaking it before handing it to me. "Come on, you need to drink this."

"I don't want to drink that, I want to know what happened back there." I stare determinedly at the side of his face, the growing fire illuminating his rusty eyes. "Something happened, please tell me what."

"I told you, I killed Sam. We had to go." He turns to look at me, and holds out the white bottle again. "Please, just drink something, and then we'll talk."

His tone isn't making me feel any better. Something bad happened, I know that much. Sam said something that drove him into a rage. But I take the bottle with a sigh, twisting off the cap and taking a swig. It's a protein shake, thick and chalky, and it coats my throat unpleasantly. But it's filling at least, and Silas's smile grows as I eventually down the entire bottle.

"I'll hunt down some proper food tomorrow." He presses a kiss to my temple.

"Proper food?" I cock an eyebrow as I gaze up at him. "You gonna fry me some roadkill?"

He chuckles, putting an arm around my shoulders. "You sound so very southern when you talk like that."

"Well you can take the girl out of Georgia…" I nuzzle into him, draping my arm across his stomach, and let out a long exhale. "I can't believe you busted me out of there."

"I had no choice. I wasn't going to let them-"

"Let them what?" I sigh heavily. "I wish you'd stop being cryptic."

"They were going to send you to Charleston." He says the words heavily, as though he has to get them out before he thinks better of it.

My breathing halts for a second as I try to absorb his meaning. *Charleston.* I hear Matt's voice, telling me about all the women he'd been forced to sleep with. All the drugs they'd fed him to get him horny and hard and all the disgusting things required to make the babies the vamps desperately need. I cough out a gasp, and Silas's grasp around me tightens.

"You mean…" I still can't say it out loud.

"They were going to transfer you to the breeding farm."

"That's why they hadn't drained me in so long." *That's why they kept me alive.* It all makes sense now. Anyone else, they'd have shot. When I tried to… To kill myself. I squeeze my eyes shut. They brought me back, got me healthy again. Sending me to the gym, getting my weight up, and then that horrific examination. It was never about *me.* "They were keeping me for my uterus."

Silas swallows hard, his body tensing under my hands. I can feel the rage rolling off him.

"Yes, they were."

"And you killed Sam because she told you?"

My eyes fly open as his fingers notch under my chin, forcing me to look up at him. "Yes. Because she made out that you meant nothing, and that I would get over you. She had no idea, *no fucking idea*, that without you, *I'm* nothing."

My eyes go damp. "They were going to make me get pregnant."

Silas growls low in his throat. "And I wasn't going to let that happen. No one, you hear me? No one hurts you. I would never let anyone hurt you, or touch you like that. Nobody, ever."

"They were going to take me away from you." I reach up and stroke his cheek, and his hand curls around my wrist. He presses a kiss into the palm of my hand, his eyes slipping closed as he inhales.

"Yes. They were." He puts my hand to his forehead, and exhales heavily. "I couldn't bear it. I couldn't have them take you away. I wasn't going to let them do that to you, to us. So I did what I had to."

He pulls me into his lap, curling himself around me as though he wishes he could slip me under his skin. The warmth of the fire begins to wash over us, and my body begins to tingle with giddiness as I realize that we're free. I clasp a hand over my mouth to stop a giggle escaping.

Silas looks down at me with a crooked grin. "Angel?"

I nod, maybe a little too enthusiastically, and then Silas's eyes widen a little as I don't stop nodding. Tears are sliding down my cheeks, and the floor begins to tilt and shift under me even though I know we're sitting still.

"Jules, I need you to calm down, alright? Deep breaths."

I'm having a panic attack, I can feel it. My hands start shaking, and Silas clasps me even tighter to him. "S-Silas." My fingertips claw into him. "Oh fuck, Silas, p-please, I don't-"

"It's alright, you're alright, I've got you." He strokes my hair. "Listen to me, focus on my voice. I'm here, and you're safe."

"I never thought-" I break off as a loud sob bubbles up my

throat. "F-five years." I almost scream the words. Five years. Five fucking years.

"I know, I know." Silas begins to rock me gently, I think. I can't be sure, as the room continues to spin around me. "I should have gotten you out of there the day I laid eyes on you. I should have run with you right then and there."

"They-they were going to l-let some man rape me. They were going to-Oh *god*." My head falls against his chest. "I never - I never want anyone to- to..." I try to breathe, clawing at him. "B-bite me. Please, I want you to make me feel good."

He tenses, his hands splayed on my back. "Jules-"

"*Bite me.*"

With a heavy breath he tips my head back, sinking his fangs into my neck. The sweetness floods my body before my mind can comprehend what's happening, and I sag in his arms. The blazing ecstasy of my orgasm pushes out all the dread and panic, leaving nothing but a white cloud of bliss in its wake. Silas's hand cups my breast, gently rolling my nipple between his fingers as his tongue sweeps across my skin, lapping up my blood.

I stay in his arms, my eyes closed, as he withdraws his fangs, licking away the punctures left behind. His hand stays on my breast, caressing me as tiny aftershocks jolt through my body.

"Thank you," I murmur. "I needed that."

"Yes, you did." His fingertips stroke down my stomach. "And I did too. But we need to be careful."

My eyes flutter open, and I frown up at him. "Careful?"

"I can't take too much blood if we don't have food for you." His hand splays over my stomach. "So, no more biting until we get you some protein."

"OK." I push the hair out of my face. "I guess you can always just give me an orgasm the old-fashioned way."

He laughs softly. "Trust you to have a panic attack and then be thinking about sex two minutes later."

"It's not my fault sex with you is like therapy."

"Well, as your therapist I'm going to prescribe you daily sessions." He chuckles as I lay my head back against his chest. "At least once a day."

"That sounds good to me." I sigh as his hand strokes my stomach. "So this colony in Roanoke, they'll let us both live there?"

Silas probably thinks I don't notice the split second hesitation before he answers, but it may as well have been a year.

"Sure, that's how it sounded."

"So you don't know?"

"Angel, you need to sleep." He strokes my hair again, brushing his fingertips against my scalp, and any protest I was about to utter dies on my tongue. "Now, we'll spend the night here, and drive the rest of the way to Roanoke tomorrow. Sleep."

And because the day was so overwhelming, I do.

THE SUNSHINE IS bright the next morning, and Silas has the solar panels set up with the generators on the porch when I walk outside.

"Good morning," he says with a smile. "You slept like a log."

I rub my eyes. "Yeah, well, when I get to sleep with you, I guess I sleep better."

"I'm glad to hear it." He looks up at the sky, and his expression shifts for a moment. "I don't much like these clouds."

The clouds swirling above us are thick and dark, almost green. The air is sticky with humidity, and the wind is blowing through the tops of the tall trees. I look back at him, and he sets about packing up the generators.

"We should move."

"OK, but have they charged enough to get us to Roanoke?"

He lifts one generator and pushes it into the bed of the truck. "I don't know, we'll try."

"But what if we don't -"

"It's alright, angel." He cuts me off with a wide smile as he picks up the second generator and deposits it back in the truck.

"You have nothing to worry about. I'll keep you safe no matter what happens."

We drive away from the crumbling house just as the first crack of thunder sounds in the distance.

"Maybe we're driving away from it," I say, gazing out the window at the clouds that just keep getting darker and darker.

"Yeah, maybe." Silas sounds as unsure as I do.

I try to ignore the impending storm, playing with my fingers as I try to think about something to talk about other than the uncertainty of our situation, but Silas beats me to it.

"Tell me about your brother," he says as we take the turn back into the highway.

"Kaden?" I sigh heavily. "Um, well, he was tall, and uh, he was on the wrestling team in high school. He was real strong, and he ate like crazy. Mom used to joke about needing a second mortgage just to feed him."

Silas laughs, his hand flexing around the steering wheel as he reaches over with the other to curl his fingers around mine. "Did he want to become a professional wrestler?"

"No, he wanted to be a cop, like my dad, but my dad tried to talk him out of it."

Silas's gaze flickers over to me. "Oh?"

"My dad hated being a cop. He said he became one to do good, and all he saw was corruption."

"Why didn't he get out of it?"

I shrug. "I guess... I think he was worried about not being able to support us, and he wanted us to be secure and out of the house before he and mom..." I trail off.

"Sorry, we don't have to talk about this."

"It's alright, I guess sometimes it still hits me that back then we thought we had so much time. All that life ahead of us, and now..." I gaze out the window. The clouds are becoming thicker, and lightning flashes in the distance. "Now, I don't even know what a future would look like."

"What did you get out of your locker?"

I fidget with a loose thread on my pants. "I have a locket, with a picture of me and Kaden in it. My mom gave it to me when I left home to go to college, because she knew I'd miss him. She'd worn it since we were kids. It's the only thing I had with me when they rounded us up. I wasn't allowed to keep the chain, but I have that at least." I gaze over at him. "And you? What did you take with you?"

"A cassette tape and a polaroid picture." His mouth quirks. "Do you even know what a cassette tape is?"

"Haha," I drawl sarcastically. "Yes I do. What's on it?"

Silas takes a heavy breath. "It's the recording of the top 40 countdown, on the radio. But in the background you can hear my... my friend and I, laughing. It's the last recording I have of her."

"Is she the girl in the picture?"

He nods, hands flexing around the steering wheel. "Yeah."

"What happened to her?" I feel like I'm prying, like he doesn't want to talk about this, but he huffs out a breath, leaning his head back as his eyes stay tilted towards the road.

"She killed herself, after... After some boys at school assaulted her."

My stomach drops, and I feel cold all over. "Oh jesus, I'm so sorry."

His hand shoots over to grab mine. "I shouldn't have said anything. I shouldn't have told you."

"No, no it's fine, I mean, I wanted to know. I'm sorry. I just... That's so sad." I realize now just what my attempt would have set off, what painful memories Silas would have had to face. "I'm sorry if I brought that all back."

He looks over at me with a heavy frown. "What? No.

That's not - Juliet, I was distraught because of what happened to *you*. Of course it brought back bad memories, but that's not what you should be worried about. I was able to help you, and save you. I..." He trails off, looking back at the road with slumped shoulders. "I mean, I hope I helped you."

"You did. Really, you did." I squeeze his hand, desperate for a change of subject. "I still remember the first time I saw you, in the cafeteria. I remember thinking you'd be attractive if you were alive."

Silas's shoulders lift as he chuckles. "Is that right?"

"In my defense, you did stare at me in a pretty creepy way."

"Yeah, I did that a lot those first few months." His mouth lifts into a grin. "Even while you were asleep."

I gasp and swat at his arm. "You pervert!"

He snaps up my wrist and hauls me into him, wrapping one arm around me as he continues to drive. "Don't even pretend that doesn't get you all hot and bothered." He chuckles as I glare up at him. "You need to accept you're a little freak."

"I guess I just needed you to help discover that."

"I guess so."

Thunder rumbles loudly, so loudly we can hear it clearly over the engine. The trees lining the highway are swaying heavily, torn back and forth by the wind that's starting to howl. I look out of the rear window, and the clouds on the horizon are a dark forest green, riddled with lightning bolts.

"This storm is getting worse."

Silas huffs out a breath through gritted teeth. "Dammit."

"Where are we?" I look around us, but we're on a stretch of highway with no discernible markers, no abandoned buildings, nothing but trees as far as the eye can see.

"We're in South Carolina," Silas says, leaning over the steering wheel to look at the storm through the windshield. "But we can't keep driving in this." Tiny hailstones begin to ping against the truck, interspersed with fat drops of rain that bead and race down the windows.

"Where do we go?" I don't like the panic that laces my voice, but for some reason the idea of being stuck out on a highway in rural South Carolina while a tornado is building doesn't make me feel good.

Before Silas can answer, a fence appears along the edge of the road, running the tree line until it leads to a huge wood and iron gate. One side hangs on just by the lower hinge, the other lies flat on the road. Overhead, in swirly black wrought iron, is the name *Chapel View*.

"That's probably an old estate," I say, pointing at the gate. "If we're lucky it's still standing, and they might have a storm shelter."

Silas turns the wheel, and we bump along what was once a nice paved drive, but is now riddled with holes, the pavers standing up haphazardly or gone completely. The space left behind by the missing gate is wide enough for the truck to fit through easily.

Live oaks line the drive, long mossy tendrils swaying wildly in the wind. It's almost a little eerie, their color stark against the bruised sky above us.

Then the house comes into view ahead, tall and grand with towering white columns. Vines have taken over much of the frontage, but it's still impressive, if a little gothic and imposing in this light. I lean forward, bracing my hands against the dash as we approach.

There's a circular drive, covered in a maze of ivy, and in the middle stands an old fountain. A statue of a woman draped in a toga, a jug in her arms from which once poured water into the large basin below, stands on top.

"Well someone was well off," Silas says as he brings the

truck to a stop. He gazes up at the big house, and shakes his head, before gunning the engine again.

"Where are you going?"

"To find something smaller." We round the house, following the ivy tracks through the trees and past an old barn. "Houses like this will have smaller houses around them, and that place is ridiculous."

Sure enough, we come upon a smaller farmhouse, and it's so perfectly preserved I have to blink several times to make sure I'm not imagining it. It has two gables, and a white porch that's only missing a few posts from the railing. There are even faded curtains still hanging in the windows.

"How is this place still standing like this?" I murmur. "It looks like someone still lives there."

Silas brings the truck to a stop and turns to me. "Stay here, with the doors locked and keep your head down, understand?"

I nod, ducking down in my seat. Silas grabs a gun from underneath his seat, even though he probably doesn't need it. He climbs out of the truck, and the locks click into place. I try not to panic again, taking deep even breaths and reminding myself that the house is more than likely empty, it probably just looks like someone lives there, it's fine.

The minutes tick by, and the thunder overhead seems to growl almost constantly. The wind swishing through the trees is almost as loud as the storm, and the truck wobbles a little as it's battered by a gust.

I inhale sharply as Silas tears the door open and climbs back in.

"All clear, just going to park the truck in the barn and then we can go and take shelter in there."

"Does it have a basement?"

Silas nods, pulling up outside the barn. "I'll go open the doors." He turns to me with a smile. "You can drive, right?"

I blink at him. "Uh, yeah, I can, but-"

"Good, I'll open the doors, you drive in." He climbs out before I can protest, and I stare at the steering wheel for a good few seconds.

I can drive. My mom taught me how, years ago. She was a good driver. I was a good driver. But my palms are clammy as I slide into the driver's seat.

My feet brush the pedals, and I grip the steering wheel as Silas throws back the doors of the barn and waves me in. *OK, this is OK. I can do this. No big deal.*

I shift into drive, and the engine roars as I realize the emergency brake is still on. I release it, and the truck lurches forward. I slam my foot on the brake, and Silas laughs, waving me on. I take a deep shuddering breath, and gently press my foot down on the gas. The truck moves forward, into the dark barn, and once I've cleared the door, I bring it to a stop.

My hands are shaking when Silas opens my door.

"See?" He grins up at me. "You never forget how to drive."

"That was so weird."

"But so cool, right?" He raises an eyebrow.

I nod, my shaking hands still gripping the steering wheel. "Yeah. And normal."

Silas's grin melts into a warm smile. "Come on then." He puts a hand over mine on the steering wheel. "Let's get inside before this rain gets any heavier."

I nod, putting the truck into park before I push down the emergency brake and kill the engine. Silas scoops me down out of the seat, and I wobble on his arm as my feet touch the ground.

"Alright?" He asks.

"Yeah, I'm fine." Why has driving a car set me off like this?

I let Silas guide me across the yard back to the sweet little farmhouse, and he pushes through the faded red door into the foyer.

It's gorgeous. Dusty, for sure. But it's all perfect, like the owners just walked out a few weeks ago to go on vacation. White stairs lined with blue carpet lead up to the second story, and a hallway leads past them down to what looks like a kitchen.

To our right is a lounge room with overstuffed sofas and a big rug with an indiscernible pattern on it. Faded checkered curtains hang on the windows, through which lightning flashes wildly. Rain begins to beat down on the roof.

"How does this place still look so nice?" I ask, taking a few tentative steps into the lounge room.

"It's like this upstairs too," Silas says, running a hand over his damp hair. "I have to wonder if someone was here until recently."

"How would they not have been discovered?" I walk closer to the fireplace, to the mantlepiece lined with candles.

"It's pretty isolated out here," Silas says, putting the bags he carried in from the truck down on the sofa. "But either way, no one's been here for a while, and we can wait out the storm." He gestures for me to follow him, and we head through a narrow hallway into the kitchen.

"Oh wow," I murmur. It's an old kitchen, still equipped with a wood stove. A table with bench seats is built into a bay window, a glass lantern hanging over it. Wooden counters with green-fronted doors are built around the edge, with a large copper sink under another window to our left. "This place is adorable."

"Dream home, angel?" Silas asks me with a smile. "And look what else I found." He goes to a tall cupboard door and throws it open. It's a pantry, completely stocked with tins of food and bags of grains. I almost shriek in surprise, rushing at the cupboard and pulling two of the tins from one of the shelves.

"Spaghetti-os?" I can't help but laugh, and Silas's eyes are sparkling as I look up at him, mouth agape. "You have to be kidding."

"Guess I won't need to go and find that roadkill after all, ey?"

I look back down at the cans in my hands. "No, these have to all be out of date."

Silas shakes his head. "Nope, I can smell that everything in here is absolutely fine. Believe me, rotten food is pungent. If it was off, I'd know."

An incredulous laugh bubbles from my lips. "I can't believe this. All this food." I shove my head back into the cupboard and squeal as my hands fall on a red and white tin. "There's beanee weenees!"

"There's *what?*" Silas asks from the stove, where he's attempting to start a fire.

I snatch up the can and display it to him proudly. "Beanee weenees! It's beans and franks! My grandma used to make them for us when we went camping."

Silas snorts and shakes his head. "And you Americans say British food is disgusting."

I hug the can of beans to my chest like an old friend as Silas gets a fire going in the stove, before lighting the lantern over the table. The storm is getting stronger, wind whistling through the eaves of the old house, but it's all strangely comforting.

I find some old saucepans under one of the benches, and Silas rinses them out with some water before tearing open the tin of beans like he's simply taking off a bottle cap. He dumps them in the saucepan, stirring them as they bubble, and the smell of my childhood fills the kitchen.

My mouth is watering violently by the time they're heated

through, and Silas laughs heartily when I start eating straight from the pan.

"Hungry, angel?"

I nod, my mouth too full to respond. I didn't even notice how hungry I was, but I'm convinced this is the best meal I've ever had in my life. My eyes damn near roll back in my head as I take one delicious mouthful after another, until the pan is practically clean.

I wipe my mouth with the back of my hand, then give Silas a small smile when my eyes meet his. "Um, I was really hungry."

He leans back against the counter, arms crossed over his chest, smiling as he shakes his head. "Well, I'm glad that hit the spot then."

I lick my lips. "It did. Very much."

"Good." He looks around the kitchen with a sigh. "Well, this is definitely the place to bunker down for the night."

Or forever. I don't say it, but the thought makes me all warm and fuzzy inside. This cute little house, just me and Silas. *Just me and Silas*. I balk a little, rubbing my arm as I try to count and remember the last time they gave me a depo shot. I do the math, then do it again, and again, and after a minute I see Silas watching my face curiously.

"Everything OK?"

I swallow hard, then nod quickly, walking over to him and wrapping my arms around his waist. "Yeah, everything's fine. More than fine."

"Good." He lowers his mouth to kiss me, and even though I know it's irresponsible to get pregnant now, and I really don't want to, the thought of it sends shivers down my spine. His hands run up and down my back, cupping my ass, and suddenly he's lifted me up and spun us so I'm on the kitchen counter. "You taste ridiculous right now," he says with a laugh against my lips.

"Welcome to the South."

He laughs again, yanking my shirt off over my head. "Indeed."

His eyes move hungrily over my breasts as he unbuckles his belt, and I lift my ass to scooch off my pants. I put my heels up on the bench as he undresses, and his naked body takes my breath away every single damn time. He's just too beautiful.

He drops to his knees, running his tongue up my center in one long lick, and my toes curl around the edge of the counter. "Mmm," he growls, "this tastes exquisite though."

I never realized how much I'd held back before, even when we were out in the forest, even when we were in Silas's cabin - there'd always been something locking me down, not letting me really let go the way I wanted to. Even when he'd been in my ass, and given me the orgasm that I thought was going to fry every neuron in my brain, I'd been aware somewhere in the back of my mind that someone might hear us, that we'd get found out and Silas would get hauled away and tortured.

But here, in this charming kitchen in a farmhouse hundreds of miles from the compound, I gasp and moan, my hands carving through Silas's hair as he sucks on my clit, screaming his name as I come. I tremble on the counter, my head slung back against the wall, as Silas rises to his feet. I open my eyes to watch him as his dick slides inside me, the sheer ecstasy on his face as he fills me completely almost enough to unravel me right then and there.

He fucks me slowly, taking his time, looking down to watch himself sink into me, pressing his thumb to my still-throbbing clit.

"Fuck," he breathes. "I could watch this pussy stretch like this for me all day." He hisses in a breath as I moan. "That's a good girl, getting so tight for me. Come on my cock, angel. I want to fill this cunt up while you scream for me."

My thighs tremble as he slams his hips against me, my body raging with desire more powerful even than the storm outside. He spits on my left nipple, and the tingle of electricity from his venom makes my back arch. His fingers work my nipple between them, and my stomach tenses as I begin to contract on his cock.

At that moment, he pulls out of my pussy and pushes his soaked cock into my ass. I squeal through my scream, my body crying out at the intrusion. I'm still coming, my body shuddering as he lifts me further, thrusting into me as I claw at his chest.

"Silas, *fuck*." The last word is drawn out on a long moan, because even though there's pain, it's edged with pleasure so intense I can't think, I can barely breathe. He pushes two fingers into my pussy, fucking me with his hand and his cock at the same time, his other hand tangling in the hair at the base of my neck to draw me to him. With a groan, he sinks his fangs into my throat, and my whole body explodes. I scream and thrash, the pain making my orgasm sing through my entire body, my face flushed with heat, sweat dripping down my spine.

Silas releases deep inside me, and I'm nothing but a spent rag doll in his arms.

"Do you have any idea how perfect you are?" He withdraws his cock, and I'm shivering like I have a fever. "Do you know how good it feels to fill you up with my cum? Knowing that you're mine."

I lick my lips, nodding. "Yours. I'm yours."

"Yes you are."

I'm aware of being carried upstairs and being deposited on a bed. Somehow, Silas heats enough water to wash us both, and there are cold tiles against my feet as he cleans me down. Candlelight flickers as lightning flashes through the windows, and then I'm in a soft bed, Silas's naked body warming mine as deep sleep claims me.

As I drift off, I can't be sure if I dream the words, but I hear Silas's voice, warm and comforting against my ear.

"I love you, angel."

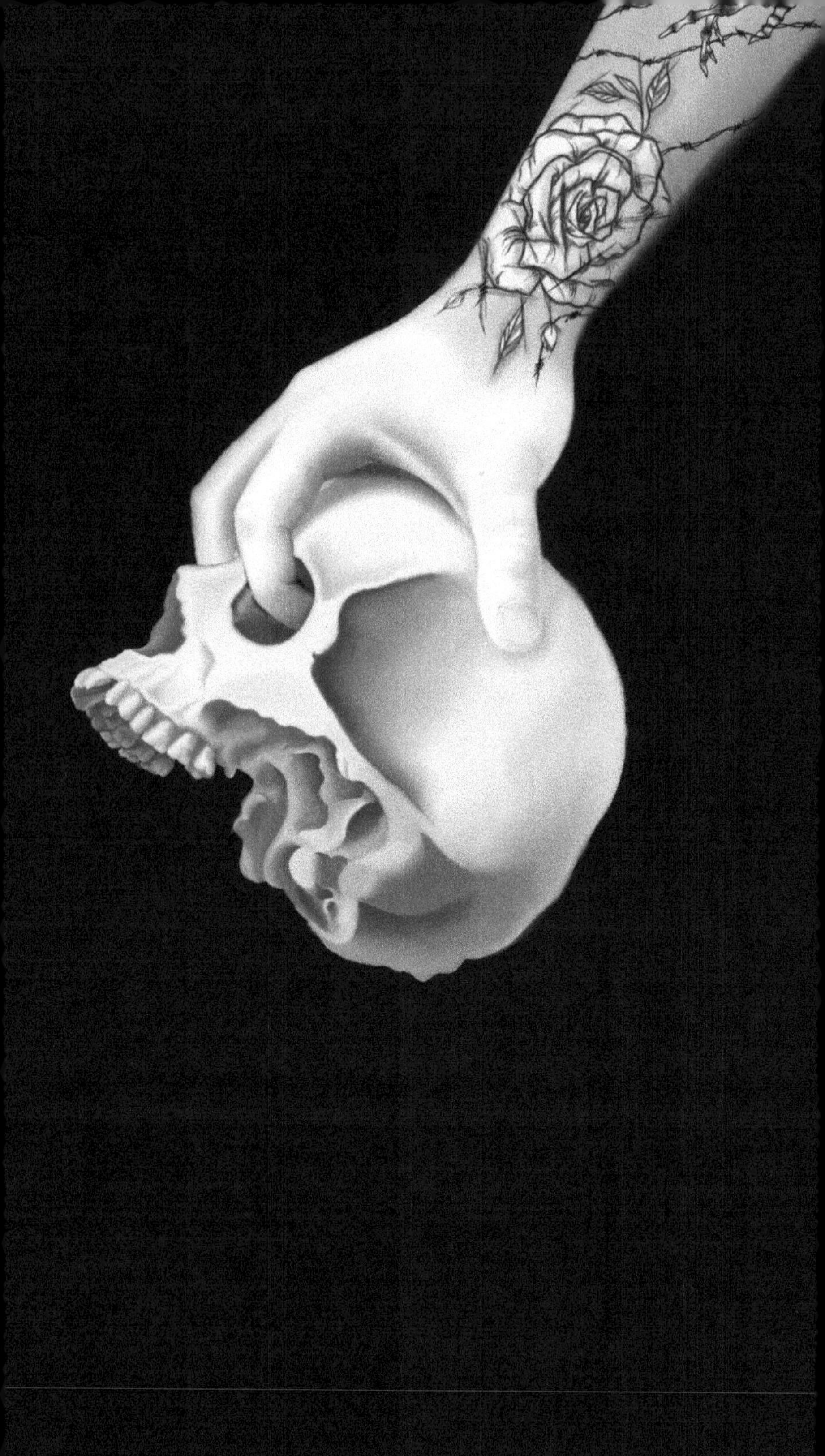

CHAPTER 33

SILAS

I WATCH Juliet as she sleeps, her breathing deep and even. She's been asleep for hours, since I fucked her into oblivion in the kitchen of our pseudo-dream house. I should have been more gentle with her. I shouldn't have taken her ass like that with no warning.

But the surprised squeak that burst from her, smelling her desire and fear mingled with that sour edge of pain - fuck, what that did to me. My perfect, dirty slut. My perfect girl. *My girl.*

She was already asleep when I told her I loved her. When I murmured to her that I wanted to put a baby in her, so that she'd be mine forever. I can't tell her that I didn't come in her pussy because I'm scared of what I want. I can't tell her that the idea of filling her with my cum til she's pregnant makes me so hard I can't think. I can't tell her that for the first time I want a future I could never envision before.

But now the thoughts won't let me go, and I shift her in my arms so she's on her back. I move over her, teasing her clit with the head of my cock. She stirs but doesn't wake, her lips parting slightly as she murmurs in her sleep.

"You're so fucking beautiful when you sleep," I tell her. I push a finger inside her, biting back a groan when I find that she's wet, practically dripping for me. She's wet enough to take me now, for me to sink into her without waking her.

I kiss her neck, smelling the blood that's gently pulsating through her body. I slide inside her slowly, watching her nipples peak as her body reacts to me. She's completely relaxed in her dream state, warm and pliant, her head tilted slightly to the side so I can see her pulse quicken.

I don't fuck her yet, just lie like that, savouring the feeling of her wrapped around my cock. I suck one of her pretty tan nipples into my mouth. She shifts lightly, the movement causing her to tighten around me, and I groan. I start to move slowly, and she gets wetter and warmer.

"Are you dreaming about me?" I murmur against her ear. "Are you dreaming about me fucking you, angel?"

She makes little sounds, tiny gasps and moans. Her eyelashes flutter, and she frowns a little.

"Oh." It's more of a breath than a word. Her hands are on my back, her body still so dreamily soft. "It's not a dream."

"No, it's not, angel." I pick up the pace, and within minutes both of us are hot and sweating, caught underneath the thick blanket. Her eyes are wide open now, gazing up at me as I fuck her hard. "Such a dirty slut," I pant, my cock hammering into her, right to her end. "Wet for me even in your sleep."

She moans, her eyes rolling back in her head. "Oh god."

I wrap a hand around her throat. "Who?"

She stutters, inhaling sharply as I press the sides of her neck. "Oh fuck... Silas."

I chuckle darkly. "Is your ass still sore, angel?"

She nods, breathing rapidly. "Don't-"

"I want my cum spilling out of this pussy." I hitch her leg higher over my hip, and her back arches off the bed. "Come for me, angel."

It only takes a few more strokes for her cunt to quiver

around me. The sensation is too much. My desire is making me foolish. I know I shouldn't, but I roar out my release, spilling deep inside her. Her fingers are clasped around the edge of the pillow, her head thrown to the side, her hair covering her face. Every puffed breath sends tendrils of that soft gold hair fluttering from her lips.

Fuck, she's perfect.

I pull out of her and move down between her thighs. She doesn't protest as I lick and suck her clit, determined to make her come again with all my cum inside her. She draws in one sharp, small breath after another, her body clenching, and with a high-pitched whimper, she pulsates on my lips.

"Good girl," I murmur against her dripping cunt. "What a good fucking girl you are."

I trace my tongue along the scars on her labia, down her thigh, my mark, my brand. I have to take a steadying breath, because the feeling of that raised skin against my tongue has me hard, and I know she needs to rest and eat before I bend her over the kitchen bench and fuck her again.

"Is it still storming?" Her voice is breathy and spent, and she blinks as I stroke the hair out of her face.

"It is, angel." Rain batters the window as I lower my mouth to hers. "No tornado, but still storming."

"Well, we'd better stay here then." She pulls me down to her, and we lie in the bed together, my arms encircling her tightly. We both doze off for a little while, but I don't sleep deeply. I'm not even tired. I'm simply happy, and more comfortable than I've been in years.

When I wake a while later, the sky is barely brighter, still heavy with angry clouds. Juliet rolls over in my arms and grins up at me.

"Good morning, again." She kisses my collarbone. "Kinda disappointed I'm not waking up with your dick inside me."

I laugh and stretch, tucking a hand behind my head. "I have to say I'm enjoying doing whatever I want to you."

"So am I." She lays her chin on my chest, gazing at me with her big grey eyes. "But not anal. I don't mind everything else, but anal, that's an awake thing. *Wide* awake."

"Understood, angel." I caress her forehead with my fingertips. "You feel like heaven when you're asleep."

She smiles at me, her eyes betraying all that simmering lust that lies beneath the surface. "I loved waking up like that. Your mouth." She presses a kiss to my chest. "Your fingers." Her tongue flicks over my nipple piercing. "Your cock. Whatever you want to put inside me while you wake me up, I don't mind."

I groan as her tongue probes my piercing again. "You need to eat first."

"Eat what?" She begins to move down my stomach, licking and kissing as she goes.

"Angel, I mean it." But I give up protesting as she moves down my body, and when her mouth descends on my cock, I simply give in to the feeling. Her tongue explores my length, flicking up and down, her teeth nipping at my piercing. She takes me deep, her head bobbing up and down lightly.

"Let's just stay here forever," I say with a groan, curling my fingers into her hair. She makes a little choking sound as I shove my cock to the back of her throat, her hands digging into my hips, urging me to fuck her mouth. "Fuck, let's just stay here, angel."

She hums, the sound vibrating straight through me, and I explode in her mouth. She swallows everything, licking her way gently up my shaft before releasing me with a soft pop. She grins at me, licking her lips.

"Too bad you don't sleep much, I could wake you up like this."

I laugh, pulling her into my arms. "I'll have to start sleeping more then." I kiss her forehead as she sighs happily. "Come on, you need to eat breakfast."

"And what about you?" She gazes up at me, her eyes suddenly full of concern. "I mean, you need more blood than what you brought with you, right?"

"I'll be alright. If you eat plenty while we're here, I can drink yours safely. I just don't want to hurt you."

"You mean I get extra orgasms in a day?" She laughs as I smack her ass. "I'm down with that."

"Right you, up now, and eat."

We pull on our clothes and head down to the kitchen, where I cook her another bizarre tin of convenience food that has her clapping her hands with glee. She eats all of it, and her cheeks are pink, her lips full, and she looks so much better than she ever did at the compound. She was always beautiful, but just two days away from that place and she doesn't look like a captive anymore.

"Did you mean that?" She asks me.

"Mean what?"

"What you said, while I was sucking your cock." She smirks at me. "About staying here forever?"

I lean back in my seat and stare out the window. Rain washes across the open field in heavy sheets, fog swirling in the tops of the trees.

"In another life, yeah. You and me, we'd stay here. Have our sweet little home. Maybe a dog. Do the hobby farm thing. Fuck all night."

When I look back at her, her expression is somewhere between contentment and sadness.

"That sounds nice." She looks down at her hands. "You know I haven't had a depo shot in a while, right?"

"I know that."

Her eyes remain downcast. "You said it was hard for a vampire to get a human pregnant."

"It is." I lean across the table, extending a hand which she takes, but still doesn't look up at me. "Do you not want me to come inside you? Is that what you're saying?"

She shakes her head, then shrugs. "I don't know. What did you mean when you said that? Like, how hard are we talking here? Like a one in a million chance?"

"I've only ever heard of it happening a handful of times. I can't be sure of the odds. You're young and healthy, maybe you'd be fertile enough... I don't know." I squeeze her hand, and she looks up at me, her eyes shining with tears. "Angel, if you don't want to run that risk, I'll pull out. I don't want you to worry."

"You like the idea though, don't you?"

I'm taken aback, combing through my memories to think if I said anything that betrayed just how feral the idea of her carrying my baby makes me. "Nothing that makes you unhappy makes me happy."

She sniffles and nods. "OK. Maybe in another life, but right now..."

A loud crash of thunder sounds overhead, and she jumps. I take her hand in both of mine.

"Guess we'll be staying here a little longer, ey?"

She smiles at me, shyly at first. "I guess so. I'm sure we'll find a way to keep entertained."

THE STORM RAGES on for days. A tornado doesn't eventuate, but I'm sure one passes not too far from us on the second day after our arrival. The wind howls and the thunder is louder than anything I've ever heard in my life.

Juliet and I stay holed up in our little farmhouse, taking strolls to stretch our legs when the wind stops howling long enough. The rain doesn't bother her at all, in fact she prefers walking in it, tipping her head up to meet the falling drops, her eyes closed, her expression one of pure bliss.

We don't see any Afflicted, and I wonder if the horde we saw on that last aborted trip to Savannah made their way to the compound. They haven't come this way, which is a relief. I'd worried at first that the farmhouse had been some sort of hideout for marauders - humans that escaped the compound and now live out in the wild, evading vamps and attacking any humans that crossed their path.

But no one returns to the house, and my exploration of the main house one day tells me no one has even looted the place. There were still plates on the table, as though the occupants had been interrupted and dragged out during a meal. It makes me shudder, but it also fills me with relief that no one seems to know about this place.

I entertain the thought of staying here several times, usually when I'm buried inside Juliet. I know I need to take her to Roanoke. I know we need the safety of bars and weapons and barbed wire. I can't keep her isolated out here forever, as much as I want to.

When we're not fucking, Juliet and I spend our time drawing, or reading one of the many books we found at the main house. Juliet reads me Shakespeare, putting on theatrical British accents that make me howl with laughter.

I hate this feeling. I hate how content I feel. We have so much time here, to explore each other, to discover each other in a way we couldn't before. I respect Juliet's wishes to not come inside her cunt, but coming in her ass or her mouth, even lashing her stomach or her back with my cum, it's all heavenly. I wake her with my cock or my mouth most mornings, unable to resist her warmth.

Several times I've bent her over the sofa or the counter with no warning, tearing her clothes off and fucking her breathless. She loves it, the fire in her eyes at being used by me igniting every single time.

I could live the rest of my life like this.

"What're you thinking?" Juliet is lying on her stomach, naked on the bed as she reads, snapping me from my thoughts.

"I was just thinking it's stopped raining."

She immediately understands my meaning, and gazes out the window. "Oh. I guess it has."

"But the generators need charging, you know. So they'll need a full day of sunlight before I can drive the truck again."

Juliet nods emphatically. "Yeah, absolutely."

"And it might start raining again." I gesture to the grey sky. "Looks heavy out there."

"It does."

We stare at each other for a little while. Juliet eventually climbs off the bed, crossing the room and straddling me where I sit on the armchair.

"You haven't had any blood today, have you?"

"I'm alright, angel." I stroke her hair back over her shoulders, running my fingers through it.

"I need you big and strong," she says, bracing her hands against my shoulders. "You need blood."

"Mmm, fine, but not from your neck."

Her eyebrows shoot up in surprise. "From where then?"

I lock an arm around her waist, carrying her down to the floor and laying her on her back. She sucks in a little breath of anticipation as I push apart her thighs.

"Do you want it to hurt a little, angel?"

She bites her lip and nods.

"Such a desperate little slut." I run my mouth along her thighs. "You'll even let me hurt you just so you can get off." I shove two fingers inside her, and she gasps. "Fuck my hand, there's a good girl."

She lifts her hips and rocks them against my hand, her hands flat on the floor as she holds herself steady.

"That's it. Fuck, your cunt is so pretty, angel." I watch her pussy take my fingers in, feel it becoming wetter as she keeps moving. I curl my fingers, and she moans as I find her g-spot. "Good girl, make yourself come, I want to feel that pussy as you come."

"I need more," she pants. "My clit, please."

I rub her clit with my thumb. "Like this?"

"Ohh, yeah. Like that." She rocks herself harder, her body moving frantically, begging for release. "Oh fuck, fuck, *fuck*."

She becomes tighter around my hand, and she trembles as her orgasm has her come undone. I stroke inside her, before withdrawing my fingers, putting them in my mouth and sucking her off them. She tastes perfect, and her sweetness spikes my own arousal so sharply that I don't even warn her before I sink my fangs into her upper thigh.

She screams, arching violently off the floor, and a gush of heat washes across my chest. My triumph is so loud I can practically hear it echoing through my skull. I gulp down her blood, hot and sweet, before licking over the wounds. I look up her body, over her quivering stomach, to her flushed face.

"Oh fuck, what the fuck?" Her head drops back against the floor. "What the fuck was that?"

"You soaked me, angel."

Her head shoots back up, eyes wide with alarm. "I what?"

"You came so hard you squirted."

She yelps, trying to wriggle away, but her body isn't obeying her just yet. "I'm so sorry!"

"It's a good thing, angel. Never apologize for feeling good."

She covers her face with her hands. "Oh my god, how *embarrassing*."

I chuckle and pull her up, holding her as she sways in my arms. "Angel, I drink blood. A little squirting isn't going to put me off in the slightest. On the contrary. Now come on, let's get cleaned up."

JULIET

ONCE WE'RE clean and Silas has assured me for the millionth time that it's fine that I squirted all over his chest, we head back into the bedroom. It's dark now, and my heart sinks a little when I still can't hear any rain. Tomorrow we'll get ready for the final stretch to Roanoke. We probably only have two nights left here.

I should be relieved. I should want to be in a safe colony, with other people. I know there's more to life than fucking Silas and existing in this little cocoon. Soon the supplies here will run out. We can't stay here forever. But I feel like a new person. I feel like I *am* a person, not just someone who exists. But it's more than just the sex, as amazing as that is. I know it's because I love Silas, even though I still haven't told him. He's made me come so hard I nearly have a few times, but I can't bring myself to say those words out loud. I don't know why. It still hurts. I'm scared that he won't be able to stay with me in Roanoke, even though he's given me no indication that they wouldn't let him. I just can't shake this strange feeling...

I brush my hair out in front of the dressing table mirror, which is dulled from age. Silas stands behind me, watching me, his gaze dark and full of desire.

"Haven't had enough?" I ask, raising an eyebrow at his reflection.

"Of you? Never."

I snort out a laugh. "Were you always like this?"

"Like what?" His voice is low and dangerous.

"You know, horny all the time?"

"Yes." He puts a hand on my hip, and the sudden heat makes my insides curl up on themselves. Just one touch does this to me. "I've always liked sex, but sex with someone like you..." He steps closer, so his erection is pressed to my back.

"Someone like me?"

He puts his hand on my other hip, lowering his mouth to my throat. "When you meet someone that you can see is just aching to be unlocked." His lips brush over my skin. "The first time I saw you, I thought you looked so pure, so innocent and angelic. But underneath this exterior, you were just waiting for someone to find that side of you. And now that side of you is mine."

"All of me is yours." I close my eyes as his kiss against my neck becomes more urgent, his hands splaying across my stomach and pressing me against him. "And what about you? Did I unlock a side of you too?"

"You didn't unlock me, angel." His fangs rake along my shoulder, drawing tiny droplets of blood. "You tore open my rib cage with your bare hands and took my heart for yourself."

"Oh, did I?" I wince as his fangs run along the other shoulder, the slight sting of pain sending a new rush of heat between my thighs. "How rude of me."

His eyes meet mine in the mirror, and his mouth shifts into a smile. "Remember what you said to me that night? What you wanted to see?"

"See?"

"See yourself, stretched around my cock." He gestures to the mirror. "This gives me an idea."

A small voice in my head asks *More?* incredulously. But I beat that voice down. Because, *yes, more.*

I let Silas lift me up so the edges of my knees are resting on the dressing table. He brackets my waist with his hands, and pushes the tip of his cock to my entrance.

"Now, watch." His breath is hot against my ear, and my eyes skate down to where our bodies are joined.

It's somehow beautiful and filthy at the same time, watching that thick cock slide inside me. My pussy stretches around him, unable to accommodate all of him at this angle. Silas forces me higher onto my knees, and more of his dick slips into me. I cough out a gasp, forcing myself to keep my eyes open.

"Look at how beautiful you are when you take me." Silas's fingers part my pussy, exposing my throbbing clit. "Look at you, just aching to come. Rub that clit angel."

I do as he says, watching my fingers move over my clit. I've never seen myself like this before, never watched as I got myself off. Silas hisses and gasps behind me. He lifts me so my feet are resting on the edge of the dressing table, his cock still inside me. He bounces me on him gently, and I careen quickly towards that edge, my toes curling and my back arching.

"Keep watching," he commands against my ear. "Make yourself come, and watch as that needy pussy throbs on my cock."

My eyes move back down to where his thick length is buried within me, and I whimper, my stomach tensing as my orgasm builds.

"Oh fuck." He sucks in a breath. "I want to come inside you, angel."

I nod against his shoulder. "Yes, yes, please."

"You want my cum to fill you up?"

"Yes, oh *god*." My fingers move faster, chasing the high.

"So fucking tight, like you'll never let me go."

"I-I won't. Never." I'm almost there, the sounds breaking from my throat high-pitched and raw with need. "I want you inside me, always. Oh fuck, *fuck*."

"I'm going to fill you up with my babies."

I let out a high-pitched moan at his words, watching as the contractions of my body make his dick twitch, my arousal coating his shaft. He digs his fingers into my hips as he fucks me hard, straight through my orgasm and headlong into another. I brace my hands against the mirror, watching his face, his eyes locked on my reflection as he slams into me over and over. He grits his teeth, inhaling sharply as he tenses against me, then with a heavy breath he spills inside me.

We just gaze at each other's reflections, panting, for a long time, as our bodies cool and calm. The desire wears off, and we both seem to realize that what we just did was pretty stupid. But I can't even find it within myself to feel bad, or irresponsible.

"I'm sorry," he says, pulling out of me gently. "That wasn't-"

"I love you." The words bubble out of me, just like they did with Matt that one time I thought I was going to die. But I didn't mean them then. I had no idea what love would feel like. That it would bury itself within my soul and tear me in half, a jagged, bleeding edge laced with so much beauty and sweetness it makes me want to cry.

Silas's eyes widen a little. "Jules-"

"I love you." I say it again, knowing I'm covered in cum and sweat, and I'm still crouched on a dressing table naked. I look a mess and I'm still trembling, and this isn't how I imagined the moment. But it doesn't matter. Nothing else matters but the look on his face right now, a beautiful combination of fear and elation. "I want you to promise me something."

Silas gathers me in his arms, turning me around and helping me down off the table. "Anything, angel. You name it."

"Promise you'll never leave me."

His mouth is hot when it claims mine, his tongue stroking in my mouth. "Never. I'm never leaving you, ever again. I'll die first."

"I can't live without you." I curl myself up against him. "I can't. Ever."

"Me neither. And you won't have to."

I don't tell him about my fears, about the sneaking dread that won't leave me alone. The awful feeling that what awaits us in Roanoke isn't a safe haven, but just another apparatus that'll tear us apart. I don't tell him that. I simply let him take me back to bed, and fuck me until the sun starts to peer over the horizon.

THE NEXT DAY, the sun shines in a clear blue sky, and Silas charges the generators. We're quiet most of the day, trying to stay close to one another. We take a walk through the forest, and he keeps his arm around my shoulders as he tells me all about London, about his adventures around the world with Margot.

He heats enough water for us to have a bath together, and he listens to me intently as I lie in his arms, talking about art and discussing my favorite books.

We spend our last night in our sweet little farmhouse in

bed, fucking with such fervor and ferocity it's as though the world is going to end.

The voice that tells me our time together is running out gets louder and louder.

My eyes open to the smell of food cooking, and more cruel sunshine washing through the window. The curtain waves gently in the soft breeze. It would be such an idyllic scene if we didn't have to leave.

I finally relent, climbing out of the bed and pulling on my clothes. I pad down the stairs to find a shirtless Silas standing over the stove, one foot tucked behind the other as he leans on the counter. I walk up behind him and wrap my arms around his waist, laying my cheek against his warm back. His fingers brush along my arms.

"Good morning, angel."

"You made me breakfast?"

"You need to eat before we go." His voice falls flat on the last word. Maybe he's having the same fears I am. Or maybe he knows something he isn't telling me.

We could stay here. We could keep living our lives out here and never going anywhere else. I open my mouth to say the words, to speak that thought out loud, but quickly snap it shut again. Just because this place has been untouched doesn't mean it will never be discovered. Silas is strong, and he'd protect me. But even he can be overpowered. And sooner or later he'd have to leave me alone, and then...

Silas is staring at me, his hand paused on the spoon he's using to stir the contents of the pan. His eyes search my face for a second, and then he smiles warmly.

"Come on, eat, angel. I'll go get the truck."

"No." I take a few hurried steps towards him. "Please stay with me. I don't want to eat alone."

He nods, looking back down at the stove. "Ok, come on

then, let's sit." He sits opposite me at the table, smiling wistfully as I eat. "You've gained weight since we've been here. Your cheeks, they're all round and rosy now."

I smirk at him. "Shoulda seen me when I was a swimmer. My back was a wall of muscle."

One of his eyebrows lifts, and he grins. "I'll bet you looked incredible."

I shrug, pushing my food around the pan. "The freckles usually put folks off."

"Well, those folks were idiots. They were the first thing I noticed about you."

Now it's my turn to raise an eyebrow. "Are you serious?"

He nods, then tilts his head thoughtfully. "Well, that and how good you smell getting yourself off."

I grunt out a laugh. "Well, at least you're honest."

"With you, always."

"Do you really think this colony in Roanoke is genuine?"

The question hangs thickly in the air between us, and Silas lets out a sigh, rubbing his hands along his thighs.

"Juliet, listen, I swore to keep you safe, and that means what it means, alright? Now, the vamps in Savannah said there were vamps living in this colony as well, and I've got no reason to doubt that." He gives me a weary smile that doesn't quite reach his eyes. "You're going to have to trust me, and we're just going to have to hope."

Before I can respond, his eyes flood with violent crimson, and he gets to his feet.

"Juliet, we have to go."

I scramble off the bench, the muscles in my legs tight as bowstrings. "What is it?"

"*Now.*" Silas grabs my wrist and pulls me along behind him, scooping up the bags by the front door before we push out onto the porch. He pauses, tilting his head, as though listening intently, before bursting into motion again, dragging me across the yard towards the truck.

"Get in." He commands as he pulls open the barn doors, shoving the bags at me. "And keep your head down!"

I scurry to the truck, pulling the door open just as I hear it - the sound of engines approaching. I hug the bags to my chest as I curl up in the seat, keeping my head low. I jerk my arms tighter around the parcels in my arms as Silas tears open the driver's side door, climbing in and gunning the engine. He throws the truck into reverse, backing out at an almost alarming speed, turning the wheel before shifting to drive. The truck shoots forward on the bumpy road, and I stay huddled down, holding my breath as I wait for us to hit another truck or for the pinging of bullets to start hitting us.

"It's alright, Jules," Silas says, his voice tight as his eyes stay fixed on the road. "It's OK. I'll get you out of here."

"Someone found us."

His eyes flash up to the rear view mirror before moving back to the path in front of the truck. "I don't know, but someone's coming and we're not sticking around to find out who."

The truck bumps violently down the uneven drive, Silas moving at a speed that makes my eyes water and my stomach churn. I clutch the bags tighter again in an attempt to stop my hands shaking. I squeeze my eyes shut, sending out a silent prayer to get us out of here, to let us get to safety. I don't believe in god anymore, in a world like this who would? But maybe, just maybe, someone's listening.

"Shit." Silas says the word just as staccato thuds start to echo through the truck. Someone's firing at us. Silas reaches out, pushing me down further into my seat. "*Stay down.*"

He weaves on the road, the strikes against the truck's exterior becoming more random. An engine roars up behind us, getting closer and closer. The truck lurches towards the edge of the road as whoever is behind us nudges the tailgate.

They're going to kill us. A bullet shatters the rear window and slams into the seat.

I have to do something, I can't just stay huddled down here. I reach under the dash, and Silas's eyes flash down to me.

"What the fuck are you doing?"

I yank out the gun he has stashed down there, and wind down my window. "Getting these assholes off our tail."

"Juliet, *get down!*" He reaches across to grab me, but I squirm out of his reach.

"Just keep driving!" I wind down the window, leaning out and raising the gun at the drab green jeep that's right on our tail. I can make out two occupants, but not much more than that. I aim straight at the windshield and squeeze the trigger.

The jeep sways as it tries to avoid the bullet, but it strikes and sends the glass shattering. The jeep shimmies and veers off the road, straight into a tree where it comes to a sharp stop in a shower of metal and steam.

I slide back into the seat, the gun clutched tight in my hands.

"They crashed." A lump catches in my throat. "Just drive."

Silas reaches over and puts an enormous hand over mine. "You did great."

"Thanks. Just drive."

Silas keeps his hand there until he turns us out onto the highway, and for the next hour, as we get as far away as possible from whoever the hell was pursuing us. He's not taking any chances.

By the time he pulls over, and takes the gun from my sweaty hands, the lump in my throat is so thick I can't even speak.

Silas pulls me into his arms, stroking my hair and telling me how amazing and brave I am.

"Did you see who they were?"

I shake my head, wrapping my fingers around the collar of his shirt.

"It doesn't matter, angel. You did so good. I'm so proud of you." He runs a hand down my back, and sighs. "I'm so sorry, angel."

"Don't be sorry." I choke out the words, hot tears stinging my eyes. "It's OK. We're both OK."

"No, I mean..." He tilts my head, his eyes searching my face. "We need to get to Roanoke. So you're safe."

"So *we're* safe."

He nods. "Of course, angel. So we're safe."

I tell myself he means it. I tell myself that in a few short hours we'll be safe in Roanoke, and it'll all be over.

I tell myself, over and over, and I still don't believe it.

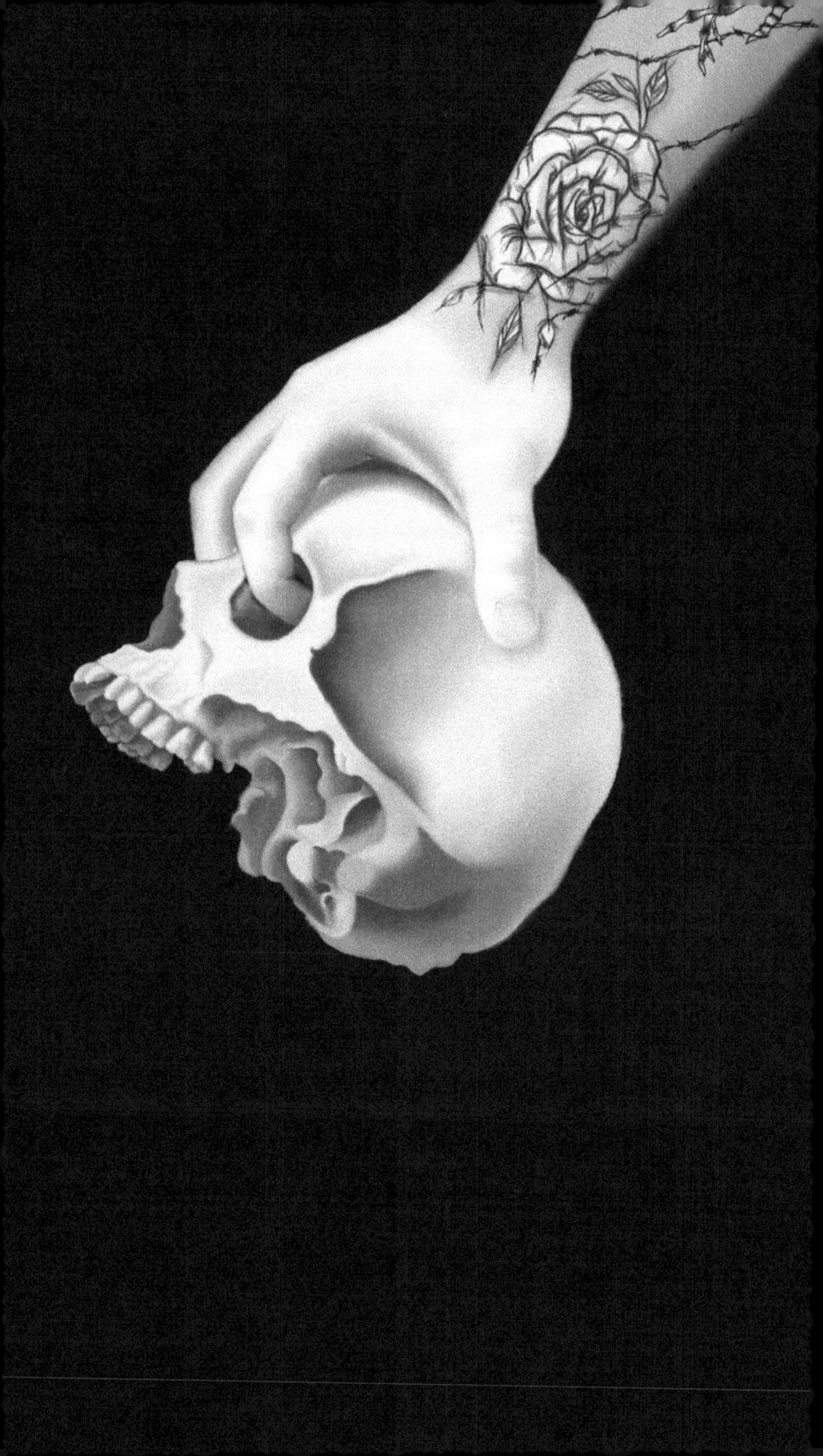

JULIET STAYS CURLED up under my arm for the duration of the drive. She stops shaking after an hour or so, and once the adrenaline wears off she even goes to sleep for a little while. But she doesn't let me go, her hand straying underneath my t-shirt to rest against my stomach.

I can taste her fear, and it's not sweet or alluring. It makes my stomach turn. It doesn't matter what I say to her, every reassurance I've given her since we left the compound. She doesn't believe me. She thinks they'll tear her away from me, and that she'll never see me again.

And the fact is, that it might come to that.

What happened this morning proved that I can't keep her safe. I can fight off a few starved marauders, sure. But not a whole horde of Afflicted. Not an organized rogue militia. And certainly not the fucking National Guard should they ever find us.

I press a kiss to the top of Juliet's head, trying to get a handle on my rage. This isn't fair. This isn't fucking *fair*. I blink my eyes hard, gritting my teeth against the sorrow that threatens to swallow me up. I'm letting her fear infect me. I have no reason to doubt the colony, the vamps in Savannah said there were vampires living there.

It might still be OK.

I drive on, the decaying towns passing us by. About an hour from Roanoke, I bring the truck to a stop, and Juliet rouses from sleep. She blinks, running the back of her hand across her face, then just gazes up at me, those eyes like a storm.

"We're nearly there, aren't we?"

I nod, stroking a strand of hair out of her face. "Nearly, yeah." I drop a soft kiss on her lips. "It'll be alright, yeah?"

She screams as something slams into the side of the car and I whip the gun up towards the window. I almost pull the trigger, but stop when I see what it is.

An Afflicted vamp claws weakly at the window. Its cheeks are completely sunken, its eyes blank. Straggly dark hair ropes from its ruddy scalp, and the sounds coming from it are pathetic, animalistic. The bloody stumps of its fingers leave dark tracks of blood on the glass.

"Oh jesus, Silas!" Juliet's head whips to look over her shoulder, before she burrows against me. "Go! Drive!"

"It's alright." I lower the gun, narrowing my eyes as the creature groans and claws at the truck.

"Silas, it's going to smash the window." Juliet's voice is wavering with fear.

"No, it's... weak. I think it's starving."

"Then it's hungry." Juliet is breathing hard against my chest, lifting her head to jerk a glance over her shoulder. "Can we get out of here, please?"

"They're dying."

The Afflicted mewls, cracked and bleeding lips torn open as it collapses, disappearing out of view.

"Silas, please, can we get out of here?" Juliet's urgent tone brings me back to attention, and I gun the engine. The tire crunches over something, and Juliet clutches a hand to her mouth.

"We ran over it," she says, breathing in deeply through her nose. "Jesus Christ, we fucking ran over it."

"That thing was in bad shape." I shake my head. "It was starved."

"How long can they go without blood?"

"I don't know, they wanted to make vampires as hardy as possible." I chew the inside of my cheek, mulling over the million thoughts in my head. "But maybe now, it's become too much. The thirst, it wore them out and now they're all dying."

"Is that likely?"

I can't answer, because I don't know. But what if the Afflicted have hit their expiry date? What if the virus that turned those vamps into zombies has ravaged their systems, leaving them to slowly die out, until there's none left? The thought is almost too wonderful to even consider. But that Afflicted was very obviously dying, slowly and horribly.

I reach over to put a hand on Juliet's knee. She clasps on to me, shaking violently.

"That scared the shit out of me." Her wide eyes turn to me, and she attempts a smile. "I thought I'd gotten a little more brave this morning, I guess not."

"Hey no, come on, those things are terrifying." I lift one of her hands to my mouth, kissing her palm. "You're so fucking brave, angel. Facing all of this out here? You did great."

She huffs out a little breath between trembling lips and nods. "Yeah." It's all she says before she huddles back in under my arm, wrapping herself around me as Roanoke draws closer and closer.

The hour slips through my fingers way too fast. We approach the outskirts, the battered city landscape stretching out before us. The truck bumps over broken roads and fallen debris, caved-in buildings on either side of us.

Juliet scoots away from me to gaze out of the windshield, leaning forward to take in the wrecks all around us.

"How do we know where to go?"

I don't even get a chance to answer, as a siren begins whirring loudly overhead. "They know we're here," I shout over the din, Juliet clasping her hands over her ears and nodding.

I turn a corner, and before us lies a huge gate. Layers upon layers of wood and barbed wire stand 25 feet high, with thick razor wire stretching the length of the city blocks. Guard towers stand at either end of the block, and I can practically feel the guns that are trained on us. The siren stops, and Juliet's hands drop from her ears.

"Halt your advance." A loud voice crackles from speakers mounted either side of the gate. "Stop your engine, and get out of the vehicle with your hands up over your head."

Juliet and I look at each other, and I give her a smile that I hope is reassuring and doesn't betray just how anxious I feel at this moment.

"Come on then, angel."

She dives across the seat and kisses me, her mouth hot and sweet. "I love you."

"It's alright." I clutch her face in my hands. "Come on, it's alright. Let's go."

We part reluctantly, and climb slowly out of the truck, walking to stand in front of it with our hands in the air.

"Do you have any weapons in the vehicle?" The voice asks once we come to a stop.

"I have two handguns!" I call back. "But only two bullets!"

The loudspeaker hums and sputters for a moment, before

letting out a high-pitched squeal, and the voice starts again. "Is the female human?"

"Yes, she is!"

"Confirm you're a vampire."

I swallow hard. "I am!"

"But he's a friend!" Juliet's voice is strained, her anxiety palpable. "He's not dangerous, he-"

"We'll be opening the gate now." The voice cuts her off, without a hint of emotion. "Do not move."

We stay still as there are loud bangs, movement in the guard tower, and finally a loud grinding noise as the gate begins to roll open. Juliet is shifting on her feet as though she wants to move closer to me, or run, or just lose her fucking mind with the anxiety that's eating her up.

"It's alright, angel." I look over at her, and her eyes are almost wild. "Just calm down. They're not going to hurt us." This is the first time she's seen this many new people in over five years. This whole situation is terrifying for her. "They won't hurt you, Jules. I promise. I won't let them."

She nods, her jaw tense. "OK. OK." The words tumble out of her, her face pale under the sprinkling of freckles.

Heavy footsteps approach, and a woman with dark brown skin and short black curls approaches, wearing dusty body armor. She's flanked by two men, also wearing armor, carrying assault rifles, which are trained on Juliet and I. They advance on us slowly, the woman's gaze measured as she sizes us up.

They stop 10 feet away, and I swallow down the rage as the guy on the left keeps his gun trained on Juliet.

"We're no danger," I say, and the woman looks at me pensively.

"And what exactly are you doing here?"

"We escaped a compound in Georgia." I gesture to Juliet

with my raised hand. "She was going to be sent off for a breeding program. So I got her out of there."

The woman raises her eyebrows, her face still mostly neutral. "Well, that was noble of you. What brings you all the way up here?"

"I'd been told that this colony was a safe haven." I lower my hands slowly, palms facing her. "I had to get her to safety."

She turns her attention to Juliet. "I'm Sutton, and your name is?"

"Juliet. Monroe." She lowers her hands to her sides, still shifting uneasily on her feet.

Sutton takes a step closer to her. "You seem a little anxious, Juliet, is everything alright?"

"Just... It's been a long time since I talked to anyone new." She rubs the heels of her hands along her thighs. "I was locked up in that place for five years. They took me when I was 19."

"I'm sorry to hear it." Sutton points a finger in my direction. "So, he hasn't been hurting you?"

Juliet shakes her head emphatically. "He saved me. He's... he's my..." She looks over at me helplessly.

Sutton raises her hand, and the men behind her lower their weapons. "It's OK, I understand. I'm glad you escaped that place. They're barbaric." She opens her hands in front of her, then clasps them together. "This colony has some strict rules, but they keep us safe. If you're willing to work hard and as part of a team, you'll have a place here. Is that OK?"

"What kind of rules?" Juliet's voice wavers.

"Nothing unusual. No fighting, no stealing, things like that. Like I said, rules to keep us safe."

"I can live with that." Juliet plays with her fingers, and Sutton's flickering eyes seem to notice the anxious movement. For the first time, her face breaks into a smile.

"I can see you've been through it, honey. No one will hurt

you here, I promise. We have families living here, kids, babies. They're all happy and healthy. You'll be safe here."

"What about the Afflicted?" I ask. "Have you been attacked?"

Sutton's shoulders square as she looks back at me. "They've never made it into the colony. Not once in three years."

"You've been out here three years?" Juliet asks.

Sutton's expression shifts instantly, smiling warmly at Juliet. "That's right. We're well established. We have gardens, livestock. Even a hairdresser if you can believe it." She gives a little laugh. "It's safe here. Somewhere you can call home after those compounds."

Juliet's face relaxes a little. "OK. Well, that sounds good." She looks over at me. "Right?"

I smile and nod. "It sounds great."

Juliet exhales and turns back to Sutton. "OK, well, if you'll have us-"

"Us?" Sutton's smile dissolves instantly. "No Us. Just you, honey."

"What?" Juliet tenses with panic. "No, no he's-"

"A vampire." Sutton cuts her off gently, before looking back over at me. "I'm sorry, but we can't have your kind in here. We did it once before, and it never ends well."

There's no point protesting. I can't negotiate my way into this. To them, I'm still a monster. I can't blame them. My shoulders slump.

"I understand."

"No!" Juliet rushes at me, throwing her arms around my neck. "No, you're not leaving me, I won't let you."

I look over her shoulder at Sutton, whose face is still neutral. "You can take care of her, right?"

Sutton nods. "Yes, of course."

Juliet spins around, tears racing down her cheeks. "He's not dangerous!" Her voice cracks, and she dashes her hands against her face. "He's a friend! He rescued me!"

Sutton shakes her head. "I'm sorry, but he can't come in."

"But they said you had vamps living here!" Juliet's voice wavers, becoming more and more strained. "They said we could be together here!"

"Jules, it's OK." I put my hands on her shoulders and turn her back to face me. Her wide eyes are red-rimmed, and she shakes her head as I stroke her cheeks. "I told you I'd do whatever I needed to do to keep you safe."

She pulls back, swaying slightly on her feet. "You promised you wouldn't leave me. You *swore* to me you'd stay with me."

I cradle her face in my hands, hating myself for the trembling I can feel reverberating through her. "I have to keep you safe. And I can't keep you safe out here, not alone. And this might kill me, but I couldn't live with myself knowing I didn't do whatever I had to do to make sure you live."

She slumps against me, wailing with grief. Time seems to slow down for a moment, as I hold Juliet in my arms. I don't even feel sorrow, I just feel empty. I know this has to be done, just like when I had to let go of Margot. I know I have to do what's best for her, even though it's leaving me hollow.

"Silas," she murmurs, grasping onto my shirt. "Please, don't do this."

"I'll find you, angel." I tip back her head, kissing those rosy lips, awash with salt tears. "I told you, I'll always find you. And one day, when the world's back to normal, I'll find you again. I promise."

An alarm starts to blip over us, and Sutton and the men tense visibly.

"There's Afflicted approaching," Sutton says, extending a hand. "Come on now, we have to get you inside."

"No!" Juliet holds on to me. "I'm not leaving you!"

"Jules." I pull her arms away from me. "You need to go. Now."

"Turn me!" Her eyes are wild, her hair sticking to the sweat beading on her face. "Turn me, and take me with you!"

I shake my head. "I'm not doing that now, not like this." I meet Sutton's eyes, and give her a nod. "Goodbye, angel."

"We need to close this gate now." Sutton gestures to one of the men. "Take her inside."

"No!" Juliet screams, her hands slipping away from me as one of the men takes her from me, holding her tightly and carrying her inside the gate as she continues to scream for me. *"Silas! Silas! No! No! Please!"*

Sutton gives me one last curt nod, before following them in. The gate rolls shut, and with a loud thud it slams home. Chains jangle as the gate is locked down, the blipping siren above falling silent as a voice announces "Lockdown is in place."

I stare at the gate for a long time. I should go, I should move, I need to get out of here before any Afflicted cross my path. But the loss is so great I just stand there, staring. My hands are cold. I'll never touch her again.

I finally climb back into the truck, gunning the engine and just staring at the dash, wondering where the fuck I even go. I can't go back to Georgia. I can't go to Boston, they'll have spread my face across the network and everyone will know to be looking for me.

Maybe I should let the Afflicted bite me. Is there any point in going on now?

I squeeze my eyes shut. There is a point. I told her I'd find her one day. And I have to keep that promise.

I pull away from the colony, watching it slip away in the rear view.

I'll find you again one day. I promise.

IT'S SUNNY. Why the fuck is it sunny? I stare blankly at the light that beats in through the window. My hair smells like green apples. They have hot running water here. I had a shower last night, and now I'm sitting here in new clothes, the first pair of jeans I've worn in years, and my hair smelling of green apples, but all I can think about is how bad my throat hurts.

I screamed for so long after they took me away from Silas that I started coughing up blood. They ended up giving me a shot to try and calm me down, some kind of sedative. That triggered an episode of PTSD so violent that I threw up until there was nothing but bile coming out of me. I wanted to die. All I wanted was to die.

But then finally, whatever they gave me worked, and I calmed down enough to have a shower, and lie down in a warm bed they assigned me. In a private room. The first time I'd slept alone for over five years.

I stared at the moonlight and listened to my breathing, my single heartbeat. Every time I closed my eyes, I saw Silas's face as they dragged me away. It all happened so fast. One second I was relieved we were safe, the next...

Now it's the morning, and I'm sitting on a hard gurney, my arms wrapped around me. A woman sits in a chair next to me, I guess she's a doctor or something, and she asks me questions that I can only answer with a nod or a shake of my head. Because my throat hurts so bad that I can barely speak.

My vision keeps clouding as fresh tears mist my eyes. Every time the realization that he's gone, that he's *gone*, weighs down on me, I'm flooded with despair so deep I think it's going to kill me.

I kind of hope it does.

The woman stops asking me questions, and reaches out to put a tentative hand on my arm. "Are you OK, sweetie?"

"No." I choke out the word through my throat, which feels like it's lined with broken glass. "I'm not."

"They said you'd come with a feeder, and he had to go."

"He wasn't-" I cut off as I cough, holding the back of my hand to my mouth. "He wasn't a *feeder*. He saved me. He was my... my... We were together."

"Did he feed off you?"

"With my consent, yes."

The woman regards me with a pinched expression, sympathetic as she nods. "I know some of them can be decent, but we can't be sure."

I lapse back into silence, because I'm not going to argue with these people. There's no point. The woman continues on trying to engage me in friendly conversation. She tells me about the colony, about how friendly everyone is, how well set up they are. I don't care about any of it. I know I should, I should be glad to be safe.

But I'm not.

"Is Sutton in charge?" I ask, cutting off the woman's words.

"Oh, yes, she is. She and ten others started this colony a few years ago. She's great, very strong."

"Can I see her?"

The woman considers my words for a second. "Oh. I mean, yeah of course, I'll ask if you can go speak to her." She calls out for a man standing in the corridor. "Could you ask Sutton if she has time to talk to the new arrival?"

The man looks at me with a kind expression before nodding, and leaving the room.

"You're going to be so happy here, sweetheart." The woman squeezes my arm, smiling softly. "Wait here, Michael will take you to Sutton." She leaves the room, and I gaze out the window.

The sun's shining on the surrounding buildings, the remains of downtown Roanoke. I'd come here as a child, one of my aunts had lived here for a while and we'd visited her. It looks a little different now, half destroyed buildings, attempts at patching them up with wood and wire dotting the walls. They're trying here, I can see that. The woman had said there were 800 people living here. Sutton said they even had children here.

Maybe I could have a normal life. Garden alongside everyone else, get older, meet someone, maybe have a baby.

My hand strays to my stomach, and I have a genuinely stupid thought. *I hope Silas's baby is in there.* Then I'd have a piece of him with me forever. But would they accept a half-vamp baby? I don't even know. I bite back yet more tears that threaten to start falling. I hang my head in my hands, wishing I could stop fucking trembling. I take some deep steadying breaths, and by the time Michael comes to get me, I'm almost calm. Mostly. Like 50 percent.

We reach Sutton's office, which looks like it once belonged to an accounting firm. She sits behind a battered wooden desk, in a black folding chair, and she gives Michael a nod, dismissing him from the room. Her eyes are kind as they move back to me, and she gestures to a chair on the other side of the desk. I don't sit down, standing behind the chair with my hands behind my back so she can't see them shaking.

"Are you feeling better this morning?"

"I guess."

She frowns sympathetically, like a worried aunt. "I'm so sorry they gave you that medication without your consent, I understand that would have been awful for you. But we were so worried."

I shrug, swallowing hard. "It's fine. You did what you had to do."

She gives a gentle nod, leaning back in her chair. "You wanted to see me?"

"Yes, I did. Have the Afflicted passed?"

"They have." She puts her clasped hands on the desk. "It was a rather large horde, it took them all night to pass. But they're miles away now."

I clear my throat, wincing a little as I swallow against the pain. "So, the gate can be opened again?"

Sutton's brow furrows for a second. "If it needs to be, sure. We'd open it."

"Great, I'd like you to open it please."

"Why?"

I take a breath through my nose, summoning all my courage to actually enact what I came here to do. "So I can leave."

Sutton's eyebrows shoot up. "Leave?"

"Yes, leave."

Sutton sighs, leaning back in her chair which creaks with the shift in her weight. "And where exactly do you think you're going to go?"

"Am I a prisoner here?"

She shakes her head emphatically. "Of course not."

"Great, so could you ask them to open the gates please?"

Sutton gets to her feet, rounding the desk to lean on the side closest to me. "Look, I understand that yesterday was an emotional day for you. That vampire obviously means a lot to you."

"He does." My voice wavers, and I clench my teeth together to stop myself bursting into tears again. "And I'd like to go and find him."

"Juliet, listen. I get it, OK?" She crosses her arms over her chest. "We've all lost a lot here. I lost my husband and my son. I understand you, I do. And I didn't stop him from staying here to be cruel."

"I know, I get it. But that doesn't change anything. I want to go and find him."

"And what if you don't?"

I shrug. "Then something else will and either way I won't be your problem anymore."

"You are not a problem." Sutton sighs heavily, running a hand over her short curly hair. "I promised him you'd be safe here. What's he going to think if he comes back here and you're gone? And we never know what happened to you?"

"I need to go and find him." I know she's right. This is dumb.

"But you're safe here."

"I was safe in Georgia, too!" I catch myself as my voice rises, breaking against the rawness of my throat. "I was safe there, locked up, for five years. I'd have been safe in Charleston too, as much as any of us can be in this fucked up world. But I don't want to be safe for the rest of my life if it's not with him."

"So, you'd rather die out there with him?"

"Sure, if that's what being with him means. What else do I have to live for?"

"You have yourself to live for."

This is stupid and toxic and what a therapist would call codependency. But I push that thought away. "He saved me. He was there for me when no one else was. He killed for me. He protected me with his life, he loved me even though it could have gotten him killed. I'm not leaving him out there alone."

Sutton pushes off the desk and moves towards me, stopping short, lifting her hands as though to touch me then letting them fall. "Juliet, listen to me. Your pain, it's raw, and new, and you're not thinking straight."

"Can I please go now?"

"What if he's gone? He could be miles away by now." Sutton's face starts to sag with defeat. "Juliet, you can have a life here, and that's what he wanted you to have."

I take a deep breath. She's right, I know she is. And Silas would be telling me all this himself if he were here. But I don't care.

"Ma'am, with all due respect, I've lived the life other people have wanted me to live for a long time now. I'm done with that. I want to live the life *I* want, and if that's short because I'm stupid, then that's on me. But at least I made that choice for myself."

Sutton exhales heavily, running a hand over her face. "Well, when you put it like that..." She trails off, looking up at me with narrowed eyes. "Michael!"

The man who escorted me appears in the doorway a moment later. "Yeah?"

"Can you organize a pack please?" Sutton says, looking down at my feet. "And go see about some proper boots. She can't walk in these flimsy shoes."

Michael disappears quickly.

"You don't need to do that," I say to Sutton. "You don't owe me anything."

"No I don't, but I do owe something to myself, and my integrity matters to me." She walks to a filing cabinet in the corner, unlocking it and pulling open a drawer with a loud scrape. She withdraws a handgun, inspecting it for a second before walking back to me. "Do you know how to use one of these?"

"Yeah, my dad was a cop, he said we had to learn how to use one responsibly."

"Good." She hands me the weapon. "I can't spare many bullets, just what's in there. But I won't send you out there unarmed."

"Thank you." I clasp the gun in my hands, which suddenly feel cold. "I appreciate it."

"And if you don't find him, come back." Sutton's mouth lifts into a wavering smile. "Don't think you're not welcome back here. I could use someone like you here."

I snort. "Stupid and irresponsible?"

"No." She shakes her head, her eyes softening for a moment. "Passionate and driven. It's easy to lose that in a world like this, where we're just surviving all the time."

I swallow hard. "Thank you."

Michael reappears with a black backpack, a pair of boots and thick navy blue puffer jacket. "The boots will probably be a little big, but they'll do better than those things."

"Thanks." I take a seat, kicking off the thin flat shoes I'd been issued at the compound, and pull on the thick socks and hiking boots. They're a little big, but the socks help. I get back to my feet, shrugging on the jacket before hoisting the pack onto my shoulders.

Sutton and Michael lead the way out of the office, and with every step I feel more and more ridiculous. I'm a fool. This is so stupid.

But by the time we reach the gate, my resolve returns. I

refuse to believe that Silas is miles away. He's nearby. He hasn't left me. He wouldn't have done that.

Or maybe he's not as dumb as me, and he actually has a sense of self-preservation.

Sutton turns to me, and smiles warmly. "I meant what I said. If you don't find him, you get yourself back here."

"OK." My stomach is a churning knot of ice.

"And if I was him, I would have headed north, further from Georgia." She gestures to her left. "That way. Follow the main road out of town. Be careful in the forests, there's marauders every now and then."

"OK." I've lost the ability to say anything but that word. I jump as the gate starts to groan, rolling open slowly.

Sutton must sense my fear, because she puts a comforting hand on my shoulder. "Be safe. I hope you find him."

"Thanks."

"And remember - you can come back, anytime." Her hand drops from my shoulder, and she takes a step back.

"OK."

I turn away from her, and walk through the gate. The guards above me look down at me, probably thinking what a goddamn idiot I am. Finally I'm on the other side, out on the road, the last place I saw Silas, the last place he held me. The gate rolls shut behind me, and then I'm alone.

For a split second my resolve nearly falters, and I want to turn and slam my fists against the gate, beg them to let me back in where it's safe. Panic rises through me, rushing into my lungs and squashing all the oxygen out of me. I lean on my knees, rasping in deep steady breaths. I'm not going to panic, I'm not going to lose it.

I can do this. I can find him. He's close by. He won't have gone far away from me.

I force my feet to move, even though they're weighted to

the ground by fear. One step, one more, and another, and before I know it, I'm out of sight of the gate. A few more minutes and I turn a corner, out onto a wide open road that stretches in front of me along a line of collapsed buildings.

The sun's beating down on me as I keep walking, and despite the cool breeze, within a few minutes sweat is running down my back. The backpack is heavy, and hurts my shoulders a little. My feet are sweltering in these boots, but at least they don't hurt. I hope I can run if I need to.

After an hour, the city has started to fall away, the road widening and rising to pass the forest that runs alongside it. I notice for the first time the mountains on the horizon. The land around the compound was so flat, and I pause for a moment to admire my surroundings. If I look past the ruined buildings, it's actually really pretty around here.

I take the pack from my shoulders, opening it to find a huge bottle of water, some packed food, some silver foil packets that remind me of army rations, and a first aid kit. I take some careful sips of water, not wanting to waste it. Is that a stupid thought to have when I don't even know how long I'll survive out here?

I look over my shoulder, back the way I came, and I'm sure I could find my way back to the colony. But how far do I go before I give up? *Give up.* My shoulders sag a little as I think about the day before. Silas gave up. He just left me here. Maybe he's far away, maybe he realized he didn't want to be with me after all.

I inhale sharply and straighten up. I'm being ridiculous. Silas just wanted the best for me, that was all. He thought he was saving me, he just wanted to see me be safe. It has nothing to do with him not wanting me. I can't help the tear that runs down my cheek, catching the cool breeze. The temperature is dropping and I hope to god it doesn't snow.

I push on along the abandoned highway, taking steps over large cracks in the asphalt, vines snaking along the ground. Nature started taking this place back a long time ago.

The road dips off to the right, through the forest, and the highway continues along ahead of me, but the road is so damaged I know that Silas wouldn't have been able to take that route. If he came this way, he had to take this road through the forest.

The hairs on the back of my neck stand up, and I tell myself it's just the wind. I'm just cold. It isn't my intuition telling me that danger lies ahead. There's no one out here. It's just me.

The feeling of dread presses down on my shoulders more and more as I advance. Something's wrong. Silas isn't down here. I stop, taking down the pack to retrieve the water bottle. I'm probably just tired and thirsty. I haven't eaten in hours. I'm hungry. My body's just reacting to all of that.

My hands are shaking so badly that I can barely hold the water bottle to my lips, and spill some of it down my chin. "Jesus, Juliet, get a grip," I chide myself quietly, but I may as well be shouting the way my voice shatters the silence around me.

I tuck the bottle away in the pack, and as I zip it shut, my scalp prickles.

I'm being watched.

I can feel eyes on me.

I slowly pull the pack on, and turn around, heading back to the highway. I try to keep my movements measured, try to stop myself from breaking into a run, as though it's a fucking bear and *you don't run from bears*. That's the advice right? My brain isn't working right.

There's a snap of twigs, and sweat erupts on my top lip. *Keep walking. Just keep walking.* The highway is in sight. It's OK. It's just an animal. Keep moving.

Then there are footsteps. Heavy slow footsteps on the asphalt behind me. Very human footsteps, followed by a throaty laugh.

"And where do you think you're going?"

I break into a run.

"Your husband, huh?" His voice is drowned out by the approach of a roaring engine, much louder than the electric trucks from the compound. An ancient pickup emerges from the trees, the hood long gone, exposing a whining spinning engine. Three men hang from the sides of the truck, and two more sit in the cab.

They all look as mangy as the one who won't let go of me now, and my mouth goes dry with panic. I can't overpower this guy, let alone six of them. Shit, this was so stupid. I'm so fucking stupid.

"What you find there for us, Earl?" One of the men jumps down off the side of the truck, ambling towards me with a limp, his clothes hanging from his malnourished frame.

"Sweet thing says her husband's huntin' out here," the one holding me, Earl I guess, says with a scoff.

The one walking towards us runs a hand over his mouth, looking me up and down as I dangle helplessly in Earl's grip. "Ooh, I don't know about you, but if this pretty girl was my wife I wouldn't let her out of my sight." He digs his hands into his pockets, narrowing his eyes. "Now tell us the truth, honey. Your husband, he's not really here, is he?"

"He is." I stick my chin out, determined not to show even a hint of fear. "He's here, and he's big and strong, and he'll fuck you up if he sees you touching me."

He raises his eyebrows. "Is that so?" He lifts one hand from his pocket and looks around him, eyes wide. "Hey husband!" Now that the engine has gone quiet, his voice bounces off the trees around us. He looks back at me, raising his finger, and poking it gently into my shoulder. "Oh husband! I'm touching your wife!" He cocks an eyebrow, his thin pale lips turning up into a grin. "Is he gonna come out and fuck me up now?"

I glare at him, shrugging him off and writhing again in

Earl's iron grip. "Get your fucking hands off me, you smell like shit."

"Well maybe we just need a woman like you to come and clean us up, huh?" Earl chuckles, then lowers his nose to the side of my face, sucking in a whistling breath. "Oh, you smell *good*." I shriek as his tongue darts out and runs up the side of my face, leaving a trail of saliva on my skin. "Mmmm, taste good too."

I jerk my knee up into his groin, and he yelps, his grip loosening for just long enough for me to slip out of it. He stumbles backwards into the skinny guy, distracting them as I pull the pack from my back and fumble with the zip.

"Fucking *bitch*." Earl clutches his groin. "Stupid fucking *bitch*."

I pull open the backpack just as the skinny guy advances on me. I bring the gun up, pointing it right at his face.

"Don't fucking move!" The gun's heavy, and I have to drop the pack to hold it with both hands. But both of them have stopped with their hands up, and the men that are still with the truck are frozen where they stand. "Anyone moves, and I'll blow your fucking brains out!"

The skinny guy attempts to swagger a little, putting his hands back in the pockets of his worn out grey pants. "Now, a little girl like you doesn't know how to use that does she?"

"Try me, asshole." I cock the gun, and his face drops. "My dad was a cop who made sure his little girl knew how to deal with creepy fucks who might try and jump her on the street."

"Come on now." He holds his hands up, palms facing me. "We just want to be friends, honey. You don't have to be scared."

"I don't need friends, now fuck off and leave me alone."

Earl seems to recover from the kick to his manhood, and his

face goes red, veins popping out from his temple. "Fucking little bitch."

The skinny one puts his hand on Earl's shoulder. "Hey man, she's got-"

But Earl is as dumb as he is big, and lunges at me. *"I'm gonna fucking kill you!"*

The gun goes off, and Earl howls, his hands flying up. The bullet has torn open the side of his face, blood spraying over the skinny one, who jumps aside with a shout. His eyes are wild as he looks back at me.

"You crazy little bitch!" He moves towards me, the shock of being showered with blood clearly making his brain short circuit because I'm still very much armed.

I squeeze the trigger, and he jerks backwards as the gun clicks - and nothing happens. I pull the trigger again, and again, but all that meets my finger is resistance. The gun's jammed. The skinny guy hesitates, but on the third click, his lips pull back in a grin that reveals his mouthful of browned teeth.

"Oh no," he tuts. "Guess you're just shit out of luck, huh?"

He rushes at me, and I raise my hands to defend myself, but he's got surprising strength, and slams his first into my cheekbone. White stars explode in my vision, and I cough as I'm thrown onto my stomach, the gun wrenched from my hands.

"Now, you little shit," the skinny guy drawls into my ear, "you're gonna listen to me or-"

He cuts off with a cry, and his weight is lifted off me.

"You touching my wife, you fucking cunt?" A voice roars. "Which hand did you hit her with?"

There's a scream of pain.

"I asked you which hand you touched my wife with, you disgusting decrepit fuck."

I roll on to my back, and through the fog I see Silas with the skinny guy dangling by the collar of his shirt. Silas looks down at me, his eyes blazing red.

"Which hand did he hit you with, angel?"

"H-his right." My vision clears but my face is on fucking fire. "It was his right hand."

Silas bares his fangs at the skinny guy. "You hit my wife with your right hand. Guess you won't be needing it anymore." He drops the guy to his feet, seizing his right arm in his hands, wrenching it from the guy's body with a loud crunch.

The guy *screams*, a fountain of blood shooting into the air. Beyond the scene in front of me, I can see the bloody bodies of the other men draped over the truck. Earl is still stumbling around clutching his face, shrieking and gurgling.

The skinny guy has collapsed to the ground, his body convulsing as he bleeds out. Silas walks over to Earl, who holds up a hand, garbling thickly through the wound. Without a word, Silas tears his head straight from his body. Earl's enormous frame collapses, spilling blood across the road.

I try to get to my feet, and Silas turns on me.

"You stay down until I say." He points a bloody hand at me. "Stay right there."

I'm so relieved to see him I burst into tears. I curl my arms around my knees as he stalks over to the skinny guy, who's about to die if the fluttering rise and fall of his chest is anything to go by.

"You dared touch what's mine."

"P-please." The guy weakly lifts his remaining hand. "Please-"

"I don't negotiate with anyone who hurts my wife."

Silas lifts his foot and smashes his boot down into the guy's head. His skull gives way with a loud crack and the sound of wet flesh. Silas takes two steps away from the inert corpse, spitting on the ground, his shoulders heaving.

He turns to look down at me, his face splattered with blood. He shakes his head, his face crumpling into an expression of tortured relief. He rushes to me and drops to his knees, pulling me into his arms. I don't care that he's covered in blood and carnage, I wrap myself around him and sob.

"What the fuck are you doing?" He cradles my head against his chest. "You absolute fucking idiot, what the fuck are you doing out here all on your own?"

"Looking for you." I gaze up at him, my lips trembling. "I came to find you."

"You're meant to be safe, angel." He strokes my cheeks. "You're meant to be safe, not out here."

"I don't want to be safe, I want to be with you."

He clenches his eyes closed before clutching my face in his hands and bringing his mouth down on mine. His kiss is hard and punishing, punctuated with sweetness and desperation as I feel him quivering with barely restrained rage. Or maybe it's love? Maybe it's both?

He pulls back from me, his eyes still glowing red, and he places one soft kiss against my forehead before hauling me to my feet. "Come on, let's get out of here."

"Are there more of them?" I ask, averting my eyes from the bodies strewn over the rickety old truck.

"I don't know, but we're not sticking around to find out." His fingers entwine with mine as he pulls me along after him, a sign of tenderness even as I can feel his anger rolling off him. I don't even care, he can be angry with me if he wants to be. I'm so glad to be back with him that I can't focus on anything but the warmth of his hand.

The truck is parked on a narrow dirt path that leads off between the trees. I squeeze past overgrown shrubs and climb up into the seat, Silas slamming the door shut behind me. He climbs into the driver's seat, putting the keys in the ignition but not starting the engine yet.

He looks over at me, his eyes finally dimming back to the usual rusty brown. His face is twisted with emotion, his jaw set as though he's biting back words.

"You OK?" I ask after a moment, and he shakes his head.

Without another word, he tears his gaze from my face and onto the road ahead, gunning the engine and turning right onto the overgrown remnants of the old highway.

She throws something at me, a stick or a pebble, I don't know. It strikes me in the chest, and her eyes are wild now.

"Fuck you!" She hisses through clenched teeth, her finger darting through the air at me.

I rise to my knees, pointing a finger right back at her. "I wanted you to be safe. I broke you out of that compound so you could be *safe,* not bloody out here and exposed to the fucking elements and getting yourself raped and beaten by a bunch of hillbillies!"

"Fuck you!" She's on her feet now, her hands balled into quivering fists by her sides. "You don't get to decide for me like I'm a child!"

I get to my feet too, rounding the fire to grab her shoulders. "Now listen to me-"

Her hand strikes me across the cheek. "No! I'm done listening to you vamps, to you fucking *men* who think you know better and don't ask me what *I want.*"

I want to fucking shake some sense into her. "I have *never* done anything you didn't want, ever."

"Except dump me with some strangers without even *talking to me!*" A tear races down her cheek, and she pounds a fist into my chest. "You swore to me, you promised me that you'd never leave me! You said you'd die without me!"

"I wanted you to be safe! Christ, Juliet, what do you think I did after I left you there?"

"I don't fucking care!" She pushes out of my arms, dislodging my grip enough for her to get a few feet before I reclaim her and push her back against the rickety wall. "Let me go!"

"Do you think I left you?"

"You did leave me!" She starts to cry, turning her face away from me. "You left me and I didn't even... I couldn't even..." A choked sob steals her words, and she squeezes her eyes shut. "You left me, and I thought I'd never see you again."

"I didn't leave you." I hold the side of her face, forcing her to turn her head, but her eyes stay firmly closed. "Fucking hell, angel, I was lost. I was a fucking wreck. I circled that colony all night, I didn't fucking know where to go. You were all I could think about."

Her eyes open slowly, more tears sliding down her face. She raises a tentative hand to my face. "You did?"

"Fuck," I breathe, clutching her hand to my mouth for a second. "Yes. My god, you're everything, angel. And then when I heard those men, when I smelled you on the breeze and knew you were in trouble. I was so scared I wouldn't make it to you in time."

She sniffs, her mouth turning down into a frown. "I was doing fine." She pushes against my chest. "I can look after myself."

I slam a fist into the wall beside her. "God fucking *dammit,* you're a nightmare."

"*You left me!*" Furious tears race down her cheeks. "You didn't ask me, you didn't talk to me, I didn't even get to say goodbye to you, and you just left me there with people I didn't even know! That *you* didn't even know!"

"You would have been safe there!"

She shoves against my chest with open hands. "How the fuck do you know?"

"Because you were away from me!"

Her eyes widen, and she sucks in a breath. My shoulders are heaving, and a scalding hot tear runs down my own cheek. I swallow hard under her gaze, and wipe the tear away with my thumb.

"Why - why would you say that?" She hiccups a little, her

residual sobs dissolving as she eyes me with confusion. "Why would you say something like that?"

"I'm not safe, I never have been." The words taste bitter in my mouth. "I've never been able t-to keep anyone safe. I knew that when I got you out of Georgia. I hoped... I hoped I'd be able to stay with you, but-"

"Is this about Margot?" Juliet raises her hands to cup my face. "Silas, I'm not her."

I push her hands away, suddenly unable to bear her touch, misery and sorrow crashing down on me. "It's not just that."

"Then what?"

"I don't fucking know!" I rake my hands through my hair. "I'm - I told you, I'm not good. And sooner or later, I'd have done something, I'd have fucked this up, I'd have stumbled and not watched you, and not kept you safe, and I would have ruined you."

Juliet blinks at me, shaking her head. "Where is this coming from? Who told you this?"

My shoulders sag. "It doesn't matter."

She moves against me, fingers cradling my jaw. "I told that woman at the colony, and I'm going to tell you now - I don't care if I die."

"Juliet, you don't understand."

"No, listen to me. I don't care. Because I don't want to live an entire lifetime away from you. I didn't care about anything until you. I stopped, years ago."

I laugh bitterly. "Not even Matt?"

She frowns, shaking her head. "That was desperation. That was loneliness. This-" She puts her hand on my chest. "You and me, this is real. And whoever told you that you ruin everything, they didn't see you. Not really. But I do. I see you."

I wrap my arms around her, clutching her to me. "I'm so sorry. I'm so sorry, angel."

She inhales deeply. "I'm not Margot. You need to stop seeing her when you look at me."

"I don't. Not once, it's not like that."

"Then what is it?" She tilts her head to gaze up at me. "I want to understand."

I gesture to the fire, and we sit down side by side, her hands firmly curled around one of my own. Her eyes are wide and searching, open and not judging me, just waiting for me to explain.

"Six months after I was turned, I went home." I stroke the backs of my fingers along her wrist. "I was clean, I'd... I'd managed to get myself together, after doing some... terrible things. Margot, she saved me in so many ways. And then I was ready to go home. To show my family that I was a different person. Yes, I was a vampire, but that was a good thing. I wanted to show them that."

Juliet stays silent, the firelight reflected in her grey eyes.

I breathe down the lump forming in my throat. "My little sister opened the door. She... She didn't recognise me at first. I'd been a scrawny heroin addict stealing the family VCR last time she'd seen me. And now I was... well. This."

"She must have been so happy."

"She was. Shrieked with happiness, threw herself at me. 'Si's home!' She just kept saying it over and over. I hadn't seen her in almost a year. She was so beautiful, so happy." Pain leeches into my bones, and I squeeze my eyes shut against the prickling threatening to throw more hot tears down my face. "My dad appeared in the kitchen doorway, my brother was right behind him. Mum came out of the lounge room. They all just stood there, staring at me. Dad saw the fangs first."

"They thought you were a danger to them?"

"My dad, he lost it. Tore my sister away from me, told her and my brother to get upstairs. Mum burst into tears, started crying, asking what they'd done to me." I shrug. "Vamps were becoming public knowledge, but there was so much fear, they didn't understand. They thought I was a monster."

"You're not, though."

I meet her eyes, and sigh. "I killed people, Jules. And not just by accident. I killed them because I was obsessed, because of what I wanted. I'm broken. I'm an addict."

"No." She clasps my face in her hands. "You're not broken. You're not just an addict. Stop saying that."

I scoff out a cynical laugh. "Maybe this is my affliction, hmm?" I stroke the hair from her forehead. "Love. Margot used to joke about it, my obsessive nature. It's a part of me, and it's ruined me, over and over again. I don't want it to ruin you too."

"Too late." Juliet brushes a soft kiss against my lips. "If this is ruin, then I'll take it. I'll take you and your ruin and your obsession, and everything that comes with it. Because I want *you*, Silas. All of you."

I pull her into my lap, wrapping my arms around her waist and nuzzling into the soft crook of her neck. "I don't deserve you."

"Yes you do. We deserve each other."

I inhale deeply, and can't help but chuckle. "You smell like green apples."

"It's the shampoo from the colony." She strokes my hair gently. "When I finally stopped screaming for you, I washed my hair."

I pull back with a sharp breath, ready to apologize for leaving her there, for my weakness and self-loathing, for causing her yet more pain. But she silences me with a kiss, her fingers spearing through my hair.

"No more," she murmurs against my mouth. "Now, you must be starving. You should drink."

JULIET'S back lies against my chest, my arms firmly wrapped around her. Her breathing is deep and even, sleep claiming her a few hours ago. I hold her and thank my lucky stars that she's here with me. I place a kiss behind her ear, and she shifts gently in my arms.

"Is it still night?" She asks sleepily.

"Yes, angel. Go back to sleep."

She murmurs and wraps her hands around my arms. "Mmm, this is nice."

I chuckle. "Sleeping on the ground in an abandoned farmhouse? Very nice."

"At least it's warm." She turns over in my arms, her eyes still closed. "You're always so warm."

I run my hands up and down her back, and she sighs.

"So what do we do now?"

"I don't know." I kiss her forehead. "Keep heading north, find somewhere to shelter, and maybe one day we'll find a colony where we can live safely."

"OK." She shifts against me, pushing a hand under my shirt. "Maybe we can find another little dream house, huh?"

"Mmm, maybe." I huff out a breath as her hand runs over my stomach, carving over my hip so she can pull me closer.

"You called me your wife." She smiles, her eyes still closed. "When those bandits attacked me, you said I was your wife."

"You called me your husband." I'm suddenly very aware of the fact that she's only dressed in a t-shirt and panties, curled up around me under the blanket. I run a hand down her bare thigh. "I heard you say it, and fuck, angel, you have no idea what that did to me."

"Guess I'm not the only one who likes the names, huh?" She giggles as I trace kisses up her throat, grinding herself against my cock. "It's not official til we say vows though, right?" She wriggles her hips as I hook a hand into her panties, helping me pull them down her legs.

"I guess not." I unzip myself, freeing my cock. I spit into my hand, rubbing it over the sensitive tip which is already leaking pre-cum because her scent is driving me fucking crazy. Juliet's eyes are still closed as I hitch her leg over my hip and push inside her with a growl.

"Oh fuck." She gasps. "This isn't the ceremony everyone tells you to dream up when you're a kid."

"But so much more fun." I slide in and out of her slowly, watching her lips as they part, her brow as it furrows. "The priest would be on the floor in shame by now."

Juliet laughs over a moan. "Just a private ceremony for two then." Her fingers dig into my shoulder, and her eyes slide open slowly. "How do they go?" She gasps as I thrust harder. "For... For-"

"For better or worse."

She smiles. "For richer, for- *Oh* - for poorer."

"In sickness and in health." I cage a hand against the back of her head, the other digging into her hip.

"Til death us do part."

"No, not even then." I roll her onto her back, pinning her hands against the ground.

She arches her back, moaning loudly. "No?"

"I'd break down the gates of heaven or trawl the depths of hell to find you." I fuck her harder as her legs wrap around my hips, her body writhing under mine. "Because nothing - not God-" She cries out as my cock rolls in and out of her, the scent of her love overwhelming. "Not death, or this fucked up world, nothing can keep me from you."

She whimpers, pressing her legs around my hips. "I'm yours, Silas."

"Yes you are angel." I kiss her hungrily, her moans and sighs meeting my lips. "My wife. My everything. I love you. Fuck, I love you."

She shudders, her hands fighting against mine. "I love you too. Let me hold you, oh god, please."

I release her, and she wraps herself around me completely, her breath mingling with mine. I lose myself completely in the moment, in her body, in the sounds she's making and the knowledge that she's mine, *mine*. It doesn't matter that we're not in a church, that she's not wearing a white dress. No, we said these vows on a blanket on the floor of an abandoned farmhouse, covered in sweat and moaning each other's names. Instead of exchanging rings and saying I Do, I come inside her as she screams, her body hot and tight as her orgasm rolls through her.

It means more than if a priest had declared we were now husband and wife, telling me I could now kiss what was mine already. When Juliet leans up to kiss me, sweat lining her lips, I can taste everything that I never knew I wanted.

My wife.

We remain tangled like that for a long time, kissing and murmuring to each other, the firelight dancing along the broken walls around us. When we curl up together, naked and blissful, Juliet's back against my chest, she sighs happily.

"I heard you that night," she whispers. "That night in the farmhouse, when you said you loved me."

"I thought you were asleep." I stroke my fingers down the curve of her shoulder.

"I thought I dreamed it." She nuzzles into my arms. "But I didn't."

"No, you didn't, angel. I love you." I kiss her neck. "I love you more than life."

"I love you too." She murmurs sleepily, and within a few minutes, she's breathing deeply.

I hold her as dawn begins to color the sky. I don't know what this day will bring, or where we'll end up. But I know that I'll keep her safe.

No matter what happens, I'll keep her safe.

I EAT the last of the food Sutton had packed for me as Silas disconnects the generator from the truck.

"I wonder if there's anything in New York," he muses out loud. "Some of the covens that were unhappy in Boston moved there."

"I went to New York once, when I was 13."

He smiles over his shoulder at me. "Oh yeah?"

"Yeah, my mom took me to MOMA."

"Oh, that place was amazing."

"You've been?"

"It was the first place I wanted to go when we landed in the states," he says with a laugh. "Sorry angel, I hate to tell you that you're married to a horrendous art nerd."

Our eyes meet as he seems to realize what he just said, and we both smile widely. *Married.* I don't care that it wasn't a proper ceremony. It doesn't matter.

"I think I can handle that." I get to my feet, and he leans back against the truck as I approach him. I drape my arms around his neck. "We can be horrendous art nerds together."

He strokes his fingers through my hair. "We can indeed."

He plants a kiss on the tip of my nose. "Now, let's get going. I want to make good ground before nightfall."

We climb into the truck, leaving the unconventional location of our wedding behind us, and my hand finds Silas's on the shift as we drive. The sun is beating down, and the sky is as blue as a robin's egg. It's a perfect day, and I keep gazing across at Silas - at my husband. God, the word makes me so giddy. He keeps his eyes on the road as he lifts my hand to his lips.

"Alright, angel?"

"More than alright." I move across the seat and snuggle under his arm. "I guess this is our honeymoon, huh?"

He laughs out loud. "You want to pull over and make it official?"

My gaze wanders out the windshield as I laugh, but it's cut off quickly. I choke on thin air as I lean forward.

"What the fuck is that?"

Silas slams on the brakes. "Holy fuck."

"Silas, what the fuck?" My head whips around to look at him. "What is that? Are those-"

"Tanks. They've got fucking tanks."

We sit on the ridge, overlooking the sprawling valley below us, and watch as the caravan of tanks rolling along behind an immense herd of Afflicted throws up dust from the broken highway. The large red and blue letters - NG - are visible even from here.

"It's the National Guard." I run a hand over my mouth, feeling sweat break out over my upper lip at the sight of all those Afflicted. "They're still using the Afflicted. What the hell is wrong with them?"

"They're headed south." Silas turns to me, his face dark.

"Where do you think they're going?"

"If I had to hazard a guess, I'd say Roanoke."

I gasp, shaking my head. "No, no way, why would they attack humans?"

"They think it's vamps as well." He looks back out the windshield. "The rumor that vamps lived there had spread to Savannah, there's no reason to think it wouldn't have spread even further."

"They're going to kill them all. Oh my god, there are *kids* there."

Silas guns the engine, throwing the truck into reverse and executing a turn amidst a squeal of tires, before shooting back down the way we came.

"We've got to warn them," he says, reaching over to take my hand. "It'll be alright, we'll move much faster than them. We'll get there, and warn them. They'll have time to get out of there."

"Do you think they'll listen to us?"

Silas's jaw ticks. "I bloody well hope so."

I'm sure we didn't drive that far from Roanoke, but my palms itch with every passing mile, every minute that ticks over. I keep checking over my shoulder, like I'll suddenly see a cavalcade of tanks behind us, or Afflicted climbing into the bed of the truck. Silas keeps trying to reassure me, but I'm beyond panic now.

Finally, we're on the outskirts of Roanoke.

"How long do you think it'll take them to get here?" I ask, scrubbing my hands along my thighs.

"I don't know, a few hours? Maybe? It's hard to say." He gazes up at the sky, where iridescent silver clouds are starting to gather. "It almost looks like snow. That'll hold them up."

"How are 800 people going to find shelter out here in the wild when it's snowing?" My eyes begin to sting, because this whole situation feels so fucking hopeless. "And there's those bandits, what if there's more of them?"

Silas brings the truck to a sudden stop, and reaches over to me. He pulls me close, kissing me hard. His mouth is so warm, and I try to steady my wild heart rate, holding on to him with everything I've got.

"It's going to be alright," he murmurs, looking deeply into my eyes. "It's going to be alright, angel. I promise you. No matter what, I'll keep you safe."

"Don't leave me."

"Come on now, let's get in there and help these people." He lets me go, and I stay right beside him on the seat as we head for the gates of the colony. Silas starts blaring the horn, and I wind my window down, waving my arms wildly as I lean out the side of the truck.

"Open up!" I shout as loudly as I can, the cold air burning my throat and my lungs. "Open the gate!"

We come to a stop and jump out, continuing to wave and shout.

"There's danger!" Silas yells to the guard tower gesturing back the way we came. "Open the gates!"

Almost immediately, the gate begins to groan and shift, rolling open slowly. Two guards emerge, having clearly thrown their body armor on quickly, the buckles on the side dangling open.

"What's going on?" One of them asks, clutching his assault rifle across his chest. At least they're not pointed at us.

"The National Guard are coming." The words bubble out of me almost hysterically. "They raided our compound down in Georgia using Afflicted, and now they're going to do the same to you."

The guards glance at each other, jaws dropping.

"What the - what do you mean?" The taller one takes a step closer, looking from me to Silas and back. "We're a human colony, why would the National Guard come here?"

"When I was in Savannah, I was told there were vamps

living here with you. It's more than likely the National Guard have heard that rumor too." Silas's voice is deep with worry, his hands spread in front of him. "We need to get everyone out of here now."

"What's going on?" Sutton's voice rings behind the guards, and they step aside, one of them jerking his thumb in our direction.

"These two think the National Guard are bringing Afflicted here to take us out." The guard rubs a hand over the back of his neck, shifting on his feet. "Jesus Christ."

"Don't panic just yet," Sutton says, eyeing us uncertainly. "Why are the National Guard using Afflicted? As a weapon? A diversion?"

"More like a battering ram." Silas replies. "They did it in Milledgeville, sent the Afflicted in before storming the compound themselves. It was a disaster. They didn't take out any vamps, but 20 humans died. It was a bloodbath."

Sutton's eyes widen slightly. "Oh shit."

"And as I was just telling your men here, they more than likely think there are vamps here. I'd heard there were, they probably have too."

"Where are they now?" Sutton crosses her arms over her chest, no doubt trying to disguise her trembling hands.

"About 25 miles north of here, or they were when we spotted them. They have tanks so-"

"Tanks?" Sutton cuts Silas off with an exclamation. "They have *tanks*?"

"Afraid so. But they're traveling behind Afflicted, so it's slow going. We have time."

"Time?" Sutton runs a hand over her head, bracing the other one against her waist. "Jesus Christ, we have 800 people in here. There are old folks, kids, pregnant folks, I mean..." She trails off, covering her face with her hands. "Oh my god."

"Let us help." I step forward and take her hands. "I know we're just two people, but we have a truck, we can take some in the back, and help you get people to safety."

"How do we know they're coming here?" She asks, clearly grasping at hope. "Maybe they're going somewhere else."

"There's nothing else around here, boss." The shorter guard's words bring Sutton's hope crashing down. I can see it in her face, as her brow furrows, her teeth clenched.

"No, I guess there isn't." She holds on to my hands, leaning on them heavily. "We worked so hard to keep everyone safe."

"Maybe we can barricade ourselves in?" The taller guard says.

Silas shakes his head. "Listen, I wouldn't recommend that. The Afflicted, they're insanely strong."

"No, he's right." Sutton nods her head slowly. "We have a better chance here than out there in the wild."

"Listen, your systems are good, but this horde is huge." Silas's voice rings with urgency. " You need to get out of here."

"And then what?" Sutton lets go of my hands, straightening her shoulders. "Then I have 800 people out there, in the woods, with no shelter, no food?"

"Please, you need to get out of here." I take a step closer to Sutton. "I don't want that to happen to you. It was awful. Please."

Her face falls with a look of defeat, and she nods. With a heavy sigh, she gestures sharply for us to follow.

"Bring in your truck, we'll send up the alarms and get folks moving."

Silas nods and turns tail, and I follow him back to the truck as Sutton barks commands to the guards.

"Thank god she listened," he mutters, driving in slowly after the guards. "I thought we were going to have a fight on our hands for a second there."

"So did I." I look over my shoulder to see Sutton talking to the gate guards. She gestures to the barrier wall, crossing her arm over her chest and casting a glance at the truck "What is she doing?"

"What do you mean?" Silas looks in the rear view, his eyes widening as the gate begins to close. "What is she doing?" He brings the truck to a stop and we both jump down as the gate rolls shut and the guards begin to chain it up. "Ey! What the hell are you doing? We need to get these people out of here!"

Sutton faces us with pursed lips. "I changed my mind."

"You *what?*" Silas holds his hands up."You have to listen to me, this is-"

"I don't have to do anything." Sutton interjects, one of the guards appearing at her side. "I have 800 people to think about here. Pregnant people, old folks, little babies. It's going to snow tonight. I can't keep 800 people safe in the woods."

"The Afflicted are going to tear those people apart!" I shake my head, moving towards her, a movement she mirrors exactly as she takes three steps away from me. "These people are going to die!"

"The National Guard aren't going to attack a human colony. I'll make contact with them, and they'll back down."

"They aren't going to give you time to do that!" Silas runs his hands over his head, turning away to brace a hand against his waist. At that moment three little kids run across the road, laughing and chasing a ball. Silas rounds back on Sutton, his expression pained. "Please, we have to get these people to safety. The National Guard will shoot first and ask questions afterwards. You won't stand a chance."

"I disagree." Sutton's face remains maddeningly calm as she looks at us both. "I appreciate the fact you came to warn us. I don't forget a favor like that, and I will pay my dues."

"I don't need your favors, lady, I need these people, these

kids, to fucking survive." Silas points behind him towards the buildings. "All these people-"

"Are my responsibility, and they're safe here."

"Well, we're not staying here." I meet Silas's gaze and jerk my thumb towards the truck. "Let's get out of here."

"That gate isn't opening."

Silas and I both gape at Sutton. "You're locking us up?" I ask incredulously.

"I'm keeping you both safe for the night. You'll be free to leave in the morning." Sutton waves to the guard. "Take them to lock-up. They're our guests til morning, then they're free to do what they like." She walks away, leaving us staring at her back.

"We are in lockdown until dawn," a staccato voice says. "I repeat, lockdown conditions until dawn."

The guard holds out his hands for the truck keys. "I'll be taking those for now."

Silas and I exchange a glance. We're powerless here. Locked in with armed guards, and innocent civilians. Fighting back is futile. With a sigh, Silas drops the truck keys in the guard's hand.

"Any firearms?" The guard asks, jerking his chin in the direction of the truck.

"Three, but no ammunition," Silas replies. "There is a bag in there I'd like to get out, if it's all the same to you."

The guard's eyes narrow. "What's in it?"

"Just some clothes, a cassette tape, notebook and a locket. Nothing that can be used as a weapon."

The guard scoffs. "No, you got those right in your mouth there."

Silas squares his shoulders. "I'm not a danger to you."

"Good." The guard nods. "Go on ahead and get your bag. Then you gotta come in here with me." He points to a building beside us with bars lining the windows. "It's the isolation wing."

"You're going to lock us up?" I ask. "You didn't lock me up when I was here."

"Well, you weren't here with a feeder then, were you?" The guard's hands flex around the barrel of his rifle. "We're not going to take any chances. Don't worry. You'll be plenty comfortable."

"Fine." Silas turns on his heel and takes the bag from the back seat, putting it over his shoulder before we follow the guard into the building. We walk through wide double doors, into the lobby of what appears to have once been a bank. The patterned carpet underfoot is threadbare but clean, the strange blue and yellow pattern faded.

We're taken through a large room and up a set of stairs. Down a long corridor, the guard stops and opens a door, staying outside as he waves us in. The room looks like a motel room, with a double bed, a lamp and a door that I'm guessing leads to the bathroom.

"Towels are in there," the guard says, pointing at the door. "Stay put and behave yourselves, you might even have a nice night here. I'll have food brought to you, but it's going to be quiet with a lockdown in place." He moves to close the door, then stops. "Oh, and don't turn the light on after sundown." He regards Silas with a cocked eyebrow. "I guess with your freaky eyes that won't be a problem."

"Hey!" I snap, but he's already closing the door. "Jesus, what an asshole."

"Can't blame him," Silas replies quietly, taking the bag from his shoulder and placing it at the end of the bed. "Not like vamps have done a whole lot to gain anyone's trust."

"He still doesn't have to be an asshole," I grumble, and Silas gives me a smile.

"So defensive, angel. Anyone would think you liked me."

"Ha, ha." I put my arms around his waist and give him a weak smile. "So, what was that about a honeymoon?"

"Locked up in an old bank while World War Three is about to break out. Truly the stuff of dreams."

I hate the feeling of dread that creeps up on me, the sick sensation of my stomach dropping as I take in what Silas just said.

"You think there's even a chance that Sutton is right? That they'll be able to contact them and stop an attack?

"Sure." Silas sweeps my hair over my shoulders, dropping his gaze from mine. "Absolutely. If they send someone out, or put up signals, anything. It could work. If they find the frequency the Guard is on, they might be able to communicate what this place really is. It could all be fine. And maybe we really are in the safest place we can be."

He doesn't sound convinced, and I chew my lip, mulling over all the possibilities. Maybe we will be safe here. Maybe we won't be. If it ends up like Milledgeville...

"Hey."

I look up at Silas, and he smiles softly.

"It's going to be OK."

I scoff out a shaky laugh. "Yeah, of course it is."

He pulls me down onto the bed with him, and I settle my head on his chest with a heavy sigh.

"Where are we going first, ey?"

"First?" I frown at him. "What do you mean?"

"When this is all over. When the world's back to normal." His fingertips stroke my cheek. "You get first pick. Where are we going?"

Indulging in the fantasy hurts more than I thought it would. Like spinning a globe in my mind, I lie there thinking of all the places I want to go, all the things I wanted to see, before. *Before.*

"Paris."

Silas raises his eyebrows. "Oh, yeah? You ever been?"

"Yeah, when I was a kid. It was amazing."

"Paris it is then." He wraps his arms around me, holding me close, kissing the top of my head. "Perfect location for a honeymoon."

A siren drones softly in the distance, and I hold on to Silas, quietly praying. *Please let this all pass. Let the world go back to normal. I don't even need Paris. I just need him. Please, let us get out of this alive.*

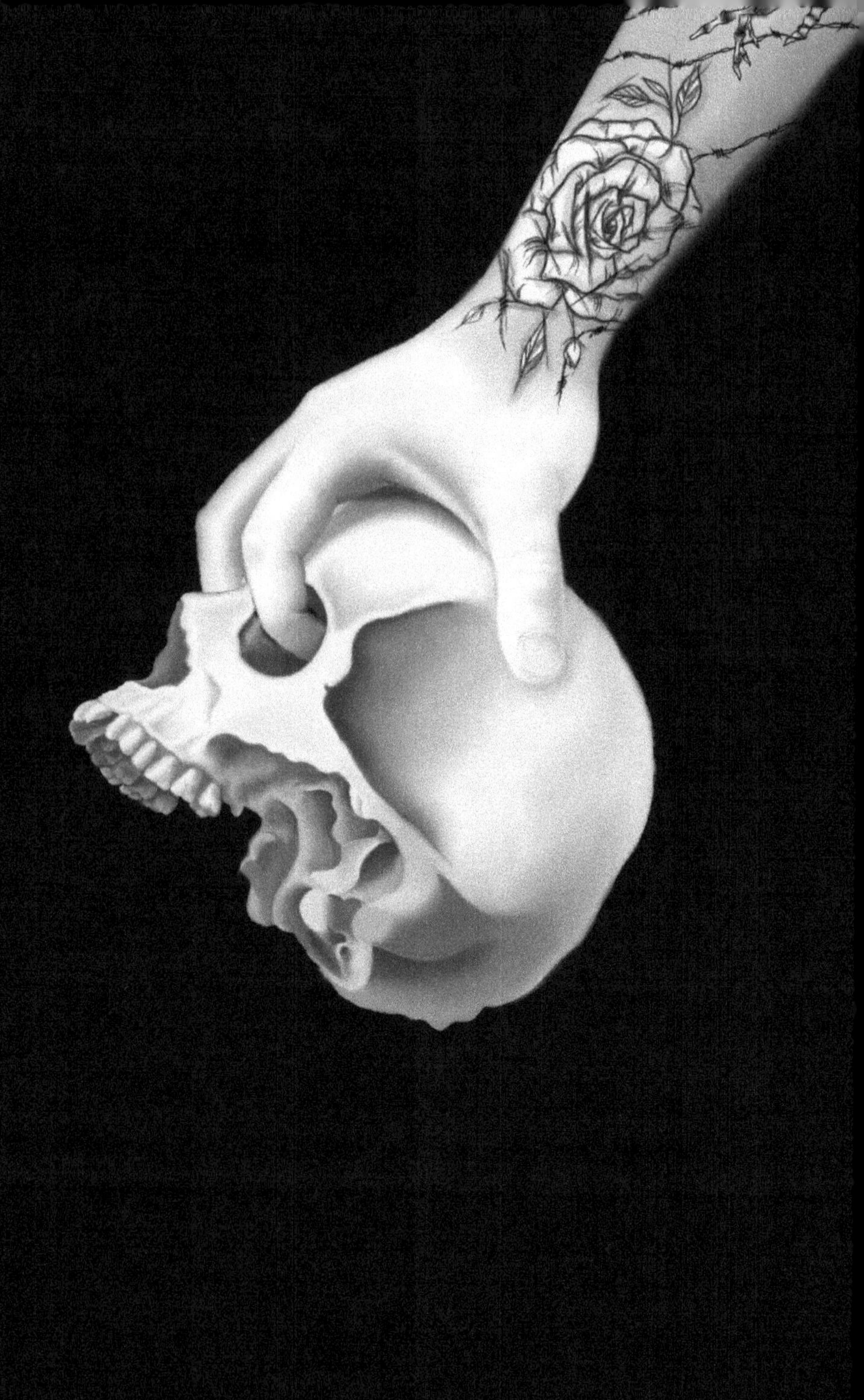

FOR A FEW HOURS, I dare to hope that maybe Sutton was right. I entertain fantasies that maybe the National Guard were simply herding the Afflicted into a death pit somewhere, exterminating the last of the vampires' disastrous medical experiment with fire. Since we left Milledgeville, maybe something had occurred, some rebuilding effort. Maybe Boston had finally gotten their shit together.

But just as the sun begins to set, the wail of a siren breaks through the deep silence. Juliet had dozed off on my shoulder, but with a start she sits up, her eyes wide.

"Oh shit," she murmurs, her hand over her mouth.

Before I can respond, there's an explosion, distant, but close enough to have the ground beneath us quaking gently. The National Guard are indeed shooting first and asking questions later.

Juliet scrambles to her feet and goes to the window, pushing aside the curtains and looking out into the growing dark.

"Jules, be careful." I'm at her back, looking out the window over her shoulder. Orange glows in the distance, over the tops of the buildings, and the siren continues to drone. "They're trying to blow out the perimeter."

"With a tank that won't be hard," Juliet says. "Dammit. She's just killed all these people."

"They might still not get in. If Sutton can communicate with them, they might stop the attack."

At that moment, the loudspeakers whistle, and Sutton's voice rings out over the colony.

"You are attacking a human colony! Halt your advance! I repeat, this is a human colony. There are no vampires here!" Sutton's voice is measured and commanding, not a hint of a waver.

Juliet exhales heavily after a moment, as though she was holding her breath. "God, I hope they heard that. They won't come in now, will they?"

I shake my head, but even as I do, I hear it. Dread rushes through me. I clasp Juliet to me, and she sucks in a breath.

"Silas?"

"Whatever happens, stay behind me, OK?"

"Silas? What-"

I press a kiss to her mouth. "I love you, alright? I need you to know that."

Her fingers curl around my shirt, her hands starting to tremble. "Silas, what? What's happening?"

Screeching and screaming starts to sound below us. Juliet's eyes don't leave mine as realization washes over her. She simply shakes her head, biting her lower lip as she nods.

"They're here, angel." I could hear them coming. The National Guard blew open that fucking perimeter and sent them in, without even thinking. Without even knowing. And now they have no way to stop them.

I can hear them bashing against the exterior of the building below us, hundreds of heavy footsteps and their shrieking getting louder and louder.

"Come on." I grab Juliet's hand and head for the door. One solid kick, and the wood splinters, the door flying outwards. "We need to get out of here."

"Where do we go?" Her voice is tight with fear.

"If we get to the roof we can avoid them, head for another building, barricade ourselves up there." I pull her down the corridor behind me, the rhythmic battering from downstairs becoming louder and louder. "Stairs, stairs, fucking stairs, where are they?"

"Silas!" Juliet jerks me to a stop and points at a blue door at the end of the corridor. We sprint for it as the banging downstairs stops, and the shrieking of the Afflicted fills the building. They've made it inside.

I push Juliet up ahead of me, and she takes the stairs two at a time, rounding each curve of the stairwell until it ends in a solid black door. She steps aside to let me shoulder it open, and it gives way with a loud groan.

Out on the roof, the last of the evening light is fading. Juliet is panting beside me as I close the door, looking around on the roof for something to barricade it with. But there's nothing, the rooftop is bare. But the roofs on either side of us are low, and within jumping distance.

"Let's go." I snatch up her hand and run for the edge of the building. Before we reach the edge, I scoop her up in my arms, and she yelps as my feet leave the ground and I jump across the distance between the buildings. As we land on the other side, the door on the rooftop we just left bursts open, and Afflicted flood out into the open. Juliet's sharp intake of breath covers a scream, and her arms wrap around my neck.

"We're alright, angel." I race for the next rooftop, underestimating just how far this expanse is. We make it, but I stumble at the other end, losing my footing and crashing to my knees.

"Are you OK?" Juliet cries.

"I'm fine, I'm fine." I look over my shoulder, at the Afflicted that are pouring over the edge of the building. They're driven purely by instinct, scenting us on the breeze and trying to get to us.

I get to my feet at the very moment that the door of the rooftop we now find ourselves on flies open, and three Afflicted stumble out, hands extended as they shriek and scream, looking for us.

Juliet claps a hand over her mouth, trying not to scream, but it makes no difference. They can smell us. I put Juliet on her feet and shove her behind me. She holds on to my shoulders, breathing rapidly.

"Oh my god," she cries, unable to suppress her scream anymore as the Afflicted begin to barrel towards us.

The first one is small and lithe, and looks as though it could snap in half. It does, in fact, when my boot lands in its middle. It folds in half like a broken clothesline, and lies on the ground shrieking, bloody fingers scraping at the ground. The next two are decidedly bigger, and have the hollow cheeks and bared teeth of very hungry predators.

The first one gets close enough that I can grab onto its arm and pull. It wails in pain as the arm detaches from its body, the sick stench of rotting flesh rising through the air. It ambles sideways, disoriented by the pain.

The third one is stronger than the first two. It wrenches me away from Juliet, who screams my name as I grapple it around the waist and slam it to the ground. Its dead, black eyes don't see me, but its nostrils flare violently as its fangs snap at my arms.

I curl a hand around its neck and slam its head repeatedly

into the ground. Bones crunch, blood starts to coat the ground, and finally there's just the wet slap of brain matter on concrete. It goes still under me just as Juliet screams again.

The one-armed feeder is making a beeline for her, and I rush at it in a low crouch. I keep running until we reach the edge of the building, and fling it down the several stories to the street beneath us.

The street teeming with Afflicted.

There's hundreds of them. Thousands, maybe.

Juliet comes to my side, and gazes down at them.

"I guess this is it then, huh?" She tilts her head to look up at me. "There are too many of them."

"We're going to get out of this, OK?"

There's shrieks and wailing in the stairwell, and Juliet gazes up at me sadly.

"There's too many of them."

I shake my head. "No. This isn't how this ends for you."

I rush to the door, holding it shut. I'm not going down without a fight. Juliet stands 10 feet away, covering her mouth with her hands.

"Tell me about Paris!" I call, putting my full weight against the door as the first Afflicted slams into it.

"What?" Juliet regards me with shock. "Are you kidding me?"

"Tell me about it!" Another slam into the door, nails scratching at the metal. "I've never been!"

"You're crazy!"

"Talk to me, angel!" Another thump, more frantic clawing.

She shakes her head, licking her lip and clenching her eyes shut. "There - there was this little cafe, and Kaden made himself sick on hot chocolate, and he threw up all over this cobblestone street."

Even in the situation we find ourselves in, death very likely imminent, I can't help but laugh as Afflicted shriek and groan on the other side of the door.

"Well, that sounds amazing!" I grit my teeth as the door shifts slightly, and I push my shoulder back against it. "What else, angel? Tell me-" The door gapes slightly, and I shove against the force of the Afflicted trying to get to us. "What was your favorite thing?"

"The music!" She's crying now, her jaw trembling as she watches me try to hold this horde back. "There was an accordion player on the corner of the street where we were staying, and he played Edith Piaf as the sun went down. It was the most beautiful thing I'd ever heard!"

My eyes meet hers, and I smile. "That sounds beautiful, angel." The door gapes again, broken, craggy fingertips curling around the edge of it. "You know, I remember the first day I saw you, I was in love with you then. You're the most beautiful thing I've ever seen. You're the best thing that ever happened to me, you know that?"

She sobs, her shoulders shaking.

"I'm so glad you're my wife."

She shakes her head. We're saying goodbye. She knows it.

"Silas-" She takes two uncertain steps towards me.

"Go on, angel. Run for that roof over there, keep running. Stay safe, OK?"

She shakes her head even more emphatically. "*No.*"

"Run, now. And don't look back."

The door creaks again, and this time when it gapes open, I can't get it back into the frame. I plead with Juliet with my eyes. *Please go. Please live. Please don't stay here.*

Her face crumples as she backs away from me, squaring her shoulders as she breaks into a run. I watch as that golden hair flails out behind her, her long legs stretching beneath her as she launches into the air. She makes the landing, tucking into a roll on the other side and quickly getting to her feet.

"Silas!" She jumps up and down, waving her arms. "Silas, *come on!*"

"I told you not to look back!"

"Get the fuck up and run!" She screams at me desperately.

I take a deep breath, and shove away from the door. It flies open with such force I'm knocked onto my back. I scramble away from the Afflicted, who are screaming and screeching.They move to descend on me with outstretched hands, and all I can hear is Juliet's cries.

The Afflicted stop in their tracks as a floodlight and the deafening whir of helicopter blades sound over us. The black hawk dips and turns over the building, and the Afflicted all stare up at it as it begins to snow.

I back away, getting to my feet. I look over at Juliet, who's holding her hands over her ears as the helicopter continues its circles over us. It does two more passes, then moves on. The Afflicted aren't screeching anymore. They're gurgling, almost like they're choking.

I look down onto the street, and the Afflicted down there begin to fall to their knees, some straight onto their backs as though they've been shocked into stasis. I turn back to look at the ones on the roof. They begin to fall, one by one.

"What is happening?" I hear Juliet's voice through a strange sort of haze.

I feel dizzy. I raise my hand to my face. It glistens with snow, sticking to my skin in the wavering glow of the distant floodlights.

No. Not snow.

My mouth goes dry, and my throat becomes tight. My heart slows.

Not snow.
Silver.

"It doesn't matter." I clasp onto Silas's hand, and the fact that it's still warm makes me almost angry. I could almost believe he was just sleeping.

The nurse puts a comforting hand on my shoulder. "Well, when you're ready, you let me look at it, OK?" She leaves without another word.

I lay my head on Silas's chest, gazing at his motionless face.

"You're so beautiful." I trace a finger along his jawline. "You can't be dead. I won't let you be dead. That's not fair. I've lost everyone else."

I curl my fingers around his, and tears slip down the side of my face. They pool on his chest, glimmering with those tiny shards of silver.

"I didn't finish telling you about Paris." I sniffle and bite my lip to stop myself from crying again. "You know, I'd have thought you'd have gone there, Margot being French and all. I guess maybe it was bad memories, huh? Anyway, I think you'd have really liked it. The galleries were amazing. They had these people set up by the Seine, they'd be there with their easels, and everyone had a different art style, it was so fascinating to watch."

I lean over him, stroking the dark tendrils of his hair from his forehead.

"I discovered macarons there, and I made myself sick with the green ones. I told you about Kaden throwing up every-where, well let me tell you that was nothing compared to me." I laugh, brushing away the tears that keep running down my cheeks. "And throwing up green, well that was so much worse."

Footsteps rush past the cubicle, voices talking about IVs and saline and *Can we get another stretcher down here?* People are hurt, people are dead. But I can't face all that and offer to help. Instead I nuzzle my face into the crook of Silas's neck.

"You know, you made me want to live again," I whisper to him. "I didn't want to when I... I went to the stream. Even though you were so nice to me, I didn't see life being any good. And then... You know what it was? You know what the moment was? When I woke up and you were there. It was like, I nearly died and then my reason for being here was there." I bite back a sob. "I thought you were a monster, I thought you were darkness and badness and all that shit, and I was so wrong. You were my light, Silas."

"And you were mine."

I back away with a gasp, my mouth dropping open. It can't be. It's not real. I'm dreaming.

Silas smiles at me weakly, his eyes a dull shade of brown.

"Hello, angel."

With a strangled cry I throw myself on him, one sob after another tearing out of my throat as he wraps his arms around me.

"Come on now." He strokes my hair, his chest shaking as he coughs. "It's alright, don't cry."

"You were dead!" I look down into his face, shaking my head. "I don't understand, you were - they dumped the silver, and you, you were - you were dead."

The curtain opens behind me, and the nurse appears on the other side of the bed. I back up as she leans over him, turning his head side to side gently, then gesturing for him to open his mouth.

"Well, this is unexpected." She regards Silas critically. "Hmm. We have a doctor here from the National Guard, he's an expert in fee - in vampire health. I'll have him come take a look at you."

"Silver should have killed him," I say stupidly. "How is this possible?"

The nurse shrugs. "No idea, I deal with humans, not vampires." She lifts an eyebrow. "You look like shit though, so that silver definitely weakened you. Stay down, and I'll send the doctor along."

She leaves, and Silas and I just stare at each other.

"Sorry I scared you." He coughs heavily, rolling on to his side with a groan. "Fuck me, I feel like shit, too."

I help him settle back on the bed, and he winces as he smiles at me.

"Guess it just wasn't my time yet, ey?"

I sit back down and take his hand. "I don't understand, but I don't really care either. You're here. I thought I'd lost you."

"So did I, angel. But fuck am I glad I'm still here."

The curtain flies open with a loud hiss, and a man in a white coat strides in. He pushes the silver glasses he's wearing up his nose, and looks at us both with raised eyebrows.

"I'm told we have a vampire who's immune to silver in the house?" He crosses his arms over his chest. "Impressive."

"Hardly immune." Silas coughs heavily, a loud rasping echoing through his chest. "I feel like death."

"Feeling like death and being dead are two very different things, my friend." The doctor rounds the bed, and I move back so he can examine Silas. He shines a light in his eyes, and grumbles something to himself. He inspects Silas's fangs, then straightens up. "When were you turned?"

"1995."

"And what do you know about your maker?"

Silas rolls onto his back, hissing in a sharp breath of pain. "I mean, plenty, why? What do you need to know?"

"Anything unusual about her appearance?"

Silas frowns, his eyes scanning the ceiling. "Um, I mean, not really."

"Nothing unusual about her eyes?" The doctor is smiling in

a way I don't understand, as though he's anticipating something amazing is about to happen.

"She had blue eyes, nothing unusual-"

The doctor hacks out a laugh and balls his hand into a fist. "I knew it."

"Knew what?" I ask. "What is going on here?"

"Your boyfriend's maker, she was an Original."

"Husband," I snap, and the doctor rolls his eyes. "What do you mean an Original?"

"That's not possible." Silas tries to sit up, but has to stop, and collapses back down onto the bed. "She was turned during the French Revolution, she told me about it, many times. She was 31 years old in 1792. She told me all about her life. She wasn't an Original."

"Only the Originals had human eye colors," the doctor says.

"That's a ridiculous myth," Silas scoffs.

"*And* they were famously the only vampires immune to silver." The doctor gives Silas a meaningful look. "She passed that on to you. Only the offspring of the Originals can withstand silver. There aren't many of you, but we've met a few and are having a lot of luck using their blood to make new vaccines."

"Is that so?" Silas sounds instantly curious.

"Sure is. It's something we should have been working on the whole time."

"So you'd want to do that with me?"

I spring to my feet. "No one's poking and prodding him when he's in this state."

The doctor laughs jovially and holds his hands up. "Relax, hon, no one's going to hurt him." He smiles warmly at Silas. "But, if you were willing, we have a big lab up in Philly. You could both move up there, we'd make sure you had everything you needed."

"There's a colony there?" I ask cautiously.

The doctor gives me a warm smile and nods. "You two probably don't know this, but the vampires and the President have signed an agreement. Rebuilding efforts are underway."

My heart drops straight down into my feet, and I collapse into the chair. Silas raises his head, alarmed.

"Jules, are you OK?"

"Yeah, yeah, I'm fine. I just can't believe this is happening."

The doctor's kind smile moves to me. "Good things are coming, I promise." He looks back down at Silas. "You'll probably feel terrible for another day or two, but we'll get you some blood and you'll be back to normal in no time. Then, if you decide you want to, I'll arrange for you to come up to Philly. I'm Doctor Harris, by the way."

"Silas." He lifts a trembling hand, which Dr. Harris takes and gives a brief shake. "And this is my wife, Juliet."

"Great to meet you both. I'll leave you to consider my offer."

"Sure thing, thanks doc." Silas raises a hand in acknowledgement, and Dr. Harris leaves with a nod.

"Jesus Christ." Silas runs a hand over his face, and it dawns on me that this is huge for him. Sure, the world is righting itself outside these walls, but within them a huge chunk of Silas's just tilted right off its axis.

I scoot forward in my chair and take his hand. "You OK?"

"Yeah, I am, really. I just..." His brow furrows, and he drags his teeth over his lip. "Why would Margot lie to me? Why would she say she'd been turned then when she hadn't?"

"Maybe she had something to hide? Maybe she was running from something?"

"It must have been something huge for her not to tell me." Silas frowns up at the ceiling. "To make up a whole life, an entire story, that wasn't true? What is an Original running from if they do that?"

"Must have been something pretty big. Maybe that was why she was a loner?"

"Even the vamps in Boston were fooled by it." He sighs heavily, before looking back at me. "Anyway, we'll never know, I guess."

"I guess not." I puff out a breath. "So, Philly, huh?"

"I want to help." Silas's voice is thick with determination. "If my blood can somehow help, can somehow make vaccines for people to be healthy, I want that."

"Of course." I grip his hand tightly, and press a kiss to the back of it. "Wherever you want to go. I'll go with you. Forever."

He pulls me down to him, and wraps his arms around me. "More than forever, angel. Forever's not enough." He kisses my forehead, and I nuzzle into him.

Everything's going to be alright now.

I'M WATCHING TV. I'm sitting on a couch, Silas sitting beside me, his fingers entwined with mine, and we're watching TV.

Folks are jammed into the room around us, so silent you could hear a pin drop. All eyes are fixed on the grainy screen as our President appears behind a lectern. I still remember her from the emergency broadcasts when the Affliction first became a concern. She looks the same, just a little older, grey strands through her brown hair.

She smiles warmly at the camera, and opens her mouth to speak.

Silas squeezes my hand as she recounts the events of the

past two weeks. The riots in Boston. The rebellion against the vampire covens in Boston by humans and vampires alike. The National Guard being disbanded for the improper use of Afflicted. The new virus they'd released that was slowly killing the Afflicted, their numbers dwindling by the day.

"All Human Preservation Compounds will be disbanded." Her voice is strong and confident. "We know these facilities caused widespread suffering, and we will provide every support necessary to assist humans to transition back into a normal life."

She turns to her side, and gestures for someone to join her. A man appears at her side, a vampire, his blonde hair hanging to his shoulders. His rusty eyes look out at us from the screen, and he smiles.

"We have made huge advancements in the creation of a synthetic blood alternative that provides identical nutrition to human blood," he says, and the room bursts into murmurs. "The harvesting of human blood will be on a strictly voluntary basis, and only until the synthetic alternative is perfected." He turns to the President, and she smiles warmly.

"He's bitten her, he has," Silas mutters under his breath. "Look how she's smiling at him."

I shove him with my elbow. "Shhh."

"Seen that look on your face before."

I suppress a giggle. "*Shhh.*"

"We will move together as one," the vampire on the screen goes on. "One people, with a common purpose - to rebuild our world. Together."

"Together!" Someone calls at the back of the room, and everyone bursts into applause.

I look at Silas, and his mouth lifts into a smile. He looks like himself again, even though his eyes are a lighter brown than they were before. He's back to full strength, with the help of a lot of blood, and a new supplement Dr. Harris developed.

I lean over and kiss him softly. His lips are so soft and warm.

"You ready?" I ask quietly as the room around us continues to celebrate the possibility of this new future.

He nods. "Sure am. Let's go. They'll be waiting for us."

We get to our feet, leaving the jubilations of the colony behind us. Outside, snow is lying thick on the ground, and a guard is sweeping it off our truck. Dr. Harris is waiting for us with two other people, waving a greeting as we approach.

"I can't tell you how glad I am that you agreed to this." He shakes our hands, and Silas chuckles.

"Happy to oblige. Sort of looking forward to a fresh start." He puts his arm around my shoulders, and kisses my temple. "Been something of a rocky start to married life as you can imagine."

The doctor laughs loudly. "A baptism of fire as they say. Well, they found you two a great apartment, everything is waiting for you."

I look up at Silas. "Can't wait."

"Me neither." He kisses my forehead. "Me neither, angel."

Our truck bumps along the road behind the doctor's vehicle, two escort vehicles flanking us as we make our way to Philadelphia. I stay under Silas's arm, watching the landscape slip by.

"You know," he says after a few miles, "now that the world's going back to normal, we might be going to Paris sooner than we think."

I can't help but laugh. "You think so?"

"Sure, why not?"

"I promise not to throw up green macarons all over you."

He laughs out loud. "Yeah, I did hear you talk about that." He smiles down at me. "Forever, ey?"

"No, not forever." I lean my head against his chest, the snow around us glittering as the sun beats down. "You were right. Forever isn't long enough."

"Not nearly long enough, angel."

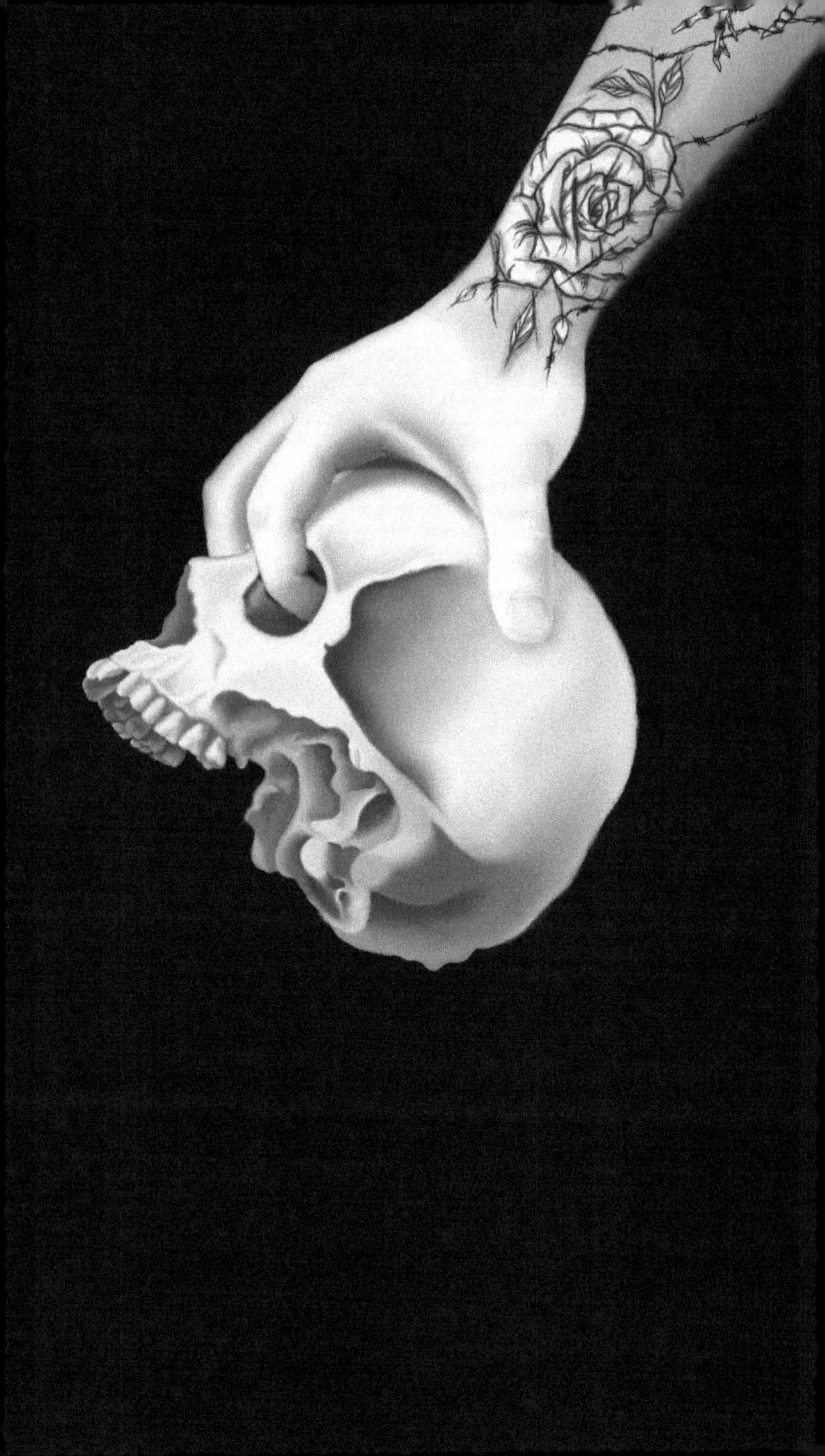

Silas

"WE CAME in here to get clean." Juliet laughs, a throaty moan escaping her as her thighs squeeze my hips.

"One last fuck as a human," I murmur against her ear. "I couldn't resist."

Hot water cascades down over us as I fuck her against the tiled wall, pooling in all the places our bodies are joined. Juliet writhes and moans, her breasts rising and falling rapidly against my chest. She's right, we came in here to clean up and get ready for what's about to happen, but having her wet and slippery right in front of me, there was no way I was going to pass up this chance.

She cries out, her fingers digging into my shoulders as she comes. I grit my teeth, holding off because I'm nowhere near done with her yet. I wait for her to calm down a little, sliding in and out of her pulsing pussy, before withdrawing from her, putting her down on shaky feet and bending her over in front of me.

She whimpers as I plunge back into her, her hands braced

against the wall. I fuck her slowly, one hand tangled in her hair, watching my cock slip in and out of her.

"Harder," she pleads. "Please, harder."

"Oh, you can beg so much better than that. Come on, little whore, tell me exactly what you need."

"I need you to fuck me harder." She inhales sharply as I yank her head back.

"Is that the best you can do? Dirty slut, you usually beg so nice for my cock."

"Please Silas," she says with a groan, her hands flexing on the wall. "I need you to fuck me harder. I want to come again."

I pull out of her, stroking my pierced tip against her clit, and she lets out a high-pitched gasp. "Oh, you like that do you?"

"Y-yes." Her legs begin to tremble.

"Is this what my filthy girl needs to get off?"

"Yeah." She moans loudly, her toes curling and her legs shaking so hard she's having trouble staying upright.

"Don't you dare come without my cock inside you."

She whimpers again, making a sound almost like a sob. Her body goes tense as she tries to hold off, as she tries to control the urge that's aching to break through her shivering body.

"Such an obedient little slut." I know my words are threatening to send her over the edge, but I'm enjoying this game too much. I push two fingers inside her, and her cunt is so tight I have to bite back a groan. A gentle pulse grips at my fingers, and I smack her ass hard. She moans loudly.

"I told you not to come."

She shakes her head against her arms. "I'm not, I'm not. Oh god, Silas, please."

I pull on her hair, harder this time, yanking her head back so I can see her rosy lips parted as she pants, her eyes clenched shut and brows drawn together as she tries to maintain control of herself.

"Tell me what you need, little whore."

"I need your cock inside me. I want your cum inside me. Please. Please."

I shove into her, biting open my wrist and coating her ass in my blood, which runs down her legs in crimson rivulets. I push two fingers into her ass and she screams. I fuck both her holes hard, unrelenting thrusts that don't ease off as she pulsates and I press my fingers against her core. She's scrambling against the wall, desperate to escape me but panting for more.

I pull out of her pussy just as my own climax peaks, my balls drawing up tight as I push my blood-soaked cock into her ass. She doesn't tense, but goes floppy like a rag doll, sagging down so I have to hold her by her hips as I spill inside her ass.

She's whimpering, murmuring my name, and I gently put my arms around her waist so her back is against my chest. My cock is still inside her, and I hold her there for a while, waiting for those perfect flutterings to stop. When I finally pull out of her and start to wash her down, she looks almost drunk. She smiles sleepily at me.

"Well, for a last fuck as a human that sure was a good one." Her face becomes uncertain for a moment. "It'll still feel good, right? I mean, you'll still want me the same, as a vamp?"

I roll my eyes as I wash blood from her stomach. "Oh my god, Jules, are you kidding me?"

"I just want it to be as good as it is now."

I sigh as I meet her eyes. "It will be, it'll be even better."

"Can I - I mean, do vamps bite each other?"

I kiss her jaw, and she shivers. "That's an extremely intimate thing that's only done with someone you love." I nibble on her earlobe. "It's extremely pleasurable for both parties."

"Well, that sounds like fun." She wraps her arms around my waist. "I'm ready now."

"OK. Let's get you dried off and comfortable."

We'd discussed this a lot over the past year. After our arrival in Philadelphia, the world had slowly begun to rebuild. Within three months, the numbers of the Afflicted had dwindled almost to nothing, as the virus that robbed them of the ability to gather strength from blood left them as nothing but starving corpses.

I worked with Dr. Harris at the lab, and the advances his team was making in vaccines were incredible. The synthetic blood alternative had been perfected within 6 months, meaning vampires no longer relied on humans, and that was when the world really started to come back to life. The city around us started to feel like a city again, and Juliet was happy teaching art when the local elementary school reopened.

But the discussions around our future were a little more difficult to navigate. Juliet's period never returned, and an examination told us that the years of depo shots, far beyond what was medically advisable, would make conception extremely difficult. It was a problem many were facing, yet another horrific mismanagement of the vamps in the preservation centers.

For Juliet, it was made even more difficult by the fact that she had a vampire partner. Even with a human, it could potentially take her years to conceive. With me, it was virtually impossible. Juliet struggled with this revelation for a few weeks, and I was unsure how to comfort her through it. All I wanted was a future with her, and if that included a child she desperately desired, I wanted to give her that.

But then one day, she began to ask about being turned. I talked her through it, over and over, until she began to become comfortable with the idea. She finally accepted that it wouldn't make her a monster, wouldn't change her at any fundamental level, it would just mean we'd be together forever.

She talked to Gina about it, who'd been moved into the same building as us after Juliet had put in a special request. Gina was surprisingly supportive. Like any mother, or someone who was close enough to being one, she simply wanted Juliet to be happy. That was the final piece of the puzzle, and Juliet told me she wanted to do it. We decided tonight, our first wedding anniversary, was the perfect night to start our new life together.

By the time we're back in the bedroom and on our enormous bed, she's wide-eyed and shaking. She lies down, biting her lower lip and gazing at me uncertainly.

"Now remember, angel, this won't hurt," I tell her, stroking her cheek. I'm a little nervous myself. I've never done this before, I'm running on sheer instinct to know when to stop. But I have to trust myself, and show her she can trust me too. "It'll be like falling asleep. You'll be all groggy, and then you'll wake up feeling like you can lift a lorry."

"A what?" She asks with a sweet little frown.

"A truck, angel."

"Oh." She swallows hard. "Am I going to get jacked like you?"

I laugh softly. "I doubt it."

"Maybe it'll all just go to my ass." She holds her hands up, a foot apart. "I always wanted a dump truck ass. I mean, is that like a request we can make?"

"You're nervous."

"Yeah." She sucks in a breath. "Just a little."

I chuckle softly and kiss her, stroking my fingers through her silky hair. "It'll be alright. I promise."

She inhales deeply, then nods. "OK. I'm ready."

I kiss her again, one last human kiss, then lower my mouth to her throat. "I love you, angel."

"I love you, too." She places hesitant shaking hands on my shoulders.

Her fingers dig in for a split second as I strike, her body reacting to the venom as it always does. She pants and moans, raking her fingers through my hair. I drink her blood down, more and more, hot and sweet as it runs down my throat.

She starts to go quiet, her body soft. Her hands lay on my back lightly, until one drops down, then the other. Her breathing is shallow. Her heartbeat slows until it's barely audible.

I pull back, tearing open my wrist and pressing it to her mouth.

"Drink, angel."

Her tongue traces along my veins, slowly, her eyes rolling back in her head. Another stroke of her tongue, and her throat bobs as she swallows. Her mouth cups the wound, and she begins to suck.

"That's it, angel."

Oh god, I wasn't expecting it to feel this fucking good. I grit my teeth, grinding my hardening cock against the bed. Fuck, what she does to me.

She lifts a hand, curling it around my arm and pressing me harder against her mouth. I can feel fangs now, scraping against my flesh. Her eyes fly open, and I'm looking into the warmest pair of chocolate brown eyes I've ever seen in my life, laced with flecks of fiery scarlet, as though they're made of flame.

She moans, the sound vibrating against my skin. She's rocking herself against my thigh, both of us hot and sweating. Suddenly she releases my arm, throwing her head back, blood trickling from the corners of her open mouth. Her fangs are bared to me, two dainty white points between her rosy lips.

"Oh fuck," she drawls. "Oh my god."

"How do you feel, angel?"

"Amazing." She gazes around the room, her eyes darting from place to place as she notices all the tiny details her human eyes missed. "I feel like I'm brand new." She lifts a hand, turning it back and forth in front of her. "Everything feels… different. Good."

"You look so beautiful." I lean down to kiss her, and she makes a small, happy sound as our lips meet. Her fangs nick me, and I groan.

She pulls back quickly. "Shit, did I hurt you?"

I can't help but laugh. "Remember what it feels like when I bite you?"

"Oh." She gives me a smug smile. "It felt good?"

"So good." I stroke her cheek. "What do you need right now? Blood? Are you thirsty?"

She eyes me hungrily, licking her lips. " No, I just need you." She flips me onto my back and straddles me. "Three days, huh?"

Christ she's strong. I laugh as I gaze up at her, my wild, filthy, sinful girl. "Three days?"

"That's how long you said you and Margot fucked when you were turned." She looks down at me with those fiery eyes, and grins, probing the tip of one of her new fangs with her tongue. "And it's a record I'd like to break."

We fuck for five.

ACKNOWLEDGMENTS

I picked this patchwork WIP back up in January 2024 during a particularly difficult time in my life. I thought my career was over, indeed I believed my life was no longer worth living.

This book quite literally saved my life, and it would not have happened were it not for the amazing people I have around me.

First and foremost, my incredible husband, Mark. You are the Book Boyfriend of my dreams. Without you, none of this would happen. I love you more and more every day.

My Mum, you herd babies and change nappies and cook lunch when I'm once again frazzled and overworked. I love you. Thank you for cheering me on every step of the way.

My beautiful children - I do this all for you. Thank you for being patient with me, for celebrating every increase in word count, and for helping me unpack all those Amazon parcels (I know y'all steal my stickers, but I don't even care). One day, Mummy will buy you a house with the yard of your dreams, and it'll be YOURS forever.

Deana, my amazing PA, you got me through so many dark days with your kindness, but also kicked my ass when I needed a shake-up. You are truly extraordinary, and I am so very grateful for you.

Marty, you're not just my Lead Artist (yes, we're sticking with that now, too bad), you are an inspiration and such an incredible friend. Your positivity got me through some truly dark times, and I cannot thank you enough. Your support means the world to me.

Avery, thank you for providing the beautiful chapter art in this book. I love working with you and cannot wait to do it again in future.

My Street Team - what can I say about you all. You're the most wonderful group of people and I love our chats. Your fierce loyalty and support is unwavering, and all I can say is Thank You, and I love you all.

My gorgeous author friends, Layla Pine and Allie Shante - thank you for lifting me up when I needed it, for sharing your dreams and art and WIPs with me, and for making me laugh. I value you both more than you will ever know.

And finally, to my loyal readers, my ARC team, the artists I've had the privilege of working with, and the Bookish Community - thank you for taking a chance on a little indie author. You've changed my life in ways you cannot even imagine.

Thank you
Thank you
Thank you

ABOUT THE AUTHOR

RD Baker accidentally writes dark and deadly spice on a regular basis. She enjoys creating Book Boyfriends that are emotionally mature but also unhinged in the very best of ways. She is highly caffeinated at all times, and has an obsession with rag doll cats.

She lives in the Blue Mountains, on Darug/Gundungurra Land, with her family.

Sign up for her newsletter a rdbakerwrites.com to stay up to date!,

www.ingramcontent.com/pod-product-compliance
Lightning Source LLC
Chambersburg PA
CBHW051115300726
48981CB00002B/138